PSYCHO GODS

THE CRUEL SHIFTERVERSE SERIES: ARAN'S STORY
BOOK 3

JASMINE MAS

Also by Jasmine Mas

The Cruel Shifterverse

Psycho Shifters

Psycho Fae

Psycho Beasts

Psycho Academy

Psycho Devils

Psycho Gods

WARNING

THEY ARE TRUE ENEMIES. This is war. It is excessively violent. This is a reverse harem. Everyone's a villain.

There are some intense situations in this book that might be triggering for some readers. If you are concerned please refer to the trigger list on my website jasminemasbooks.com, click on the black "Trigger" tab at the top right of the page for the list.

Please beware, the last chapter of the book might cause you to laugh so hard that you cry :).

"The effects of unresolved trauma can be devastating."

—Dr. Peter Levine

A regular person can survive only **three hours** without warmth.

INTO THE STARS

ALL MYTHS ARE ROOTED in some truth.

This series is about different planets connected by black holes.

Aka, realms attached by portals with inhabitants you've heard of in myths and dismissed as fairy tales.

There are politics, deceptions, and secrets on the macro scale. And they vary from realm to realm.

In the human realm, the inhabitants learn they live in an anarchic system, that there is no supreme authority over different countries.

They're wrong.

The High Court secretly reigns sovereign over *all* the worlds. "Realm-Wide Peace" is their motto.

Monsters enforce this peace. A next-to-impossible task because wealth corrupts, but power destroys.

And among the hundreds of planets with sentient life, a few special individuals possess power on the nuclear level— more energy in their cells than an atomic bomb.

The truth: Most individuals go their entire lives without

knowing or caring about the other realms or the creatures within them. They live in bliss.

In this series, ignorance isn't an option for our main characters.

Through birthright or circumstances, they're players in the macrolevel game.

Now all they must do is survive.

PART ONE
CLINOMANIA

The games of the gods will corrupt your head.
Those who survive—were already dead.

CHAPTER 1
ARAN
FATHERS

CLINOMANIA (NOUN): an excessive desire to remain in bed; morbid sleepiness

I stumbled down the empty black marble hall of Elite Academy.

My footsteps echoed loudly.

Orion ran silently behind me. He was my escort because of the bond sickness. My silent shadow.

Crack. Lightning struck the walls, and electricity made the hair on my arms stand up as white spots danced in my gray vision.

I slipped on a patch of ice and barely kept myself upright.

Stained-glass windows mocked me—maroon was splashed across gruesome battle scenes; slain soldiers clutched their swords as their souls were taken into the valley of the sun god.

My stomach churned because the Legionnaire Games were over, and I was going to war.

Soon, I'd be the downed soldier in the window.

It would be my blood.

Today was the day we left the academy for the realm overrun with ungodly. In a few hours, I'd RJE to a military base and become a war leader.

I felt sick.

Ice crackled, spreading across my fingers, then slowly crawled up my forearms, and I curled my hands under my armpits.

I looked back over my shoulder.

Shivered.

My teeth chattered from the pervasive chill that was emanating from my bones.

There was a path of cobalt ice coating the marble floors behind me, and as I zigzagged across the hall, the ice snaked and followed me.

Orion stared at it with shocked wide eyes.

Pressure built in my empty chest.

I wanted to scream.

I'm just an angel. I know what I am—I'm just an ordinary angel.

The pressure in my shoulders from my retracted wings told another story, and I grimaced because everything was falling apart.

I'd stayed up all night, twelve hours of straining with my wings spread wide, and I hadn't risen an inch off the ground.

Nothing had happened.

I couldn't fly.

Then I'd envisioned an angel's ice sword forming in my hand, but yet again—nothing.

Instead, as if mocking me, cobalt crawled along my fingers like gloves and spread across the ground with every step I took. I had zero control over it.

The ice was useless.

I was useless.

It was simple: angels were powerful, and I was weak.

My footsteps echoed louder as I sprinted down the marble hall toward Lothaire's office. A servant told me that my vampyre/tormentor/commander/sire wanted to speak with me.

Lovely.

Does he know what's wrong with me?

When I got to Lothaire's office door, I went to open it but stopped. Frozen with numbness, I watched ice spread from my feet and crawl up the wood like an infection.

Time warped, and I stood still as a statue.

Eyes wide.

Unfeeling.

Sightless.

The door slammed open, and I jumped as Lyla walked out. The witch's otherworldly eyes stared through me, and I averted my gaze, staring down at my ice-coated feet.

You didn't look fate in the eyes, especially not when your fate was as corrupted as mine.

In my peripheral vision, Lyla's forest-colored hair blew on a phantom breeze. White runes glowed across her dark skin. She stood inches away from me and waited silently.

She smelled sharp, like grief mixed with destiny.

Pressure built in my eyes, and suddenly I was hyperaware of the gaping emptiness inside my chest.

A horrible sense of foreboding slammed into me—things were going to get dark. A long stretch of merciless night spread before me.

Lyla leaned close and whispered so quietly it took me a few seconds to process what she'd said.

"You must embrace the dragon."

Her soft words hung insidiously in the air between us.

"She's here," she said loudly as lightning struck, then she walked away and disappeared down the hall.

Lothaire responded. "Come in, Aran." His voice had a strange inflection.

Orion sat down in the hall to wait for me.

I gingerly entered.

He stood up, single eye wide as he stared at the ice that spread out from underneath my feet.

I hid my hands behind my sleeves and cleared my throat. "You called for me, sir?" I asked awkwardly.

Bowed my head.

Stood at attention.

He made a strangled noise and said, "Please, don't do that—just stand normal."

My shoulders slouched as I stood normally. "Yes, sir," I whispered.

He flinched like I'd slapped him.

Silence spread between us, and the temperature in his small office plummeted. Ice crackled as it trailed up my arms beneath my sweatshirt, toward my heart.

Lothaire cleared his throat a bunch of times. "Lyla has hinted that there are—things I don't know about you."

I harrumphed.

Understatement of the year.

I picked at my lip and waited for him to demand answers. I waited for him to get aggressive and pry, but he didn't do any of that.

Instead, he started talking.

He told a story about a man with excessive power who'd committed horrible atrocities in his youth and was owned by the High Court as a result. He told me about how he'd been forced to conceive me with Mother. How he was trapped and had no choices.

He said he'd thought I was better off with her.

He said he'd thought I was safe.

He said a lot of things.

Finally, he pointed to his missing eye, then pointed to mine, the one that had a little more gray in it than the other.

He explained how he'd pulled it out of his eye socket for me, then he'd slashed his own face.

He was the reason I had two eyes.

The reason I could see.

My shivering intensified, and ice crawled up the outside of my throat.

I was numb all over.

I felt as if I hovered outside my body and watched him talking to me from a faraway vantage point.

Finally, he finished his heart-wrenching tale.

We stood in more uncomfortable silence.

I pulled my pipe from my pocket and inhaled enchanted smoke.

The room was freezing, and our breath puffed in frosty clouds between us.

I realized it was my turn.

Lothaire waited.

Silently.

Calmly.

With unfeeling lips, I began to talk.

I told him about the nightly tortures and the constant beatings, the harsh tutors, and even harsher guards.

The air was suddenly too thin, and it was hard to breathe.

Between shaky gasps, I told him the things Mother used to say to me. The things she'd done.

The many nights I lay sprawled across the floor on fire, screaming while I prayed someone would save me.

How no one had.

The days I was barely able to endure because I'd been so terrified about what was to come later. Anticipation eating at my stomach until I was physically sick.

When I was done speaking, Lothaire's tanned skin was a sickly shade of pale.

He stared at me like he'd never seen me.

Then his face crumpled, and he staggered backward with a wail. His back hit the wall, and he cradled his head in his hands as he let loose an unholy sound. Sparks of power popped in the air around him.

He was a broken man.

Shattered.

Thank the sun god I didn't tell him about the slur on my back.

"But it's over now," I said, my voice hoarse as I inhaled smoke like it could save me.

He dropped his hands and stared at me, an unfamiliar expression on his face. "How can you say that to me? How are you standing here?" He inhaled shakily. "How are you functioning—I've failed you."

I tried to smile sheepishly, but my face muscles weren't working.

I shrugged.

"Describe *functioning?*" I asked with a weak chuckle, then sucked in enchanted smoke until my lungs burned.

The joke fell flat.

Awkward.

He stood up straight abruptly and searched through his desk until he pulled out an RJE device.

I waited for him to explain, but he said nothing.

Instead, he walked forward until we stood about an arm's distance apart. "Can I—hug you?" he asked softly.

I grimaced. "Sure?"

The towering vampyre enveloped me in a tight hug. Tentatively, I brought my arm up and patted his freakishly muscled back.

"It means nothing," he whispered, "but I'm so sorry. I thought because of my agreement with the High Court that you'd be protected—I thought you'd be safe."

He squeezed me tighter.

"Well, I'm alive," I whispered. "I'm fine now." The lie tasted sour on my tongue.

"After the war—we'll talk more," Lothaire said. "For now, you need to concentrate."

The war.

Queasiness returned at the reminder of what we were heading into.

He must have felt me stiffen, because he pulled back and patted the top of my head fondly.

His tone was serious as he said, "One thing you'll never be is weak. You're more capable than you give yourself credit for. The war will be easy for you—it's the weaker soldiers who should be afraid. Not you—not *my* daughter."

I winced.

He doesn't know I can't fly or wield an ice sword. He leveled cities, but I can't even control a little ice.

Lothaire shook his head like he could read my mind as he reached forward and squeezed my shoulders. "I promise, you are more powerful than you can even imagine. Remember, I've tasted your blood when I tested you for Elite Academy—I know these things."

I shrugged with embarrassment.

Parents were supposed to tell their children lies to make them feel better. It was my first time experiencing it, and it was strange.

"Okay," I said as I rubbed the back of my neck and stared down at the ice-covered floor.

Lothaire tipped my chin up and bared his canines as he grinned. "Don't fret, war can be fun."

There it was.

For a second, I'd forgotten he was *certifiable.*

"For sure," I said sarcastically as I rubbed at my face.

He ruffled my blue curls and spun the RJE device in his hand. "I heard through the academy grapevine that Ghost wanted to say goodbye to you." He frowned. "I have no idea why that sadistic poltergeist librarian would want to—"

I cut him off and clutched at my heart. "Aw, how sweet of him."

It was Lothaire's turn to look at me like I was crazy.

I shrugged as I smoked. "We have a bond."

"You know he's murdered thousands of people, right?" he asked with confusion. "And he tortures students for fun?"

I rolled my eyes. "He's chill. It's not that serious."

Lothaire muttered something about daughters under his breath, then leaned forward and pulled me into another hug.

Finally, he backed away. "I need to give something to Corvus. Don't take too long saying goodbye. We leave soon for the war camp."

I exhaled heavily. "I know."

A few minutes later, I sat in the library with my pipe held out while Ghost, the unfriendly poltergeist and inspirational figure in my life, sucked on the enchanted smoke. Orion stared at me with wide, unblinking eyes.

The stained-glass windows of Elite Academy glimmered as they filtered dark blood-soaked light, and the air was rich with the musty scent of books. Students sat at tables studying, and lightning crackled in the halls.

There was a loud cough at one of the tables in the back.

Ghost tipped an invisible hat to me, then he floated away to put the criminal into a coma for violating the sanctity of the library.

I looked after his retreating figure fondly.

I'd miss him.

I curled my fingers around my pipe as trepidation mingled with anxiety.

It wasn't until we were leaving the library that I realized I'd forgotten to ask Lothaire what he had to give to Corvus.

CHAPTER 2

ARAN

DARK REVELATIONS

LUGUBRIOUS (ADJECTIVE): dismal.

"On the Creature Classification Scale—a one-to-five ranking system, with five being the danger level of certain gods—the ungodly are ranked a four," Dick said harshly, his expression bleak.

My ears echoed with the phantom screams of the dying and ripping flesh, and I shuddered.

What kind of monster would a five look like?

I couldn't even imagine it.

In the chair in front of me, Jinx shivered and slumped lower in her seat like she was also horrified. I smirked smugly because something had finally scared the haughty know-it-all.

You're smiling because a child is terrified. Nice one, Aran.

I grimaced.

It was hard growing up to be the villain, but here I was, sitting in a room, getting lectured about war while I fantasized about making a youth miserable.

Life comes at you fast.

We'd relocated to Planet 003FX—the realm infested with ungodly—and were in the newly constructed strategy room, getting lectured at by the High Court, aka Dick.

As Dick spoke, a figure in a black cloak with glowing blue eyes stood in the corner with their features obscured. From the person's towering height and width, they were a man.

I knew him well.

It was the same cloaked figure who'd taken Sadie to the war camp in the shifter realm. The same person who'd helped me escape the fae realm. The last time we'd seen him was at the ball in the beast realm.

Now he watched us silently, cloaked in shadows and darkness.

Another sycophant of the High Court lording over soldiers in the isolated valley of a war camp.

I ran my tongue across my teeth and tasted the power that stained the air. Goose bumps erupted down the back of my neck.

We were the champions of absent gods. Pawns for slaughter or icons of victory? Only time would tell.

Jinx and the demons were in the front row.

Twins to my right.

Sadie and her men to my left.

Devils in the back row. Orion leaned his head against Malum's shoulder, and the leader of the kings played with his blond hair with one hand and had his other hand draped over Scorpius's shoulder protectively.

A strange feeling flipped over in my stomach because they were obviously perfect together.

I didn't fit in with them.

It was a cruel joke that I was their Revered.

I resumed studying my surroundings. Concrete walls

glowed blue with the remnants of construction enchantments, and the space stank of frost, dirt, and leaves.

There were no windows.

A small orb in the corner was the only source of light.

Oversize wingback chairs faced the chalkboard, and a long table with an enchanted tablet built into its surface spanned the front of the room. Shelves lined the walls, filled with binders overflowing with information on the ungodly, the realm, and war strategies.

Binders were open on our laps.

Dick stood unnaturally still in front of the chalkboard as he lectured.

I slumped low in my leather chair.

This was our twenty-something-eth strategy meeting in the past week, and I was tired of being talked at; any adrenaline from surviving the Legionnaire Games had dissipated, and my attention span was ten minutes. Max.

Dick's lips were moving, but I only heard every third word.

He flashed a tray of gas canisters, put them in a drawer, then ranted about not using anything in the drawers because you would face criminal consequences.

He went on and on about prohibited weapons.

If they were prohibited, then why would they have them on hand? What idiot would actually pay attention to this deranged presentation?

I picked at the leather cushion beneath my thigh and concentrated on mimicking a rock: hear nothing, see nothing, sit still all day, and sometimes fall over and crush people to death.

Goals.

Next to me, John raised his eyebrow, dark eyes questioning, and I sank lower with boredom. He nodded in understanding as he absent-mindedly played with one of my curls.

Beside him, Luka leaned forward and looked back and forth between the two of us with his brow furrowed. His fingers were wrapped around John's wrist in a vise.

I'd noticed lately that the three of us were always connected.

One twin looked down at me with intense dark eyes, while the other flashed dimples, and a tendril of warmth flowered in my stomach.

Pain streaked down my spine.

I winced.

John wrapped my curl tighter around his finger, and Luka's olive knuckles turned white as he gripped his twin fiercely.

I sank back with a sigh.

On my other side, Sadie was sleeping in a seated position with her eyes wide open. Equal parts envious and creeped out, I poked at her side.

She slowly turned her head in my direction—red eyes wide and unseeing as she stared at me for a long minute— then she slowly turned her head back forward.

I made a mental note to unfriend her immediately.

"Don't you dare wake her up," Cobra mouthed next to her.

I rolled my eyes.

Blah, blah, blah. I'd rather be at Elite Academy, drowning in the black sea, than sit through another of Dick's sanctimonious explanations on battle strategy.

But here I was.

Time plodded forward.

When I was three seconds away from a self-induced coma, Dick said, "Please close your binders."

Thank the sun god.

I unrolled my hunched spine and patted the already

closed binder on my lap. I hadn't bothered to flip through the summarized list of policies and strategies, because I'd memorized it the first time he'd covered it:

- Don't eat any food from Planet 003FX.
- Don't make loud noises.
- The objective is to eliminate the ungodly quietly and efficiently before they realize they are under attack.
- The civilization indigenous to Planet 003FX is unknown because of the treacherous nature of the realm's terrain. Their new name: the infected.
- Recent intelligence indicates the civilization is composed of remote city-states called compounds that are located in mountainous valleys.
- The planet has a twenty-four-hour day and night cycle, like most realms with life.
- Experts theorize it will take days for information to spread among the settlements. Since not all the portals in the realm have been located, the ungodly must be eliminated before they can flee.
- Only wear your standard-issue battle gear. It is camouflage to the terrain.
- Keep your hair pulled back from your face.
- ~~No smoking, drugs, or alcohol use during the war~~.
- Always keep track of your weapons.
- Use your weapons, holsters, and straps.
- Enchanted bullets do not work against the ungodly. Rely on other weapons.
- Treat other soldiers with courtesy.
- Study the ranking officer chart and always listen to your commanders.

- Leadership chart in descending rank: champions, generals, spies, assassins, foot soldiers.
- Champions and generals have access to the strategy room for planning and will give the rest of the war camp their assignments.
- The champions have the ultimate say.
- The current theory is the ungodly infect their prey by forcing them to swallow their eggs. Do not swallow any eggs. It is theorized the warm temperature of the planet has allowed them to infect and spread at an abnormal rate.

I'd crossed out the drug policy because I didn't follow bad laws.

My new life motto: stand for something or fall for everything. Yes, I was standing for drug use.

Someone had to.

And the next person who reminded me not to eat food from the realm was getting stabbed in the throat. I was tempted to eat a leaf off a tree just for fun, bonus points if it killed me.

Also, whoever had written the last bullet point deserved to be institutionalized.

Who the fuck would voluntarily eat the eggs of a parasitic monster with pincers?

Controversial take—that person deserved to be infected.

"Write what I'm about to say down." Dick pointed to the pens attached to our binders.

I unclicked the pen and doodled a dying stick figure shooting a rifle at another dying stick figure.

Art imitated life.

Dick frowned. "This information is crucial."

Apparently, he was incapable of getting to the freaking point.

Sadie snored softly.

Dick's posture was rigid as he said, "You're probably wondering why we've had so many meetings."

*"No one cares!" I shouted and made an obscene hand gesture…*in my head.

"Your role"—Dick's ruddy complexion flushed as he glared at each of us—"is more important than you know."

No one blinked.

Where Lothaire would yell and smack a baton, Dick spoke with zero inflection, which was somehow ten times more terrifying.

There was a strange intensity around the High Court leader that no one, not even the kings, dared to challenge. With his wings retracted, I'd never have guessed that Dick was an angel. He didn't have the poise and aura of arrogance they all seemed to possess.

He looked too ordinary.

Although…I'd never thought I was an angel, and now I was one that couldn't fly.

Current life plan: throw myself off a cliff as soon as possible.

If I flew, I flew.

If I didn't—slay (in the slaughter sense).

Dick lowered his head and said, "What I'm about to say will change everything you thought you knew about this war."

I have syphilis.

I barely stopped myself from laughing aloud at my joke.

As far as I was concerned, he didn't deserve anyone's respect.

First, he was a man.

Second, he'd taken me from the fae realm as a child and beaten Sadie into her powers as he masqueraded as a beta shifter. He'd stood beside me in a gladiator arena when I'd consumed my mother's beating heart. He'd spread angel wings wide in the beast realm and represented the gods in the Legionnaire Games.

Dick was always there when our lives hit rock bottom.

His nostrils flared as he enunciated each syllable. "The reason we've been lecturing you continuously—"

He paused.

I drew another dead stick figure on my palm.

"—the Official Peace Accords, otherwise known as the OPA, doesn't just ban the involvement of gods in war as you've been told."

Déjà vu skittered down my scarred spine.

A lifetime ago, I'd learned about the OPA in the fae palace, but the memory was sand, and it dripped through my fingers.

Dick's eyes flashed. "The OPA also bans the involvement of the High Court in any battles or strategy."

I drew another dead figure.

So we were alone? *Nice.*

Dick inhaled deeply. "The OPA also bans the realms within the High Court from establishing an independent militia of greater than one hundred soldiers."

The room was dead silent.

There would be no sprawling army fighting against the ungodly, just one hundred people versus a planet of parasitic monsters.

We were doomed.

Dick seemed to grow taller as he said, "The OPA were

enacted as an *ignorant* reaction to the last major war." He flung his arms wide, and the movement was startlingly violent compared to his usual stillness. "Just because there were some—unexpected casualties in the previous war led by the High Court, everyone panicked. *Cowards*."

What?

I couldn't breathe.

One. Hundred.

I honored those who'd panicked in the past by panicking in the present.

Dick's face flushed and twisted with disgust as he continued, "The High Court needed a scapegoat in the last war, so they blamed the god who saved them *and* the soldiers who died for them. They enacted the OPA as a cowardly way to restore faith in governance and absolve themselves of guilt in future wars. The High Court and gods bound themselves with enchantments that cannot be broken."

Only one hundred soldiers, repeated in my head.

"Now the time has come for that future war, and you must pay the consequences of past failures." He didn't sound apologetic. "We kept this from you, so you would focus on our lessons and not panic about the task ahead."

What a great plan—save the upsetting information for three seconds before a war starts.

Why was he looking at me?

Why was he pointing at me?

Click. I stabbed the pen into my hand and made a hole in the forehead of the stick figure.

He said, "We have given you every tool we can to help you, but victory is up to you—study everything you've learned over the next week and prepare to adapt." He nodded. "The angel scouting party is identifying the location of the first settlement. When it is time for battle, you will be notified—good luck."

He stalked out of the room, and the cloaked man followed.

The door slammed shut behind them.

Fugue was too mild a word to describe what came next.

Paranoia devoured me.

John threw his arm around my shoulder, and Sadie sleepily leaned against my side as we left the strategy room. The kings followed behind me like unwanted shadows or looming specters of death.

Physically, I went with the group to the cafeteria, but mentally, I disappeared.

I'd learned about the peace accords before, and it was imperative that I remembered. So I threw myself into the dark recesses of memory.

I dove into my mind.

We left the cafeteria.

Time warped.

I blinked.

I sat on the floor of our tiny new shower, arms wrapped around my legs as the frigid water kept me focused on my task.

Someone banged on the bathroom door and told me to hurry up.

I didn't respond.

On the outside, icy drops pelted skin.

Inside my mind's eye, I reconstructed the fae library stacks spine by spine, and I rebuilt the towering mental shelves I'd once lived within.

It was painstaking work.

The first lesson a fae tutor had ever taught me was how

to create a memory palace. Knowledge was useless if it had nowhere to go.

Step one: meditate.

As a child, I'd spent days, months, and years mentally building a library that mirrored the one on the top floor of the palace.

Step two: memorize.

Every day, my tutors would ask me about the contents of random pages in books I'd read. If I couldn't remember, I'd read the book again and mentally reshelve it.

The one time I still couldn't remember, my tutor had hit me. Hard.

I hadn't cowered like a princess was supposed to; instead, I'd hit him back harder.

He'd beaten me bloody and dragged me to Mother, who'd gladly lit me on fire for hours.

I'd never forgotten a book since.

When I'd turned ten, recalling was no longer sufficient for my tutors, and they'd demanded I start applying what I'd read to hypothetical situations.

There was a reason I could expertly give a detailed examination of the elements of a problem.

It wasn't nature.

It was nurture.

Brutal. Fucking. Nurture.

With me being tortured at night by cold flames, pushed to mental limits during the day by emotionless tutors, my childhood had been horrific.

But the lessons were effective.

Now, as an adult, inch by painstaking inch, I meditated and rebuilt my old memory palace under the spray of a cramped shower.

Time warped.

I blinked back into the present.

Luka cut up fruit and gave it to his twin as the kings glared at me in the dining hall. We were having another meal.

John hand-fed me fruit.

I tried to smile at him in thanks, but I was too deep in my mental library.

For some reason, the section I'd read at fourteen years old was blurry, the spines and words much fuzzier than the rest of the mind palace.

"Something is wrong with her," Malum snarled. "We need to bring her to the medical room."

Luka shifted in front of me protectively but didn't respond.

John said, "She said she's fine and that she just needs to think. Just let her do what she needs to do."

"She's not fine, she's fucking catatonic," Scorpius exploded. "She's barely breathing."

"Leave her alone," John said harshly and shielded me with his body.

I blinked.

Time warped yet again.

I was lying on top of the covers in a narrow bunk bed that was cramped to discourage fraternization between soldiers. A distant part of me recognized that I was back in our new room, and it was night.

Mentally, I grabbed books off shelves and opened to their cover pages. I'd gone through thousands of books.

I opened *The History of Rare Fae Beasts*.

I closed it.

I opened *How to Cultivate Plants*.

I closed it.

I opened *The Enactment of the Official Peace Accords*.

I close—

Finally, I found what I'd been looking for. I flung open the book and devoured its contents. It read,

Thousands of years ago, an endless army of human soldiers set out to conquer the realms. In response to the invasion, the High Court mandated all able-bodied men and women eighteen years and older fight and defend their respective realms.

Millions were conscripted and fought in battles that spread across the realms.

The human soldiers had the strategic advantage.

Towering catapults flung flaming boulders across the horizon, and long pointed poles and swords skewered, as the armor-clad humans shot flaming arrows off the backs of powerful horses.

In contrast, the realms of the High Court had never developed weapons, because individual powers had always been sufficient in eliminating invaders.

It was a grave miscalculation.

The armies of the High Court were slaughtered.

When it seemed like complete annihilation was inevitable, the sun god took matters into his own hands.

Midbattle all the realms' suns unexpectedly burned fifty degrees hotter.

The god of light boiled the lands.

All the people, plants, and animals were decimated, and anything that didn't have a natural resistance to high temperatures died within a few hours of intense heat exposure.

The humans tried to flee back to their realm, but most dropped dead from dehydration as they ran for safety.

The sun god followed a few humans back to earth in order to identify the location of portals. Guards were subsequently stationed, and by all accounts, the human species have never tried to set foot in another realm since the war.

Smugglers who have illegally traveled through these portals tell tales of the sun god punishing the earth realm with extreme heat. They claim humans live in perpetual fear of annihilation. None of these reports have been substantiated.

After the High Court won the war against the humans, there was a consensus in the realms that the price of victory was too high.

Populations were decimated, and even after the sun god returned the realms' temperatures to normal, devastating climate effects persisted.

The shifter realm plunged into a never-ending ice age as hundreds of glaciers melted and poured cold water into the warm ocean currents. In ten days, the planet froze over.

The sun god made a public apology to the realm and offered to increase the temperature, but students from the historic University of Enchantments calculated the planet would become uninhabitable if there was another warming.

The High Court declined to comment.

The shifter realm has not since recovered.

In the fae realm, seasons disappeared and were replaced with an endless summer. The monarchy became isolationists and banned advanced weapons development.

The moderate climate of the beast realm also disappeared, and the land has since been plagued with perpetual rain. Unlike the fae, the leaders invested heavily in the production of expensive weapons, and a few centuries later, they created the first enchanted guns.

A powerful realm was also divided into two; one side of the planet iced over like the shifter realm, while the other burned with perpetual fire.

For unknown reasons, the humans never invaded, and the Olympus realm was left unscathed. The few humans who survived the warming, but did not make it back to the human realm, were taken as prisoners of war to the underworld, Olympus's maximum-security prison.

Planetary climate effects aside, at the end of the war, there were no armies to congratulate, because only a hundred of the strongest soldiers from all the realms survived the battlefield. Soldiers were either slaughtered by human weapons or succumbed to severe temperatures.

The Official Peace Accords, the OPA, were passed unanimously by all realms and executed with enchanted bindings. The peace accords were signed by the High Court and the sun god, and the mostly uninvolved moon goddess, in order to prevent future atrocities.

Narrow understanding expanded into a wide frame as context colored everything in shades of black and gray. The lack of human presence in the realms wasn't because they were primitive and weak like everyone was taught.

A sinister false remembrance.

I stopped clinging to the spatial illusion, and books tumbled off shelves. Hundreds of stacks fell over as my mind palace crumbled into nothingness.

SNAP.

Consciousness returned.

Pain stabbed across my skull like a hot poker, and I sat up and heaved.

Luka's arm was hanging over the side of his bunk, and I was gripping his hand.

My head throbbed.

My gasps were loud in the quiet room as the rest of the legion slept in their bunks.

I started to shake.

How had I forgotten such terrifying information about the sun god? It hadn't been Jinx, because she'd said the memories she'd taken were unrecoverable.

Why were my memories from fourteen so shrouded in fog?

My bunk trembled from the force of my convulsions, and Luka's thumb stroked against the back of my hand like he was soothing me in his sleep.

I pressed my quivering left palm into my eyes, then grabbed the diamond of death that hung heavy against my chest. It felt warm against my frozen fingers and vibrated at my touch.

I dropped it, and it went still.

Sweat dripped off my forehead and streaked down my sides, then stopped its trail as it froze to my skin.

Frost covered the bedsheet beneath me.

I felt sick.

After the Legionnaire Games, Lyla had spread her arms wide and said, "Every few millennia, a red giant explodes in the galaxy. It collapses in a solar system that contains a portal connecting it to realms within the jurisdiction of the High Court."

My vision blurred.

History was repeating itself.

The last invasion had nearly destroyed us all, and now it was the ungodly's turn, but there would be no sprawling army at our backs.

There would be no gods to save us.

We were sacrifices, fodder for slaughter, collateral.

I squeezed Luka's callused hand until my fingers turned white.

Then I closed my eyes.

I didn't want to be awake anymore.

CHAPTER 3
LUKA
CODEPENDENCY

Amorist (noun): a person who is in love.

Aran wasn't speaking.

I didn't like it.

I was the one who stayed quiet, and she was the one who hung off John's shoulders while cracking inappropriate, morbid jokes.

My twin had his arm slung over her shoulder, but they weren't leaning against each other like usual.

No.

Crystal-blue eyes were wide and unseeing as John dragged Aran through the trees.

Lilac sunlight and emerald from the valley forest reflected across the shimmering clouds. The new realm was colorful, and the weather seemed mostly mild.

The sun warmed the snow, and it melted immediately.

In contrast, the air around Aran was chilled like she was radiating frost. It was noticeably colder than the rest of the realm.

I was concerned.

She'd said she needed to think, but she was practically catatonic as John pulled her down the dirt path connecting the twenty freestanding concrete structures that made up the war camp.

The base was constructed in the valley surrounded by towering mountains and low-ceilinged buildings were camouflaged by trees and snow.

The new realm was a strange amalgamation of different elements.

It reminded me of a chimera, the beast was a mind-bending hybrid of a goat, lion, and a dragon. When you saw one in person, you were struck with one thought: *this shouldn't exist.* The realm was the same way.

Snowflakes fell, sizzled as they touched the warm ground, and evaporated into a low layer of steam.

Above, the lavender sky sparkled.

I barely noticed.

We hadn't eaten for hours, but I wasn't hungry as our two legions walked side by side to the cafeteria.

Sadie pulled back to walk beside her men, and all my attention was focused on where turquoise hair was supported by olive skin.

Back in the strategy room, Aran had shut down and John's eyes had crinkled when Dick announced there would only be a hundred soldiers fighting.

I wasn't worried.

Unlike my more socially aware twin, I didn't care about the events that unfolded around me.

I couldn't even pretend to give a shit.

All my energy was captured by the two people walking in front of me, and my skin crawled with worry that they were mentally struggling.

It had always been that way for me. My codependency issues were so strong that they manifested into physical pain.

John stumbled, and I lunged forward to steady him. Aran's lips curled up into a small smile as he exhaled with gratitude.

Pine trees swayed on Planet 003FX as I held on to Aran and John, gripping my twin's hand tightly.

Wide shoulders radiated strength as my brother looked down protectively at Aran leaning against us, blue curls wild.

She was ours to shield.

My discomfort abated slightly, but it didn't disappear.

It never would.

Years ago, an oracle had confirmed it.

I clutched my twin's hand while the oracle of Delphi danced around us. She spread her arms wide, brown hair flowing to her toes, as she inhaled the fumes of the ancients.

"You are crippled with codependency," the oracle sang as she twirled mindlessly. Misty eyes widened, and her lips pulled into a smile. "The lost princes have returned to the king, but they are no longer whole. Neither is the other. They will suffer unbelievable agony on behalf of the other, and all of them will be partial together."

The oracle cackled madly, and John trembled with fear. I stood in front of him, spread my short limbs wide as I prepared to do anything to protect him.

In the present, I smiled down at my wide-shouldered reflection as we walked among the trees.

Snow dusted John's cheeks.

He might have grown into a formidable man with whip-cord strength and a mischievous glint in his eyes, but he'd always be my younger twin. The boy I needed to protect.

The compulsion that lived within my skin ensured it.

Trauma had changed me.

Twisted me into something unrecognizable to others.

As we had grown up in the human realm, the foster parents had beaten both of us regularly, but John had had it worse because he'd had less control of his darkness.

One day, he accidentally dropped a glass, and it shattered on the linoleum kitchen floor. I tried to pick up the pieces, but it was too late. The foster father lunged toward John, and darkness flooded from his pores defensively.

He recoiled, called him a demon, demanded an exorcism, and shouted about a false god.

It all happened so quickly.

Everything blurred as a baseball bat broke our bones, and we were shoved into a car and brought to a cliff.

I gaped in stunned horror as he threw John over the edge.

I went into shock, and darkness exploded from me in a wave. The foster man disappeared, but I was too late.

Stumbling out of the car, I sobbed on my knees as devastation flatlined my existence.

I threw myself forward off the cliff to join John.

Lothaire materialized, grabbed me, and in one motion, jumped off the cliff and landed beside my injured twin. Before I could process what was happening, we RJE'd to another realm.

Lothaire told me the energy I'd emitted was so high that he'd been sent by the High Court to recruit me.

I ignored him and focused on John.

It took three weeks in a witch-induced coma for John to come back to me.

During that time, I didn't care that vampyres existed and there were multiple worlds. I didn't care that Lothaire recognized our darkness and knew who our biological parents were.

None of it mattered.

I had sworn on my life that I would never fail John again.

The past blended with the present.

"Give us the prophecy, oracle," the king demanded harshly. *"Stop speaking in riddles. You're scaring them, and they've been through enough."* I gripped John's hand with so much force my fingers cramped.

In the present, we arrived at a building hidden by snowy trees. "Cafeteria" was written above the green door.

John tried to pull away to open the door, and my throat closed with panic. Itchiness exploded across my skin, so I tightened my hold on him and Aran. He stopped reaching as he recognized what was wrong.

I couldn't stand to part from him.

Not after we'd been separated for so long.

Never again.

I breathed shallowly.

"Of course, my King, let me be clearer." The oracle giggled and swirled her hands in the air. *"I speak through the mouth of the stars as I proclaim this fate."* I shoved John further behind me, heart pounding with fear as I protected him with my scrawny frame.

The three of us sat down together at the table as food was passed out by workers.

I slid my chair closer to John, and he slid his closer to Aran. We sat pressed against one another.

Breathing deeply, I searched for calm.

Voices spoke around me, but I didn't hear a word they said, because I didn't care about them.

I didn't make friends.

I ignored everyone.

I didn't talk or interact.

No one existed but John—and now Aran. Two people were the center of my world.

They *were* my world.

The fateful day on the cliff had solidified my attachment to my twin into something that defined my being.

Codependency consumed every moment of my life.

It *was* me.

We were two halves of a whole, and even though John could put on a mask and socialize, he suffered from the same dependency.

Memories swirled around me.

The past was alive, and it reached for me.

The king had never revealed to the realm that the lost princes had been found, because you couldn't lead a powerful realm if you refused to acknowledge that anyone else but your brother existed.

You couldn't play the political game of survival if everyone else was already dead to you. So the lost princes had stayed lost; we'd been nothing more than rescued humans living in a foreign realm.

We'd liked it best that way.

But over time, the king had grown disappointed because he thought I'd grow out of my issues. He'd thought John would help me change into someone different.

My twin loved me the way I was.

As a result, when Lothaire returned years later to take us to Elite Academy, the king made a horrible decision: he blackmailed Lothaire with secret information in exchange for keeping our identity a secret. Worst of all, he convinced Lothaire to let only one of us attend Elite Academy at a time.

The king claimed it was because he needed our abilities to run the realm.

He lied; it was a desperate bid to fix our crippling dependency problem.

The king pulled us aside and promised we could be

reunited if we could prove we'd both formed a relationship with someone else.

What proceeded were the worst years of my life training at Elite Academy.

They thought I was John, and I never bothered to correct them because they didn't exist to me. Not in any way that mattered. I let my twin do the socializing for both of us; it wasn't for me.

In the beginning of my time at Elite Academy, I was alone in a sea of faces.

Desolate.

Unmoored.

Until a blue-haired boy with haunted eyes and a mouth dripping in sarcasm draped his arm across my shoulders and called me John.

I tried to ignore Aran, but it was impossible.

For some confounding reason, I wanted to help the pretty boy floundering to stay alive in the dark sea. My heart pounded wildly in my chest as a pipe was pressed against my lips and a joke whispered in my ear.

Aran refused to leave my side.

And for the first time in my life, I latched onto someone that wasn't John.

I *saw* someone else.

The twin that refused to interact with anyone besides his brother was cured.

Months later, the king wept with relief and rejoiced with his family when we asked for Aran's hand in marriage. Everything he'd ever wanted had come to fruition.

But when all three of us had been reunited, I'd immediately realized the king's plan hadn't worked at all.

I was no longer codependent with one person.

I was codependent with two.

It was like the oracle had prophesied that fateful day in the cave.

Her eyes rolled back in her head, and she spread her arms wide, the prophecy exploding from her lips. "The master number surrounds the lost princes. The strongest of them all; two will become three. Multiples of three are golden, you see. The broken soul leads them down a twisted path of darkness, but they will remain the three of three. Eternally."

I didn't need to smoke the blessed fumes at Delphi to confirm that Aran was the third from the prophecy.

I knew it in my soul.

Now, beside me in the cafeteria, Aran leaned her head on her hands and stared off into space as I cut up fruit into bite-sized pieces and gave them to my twin.

John didn't have to ask what they were for, because we were on the same wavelength; the Greek letter lambda was tattooed on my back for a reason.

He hand-fed her bites of food.

Together we took care of her.

Across the table, the devils said something, but I didn't register their words; my attention was wholly focused on Aran.

My skin crawled with the need to feed her.

For the entirety of my life, when my twin suffered, I suffered.

Now when Aran suffered, I suffered.

It was how I operated.

After the cave, the king was unhappy with the oracle's prophecy. He raged to the other kings and queens about how unfair it was because we'd already known darkness. The kings and queens shook their heads as they muttered about the poor Princes of Darkness.

We nodded back sullenly.

That night John and I giggled with excitement in our shared bed because we knew what three meant. It wouldn't just be the two of us for our entire lives. We'd find someone else to love.

John caught my eye as Aran delicately ate the fruit he handed her, and he smirked.

Leaning over the table, I put my arm around his shoulders and tangled my fingers in curly turquoise hair as I made sure they both ate.

My stomach grumbled, but I didn't care.

I pushed more food onto John's plate, and he smiled.

His dimples were my home.

We clasped our hands together under the covers, and John's dimples were stark on his cheeks as he laughed. I rolled onto my back and clutched my stomach as I joined him.

I watched Aran and John eat with rapt attention. The two of them would never be parted from me—if they were, I'd be dead.

The next day at breakfast, the king ranted to the two others about how the oracle was a fraud. He went on and on about how we deserved light in our future. The queen smirked down at us from her silver throne covered in violets as intelligence sparkled in her majestic eyes.

I smirked back.

John winked up at the queen and held up his fingers. She tipped her head back and laughed.

"Three of three. Eternally," he whispered to the queen as he covered his smile with his small hand.

The queen laughed because she saw what the king couldn't, and she beamed down and said, "Lucky boys."

We nodded in agreement.

The queen was one of the foremost scholars of enchantments in the realms because she could often see what others couldn't. This time was no exception.

Under the table, John smirked as he poked his three

fingers gently against my thigh, and warmth flooded my chest at his gesture.

After the meal, with John's hand wrapped around Aran's, I carried her down the tree-lined path toward our legion's sleeping quarters. The shifter legion branched off toward their barracks. The kings walked behind me, bristling with agitation and growling under their breath.

I barely noticed as I clutched my treasure.

Aran mumbled about lost books and palaces as she cuddled into me while holding my twin's hand.

Snowflakes dusted turquoise curls as I shielded her from the chilly air with my chest.

The position was familiar.

Back at Elite Academy, she'd clutched onto my arm for hours in the black sea, hanging off my shoulders as she quivered from exhaustion. Her arms had tightened around my neck as I'd hauled her across the rocky shore to safety, and we'd fallen asleep cuddled together on a broken cot.

In the present, snow kissed her rosy cheeks. Frost clung to her cheekbones like decoration.

Her breaths came out in dainty puffs of ice, and I stared, enraptured by the graceful column of her pale neck and the slight ripple of her pulse.

She looked like a dream.

Her existence provided me with a shelter from the world, and just like my twin, she was home.

When we were finally back in the warmth of our room, I cupped the back of her curly head protectively and laid her onto her designated bunk bed.

She sighed with relief.

Unlacing her combat boots, I gently tugged them off her feet and pulled the covers up over her chest.

I brushed a curl off her forehead.

Dark lashes fluttered.

John leaned against me, and I relished his proximity. Together we watched her. The bonds of brotherhood and love strummed between us like a golden ray of sunshine on a cloudy day.

Slowly, John kissed his three fingers, then pressed them against Aran's flushed cheek. He kissed me on my cheek, then climbed up to his top bunk.

I stood frozen.

Emotional.

Overwhelmed.

Tucking Aran's feet underneath her blankets, I climbed into my bunk above hers with one arm hanging down toward her like I did every night since we'd moved into the war camp.

Delicate fingers tangled with mine. Cold and pale contrasted with warm olive skin.

Even half-asleep, Aran had reached for my hand.

The position was uncomfortable for both of us, but neither of us could sleep without the other's touch.

I exhaled tension. Compulsion turned into something warm, something new and precious.

"Sleep well, brother," John whispered from above. "I'm grateful for every day that we get to spend together."

My voice cracked as I responded, "Every day together is a blessing—I will never leave your sides again." I'd survived the hellfire of separation, and now life beside them felt like a dream.

"Eternally," he murmured.

It didn't matter that we were going to war. Unlike other people, I never got caught up in circumstances. It was the people closest to you that made up your life. Period.

Other people never seemed to understand that.

Dainty fingers curled against my palm in agreement.

The narrow bunk above me creaked as John draped both his long arms off the front of his bed and buried his hands in my hair.

Every night, the three of us slept contorted in awkward positions.

Tethered.

Touch reflected our souls.

As I drifted into oblivion, a smile curled my lips because the queen had understood a decade ago what the king still could not fathom: you didn't fear darkness if together you were light.

The prophecy was not a bearer of doom; it was a promise of paradise.

The last few years at Elite Academy, I'd suffered true darkness: loneliness.

I'd suffocated in desolation as my skin crawled, alone and unmoored in a universe filled with people who would never understand. I'd degraded at the edges until I was nothing.

I'd been no one.

Now the ones I loved pressed their warm fingertips against my flesh, and our blood pounded in tandem through corporeal forms.

We were connected.

Forever.

I was never letting them go.

The betrothal jewelry hanging around Aran's neck and wrist was a testament to that promise. The pieces were price-less, imbued with rare enchantments that sensed a person's soul and connected them with the givers of the jewelry.

Until we held a marriage ceremony and said the official bonding words, the enchantment was mostly inert. All the jewelry would do was familiarize itself with Aran's soul.

At least, that was what the queen had told us.

The enchantment was an ancient one that was only used by the leaders of our culture, and even then, the last time it had been used was thousands of years ago when the queen had gotten married.

Aran was worthy.

Even though it was mostly dormant until the ceremony, it was still symbolic of the promises we'd made for one another, and that meant something.

One day, we'd complete the bonding, and the enchantment would tie our souls together.

Until then, all I could do was hold on to Aran.

My soul was already hers.

As I rested, a tear of pain streaked down my cheek because the High Court had scheduled her and the kings to have therapy in the shifter realm, which meant we would be parted.

It would be pure torture.

CHAPTER 4

ARAN

THERAPY

FERINE (ADJECTIVE): feral

Tick. Infinity. *Tock.*

The hands on the clock moved unnaturally slow as flaps of yellow wallpaper peeled off the office wall like tears.

Voices warbled in the background.

The foreground was nebulous.

It had been that way ever since we'd learned the truth about the war against the ungodly.

Sweat dripped down my rib cage as the air conditioner spewed cold air onto the top of my head. Rain battered against the cramped office's single window.

My teeth chattered.

Outside, the climate was dreary; inside, the climate was lachrymose.

The sky was bloated with water, and the room was overflowing with regret, shame, anger, and every other unsavory emotion that no one wanted to talk about.

Feelings that destroyed.

We sat in morbid silence.

A reprieve from the war—lately words were our guns and lies our enchanted bullets.

"Aran, are you paying attention to me?" Dr. Palmer snapped her fingers in front of my face. Unfortunately, one person hadn't gotten the "sit quietly and mope" memo.

I blinked.

She snapped her fingers again.

"No." My voice cracked, and I wet my lips. "I wasn't listening to you."

My therapist breathed deeply. "The High Court says these men are your fated soulmates and you need to cooperate with them for the war effort. They've mandated these therapy sessions because you all need to learn how to work together and unlock the full extent of your powers."

The only thing I would be unlocking was a muzzle for Malum.

She pointed her pen at the three devils sitting beside me on the threadbare couch.

The four of us shifted.

"But you said last week that you loathe them?" She frowned. "And then you refused to elaborate."

I didn't understand her bewilderment.

My loathing should have been a statement with a period: a form of punctuation used to end a complete sentence.

For some reason, no one wanted to accept my hatred as final.

The kings.

Dr. Palmer.

The High Court.

Everyone was waiting for me to change my mind.

Ice traveled down my limbs until I was completely numb,

sitting still while simultaneously tumbling deeper into noth-ingness.

Space buckled.

Tick. Infinity. *Tock.*

Dr. Palmer pursed her lips. "Aran, could you answer the question?"

I stared back at her blankly. The ice had frozen my eyelids and embalmed my corneas.

"You hate these men?"

She pointed again like I needed the reminder that I was sandwiched beside my enemies in a claustrophobic room meant for two people.

I refused to turn my head because I'd seen enough: freak-ishly wide shoulders, long pale fingers, callous demeanors, warm brown eyes, cheeks that blushed pink as they betrayed me. Three disturbingly handsome faces.

The problem had never been their looks.

"Um—" I broke out into a coughing fit.

The tension in the room increased tenfold as everyone focused on me. I would have been embarrassed, but I'd stopped feeling anything meaningful ten years ago.

I'd stopped feeling anything *at all* last week in the war camp.

Dick had spoken, and the lies had crumbled.

The truth—ancient peace accords—was a heinous beast.

Now Dr. Palmer handed me a half-filled cup of luke-warm water, and I gulped it down until I choked.

Liquid spilled onto my shirt.

Orion patted my back, and I flinched away from his touch. He made a soft, wounded sound as he pulled his hand away.

The air conditioning buzzed loudly.

A gust of wind slammed rain against the side of the building with splatter.

I focused all my attention on choking to death on the water—vexingly, it didn't work, so I redirected my concentration into slouching my shoulders until I was concave.

Placing the half-empty water cup by my feet on the once white but now light-brown carpet, I pretended not to notice that Dr. Palmer scowled at it like she knew I was going to forget to pick it up.

I cleared my throat three times.

Coughed.

Wet my lips.

"Aran, please take all the time you need." Her mouth said one thing, but her narrowed eyes and pinched lips said another.

"Okay." My voice sounded far away, and it felt like someone else was speaking.

Her right eye twitched. One. Two. Three. Four times.

I rotted on the couch.

"Aran." Dr. Palmer snapped her fingers twice in rapid succession, and it sounded like a gunshot.

I sat up with a start.

She pointed her pen at me.

A weapon.

You could puncture someone's corneal artery with a pen. You could gouge someone's eyes out. You could shank them in the stomach.

"Aran," Dr. Palmer said harshly.

I blurted, "Yes—I hate my mates. In fact, they disgust me." I stuck my tongue out and pointed my finger at it while I gagged, just in case she wasn't picking up what I was putting down.

The good (annoying) doctor wrote something down on her clipboard and nodded as my eyes grew heavier.

I was barreling into a war blind.

Free-falling.

I tried to sit up straight, but my shoulders slumped.

My back muscles burned with the phantom weight of retracted wings that I couldn't get to work.

Even back in the Legionnaire Games, I'd never actually *flown*. I'd just tumbled toward the dirt and used my wings to slow us down before crashing into a pole.

At least I'm good at throwing myself off high heights. I should be a professional cliff diver.

Time warped.

"Your soulmates disgust you and you hate them?" Dr. Palmer spoke slowly and overenunciated "disgust" and "hate" like she was making a point. "That's what you said last week. Correct?"

If she was hinting at something, I wasn't getting it.

I nodded and tugged at the permanent scab on my lower lip.

"Stop picking," Scorpius ordered harshly.

I jumped and pulled my hand away from my face.

A pen scribbled across paper.

Was she writing about me? Rude.

I rolled my eyes, brought my fingers back to my lip, and ripped off a juicy chunk of skin.

"I told you not to pick," Scorpius said. "Orion, pull her hand away."

Anyone else plagued by men? Just me? Nice.

"Touch me," I said tiredly, "and I'll kill you." I left off the "I'll kill us all" because of the doctor.

All I needed was to be diagnosed as a serial homicidal maniac.

Was I one? Maybe. Did I want to be heavily medicated

and locked in a room for the rest of my life? Also, maybe. It depended if Sadie was there.

Orion stared down at me.

I stared at the wall.

I wasn't the type of person to play favorites, especially not when it came to my enemies—but Orion was my favorite, and Malum was my least favorite. One hundred percent.

I was grateful the quiet man was a buffer between me and Scorpius and the two of them blocked my view of Malum.

The kings were seated in order of descending awfulness.

They had their arms draped over one another's shoulders and whispered among themselves as Dr. Palmer talked.

The three of them fit together.

Then there was me.

Scorpius leaned forward to glare at me, and Orion's muscular thigh pressed indecently against mine. We were both wearing sweatpants, but pain streaked down my back.

I exhaled harshly and managed not to whimper.

It was funny how pain felt sharper in certain situations. Sometimes adrenaline and depression masked the hurt, and other times they amplified the agony.

Nothing was masking it now.

I was raw.

Life's a cruel bitch.

"Lean back." Dr. Palmer glared at Scorpius until he settled back against the couch with a huff.

"I want to remind you all that these sessions are for *your* benefits." She scowled at each of us. "I'm not the one the High Court forced into therapy—I'm not the one suffering from bond sickness with the people I have to *lead* a war with." She scoffed, like if it were up to her, she would never have chosen us as leaders. "But you do."

Her glare was cutting.

Why hadn't we recruited her for the war effort? She'd make a good general.

As if she read my mind, Dr. Palmer narrowed her eyes.

I could so see her stabbing people.

Scorpius barked out a string of profanities.

E-x-h-a-u-s-t-i-o-n.

It pulled me apart.

"You should join the military," I said, and at the same time, she asked, "Aran, how do you feel?"

She gave me a withering look. "Don't speak unless spoken to."

"Yes, General," I whispered.

A rain droplet left a trail across the glass.

"So can I speak now to answer, or is there a time limit?" I asked as I debated how to tell her I felt like I'd been run over by a truck.

"Aran." She said my name like a curse and took a deep breath. "Moving on, how do you feel when Scorpius tells you what to do?"

I dug my nail deeper into my lip.

"Do you not like when he orders you around?" She pointedly looked at the blood dripping down my chin.

I scoffed. "*Obviously* not." I tried to wipe the copper taste off my tongue with the arm of my sweatshirt.

A beating heart throbbing against my tongue. Mother's blood down my throat.

"The fact that he told you not to pick at your lip—" Dr. Palmer nodded like she was realizing something (she was delusional). "—is making you act out of spite. Spite is an intense psychological response to a negative valence such as disappointment or betrayal."

Rain streaked drearily across the window. Cold air blew on the top of my head. Orion's thigh pressed against mine.

"Have these men betrayed you?"

Scorpius's chuckle was harsh, as if he wheezed with pain.

I would have joined him, but I didn't laugh with men. I only laughed *at them.*

A voice in my head laughed at my joke, like a monster that didn't exist, like the Angel Consciousness that did exist allegedly, like an angel guardian, like ancient peace accords that left us stranded, fighting a war.

It's fine.

I'm fine.

I understand my brain, I reassured myself.

The paradox of the liar—you couldn't lie if you knew it was false, but if it was false, then you were a liar. The cycle spiraled into infinity.

I rubbed at my wrist where the heavy diamond bracelet tingled like it was alive. It pulsed warm, then stopped, and I couldn't decide if I'd imagined it.

My subconscious screamed something to my consciousness, but there was a dead space inside my brain that I couldn't understand. There was an emptiness where knowledge fizzled. An abyss.

Perhaps it was hours spent screaming on a palace floor.

Perhaps it was the little sister I'd never had who'd stolen my memories.

Perhaps it was three men who'd tormented me.

Perhaps it was me.

I wanted to slam my skull against the wall.

"Your emotions make sense and are valid, especially if

you feel betrayed," Dr. Palmer said slowly, like I was an imbecile.

I stared at her deadpan.

"Perhaps you're feeling spiteful because of your own deep sense of hurt based on their actions?" She nodded. "Have they done anything to make you feel especially disappointed?"

Black ice scorched my throat, and I needed to wipe the patronizing smirk off her face.

I blurted out, "Malum set me on fire until my face melted off—and he never apologized for it."

Dr. Palmer stopped writing and blanched.

Both her eyes twitched. One. Two. Three. Four. Five. Six. Seven times. A new record.

Three men stiffened beside me.

Dr. Palmer opened and shut her mouth a few times. When she finally spoke, she overenunciated each word. "You're telling me that your—" She cleared her throat and checked her clipboard. "—Ignis set you on fire—the mate whose role is to love and cherish you?"

She showed more emotion now than ever before.

She hadn't even blinked when she'd learned I'd been disguised as a male because I was the wanted fae princess who'd murdered her mother, but now her eyes rounded with horror like she understood why the therapy session was awkward.

Finally.

Scorpius scoffed loudly. "An Ignis does not just love and cherish his Revered. That's a provincial and pathetic description. His life's purpose is to *worship, provide, shelter, and obsess* over his Revered—it's nothing as menial as love."

"It's disrespectful to insinuate that I would only love her," Malum said.

Ever completely missed the point of a conversation?

Dr. Palmer gaped at the kings with incredulity, and her complexion paled.

I smiled.

Everyone knew the point of couple's therapy was to make your therapist like you more than your partner —I'd won.

"You want to talk about caring for your Revered, yet you set Aran on fire?" Her voice pitched uncharacteristically high as she gaped at Malum.

Abruptly, a picture on the wall burst into red flames, and two shifters frolicking in a field of rolling hills melted into ashes.

Dramatic irony.

Dr. Palmer's voice climbed up another octave. "You're telling me that Aran is your *Revered?*" She didn't even glance at the flaming wall. All her attention was on the leader of the kings. "And it is your life's purpose to care for her?"

Malum grunted in agreement.

"Yet you lit her on fire until her face melted off?"

He grunted again.

When she put it that way…he *sucked*.

She scribbled furiously on her clipboard and pushed her glasses against the top of her nose with so much force the wire bent. "Don't you think that is something you should apologize to her for?"

Orion grimaced and pressed his leg harder against mine. Scorpius muttered something under his breath. I put my hand into my pockets and fondled my pipe.

Making the leader of the kings apologize was like trying to have a healthy relationship with a man.

Impossible and upsetting.

Malum gnashed his teeth. "She was disguised as a male

at the time. I didn't know she was my Revered. It was—different." His voice was harsh and gritty.

The doctor turned her chair toward me. "How do Malum's words make you feel, Aran?"

I brought my pipe between my lips and inhaled harshly.

For the first time since I'd seen her with Sadie months ago, she didn't comment on my smoking addiction.

"I feel like I want to light him on fire until his skin melts off," I said in a monotone voice.

"Then do it," Malum snarled, and I was jostled as he leaned forward to glare at me. "Stop whining about it and light me on fire, and then we'll be even—I don't understand why you keep fucking bringing this up? Just let me care for you. We need to move past this—we have enough to worry about with this fucking war."

Steel-gray eyes pinned me to my seat.

Flames cackled, and the awful scent of burning carpet filled the room.

No one moved to put it out.

I leaned forward and glared back. "*Exactly*. Since we're already doomed, why should I care about your pathetic bid for forgiveness? Have you ever thought that maybe I *want* to hold a grudge?"

"How does holding a grudge make you feel?" Dr. Palmer cut in.

"Wonderful," I said sarcastically.

Malum's cheeks flushed. "Do whatever you need to do to forgive me—I've already said you could light me on fire." Silver eyes softened. "I don't know if it's possible." Malum cleared his throat. "But I will try to reject my abilities and let flames consume me—for you—so you can have your revenge."

A pen dropped against a clipboard.

I gaped at my arch nemesis, and his cheekbones flushed redder the longer I stared.

"Okay, we'll try it." I nodded. "Get me a match and kerosene and I'll do it. Right here, right now, since you're asking for it."

"I have a lighter," Orion whispered. "But I don't want Corvus to get hurt."

Scorpius drawled sarcastically, "There's no way it would work." He wrapped his long fingers around Malum's neck, then leaned over and gave him a kiss on the cheek. "He's literally made of fire—he'll be fine."

Malum tried to pull away from Scorpius, but as his mate held him close and dug his nails into his skin, he gave up struggling.

Molten silver hardened into steel as he looked over at me. "I already fucking said you could do it." He spread his arms wide. "I'm waiting. Between the two of us—I'm not the coward."

"Give me the lighter." I nudged Orion.

He hesitantly reached into his pocket.

"*Stop!*" Dr. Palmer's shrill voice made all four of us wince. "No one—" She breathed deeply like she was trying to get control of herself. "—is lighting anyone on fire in this room."

"So we should do it outside of the room?" I asked.

Knuckles whitened against a clipboard, and she stared at the ceiling like she was having a mental breakdown. *Extremely relatable.*

A timer went off.

With a fluid movement, she sat up straight and smiled at us. Her voice was honey sweet as she said, "Your hour session is over. Please leave."

I stood and stuck out my hand for her to shake.

"Get *out* of my office." She held her clipboard tight to her chest.

I let my hand drop and nodded as I took a long drag from my pipe. "You're truly a goddess at your craft. Great stuff—I really liked how you just repeated the same phrases."

"*Out!*" she snapped.

"I'll let you know how lighting him on fire works." I yawned.

"I *didn't* suggest that." Her pen snapped. "As an accredited professional, I'm informing all of you right now that I will report you to the relevant authorities if any of you light each other—or anyone else—on fire."

The smoldering picture frame fell off the wall.

We all knew there were no authorities that would punish the champions of the gods. We were the appointed authorities. More proof that lunatics ran the realms.

Who looked at Malum and thought, "That man seems stable. Let's give him insane powers and put him in charge?" I'd like to speak to that person's manager…and shank them.

The kings stood up and embraced one another.

Then they turned, and all three of them crowded my space.

I looked down and noticed the water left in my cup had frozen into solid ice. Peculiar.

Shadows and muscles widened around me.

I pulled the RJE device with "therapy" engraved on its surface out of my pocket and grabbed Orion's wrist. Scorpius and Malum wrapped their fingers around my forearm.

They could have just grabbed Orion, but in the last three weeks, they pointedly touched me every time we RJE'd.

As if the split second of contact meant something to them.

They were trying to show they chose me.

Like it wasn't too late.

It was.

Fat droplets streaked drearily across the window, and I said cheerily, "I'll keep you updated." I pressed the glowing device.

Dr. Palmer shook her head frantically. "Please, don't."

"I will," I whispered as I blinked and the therapist's office disappeared.

Crack.

The air stank of wet dirt, regret, and secrets.

Location: the war camp.

CHAPTER 5
ARAN
THE WAR CAMP

Brume (noun): mist, fog.

I knelt on warm dirt as steam evaporated onto my face.

Pine needles rustled.

The new realm was colored in shades of gray.

It was depressing.

Hundreds of snow-frosted trees swayed as the therapy RJE fell silent in my hand. Condensation from steam froze across my face as I stood up.

The air was chilly, but I was colder.

A shiver racked my frame.

The tension from Dr. Palmer's office still clung to my skin, and I concentrated on my surroundings.

All was hushed.

I'd assumed the base for a planetwide war would be enormous and filled with thousands of soldiers. That it would be loud and messy. Chaotic.

It was painfully quiet.

Only a hundred soldiers.

We were alone.

Abandoned.

I pressed my pipe between my lips and inhaled deeply, and it clattered against my teeth. Horse cawed as he circled through the snow above my head.

Squinting, I studied my crow's feathers and tried to remember if they'd always trailed after him in such a long plumage.

He twirled lazily on a breeze and screeched his enjoyment.

I shrugged and blew out a cloud of smoke, my nose burning from the chilled air.

Glaring up at the towering white-peaked mountains that surrounded the valley, I pocketed the RJE device.

Thick snowflakes fell softly in the gray.

Storm clouds drifted through an atmosphere.

I inhaled smoke sharply and tried to forget that Lyla had lied by implication when she'd given our legions separate designations.

We weren't here to lead an army of thousands; we were here to fight against a planet full of monsters.

We were here to suffer.

I exhaled and pretended the gods weren't useless beings who'd abandoned us.

Snow drifted through the frigid air, then sizzled as it hit the hot ground and evaporated, and water hissed as it rose from the planet's surface in a thick layer of fog.

Planet 003FX had an immensely hot core that heated the ground to around eighty degrees Fahrenheit and a freezing atmosphere.

At least, that was what the High Court's informational packet said.

I said it sucked.

Freezing temperatures, perpetual falling snow, a foggy surface, and gray sky.

A boring place to die.

If I squinted, I could just barely see a tiny shimmer to the air. The High Court speculated that rare bioluminescence in the soil evaporated into the atmosphere and created the effect.

Since it was barely noticeable, I don't know why they bothered to discuss it.

The kings followed as I walked through the war camp hidden beneath glistening heavens.

Snow-dusted trees camouflaged the camp.

I had yet to see any evidence of animals.

"Aran, you're back." John burst out of our legion's designated bunker and threw his arms around me. "*Thank the sun god*, Luka's in a silent mood, and he refused to laugh at any of my jokes."

I didn't point out that Luka was *always* in a silent mood; it was part of his charm. Instead, I inhaled the rich scent of sandalwood and slumped forward.

John held me up.

Snowflakes danced around us as our breath mingled in frosty puffs.

Our chests pressed together, hearts thumping in rhythm, I burrowed into his arms like I could crawl under his skin.

Disappear into his warmth.

"How was mandatory therapy? Are you okay?" John whispered in my ear.

I pressed my face deeper against his warm shoulder and groaned, "Horrible. And no."

Arms tightened around my shoulders as he squeezed me three times in quick succession.

My heart stuttered.

I squeezed back four times as hard as I could.

His breath caught.

We both knew what it meant.

"Anything I can do to help?" John's fingers gently tipped my chin up, and he brushed snow off my face.

"Beat me to death with a shovel," I offered.

He chuckled, and the sound was deep and rich as he swooped down and booped my nose, holding me close as I struggled to get away.

"Is she hurt?" Luka asked behind him. "Did something happen to her face?" Unlike John's relaxed posture, Luka was rigid.

Tense.

He was focused on the two of us.

At all times.

Luka's dark eyes flashed with concern as he stared down at me, so I wiggled out of John's arms and jumped to give him a quick kiss on the cheek.

His fingers pressed reverently against where my lips touched.

Pinpricks of pain trailed across my back. There was something so heartbreakingly sweet about Luka that it made me want to latch onto him and never let him go.

John pulled me back beneath his arm and answered his twin, "Nah." He flashed his dimples and tried to tweak my nose again, but I ducked. "My *wife* is perfect."

"Our wife," Luka corrected.

Malum said, "She's *not* your wife."

The kings glared at the twins like they were a threat. Malum's flaming arms were draped over Scorpius and Orion protectively.

For a few seconds, I'd forgotten they existed, and I missed that time because it was peaceful.

The devils moved together and crowded our space as Luka stepped forward protectively.

"Not our wife." John winked dramatically. "*Yet*."

I rolled my eyes. "Whatever you say, *husband*."

My stomach swooped, and the pain intensified.

"Shut the fuck up and be quiet," Malum snarled. "You both know the rules."

What a sweet man. There was that sunshine and rainbows attitude everyone knew and loved.

His knuckles were white from how tightly he was gripping his mates for support.

Therapy had clearly mellowed him out. Not.

He needed electric shock therapy, or a lobotomy, or both.

I was willing to experiment.

John opened his mouth to speak, and the glare Malum shot at him would have brought a lesser man to his knees.

Central to the war effort was remaining undetected by the ungodly. Since the High Court didn't know what technology the planet possessed, everyone was ordered to stay indoors as much as possible, and if you were outside, you had to be quiet.

Red flames flickered on bronze shoulders, and the snow falling around us turned into rain.

The kings stared at me with intense emotions.

I stared back with deadened eyes.

I'd stopped caring when he'd forced me to stand out under a sky that rained glass.

"You're just calling him husband to get on our nerves," Scorpius sneered.

I sighed heavily. "You think you're so important. Newsflash, I'm calling him my husband—because that's *exactly* what he's going to be." I scoffed. "Everything isn't about you. Grow up."

Scorpius's razor-sharp jaw twitched, red flames multiplied, and Orion frowned at me like I'd disappointed him.

I leaned against John, and Luka rubbed my back. I smiled with contentment and said softly, "My *husbands* are important to me."

The battle lines between us were clear.

Three versus three.

Scorpius grunted at my words like he'd taken a punch to the gut.

I smirked.

Of course, I was only doing it out of spite; I might be depressed, but at my core, I was a hateful bitch.

"Stop calling them that," Malum burst out loudly, red staining his bronze cheeks as he stared at me like he was embarrassed that he couldn't control his temper.

We were all embarrassed for him.

"Let's go inside, *husbands*." I ignored the kings. "Some people don't know how to obey the rules of the camp."

John flashed his dimples, and Luka grunted as I pulled them inside the room that was our legion's sleeping bunker.

A seven-foot-tall flaming blight on the history of womankind stomped in behind us. "I told you to be quiet first," Malum said unhelpfully.

The fact that *this* was him trying to grovel to me was beyond disturbing.

"And I told you to shut the fuck up and die." I yawned. "What's your point?"

The temperature spiked.

What could I say? The therapy session was making me feel reckless. I wanted payback.

I breathed into my cupped hands to warm them.

Malum's fists trembled at his side, and his face exploded in scarlet flames.

Orion roughly pulled him back, and Scorpius shouted in his face, "Snap out of it! You're in control—the fire does *not* control you. Breathe with me. You're okay."

I rolled my eyes as Scorpius talked Malum off the edge of a total inferno for what felt like the millionth time this week.

"Just to play devil's advocate—" I chuckled at the double entendre. "—he doesn't *seem* in control to me."

Malum growled like a wild animal.

Never forget three weeks ago at the end of the Legionnaire Games when Malum said he was going to cherish and take care of me and promised it would be different.

Baby girl needs to focus on what he's manifesting because it's not working. I opened my mouth to tell him so, but—

"I can't do this!" Malum screamed, and flames shot out of his mouth like a dragon. "I can't watch you hang all over other men and call them your husbands without reacting. You're *mine*."

Eh, I'll tell him later.

He fell to his knees.

My headache intensified.

I kicked off my heavy combat boots, lay down in my narrow bunk bed, and pulled the blankets up to my chin.

John kissed my forehead and climbed up to the top bunk. Luka gave me a soft kiss on the cheek and climbed into the bed above mine. A zip of pain traveled down my spine.

Fondness spread through me.

All three of us sighed.

Our new bedroom was low, narrow, and sparse, with a single window that had a view of the trees. A sliver of mountain was visible if you pressed your face against the glass and looked to the left.

Yes, my cheek print was still on the glass from looking.

The space also had matching three-person bunk beds on the walls going longways and a two-person bunk that framed the window. A narrow dresser in the corner had eight drawers, one for each of us, and a laughably small bathroom with barely any room to move.

Overall, it was sufficient.

Better than a wall in front of a toilet and a broken cot.

"You can't be with them." Flames swallowed Malum whole in the center of the room, and Scorpius grimaced as he held on to his crazed mate.

Orion glared at the twins like it was their fault.

The room sizzled with heat.

I snuggled deeper into bed and enjoyed the cozy warmth as my chilly skin thawed. Malum made a nice bonfire.

I'd been surprised by how accepting the kings had been of the twins over these last few weeks. I'd gaslit myself into thinking just maybe they weren't totally insane.

Glad we'd cleared that up.

Malum having a total meltdown felt right. The failed therapy sessions and close proximity didn't help. Neither did a looming war.

From what I'd gathered, the kings were desperate to prove to the sun god that they were worthy kings, and they were devastated that they wouldn't have an army to back them.

I also would have been depressed if I was passionate about winning.

Good thing I was depressed for other reasons.

"You should probably cry about it more," I said to Malum, who was still fully on fire. "That will *definitely* help the situation."

Yes, I was being a raging bitch to the kings whenever I

could, which objectively wasn't helping the situation; however, subjectively, it was making me feel better.

A win-win.

Flames roared.

"He's not wrong," Scorpius sneered as he gripped his lunatic of a mate. "At the end of the day, you're *our Revered*. You're fated to be with us—not them. You need to grow up and stop pretending. You're already one of us."

Orion nodded in agreement, and light pink petals drifted across his neck as captivating brown eyes glinted with anger.

I yawned sleepily.

Who was going to tell them I was way too fashionable to be one of them? Our lifestyles had a fundamental conflict—I wanted to lie in the sun all day and do nothing, and they wanted to kill things for fun. I wanted to nap under a tree as a warm breeze rustled my hair, and Malum wanted to set the tree on fire and scream at it.

I shuddered.

We were never going to work.

Luka draped his hand down over the side of the bunk, and I threaded my fingers through his. The only good thing about the suffocatingly close bunks was we could easily reach one another.

I'd gotten used to waking up with a numb arm.

I needed Luka's touch because nightmares stalked me when I closed my eyes, and his grip was my only tether to reality.

"As your Ignis, I order you to break off your engagement," Malum snarled harshly.

A callused thumb brushed back and forth against the back of my hand comfortingly.

I snuggled deeper into my covers and said, "As the hole in the room—I order you to stop ordering me around."

Sleep pulled me under, because unlike the plush beds at Elite Academy, my mattress was hard as a rock. I loved it.

"You're not just a hole," Malum snapped.

"Wait, really?" I asked in mock confusion. "That's news to me."

"Obviously," Scorpius spat. "Don't be ridiculous. He's already apologized for that—we're trying to move forward."

"Technically," I whispered, "I have three holes. So I'm holes. Plural." I chuckled to myself as darkness wrapped around me.

I drifted away into sweet unconsciousness.

"Do *not* talk about yourself that way. I won't fucking have it," Malum barked, and I immediately jolted back awake.

Sun god forbid the hole in the room have a moment of peace.

"Is Malum having a meltdown again?" Vegar asked from the other set of bunks. Our demon teammate's voice was scratchy, like he'd just woken up from a nap.

Zenith grumbled above him.

"Oh yeah," John answered.

The demon lovers were grumpier than usual because they couldn't fit together on the narrow beds. Add into the mix a seven-foot-tall soldier of death with the constitution of a flaming, deranged donkey and you had a recipe for uncomfortable living.

Malum screamed, "*I'm not having a meltdown!*"

Convincing.

Vegar resumed snoring.

"Okay, Mitch," I mumbled.

"What?" Zenith asked.

"Male bitch."

"Oh," Zenith said, "makes sense."

The leader of the kings let out a war cry.

"Save it for the battlefield, Mitch." I pulled the blanket

over my head with my free arm and tried to suffocate myself to sleep.

Luka squeezed my hand, and I relished his touch.

"Can you stop antagonizing him?" Scorpius sneered. "You're not helping the situation."

"You're doing this to me, Arabella," Malum said harshly.

What a charming individual.

"No baby girl, that's all you." I yawned. "Also, that's something a Mitch would say."

Someone let out a barking laugh, but sleep swallowed me, and I couldn't respond.

I jolted awake.

Soft snores and the whisper of sheets echoed.

It took my eyes a moment to adjust to the darkness. The room's single window was dark with snowfall, and there wasn't a star in sight.

The covers pulled up to my chin crackled with frost, and my breath came out in a visible puff even though the room was warmed by enchantment.

I couldn't find the energy to be surprised.

Lately, the cold stalked me.

Diamonds flashed as I moved the wrist clasped in Luka's grip. My other hand was filled with cold metal and paper. I brought my palm to my face in confusion.

Recognition dawned.

A lighter and a tiny piece of paper, which read, "Please don't hurt Corvus, he doesn't mean what he says."

Orion was trying to help.

Bless his delusional, psychotic heart.

He didn't realize his mate was beyond saving.

For a second, my heart panged as I thought about how much the kings all cared about one another. They didn't want to see Malum hurt, and truthfully, neither did I—I wanted him obliterated. Complete annihilation.

There was nothing more satisfying than a grown man crying.

Empty anger welled.

I was vengeful because of what he'd done to me.

He'd made his choice.

He'd sacrificed me in the games.

He'd discarded me like trash.

I needed payback—I needed to do something.

Gently detangling my fingers from Luka's, I slipped out of bed and tiptoed across the barely three feet of space that separated one end of the room from the other.

Kneeling in front of the lowest bunk, I brought the lighter up.

Flicked it.

A yellow flame danced, and I held it against the white sheets. It crawled across fabric and left a scorch of black, and the harsh scent of burning cotton was noxious.

Fire multiplied.

Harsh bronze features in repose flickered with shadows. Asleep, Corvus Malum looked more like a man and less like the angry instrument of the sun god.

Silver eyes opened and glinted with a green sheen.

Yellow flames intensified.

Malum stared at me and didn't move as his bed went up in flames.

"Can you turn off your powers?" I whispered.

Bronze skin rippled as he leaned forward, and I scrambled backward as he climbed out of the yellow inferno and unfurled to his full height.

For a long moment, he stood before me, burning.

His brow crinkled, and he fisted his hands and scrunched his lids shut like he was concentrating on letting the fire consume him.

Lashes fluttered.

Silver eyes pooled with sadness.

"No," he said brokenly. "I can't turn it off."

As he stood before me, half-naked, layers of bronze rippled across his immense torso, his shoulders hunched forward with defeat like he'd thought this could save us.

A ripple of pain shivered down my spine, and I pretended not to feel it.

I mumbled, "At least you tried."

We both knew it wasn't enough.

We'd both heard my screams.

"Look at me."

I stared at the floor.

"Please," he begged.

I glanced up.

The flaming devil took a step closer, and his expression fell as he whispered, "I'm sorry about how I spoke to you earlier. I was out of line—and it does hurt."

A blush stained the tops of his cheekbones as he stared down at me.

His silver eyes were pleading.

Scorpius swore as he scrambled out of his bunk and smacked at the flames, and the rest of the room woke up around us. Men shouted. Someone grabbed a bucket from the bathroom and threw water on the flames. There was chaos all around.

Neither of us moved.

"Just not how you meant, Arabella." His baritone voice was soft.

He leaned closer and breathed out.

Our breath mingled.

Surprisingly soft lips pressed gently against mine, and they were incredibly warm. "I'm so sorry," he whispered against my mouth. "Please forgive me." Wide palms cradled the sides of my face, and heavily callused fingers traced gently across my cheekbones.

Pain streaked sharply across my back.

Heat burned against my mouth as a different type of fire spread inside my chest.

As his tongue battled against mine, I tasted whiskey and tobacco. My skin tingled with awareness.

Knees went weak.

The bed burned and men yelled. As they tried to put out the fire, Malum kissed me like he was trying to devour me.

Pain streaked hotter down my spine.

It reminded me.

I was embracing the devil.

I yanked away from him and stumbled until I bumped into my bed. Regret filled my throat and closed my airways for acting rashly, and I wished I hadn't woken him up.

I should have kept ignoring him.

Flames boiled me alive. Water filled my lungs. Glass shredded my skin. Jinx screamed in pain. He looked at me. "Women are nothing but holes."

He whispered brokenly, "It hurts because you're already killing me." A bronze hand reached out toward me. His lips were swollen. There was a handprint of ice in the middle of his chest where I'd touched him.

He looked ravaged.

I shivered uncontrollably as blue ice spread beneath my feet.

"I will make the past up to you. I swear on my life." His voice dripped with sincerity.

He sounded agonized.

The handprint sizzled as it melted.

I climbed backward into my bed, and bronze fingers curled slowly into a fist and fell down with defeat.

Dr. Palmer had said my feelings were valid.

I felt like Malum didn't care about me; he just wanted his Revered. He wanted a perfect ideal, not an imperfect person.

I counted desperately under my breath. "Two. Four. Sixteen. Two hundred and fifty-six. Sixty-five thousand, five hundred, and thirty-six." The numbers blurred.

I pressed trembling fingers to my lips.

They still tingled.

Whiskey and tobacco lingered on my tongue like the most depraved aphrodisiac.

I reminded myself that Aran would never be enough for the kings.

The three of them whispered and held one another in the middle of the room as they made sure Malum was all right.

Luka made a disgruntled noise and flexed the hand hanging over his bunk like he was agitated.

I wrapped my fingers around his.

He sighed with relief and squeezed tightly.

The hollowness in my chest receded, but as my eyes closed, nightmares sank their claws deep and pulled me under.

Fire burned all around.

One. Two. Three. Four. Five. Six…

Even in my sleep, I counted.

Desperately.

CHAPTER 6

SCORPIUS
THE FIRST ASSIGNMENT

Facinorous (adjective): atrociously wicked.

"*The angels have returned from their scouting mission!*" The alarm blared over the room's enchanted speaker system.

Pain stabbed my temples.

The alarm burned my overly sensitive ears.

"*The first ungodly infestation has been located, and RJE devices have been calibrated for coordinates. All legions and soldiers report to the cafeteria in .03 hours. Repeat. All legions and soldiers report to the cafeteria in .03 hours. Reminder to move stealthily, quiet must be observed in open areas. Do not compromise the base.*"

I climbed out of my bunk.

Clothes rustled and voices swore as my legion mates rushed to pull on their standard-issue military gear that Orion said was all black: insulated undergarments, flexible snow pants, a thin but warm jacket, and heavy combat boots.

I was already fully dressed.

Ever since we'd moved into the war camp, I slept fully clothed.

I was always more prepared than everyone else. Planning ahead for every situation and iteration to make sure I didn't inconvenience those around me.

My mates never judged me, but the rest of the world did.

I was the blind one.

I'd always be weak, no matter how many times I proved I was strong.

My ears rang as the high-pitched sirens wailed, and a crippling headache pounded against my temple.

"Are you okay?" Corvus asked as he massaged the base of my skull like he always did when I was around headache-inducing sounds.

I nodded at him.

Orion gave me a gentle kiss on the cheek, and I basked in his tenderness, then I pulled away regretfully.

We had obligations.

War.

Adrenaline pounded through my veins, and I cracked my neck back and forth.

Ever since we'd learned how alone we were in this war, I'd been itching to do something. I needed to take action. It was obvious that the High Court was wholly unprepared for what was to come.

Sounds erupted as my teammates scrambled to get dressed.

The voice that haunted my dreams swore softly, and I stalked across the room toward them.

"Do you need help?" I asked, every cell in my body highly attuned to her presence.

Arabella grunted. "I can't find a hair tie, and my stupid curls are—"

I pulled the band off my wrist and held it out to her.

"Where did you get that?" Her voice was accusing, and she didn't take it.

I sighed with annoyance. "Take the fucking hair band."

"Explain." She snatched it from my fingers.

"I have it on me in case Corvus needs to keep his pretty hair pulled back," I sneered sarcastically.

There was a scratching noise as my Ignis ran his hands over his shaved head and snapped, "Really?"

Arabella chuckled, then stopped like she'd remembered who she was laughing with. "Tell me why you have it." Two palms pressed against my chest and pushed me backward.

She was trying to be threatening.

I swallowed down a moan.

My Revered's hands were on me.

She'd voluntarily touched me.

Ten cold fingers had splayed against my shirt for .2 seconds, and it was just long enough to send streaks of lust exploding across my senses.

I readjusted my pants.

"Tell me!" Arabella pushed me again.

I put my fist to my mouth and bit down to stop myself from giving her an explanation. I needed her to keep touching me like I needed to breathe.

It was fucking crucial to my survival.

She *was* my survival.

Nobody could understand but us.

Unlike other relationships, devil mates weren't symbiotes of compatible souls that joined together.

A Revered *was* a male devil's soul. Period.

Without her we were soulless monsters.

An enchanted voice boomed, "*All legions and soldiers report to the cafeteria in .01 hours.*"

"We need to go now," Corvus barked over the sirens.

"Come on, Aran," Luka said gruffly, and there was the sound of flesh against cloth as he pulled her away from me.

"Stay calm," John murmured to her.

As our legion exited the room, Orion and I ran forward in unison and placed ourselves in front of Arabella. A Protector shielded his Revered.

Always.

Orion grabbed my elbow as he jogged beside me and led me down the paths.

I nodded my thanks in his direction.

We were on the same page.

Behind us, Arabella whispered, "Get out of my way." She pushed gently against my back. "Also, explain the hair tie."

I grunted from the ecstasy of her touch.

Chilly air slapped my face, and steam sizzled as the pine needles whispered, snow falling gently all around.

I tasted the cold radiating off Arabella; it was like a shot of adrenaline straight into my veins. It was addicting.

The noises of the new realm were foreign and disorienting. The landscape was quietly loud in a cacophony of hushed sounds. I'd never heard anything like it.

Orion and I fell back so we were closer to Arabella.

She huffed and tried to jog faster to get around us, but we picked up our speed and shielded her with our bodies.

She didn't get it.

We were never leaving her unguarded.

Not in a foreign realm.

Not during war.

Not in a time of peace.

Never.

Flames crackled on Corvus's shoulder as my Ignis ran at

the back of the group, his breathing steady and controlled behind us as he protected our Revered's flank.

Not for the first time, I marveled at how truly opposite they were—ice and fire. It was highly unusual because an Ignis and Revered were renowned for complementing each other's abilities.

It seemed strange that they would be true opposites. The only complement they could provide was to stop the other. With Corvus's tenuous control over his flames, a part of it made sense that Arabella was meant to ice him out when he lost control.

I grimaced.

There was something wrong with that dynamic.

It was utilitarian in its brutality, while an Ignis and Revered were supposed to be something *more*. Destined to help each other, not hurt.

My gut screamed at me that Arabella's role wasn't just to stop Corvus.

Last night, Orion had whispered in my ear that Corvus had kissed her like he was a dying man, and she was oxygen. I'd had to adjust myself in my pants.

Fuck, I wanted them both so badly.

In the present, scarlet flames crackled louder around Corvus; the temperature around Arabella dropped several degrees colder.

Instinct warned that their powers unleashed together would be cataclysmic and painful.

That was fine with me.

I welcomed the fallout.

Everyone else, including the soldiers we jogged beside down the path, were collateral. It had always been about her, but we'd been stupid fools unable to recognize it for what it was.

Now no one mattered but Arabella.

Period.

I was a Protector through and through.

When we entered the cafeteria, it was uncomfortably warm.

Soft breathing, rustling, and anticipation filled the largest structure of the camp and indicated about a hundred soldiers were present.

We gathered inside and stood at attention beside the rest of the camp.

Dick spoke loudly from the front of the hall, "The angels have located the first city-state and returned with coordinates. As you've been informed, this planet is composed of valley settlements separated by treacherous mountains."

Steps echoed with the telltale click that all the boots of the High Court workers had as a person walked among the lines.

A worker shoved metal against my chest harshly.

I grabbed the sword and sheathed it.

"Don't touch him like that," Corvus threatened the worker softly beside me.

Orion breathed roughly through his nose.

As the only blind soldier at the base, I was used to the rough treatment and the whispers that followed me. I could practically taste the doubt radiating off the High Court workers in my presence.

I heard the whispers.

They didn't think I belonged.

Corvus growled, and the worker gulped loudly.

Dick announced, "We will reiterate one last time that we suspect there to be dozens of portals hidden in this planet's geography connecting it to other High Court realms."

He paused.

A worker cleared their throat in front of me, and I held my hands out.

Knives were placed into my palms gently, and I threaded them through the straps on my belt.

"Better," Corvus said as the person scurried away.

"As we've said before"—Dick sounded annoyed that he was repeating himself—"our data indicates there has been no coordinated push to escape through the portals. They seem to travel at random in small segments, and the High Court has had success eliminating those small sects. These operations do not amount to war."

Arabella murmured under her breath beside me, "No. *We've* had success eliminating them."

I agreed.

"The ungodly need to be dealt with at the source," Dick said.

Feet shuffled, and a few men gulped.

The High Court kept dancing around explicitly saying that we had to eliminate an entire planet before they realized they were under attack.

A mass extermination.

"As I've stated before, the OPA forbid the High Court from waging direct war against another sentient species. This is the first and only mission we will be a part of. We have given you the tools and ability to locate the threat."

The worker handed me a sword, and I sheathed it.

"Going forward, the shifter and academy legions will be in charge," Dick said with authority. "The angel legion is second-in-command to them. They will convene and plan in the strategy room. Everyone except Jinx will RJE there. She stays at the base."

Soldiers whispered.

I recognized a voice.

Knox, the angel captain with heterochromia, called Jinx a string of expletives, which was strange because he was usually polite and collaborative.

I narrowed my eyes.

We'd spent a lot of time with the shifter legion, and I'd come to enjoy Jinx's presence.

I didn't like his fucking tone.

Dick continued, "We have no knowledge about the civilization the ungodly have taken over. We recommend conserving your abilities and only using weapons in this first meeting to identify as much information as possible about your foes."

The worker handed me a small silicone device and explained hastily, "It's an enchanted earpiece so the champions and generals can communicate with each other. Press down on the top button once to speak. Hold it down to turn it off."

I nodded and placed it in my ear.

It fit snugly.

"Per the OPA, all high-ranking members of the High Court will leave this camp immediately. How you choose to proceed is up to you. We are giving you all the tools you need to succeed."

A rustle of unease spread through the room.

"A team of healers, weapons strategists, enchanters, and food workers unconnected to the High Court will remain to assist with the base operations. All concerns can be sent to the High Court through a secured, enchanted tablet, but note we may not be able to respond."

Boots shuffled back and forth on concrete.

"Corvus and Jax have been handed RJE devices to the settlement. Wait for their directions. Good luck, soldiers. The fate of the realms is in your hands."

There was a whirring noise. CRACK. Dick was gone.

The room erupted into motion.

Arabella scoffed beside me, "I can't believe they just abandoned us here."

"Don't be stupid," I sneered. "People in power always leave their messes to others. It was always going to be this way."

"It's still stupid," she muttered. "Personally, I think we should let the ungodly do their thing. Who are we to intervene?"

Corvus huffed, "We're the sun god's kings. We're built for war."

"No," she said. "*You're* kings, *I'm* a queen. I was built for shopping and leisure."

My Ignis choked, and I chuckled at how ridiculous she was. It was adorable. If I hadn't fought beside her in gruesome battles, I would think she was serious.

My Revered liked to pretend she was a privileged despot. It was part of the reason we'd judged her so wrongly.

She hid her fierceness behind masks of sarcasm, but there was no mistaking that she was a force of rage and power.

She was savage.

And I couldn't stop obsessing over her.

I grabbed her hand and threaded our fingers together, and hers were frozen like she was sculpted from ice.

Tension dissipated from my body at the contact, and I rubbed my thumb back and forth over hers. She tried to pull away, but my grip was steel.

The others gathered around.

"The champions and angels are going to RJE to the location for surveillance. Wait here for further orders. When we return, we go to war," Corvus barked loudly in the quiet room.

"Yes, sir!" soldiers chorused back.

There was a clattering of wings as the angels walked over.

"You didn't join us for the scouting trip," Knox said in a smooth tone beside me. "We missed you."

I bristled.

He hadn't earned the right to miss her.

How fucking dare he talk to my Revered like he knew her? Orion put his arm around my shoulder and held me back.

Arabella chuckled awkwardly. "Yeah, well I can't fly yet. I'm still working on it."

"You'll learn to fly," he responded curtly. "You'll train with us after this battle."

"Don't fucking tell her what to do," Corvus snarled aggressively, and heat poured off him.

"That would work for me." Arabella clicked her tongue. "But I'm really big on rest days. So let's circle back to that idea next week."

"Soon," Knox said. "Until you learn to fly, you're weak. You need to master your abilities."

"Thirty seconds until we all RJE," Corvus said. Wings clattered, and Knox made a sound like he'd been pushed to the side.

Jax replied, "Remember, we need to be discreet, no loud noises."

"Got it, make loud noises," Sadie drawled obnoxiously.

Arabella laughed.

It wasn't funny.

Warm breath suddenly fanned against my ear. "Why did

you have a hair band?" Arabella whispered so closely that she must have been on her tiptoes.

I closed my eyes and inhaled her intoxicating icy scent, and my heart pounded erratically like I'd taken a shot of caffeine.

"Tell me." Her nails dug into the skin of my arm that was still gripping her wrist in a vise. She drew blood.

A shot of pure lust clouded my thoughts. *Does she know what that means to me?* Pain was my love language.

Her cold touch burned deliciously, and I grunted softly with pleasure.

The RJE device whirred as Corvus said, "Three seconds."

I bent forward so my lips brushed against her temple. "Because you kept complaining about losing them, and I wanted to be helpful."

CRACK.

The sound of jumping through time and space muffled Arabella's harsh inhale, but I didn't miss it.

I'd surprised her.

Cold air stung my cheeks, and I knelt on icy rocks. From the lack of hot steam, we were on the side of a mountain.

"Let go of me." Arabella's breath came out in uneven puffs.

My lips were still pressed against her icy skin, and it was like touching lightning in a blizzard. Electricity crackled between us.

"Never," I promised as I released her hand.

She let out a little gasp like she was in pain, and I frowned.

Nothing should have hurt her, yet her breathing pattern clearly changed like it did when she was getting stitched up.

I didn't fucking like it.

"Stay low, follow me. We'll climb down the mountain-side." Corvus's voice spoke loudly in our enchanted earpieces.

Arabella tried to take a step away from me, but I stepped closer. The battle might be starting, but a campaign was already being waged, and failure wasn't an option when it came to her.

I would figure out whatever pained her, and I would destroy it. My Revered would never suffer in my presence, never again.

Orion's touch guided me as we stayed close to our Revered and followed our Ignis into war.

CHAPTER 7
ARAN
PREPERATIONS

QUERENCIA (NOUN): an area in the arena taken by the bull for a defensive stand in a bullfight.

The infected settlement was a sprawling palatial structure, which filled the valley. It was composed of red bricks and arches that were dusted in snow.

In the center of it all, a sprawling courtyard was filled with trees wrapped in twinkling lights.

It was pretty.

Malum swore viciously as he lay on his stomach with binoculars pressed against his face. Jax was beside him in a similar position, frowning as he watched the valley below.

"What is it?" Cobra asked as he squatted under the low-hanging rocks with the rest of us.

Six angels.

Four shifters.

Three devils.

Two demons.

Two Princes of Darkness.

One half-breed.

And one fae queen who'd recently discovered she was an angel.

Nineteen people who would never have crossed paths if it weren't for nightmarish monsters, truant gods, and a controlling, oligarchic regime.

The twins sat behind me, and I leaned back against them with Sadie resting across my side as I inhaled her familiar cranberry scent.

Once again, we were together on the side of a freezing, snowy mountain.

Why weren't more wars held in tropical locations? That was the real question.

The sun set on the horizon, and the sky was a dark gray.

Horse settled onto my shoulder, his long tail feathers hanging off the side of my arm majestically. At least someone was looking good these days.

"Fuck this," Malum whispered. "Could one thing go right for us in this blasted realm?"

"What is it?" Scorpius asked, his arm draped over Orion's shoulders protectively.

Jax and Malum dropped their binoculars and looked at each other. Ever since Dick had started preparing us for war, they'd been sharing silent glances and nodding. Like they could read each other's minds.

"I'm getting worried," Sadie whispered next to me.

I blew onto my stiff hands to warm them and replied, "Don't worry. I'll save you, princess."

She stuck her tongue out at me, and I tried to grab it while she squealed.

My head still ached from building my mind palace. My shoulders also hurt, and I rolled them to relieve the dull pain that had appeared after I'd sprouted wings that didn't work like a demented butterfly.

Life was truly marvelous.

At least I hadn't been born a man; that would really suck…although, my penis would be huge.

Luka's hands traced patterns absent-mindedly across my back, and John played with my curls as he whispered something under his breath to his brother. The jewel of death hung heavy against my chest, and a diamond bracelet glinted on my wrist.

I slumped back against the warmth of the twins and cherished their proximity.

Lately, they were one of the few things that staved off the madness.

The perpetual cold inside my bones, headaches, and pain in my shoulders were overstimulating at best and torturous at worst.

Sadie patted my head and sniggered, "Please, I don't need you to save me—remember, I can enslave you at *any* time." She winked. "Plus, we get to battle beside each other in an intergalactic war to save the world. It should be fun."

I pulled out my pipe and inhaled deeply. "False." I blew smoke in her face. "Fun is a shopping trip, or when we tried to lose our virginity together at the fae sex clinic."

We both frowned as we thought about how that day had gone horribly wrong.

I chuckled. "Never forget we both checked yes for elbow play."

She grimaced and clutched her arm protectively. "I still have nightmares about someone violating them."

I squinted. "I never thought about it—but how would that work? What is sexual about an elbow? I have so many questions."

She made a face. "I think it's *pretty* clear."

It was times like this where I worried the most about her.

"What do you mean, it's clear?" I asked. "Nothing about something called 'elbow play' is clear to me."

The twins made a choking noise behind me, and we ignored them.

"Grow up, Aran," Sadie said as she shook her head like I was being stupid, then she snatched the pipe from my fingers before I could react and took a long drag. "Damn, I forgot how much this stuff hits."

I rolled my eyes at her.

Obviously.

I only smoked the best.

"Drugs are not allowed in battle," a high-pitched female voice said haughtily from a few feet away. "It was stated in the High Court's informational packet, multiple times."

Sadie, Horse, and I turned in unison to stare at the gorgeous woman who crouched against the rocks.

Black-lipstick-stained lips contrasted with her cornflower-blonde hair. She was the angel who'd slaughtered the devil and assassin in the Legionnaire Games.

Horse looked away and dug his beak into his wings to groom the new feathers along the tips. He was clearly unimpressed with what he saw.

"What's your name?" I twirled my pipe with my tongue, and Sadie's eyes glowed intensely, a scarlet sheen reflected off the snow.

"Rina," the angel answered through gritted teeth.

"Well, Rina," I said slowly with a false smile. "The High Court has *abandoned us*, and we're all probably going to die at the hands of parasitic monsters."

She frowned.

"Violently."

A few feet away from me, the demons shook with silent laughter.

I inhaled enchanted smoke. "Personally, I'm going to keep smoking. If you want to die stone-cold sober, then be my guest. But worry about yourself."

"You know, I've never thought about it that way," Sadie said as I passed her the pipe. "It really makes you think about things."

"What things?" I asked.

She stared at the smoke. "Things." She spoke like she was saying something deep.

There's my special girl.

"You're so right." I nodded in agreement and let her have her philosophical moment. I was nothing if not supportive.

Rina wrinkled her nose. "It's against the rules for everyone, especially us. We're the leaders. We need to set a good example."

"That's not really our thing," Sadie mumbled as she smoked, and I nodded in agreement. We had a reputation to uphold, and it involved drinking excessive amounts of demon brew and making questionable life choices.

Rina's pretty face contorted. "I wasn't talking to you, half-breed mutt."

Stunned silence.

"What did you just call my mate?" Cobra's voice was serrated, and there was a loud *schhhhhk* as Xerxes pulled out his knives.

I started to stand up, but Sadie pulled me back down.

No one stopped Cobra.

He stalked across the narrow rocks and glared down at Rina with slit pupils as black shadow snakes slithered across his exposed skin.

The hairs on the back of my neck prickled.

Danger intensified.

Knox moved in a blur until he stood nose to nose with Cobra. One of his eyes gleamed black, while the other glowed yellow, and his expression was cruel.

A low hiss erupted from Cobra's chest.

Knox's features smoothed into a pleasant expression, and he took a step back. He relaxed his shoulders like he wasn't a threat and said suavely, "She doesn't interact with grounders often, forgive her. She's forgotten her manners." He glared down at Rina, who visibly cowed beneath his censure.

"Grounders?" Vegar asked.

The blond man kneeling next to Rina tilted his nose up. "It's what we call people who aren't angels." He was equally gorgeous and gave off the same haughty air. I believed his name was Arthur, and they were clearly siblings.

"We mean no harm from it. Excuse us," Knox said smoothly as he bowed his head.

His words fell on deaf ears. Tension expanded across the outcrop as the legions sized each other up.

Eyes narrowed as everyone realized at the same time that the angels were prejudiced against other species.

A headache pounded in my temple.

Working with them would be fun.

Not.

Xerxes cleared his throat and turned toward Jax and Malum pointedly. "Why were you two swearing? What did you see?"

The obvious attempt to change the topic worked because Knox backed away from Cobra and everyone focused on why we were freezing our butts off on the side of a mountain in the first place.

"We can see people in the courtyard," Jax said slowly.

I squinted, but it was too far to see without binoculars.

Malum frowned. "These people, who we're calling the infected, look like the villagers we've fought before."

"That's good," Vegar pointed out, and Zenith nodded in agreement as he said, "Those people were mostly powerless and seemed primitive—"

"We should worry," Malum cut him off.

Jax exhaled roughly and dragged his fingers through his long braids, gold chains tinkling as he said, "Their architecture is advanced, and they appear to have technology."

His words sank in.

"Still, they could be mostly peaceful, and we could catch them unaware like we did in the other realms," John said hopefully as he tugged on my curl.

Jax and Malum looked at each other.

Fire spread across Malum's bronze head, and the flames reflected in silver eyes. His baritone voice was soft as he said, "Every woman and man who has walked through the courtyard has a long sword on their hips. They glow with blue enchantments. Every single one of them."

No one spoke.

There was nothing to say.

Nauseousness made my head light because enchanted steel could slice through anything.

The slur on my back burned.

Enchanted weapons were extremely rare because metals naturally repelled enchantments. They were next to impossible to forge and extremely expensive.

I breathed unevenly.

These weren't primitive, unarmed civilians like the ungodly we'd previously fought on mountainsides.

"What does this mean?" Rina asked.

Scorpius's milky eyes stared off, far away, as he sneered,

"It means we have to kill armed civilians and *then* the ungodly."

"We can't fight them like we have before." Malum's mouth pulled tight with worry.

Lothaire had insinuated months ago that the ungodly we fought were weaker than others.

Had he known?

Even back then?

Suddenly it made sense why he'd only let us fight with daggers.

It had been a warmup.

"We'll use our powers and our weapons strategically," Knox said as a broadsword of ice formed across his back. Six more crackled into existence on the backs of the other angels.

The air temperature dropped several degrees.

Frost burned my nose.

I silently stared at my frost-covered fingers and imagined a sword forming.

Nothing happened.

I was useless.

Flames spread down Malum's head, across his shoulders, and he stared at Orion and Scorpius. "Yes." His voice was rough like broken glass and whiskey. "We'll have to use our powers."

Silver liquefied into molten steel.

He exhaled roughly.

My heart rate increased, and I struggled to swallow as the leader of the kings pinned me with his gaze. The reason the High Court mandated group weekly therapy sessions was suddenly disturbingly clear.

They'd known the enemy had enchanted weapons.

Sweat dripped down my sides even though the temperature was freezing.

They'd known what we'd have to fight against.

I remembered the fear.

Petals swirled as Orion sang and entranced. Scorpius's third eye opened wide and revealed the secrets of souls. Malum pulled a dagger from his flesh, and his red flames incinerated.

Bile scorched the back of my throat, and I pressed harder into John and Luka's warmth. Arms wrapped around me and held me close.

I'd been pretending I had a choice.

Subconsciously I rubbed at the space on my hip where an enchanted tattoo used to be; like a fool I'd thought I could cut it away and be free from the kings.

I couldn't even leave their presence because bond sickness still strummed through my veins.

The men who were instruments of mass slaughter depended on me because I was the only one who could stop them once they started killing.

The High Court had known all along what I'd have to do in this war.

They'd known my soul was tethered.

They'd known I would never escape.

Because at the end of the day, nothing had changed.

I was still enslaved.

To monsters.

PART TWO
CONFLAGRATION

"Whoever fights monsters should see to it that in the process
he does not become a monster. And if you gaze long enough
into an abyss, the abyss will gaze back into you."

—Nietzsche

CHAPTER 8
ARAN
WAR

CONFLAGRATION (NOUN): a large disastrous fire.

DAY 1, HOUR 3

I fantasized about slamming my head into the chalkboard.

Eight hours ago, when we'd returned from our scouting mission to the first ungodly settlement, Jax sent the soldiers back to their barracks to await instructions. The shifters, angels, and our legion piled into the strategy room to plan.

After two useless hours of trying to brainstorm as a group, Jinx, Malum, and I had been elected as the unofficial war strategists.

The planning was better now that the angels weren't arguing with everyone and Sadie wasn't giving inane suggestions every five minutes.

It still wasn't going well.

"We forgot to factor in that we need to move quietly. Erase it and start again," Jinx said with exasperation.

She sat on the long table in front of the chalkboard with

a ferret draped across her shoulders like a scarf. Warren hung limply with his tongue hanging out of his mouth.

He appeared dead, but I knew we weren't that lucky.

Jinx held out her pointer stick and tapped it on the board demandingly. Pillows were piled up behind her back, and the remaining portion of her leg was wrapped in white gauze.

We were still waiting on an enchanted prosthetic, or even a hover chair. How the High Court had not acquired either by now was beyond me.

Jinx scowled at me like I was an idiot.

I glared back.

If there were a window in the strategy room, I would have chucked myself out of it eight hours ago. There wasn't. I'd double-checked.

Instead, I gritted my teeth as I erased the battle strategy from the board that we'd spent the past hour working on.

The worst part was that she was right.

Again.

We'd stupidly forgotten that we had to eliminate the ungodly quietly.

The numbers on the board mocked me: eight academy, five shifters, six angels, four assassins, three devils, six leviathans, sixty-eight foot soldiers.

One hundred soldiers total.

It wasn't a large number.

The best part of it was if anyone died, they couldn't be replaced, compliments of the dumbass contract signed by the High Court and the sun god.

Loophole-proof.

Depression-inducing.

Mania-fueling.

I was exhausted after trying to consider the strengths of all our fighters, the best way to kill the ungodly, battle formations, and how to secure the perimeter of the palatial settlement.

Jinx pushed her black sunglasses higher up her nose.

The room was dimly lit, but she wore them as a peace offering to show she wouldn't erase our memories anymore.

My right eye twitched.

I wasn't mollified.

Jinx could be altering our memories every day and we'd have no clue. Sadie was a big advocate for the glasses, and the shifter legion seemed to think they were sufficient, which made sense—they were all idiots.

Said idiots were currently sitting on the floor in the back of the room playing a card game with Orion and Scorpius to pass the time, as if we were at a social gathering and not preparing for war.

The demons were the only people in the room who had the decency to sit slumped over, looking depressed.

Everyone else was smiling and chitchatting.

A headache throbbed harder in my temple, and the eraser in my hand was streaked with ice as cold burned my fingertips.

Lately I was covered in ice, and it seemed to expand out around me.

I shivered as I remembered the blue flames that had trailed off Mother's fingers when she was feeling emotional.

Was I becoming just like her?

Sweat dripped down my temple, and I wiped it away before it could freeze.

One. Two. Three. Four. Five. Six.

I focused on the numbers and not the emotions scouring my insides.

An angel laughed loudly, and I jolted.

They lounged in the leather chairs and sipped from china

cups like aristocrats suffering ennui. Rina had made a call into her earpiece, and a worker had appeared with a tea cart and finger food.

I fantasized about bashing the kettle over their heads and shoving mini cucumber sandwiches into their unconscious mouths, pressing my hands to their smiling lips and freezing their mouths closed, turning them into blocks of…no. I was not going there.

"How did we forget such a pertinent factor?" Jinx slapped her palm to her forehead as she stared at our strategy board. "We're being stupid and careless."

I rubbed my aching forehead in agreement.

We'd been strategizing for what felt like an eternity, and we were working in circles.

Chalk scratched loudly against the other end of the blackboard as Malum added "stealth" to the list of factors we needed to take into account.

The enchanted binoculars had mapped the structure that filled the valley, and the visual was projected onto the blackboard. Jinx tapped on the tablet, and the enchanted swords also appeared.

"The infected will cut through our weapons," I pointed out.

Malum scribbled down the information onto the board.

Jinx looked at me and said, "Duh."

"I was just saying," I mumbled.

Jinx patted Warren's furry head. "Well—don't say stupid things."

Chalk cracked between my fingers, and I breathed roughly through my nose. My breath froze into tiny pieces.

Five. Ten. Fifteen. Twenty. Twenty-five.

"Hopefully not everyone in the compound is armed,"

Malum said as he studied the list of objectives we had written out. "We need to eliminate the armed people first."

Jinx looked at him like he was an idiot. "*Obviously.*"

Malum's jaw clenched, and his shoulders smoldered with fire. After a long moment of him breathing harshly, the flames disappeared.

Too bad.

I was hoping he'd explode and kill us all.

It was a minor consolation that Jinx was torturing someone besides me.

One thing about the fourteen-year-old was that she was going to make you feel stupid, no matter who you were. It was usually one of her best traits, but right now it was hellaciously annoying.

Every time we thought we had a plan of action, Jinx remembered another factor that rendered it impossible.

The root problem: how did you eliminate a sprawling compound filled with an unknown number of parasitic monsters without alerting them to your presence?

Trick question.

You didn't.

You gave up and let the murderous parasites take over the universe because frankly, it wasn't my business what the ungodly did.

Too bad the others didn't see it that way.

The shifters, the angels, and my teammates were outraged that the ungodly could spill out through portals and end civilization as we knew it. They acted like it was *personally* offensive.

Personally, I hoped the ungodly won.

People were annoying, and if it was my time to be the host of a monstrous crustacean, then that was my destiny.

It was called *giving up,* and everyone needed to practice it more.

"We can't forget about the portals," Jinx reiterated.

I doodled a self-portrait with chalk and said, "Best-case scenario, they don't have any portals nearby." The chalk scratched loudly across the board as it turned to ice, and I picked up a new piece.

Malum countered immediately, "But the worst-case scenario is they have a portal in the center of the base."

I pretended not to notice how gruff his voice sounded.

Pain definitely didn't streak down my back.

My lips most certainly didn't tingle as I remembered how he'd kissed like he was trying to devour me.

Nope.

I added more blood to my dying stick figure, but since the chalk was all white, it didn't give the visual effect I was going for.

Pitiful.

Malum cleared his throat harshly, and I glanced over with exasperation to find him looking smug. It took me a second to realize he thought he'd one-upped me, like we were back at Elite Academy, competing to see who was the smartest.

Who was going to tell him there was no competition?

I was already winning.

"Most likely scenario is there is a portal because of their weapons," Jinx said in a duh tone like we were both stupid. "But it will probably be located outside the base—likely in the surrounding mountains. The energy field from portals disrupts matter and makes it difficult to build around. You need advanced enchanted materials, and the city appeared to be constructed from bricks."

"So back to plan A." Malum's chalk squeaked loudly as he wrote. "Surround the base and trap the ungodly."

"Have we tried to negotiate with the infected?" A male voice asked from across the room as the angel named Arthur looked at us expectantly. "Why don't we try to talk to them first?" He pursed his lips. "It can't hurt."

I covered my mouth to stop myself from saying something I'd regret.

Some people needed a chair to the face.

In the far corner, Zenith muttered something about idiots as he played with Vegar's hair, and both demons looked disgusted.

Chalk creaked in Malum's fingers, and we shared a long-suffering glance of disbelief.

For the first time, we were in complete agreement.

A long moment passed, then Malum raked his hands across his shaved head and said, "No, we have not tried to negotiate with the *parasitic creatures*."

Arthur scoffed, "Well, we should try."

Jinx turned around on the table and asked, "Who?"

"Are you speaking to me?" Arthur looked pointedly at where Jinx was missing a leg, and the unspoken insult hung heavy in the air.

Rage flared across my sternum.

Knowledge that Jinx would eviscerate his existence was the only thing that held me back from stomping on his throat and painting the floor red.

At the back of the room, Orion whispered into Scorpius's ear, and the blind king shot to his feet. His high cheekbones were sharp as knives, as his face tightened with rage on Jinx's behalf.

"Who do you want to negotiate with?" Jinx elongated each syllable like she was talking to an infant.

Arthur opened his mouth.

"Wait, I know." Jinx's tone was deceptively nice. "The confused civilians who are cognitively unaware that they are infected with parasitic creatures?"

She laughed cruelly.

"Or do you want to negotiate with them when they lash out violently, controlled by the monsters inside them? When they scream mindlessly about death?"

Arthur paled.

Jinx continued mercilessly, "Or perhaps you wanted to talk to them when they're being ripped in half?" Her fake smile dropped. "No—I get it. You want to wait to talk to the crustacean-esque creatures who each have an exoskeleton mask for a face and six legs with pincers. The ones who rip the people in two and emerge from their desiccated carcasses. The ones that bleed green and are expanding through the realms."

No one spoke.

Arthur put down his teacup with a loud clatter.

"Any other inane suggestions that anyone wants to waste our time with?" Jinx spread her arms wide to the rest of the room.

"Someone did not read the informational packet," Sadie muttered loudly. "Stupid airers."

Scorpius chuckled and sat back down.

It took me a moment to realize that my best friend had come up with a derogatory slur for the angels because they called people grounders.

I pinched the top of my nose.

I no longer supported women's rights.

Jinx turned back around and rapped her pointer against the board next to my face. "Concentrate. We still have a stealth problem."

I banged my head gently (as hard as I could) against the board.

Infected with enchanted weapons, ungodly, a compound full of both. We had to kill them all quickly and efficiently without giving them enough time to flee.

How?

I rolled the elements around in my head and considered different tactics.

Malum spoke up and sounded assured. "Orion entrances everyone with his voice, then we eliminate them while they're unconscious." He nodded. "It's the only thing that makes sense."

I hit my head harder against the board and said, "Except we don't know if you would entrance and kill all our soldiers." *Like you did with Jinx*, was left unsaid as I continued, "We've been over this. Murdering the few soldiers we have aside, we also don't know if I can stop you again."

"You're our Revered, and you've stopped me before," Malum replied forcefully. "It should have been impossible, but you did it. You're ice for a reason—you're destined to put out my fire when I lose control. It makes perfect sense."

I cracked my forehead against the blackboard.

"Stop hurting yourself," Malum snarled.

I hit my head harder.

A flaming hand yanked me away from the board. "What the fuck is wrong with you?"

Did he want a list?

"Don't touch me." I shoved at him, and for a second, we wrestled with each other. His muscles bunched as they tensed, and I pretended not to notice pain streaking across my back.

He smirked down at me as he easily countered my movements, since he was built like a tank and at least had one hundred pounds of muscle over me.

His fire was momentarily doused by the ice that radiated off me.

Silver eyes flashed with mirth.

He loved that it was easy to overpower me.

Sun god, he was such a bully.

I kicked him in the shin with all my force, and he squinted with pain. When he released me, I brushed my shoulders off with as much decorum as I could muster.

Which unfortunately, was none.

Malum winked at me. "If you wanted to put your mark on me, all you had to do was say so. I'd get a tattoo for you any day, ice princess." His voice was gravelly as he stared down at the blue streaks of ice I'd left across his sweatshirt where I'd touched him.

I pretended not to notice that he adjusted his belt.

Instead, I pressed my legs together and rubbed at my temples as I took a deep, calming breath. "First, I'm a queen, not a princess. Second, my life's purpose is *not* to put out your messes." Ice crackled as it spread up my forearms.

He mumbled something under his breath that sounded a lot like, "*You can be my princess.*"

I choked on spit.

He slapped his hand on my back and said, "Careful. Go slow. Take your time swallowing." His expression was wicked.

Pain exploded down my spine as I realized his double entendre.

Malum trying to be seductive was a dangerous thing.

My face flamed with heat.

"She's right," Jinx said, and both of us snapped our attention toward her. "If you use your powers, you could wipe out our soldiers."

We sighed with relief.

She continued, "We can't afford to lose people because of your carelessness. Also, all four of you passed out after she stopped you from attacking me. You can't risk unconsciousness in the middle of a battle."

Malum raked his hands down his face.

Flames danced across his fingers.

"Exactly." I nodded and crossed my arms over my chest protectively.

His plan was stupid, and I was smarter; it was confirmed.

Jinx continued, "Aran, you'll have to find time to practice so you can eventually unleash your abilities in battle." She tapped distractedly at her tablet. "We'll need your skills as the war continues."

"Excuse me?" I whirled around to glare at her, but she refused to look up from her tablet.

I huffed and said sarcastically, "I'll just pencil in stopping psychotic devils in between flying lessons and fighting the ungodly."

"Good." Jinx kept tapping.

Malum looked smug as he grabbed a piece of chalk and walked back to his list of strategies. "Don't worry, we'll practice."

"I'm not practicing anything with you," I snarled back.

He smirked but didn't elaborate.

My lips tingled.

We both knew what would happen if we were stuck spending more time together. There was no avoiding it.

I hadn't felt this sick since I'd learned fifty-one was divisible by seventeen.

Jinx rotated the structure on the tablet, and it spun on the board. "If we don't contain the perimeter, potentially hundreds or thousands could flee to the portals. One hundred to one million people could be living in the valley."

My jaw dropped. "One fucking million? Are you serious?"

Jinx pushed her sunglasses up. "The structure could continue underground for miles for all we know. I'm being *realistic*."

She wanted us to die.

There was no other explanation.

"No," Malum countered. "We know this planet's core has a unique high temperature. It is unlikely life could be sustained underground."

"He's right." I stood up straight.

Jinx mumbled under her breath, "The civilization could have adapted to higher temperatures. But fine, probably four thousand people." The edge of her mouth curled up in a smirk.

I gaped.

Had she been making a joke?

We'd been working for so many hours that delirium was setting in, and I honestly couldn't tell.

Movement in the back of the room caught my eye, and suddenly I wasn't tired. My jaw clicked shut, and I said, "I know what we need to do."

A good strategist always had multiple iterations of a plan. They also used their best assets strategically to accomplish the hardest tasks the most efficiently.

"We're going to enslave the ungodly," I whispered, and Jinx sat up straighter.

"Fuck. You're right," Malum said softly, and the air beside me warmed as he walked over beside me.

The potent scent of tobacco and whiskey flooded my senses, and I swayed closer to the intoxicating aroma.

Bronze cheeks blushed scarlet.

A dagger glinted as he swallowed, Adam's apple bobbing.

Malum wet his lips and said softly, "I like your plan." For a second, as he stared down at me, harsh bronze features softened. Silver eyes seemed pleading.

His mood swings were giving me whiplash.

The energy between us was volatile.

An ache pounded in my sternum.

"Let's draw it up." Malum nodded at the blackboard, and I followed his gaze as if I was in a trance.

We moved at the same time to the list, and he stepped back to let me pass. A palm splayed across my entire lower back as he guided me to the board.

I forgot to shove him away.

His fingers burned with heat.

Goose bumps exploded across my body, and streaks of agony shot down my spine as I stumbled away from his touch.

I expected him to get angry, but Malum stood still beside me, staring down at his hands as he flexed and unflexed them like he was confused.

His features sharpened, and something dark flashed in his eyes. He took a step closer and crowded into my space so he was centimeters away from touching me. He never made contact.

"Write out your plan on the board, Arabella—now," he whispered darkly. The *or else* hung in the air between us.

I gulped, unsure of what was happening between us.

The reflection of flames burned in his eyes as he stared down at me, and his bronze cheekbones flushed red.

My stomach fluttered.

The next minutes passed with horrible tension as my chalk scratched in the mostly silent room.

Malum pointed out a few corrections, but for the most part, he loomed over me. Every few seconds, he'd look down at the hand that had touched my lower back and flex it.

Was he fantasizing about lighting me on fire?

I never knew where I stood with the leader of the kings, and he never failed to put my teeth on edge.

There was no way around the truth: he was *terrifying*.

"It makes sense, but the leviathans are better suited to guard the perimeter," Jinx said as she tapped her pointer stick against my plan, and Malum stepped away casually like he hadn't been seconds away from losing control in a crowded room.

I shivered and wrote down the change of personnel, too frazzled to argue with Jinx.

Whiskey and tobacco filled my senses.

Little streaks of pain shot down my spine with each breath.

When the three of us turned to the room to present our plan, I flushed, embarrassed that they'd seen me acting like a simpering fool around Malum.

Surprisingly, no one was paying us any attention.

The angels, shifters, and demons were all talking among themselves.

Only four men noticed.

Luka and John were both staring at me, but neither seemed annoyed, because their expressions could only be described as adoring.

Enraptured.

Loving.

In contrast, Orion sat next to them with his stunning brown eyes narrowed as he whispered into Scorpius's ear. The quiet king also stared, but his expression wasn't soft and loving like the twins'; it was harsh and obsessive. He stalked me with his eyes.

I shivered.

Orion had chased me down the marble corridor.

My exhaustion ran bone-deep.

The room's temperature became oppressive as Malum shifted so his forearm was pressed against mine.

It was an innocent touch, yet I burned alive.

"Listen up, everyone," Malum said loudly, and his baritone voice reverberated through my bones. "We have a plan."

Everyone in the room stopped talking.

Malum nodded down at me like he was letting me take charge.

I grimaced back, pressed my pipe between my lips, and inhaled greedily. I'd never loved being the center of attention; that was more Sadie's thing. I'd rather fade into the background. Disappear.

Public speaking was onerous, and I was already tired enough.

"This is what you're going to do," Jinx said with authority, and I stopped paying attention to my surroundings.

No, I didn't care that a child had more leadership skills than I did. I was too busy enjoying my smoke.

A few minutes later, alarms were blaring inside the buildings of the war camp. "Jinx, you stay at the camp, and Warren, you guard her," Jax ordered as we left the room.

We reassembled in the cafeteria.

John and Luka were frantically patting over my body, pulling at my weapons and holsters to make sure I had everything.

I rolled my shoulders and tried to ignore the persistent ache beneath my skin where my unused wings lay.

I pretended the floor wasn't growing icy beneath my feet.

As far as I could tell, none of the other angels radiated ice. They wielded it expertly in the controlled form of their swords.

Jinx was tight-lipped about the whole affair, but she'd revealed the Angel Consciousness had removed the blocks on my power because I'd proven myself selfless enough with control over my temper.

I bit down on my lower lip until I tasted blood.

My gut churned.

I had a feeling it wasn't normal for an angel to radiate ice. I had a bad feeling that I wasn't in control at all.

Good thing I was an expert at coping—I ignored my problems and pretended they didn't exist.

"You need to be alert," Orion mouthed as he shoved a cup full of cold liquid into my hands. "It's—"

I threw the contents back and gulped it down before he could explain.

"Iced coffee." He narrowed his eyes, long dark lashes fluttering, as he whispered angrily, "You shouldn't consume any substance without knowing what's in it. It's not safe."

John and Luka continued checking my holsters diligently, like they were terrified they'd missed something.

I rolled my eyes at Orion.

The coffee was strong, and already I could feel the caffeine waking me up. I took a long inhale from my pipe and let the combination of drugs revive my will to live.

Jitters replaced my exhaustion, and I bounced back and forth on the balls of my feet.

Jax and Malum shouted the plan's directions to all the soldiers.

"Can I have a second coffee?" I held out the empty cup to Orion as Luka checked my earpiece.

"No." Scorpius seemed to appear out of nowhere. "Take that pipe out of your mouth or I'll rip it out."

Sometimes I thought the blind king was calmer and more approachable than Malum. Other times, he was abrasive and cruel. Scathing.

Like a bad trip.

Luka moved with a blur and pushed me behind him, darkness glimmering around him.

"Don't speak to her like that," John said in an annoyed tone as he checked my bullet cartridges. "But he's not wrong, Aran. Put the pipe away."

Scorpius smirked maliciously and sized up John like he was seeing him for the first time. "Don't tell me what to do."

John glared and drove his shoulder into Scorpius's side. "Oops," he said sarcastically.

A muscle in Scorpius's jaw ticked. "Be careful, *human*. You don't want to mess with me."

Instead of backing down from the devil, who was half a head taller than him, John scoffed. "I'll do what I want."

Scorpius arched a brow, clearly unused to other men challenging him. "Is that so?" he asked wickedly.

I grabbed John's shoulders and pulled him away from the sadistic bastard who would tear him to pieces. "Can you not start a fight right now?" I asked him.

John grumbled, "I wouldn't just start a fight, I'd end one."

Scorpius barked with laughter like the idea of John beating him was hilarious, and I grimaced because I had to side with the king on this one.

"You're going to be the death of me," I groaned.

John pulled on my ponytail. "Cheer up, little Smurf. Before you know it, the ungodly will be dead and we'll be back here hanging out. Rumor has it the High Court is going to let us party to blow off steam." He wiggled his eyebrows up and down suggestively. "Plenty of drugs to do later."

He pretended to smoke an imaginary cigarette, and I laughed at how ridiculous he looked.

Scorpius muttered something under his breath that sounded suspiciously like, "*I have something you can blow.*"

We ignored him.

"Fine, but I want demon brew," I said.

John winked. "Of course."

"And I want to…" I trailed off and mimicked him by wiggling my eyebrows.

John's lips curled in a mischievous smile, and he pressed a soft kiss to my lips. "Anything for you, darling," he breathed into my mouth.

I tasted sandalwood and musk.

His lips were soft and warm.

Familiar.

Luka stroked the back of my head as his twin kissed me.

The pain that scoured my back was so strong it was like being doused in ice water.

Scorpius made a harsh noise in his throat, and when I looked over, he was flushed. *Strange.*

Orion gritted his teeth.

My skin prickled, and the pain intensified.

A spiteful part of me enjoyed knowing that the kings were watching me kiss John.

I wanted them to see what they would never have.

I wanted them to hurt like they'd hurt me.

Backing away from John, I nodded. "Let's do this."

I pulled the black elastic hood up and over my head, then tugged it low so it covered my entire face. The material appeared solid from the outside, but it was deceptively breathable and easy to see through.

Everyone did the same.

Clad head to toe in black, we became shadows with no discernable features.

In the middle of the room, Jax counted down from ten, and everyone gathered around the RJE devices. The twins grabbed my hands, and Orion grabbed my arm.

Sharp nails pressed through cloth into the back of my neck, and I startled at the intrusive touch. Pain traveled across my nerves and flared down my spine.

"Stay close, my Revered," Scorpius whispered against the shell of my ear. "Don't forget the bond sickness."

I shivered.

As if I could ever forget my shackles.

Crack.

We disappeared.

CHAPTER 9
ARAN
BATTLE

BALEFUL (ADJECTIVE): foreboding or threatening evil.

DAY 1, HOUR 4

"Stay low." Jax's voice crackled in my earpiece as we moved through the empty courtyard.

Festive bells were strung across the yard, and they tinkled prettily in the icy wind.

They grated across my nerves.

Our attacking group was composed of the champions, the generals, and the four women of the assassin legion, who slithered through the shadows of night.

They were nothing more than a blur.

None of us were.

We were the only soldiers going *inside* the compound, since we were the strongest and largely had no idea the numbers we'd be coming up against. We had the best chance of escaping if need be.

The rest of the foot soldiers were currently creeping

through the valley and creating a perimeter to ensure none of the infected got away.

Jax and Sadie led our group forward.

I was at the back, surrounded by shadows.

The twins guarded my front, and the kings guarded my back. Intensity radiated off them as they slunk silently through the snowy night.

Dread slithered down my spine.

The Necklace of Death pulsed, warm, against my sternum like it was trying to reassure me.

It didn't work.

I breathed shakily.

As soon as we'd RJE'd and climbed over the high wall of the empty courtyard, the men's energy had changed. Even John was different.

They'd shed their masks of civility. They were no longer the men I spent my days arguing and laughing with.

They were draconian, more killers than men.

And I was one of them.

We were like the soulmancers of lore, a people so deadly and terrifying they were more myth than reality.

The monsters of all monsters.

Air left my lips in frosty puffs. Thighs trembling, sweat streaking down my forehead, I squatted low and moved swiftly with daggers clenched between frozen fingers.

My eyes watered from the frozen air.

Snow drifted down lazily, and I blinked to clear the wetness off my eyelashes.

The pine trees in the courtyard were wrapped in fairy lights, and the distracting shards of light streaked across my peripheral vision. Bricks were warm beneath my heavy combat boots.

Tendrils of steam evaporated into the starry night.

Jax's voice was loud and crisp through my earpiece as he whispered, "There are four entrance points. Everyone stays as a group like we planned. Sadie in the front, and no splitting up. Follow me."

We entered the compound and walked directly into a long, windowless brick corridor.

I shivered as the temperature plummeted and a heavy stone floor blocked the steam and heat from the ground. The only light was flickering torches.

It was musty.

Damp.

Insidious.

My lungs rattled loudly in the quiet, and I held my breath.

One. Three. Six. Nine. Eleven. Thirteen. Fifteen. Seventeen. I counted as we moved silently, a unit of highly trained murderers.

There were no doors, and we appeared to be inside an endless stretch of silent corridor. If I hadn't known better, I would have thought we were in an abandoned building.

Goose bumps broke out across the back of my neck. How could anyone live in this austere, rank atmosphere?

From the quiet, the infected must have a lunar sleep cycle.

At the front of the group, Jax stopped suddenly and held up his hand. Surrounded by darkness, I could barely make out him signaling that the corridor branched off up ahead.

We followed him as he made a sharp right.

We moved silently.

Deeper into the compound.

I scanned the corridors, but there didn't appear to be any doors or signs of life, which made no sense.

The quiet expanded until I could hear the frantic

pounding of my heart in my ears as blood mixed with adrenaline.

Sweat poured down my sides.

My fingers cramped around the hilts of my daggers.

"Did you see something?" an accented foreign voice asked loudly, and all of us stopped moving.

Another accented voice responded, "What are you talking about?"

Down the dark hall, two streaks of glowing blue approached where we waited in the shadows.

It was the infected.

We crouched lower, nobody twitched, and nobody breathed.

"Now, Sadie," Jax whispered quietly over the radio as we followed the plan.

My toes cramped as I squatted lower, muscles trembling. I was shaking, and it had nothing to do with exertion.

As the blue glow drew closer, I made out the outline of two figures.

The infected started to run towards us.

One of them shouted, "What is—"

"STOP!" Sadie yelled, and the man never got out his question.

The two infected stopped moving—they were frozen, Sadie's blood coursing through their veins and taking them over from the inside out.

They didn't move.

They didn't speak.

"Everyone, move closer," Jax ordered, and we approached as a unit.

"It's hard to hold them," Sadie said over the radio through gritted teeth. "It must be the ungodly inside them. I can only use these two."

"Don't you dare overexert yourself," Cobra whispered back angrily.

Sadie scoffed, "I'm fine."

"You better not hurt yourself."

"You better shut up."

"We're not doing this right now," Jax snarled, and the line went silent.

The two infected held glowing blue swords that were pointed directly at us.

I stumbled back instinctively.

The infected turned like mindless zombies and positioned themselves at the front of our group, spinning their swords, a glowing blue blur in the darkness.

They were on our side now, enslaved fully by Sadie's blood powers.

They led us forward.

Deeper.

Into the compound.

We followed the corridors into the structure. Their swords whooshed as they sliced through the air. Tension gradually released as we explored and didn't find any more infected. The sprawling structure appeared to be mostly abandoned.

Our plan was overkill.

This is going to be an easy mission.

As soon as the positive thought flickered through my mind, shouts erupted, and infected appeared seemingly out of nowhere.

Blue swords clashed.

Ink dripped off the demons and formed black swords as the angels unleashed their swords of ice.

Someone screamed as they went up in flames.

Daggers whistled through the air.

Crystal wings flapped.

An animal roared.

The kings disarmed the infected and ripped them apart with their bare hands; bones snapped as necks broke.

The twins were equally vicious.

There was a grotesque ripping sound followed by the splatter of water. I stumbled as a familiar, awful chittering sound echoed down the corridor.

It hadn't been water.

It was blood.

The ungodly were here.

I staggered tiredly as I rounded a corner, slipping on a patch of ice—a trail of cobalt spread beneath my feet and created a path behind me.

I had no idea why I was shedding ice, and I had seemingly no way to stop it.

For the millionth time, I concentrated and imagined the cold forming into an ice sword.

I slipped as more cobalt spread out beneath my feet.

No sword formed.

Frustration welled, and I wanted to scream. My gut told me this was yet another gift from my messed-up heritage.

Far away, a bear roared.

I stopped to listen, then turned and ran toward the sound.

The kings must be nearby, because the bond sickness hadn't hit, but the compound was a confusing maze of corridors and hidden rooms. We'd explored most of them, but more kept popping up out of nowhere.

It was exhausting.

Another roar made the stones vibrate beneath me.

I could hear the shifters fighting, but I couldn't find them.

I was alone.

"*Scorpius!*" I yelled into the darkness because he had the best chance of finding me amid the chaos of the battle.

Another faraway roar, but no one responded to my plea.

The men must have been on the other side of the wall, in the large room filled with hundreds of people where the sounds of heavy fighting were still concentrated.

Acting without thought, I threw myself against the closest corridor wall. I groaned as fresh pain agitated the many battle wounds I was sporting.

Sun god, that had been a stupid idea.

I low-key loved that I thought I could just throw myself through a heavily fortified brick wall and it would break. Where had that confidence come from?

Limping, trembling with exhaustion, body bruised and aching, I forced myself to keep running forward.

I needed to find everyone.

It had all been going to plan—we'd been fighting as a group and staying together as we traveled deeper into the compound.

I'd cut down infected and ungodly with the twins at my front and the kings at my back.

I'd dodged—they'd attacked.

They'd dodged—I'd thrust.

On repeat.

For hours.

We'd picked up the discarded weapons of the infected, and all of us had fought with the more dangerous enchanted swords while the infected screamed and ungodly screeched in the darkness.

It had been hard to discern the locations of my teammates as they'd moved like shadows around our foe.

It had been messy.

Disturbing.

I'd only used the sword and had hesitated to fling daggers because I could not ensure that I wouldn't hit someone on my side. It had been hours of close combat.

My arms had trembled from exertion.

Then, about an hour ago, a sudden explosion had collapsed a portion of the large room where the fighting was concentrated, and my earpiece had fallen out.

Enchanted swords had swung through the rubble in a blur of bodies. Ungodly had screeched and attacked beside them.

I'd stumbled out into a hall.

I'd barely had time to throw a dagger at an ungodly's neck as I'd brandished my enchanted sword.

The ungodly had surrounded me.

Dust had been in my eyes, and bricks had been falling.

Bedlam.

I'd turned and sprinted, fighting off ungodly as they chased after me as I ran into the dark. It was disorienting.

The building was a maze of overlapping narrow halls. False walls and dead ends.

That was about an hour ago.

In the present, I sprinted around yet another corner, struggling to breathe as frustration made me panicky.

Squelsh. I kicked something wet.

Torches flickered and illuminated the streaks of gore and entrails that covered the corridor.

Had I already run past that severed head? Was I going in circles?

I kept running forward, refusing to look down at the

severed body parts strewn over the stone floor like discarded clothes.

The stench was awful.

Gore covered mostly everything in the compound.

Every hidden room.

Corridor.

Crack and crevice.

I struggled to breathe, and ice crackled as it spread out around me and encased the body parts.

"Stay calm, find the rest of the team," Jinx's voice echoed fuzzily in my head.

A part of me was convinced I was hallucinating her voice and I just wanted it to be our guardian-angel connection.

I was lost.

Bond sickness made me queasy, but it wasn't unimaginable pain, which meant the kings still had to be nearby.

I was most likely running in some sort of circle outside the big room where the battle was concentrated. What didn't make sense was that I should have run around and found the entrance by now.

The only logical explanation was I was going in a circle.

A scream bubbled up my throat.

Stupid corridors.

I ran faster through the dark, stumbling and desperate. Panicky.

If only I could find them.

A bone-chilling bear's roar echoed louder than before.

Shadows stretched and contorted around me as the silence smothered.

I was losing my mind.

Without sunlight, I couldn't tell if we'd been fighting for hours or days. The compound housed thousands of people, and the battle felt never-ending. It didn't help that almost every infected was armed.

I was lost in a sprawling compound filled with trained warriors.

A mecca of ungodly.

My foot cramped in my boot as I turned another corner, arches burning as I searched desperately for a door out of the maze.

I slipped again but kept my eyes straight ahead as I pretended not to see the streaks of gore in my peripheral vision.

The corridor was gleaming in cobalt ice.

I was losing control.

Walls and floors melded as my vision blurred. Everything was spinning.

I was losing my mind.

I turned down another dark corridor, then skidded to a stop, then doubled back—it was the outline of another hidden door.

Tightening my core, I kicked and prayed it was an entrance to the main battle where I'd lost my teammates. I prayed the men were inside.

Wood splintered, and it whipped open.

I was wrong.

An infected woman screamed and swung a sword at my face.

My reflexes were the only thing that saved me as I brandished my stolen weapon.

My stomach sank as I took in the cramped dark bedroom.

Sparks flew as steel banged together, and I towered above my foe, taller and stronger. I easily overpowered the infected and pushed my sword closer to her neck.

Her features glowed in the blue light of our enchanted swords.

Innocent eyes were wide with fear. "Why?" the woman whispered brokenly.

A screaming sound started in my head.

My vision wavered.

There was a scraping sound, and I whirled my head to the right to find more women hiding behind her. They were unarmed.

My mind fractured.

"I-I," I said uselessly, my voice hoarse from hours of exertion. It didn't matter anyway; there was nothing I could say.

My limbs went numb.

I drowned on air. It felt like I'd plunged into a lake and it had frozen, crushing my organs.

Jinx said inside my head, *"Calm yourself, they are already…"* Her voice warbled and disappeared.

The woman pressed her glowing sword back toward my neck, and I couldn't find the strength to resist. I hunched low so we were at eye level.

Her sword hovered inches from my face, sizzling with the blue enchantment that sliced through bone like butter.

She pushed me backward across the room.

I was powerless to stop her.

Time warped.

The dark room and glowing blue swords faded into shades of morbid gray as a hush descended over the world and blanketed me in stillness.

Outside in the hall, a familiar male voice shouted, but it was an indiscernible garble.

The woman said something, but I couldn't hear.

I was lost.

In the haze.

The woman must have realized I wasn't fighting, because suddenly she pulled her sword back and thrust it forward.

The descent happened in slow motion. Millions of seconds of possibilities and avenues of action unfolded before me.

I was emotionless.

Unfeeling.

The haze took everything.

I was numb.

In my imagination, I raised my sword and gutted my attacker before she could land a blow, and then I killed the ungodly as it ripped from her flesh. I killed everyone in the room.

In reality, I didn't move.

"You'll always be weak," Mother said as I screamed on the palace floor. "You'll never amount to anything. You'll never be like me."

A towering shadow burst into the room and watched as the steel sliced through my skin, and relief filled my lungs.

Silver eyes glowed through a black hood.

I didn't know if not killing her made me good or evil; all I knew was it made me feel less like Mother.

In slow motion—I crumbled toward the ground.

Terrible agony screamed along my neurons, and my eyes watered as I crashed to the stone floor. It echoed like it was hollow. It was warm. I was glacial.

If I were anything less than the reigning Queen of the Fae, I would have blacked out.

I stayed awake.

It had all happened in a split second—and Malum had seen it all.

Four other men burst into the room behind him, but they were too late.

Only *he* knew.

The woman backed up, her green-tinted eyes widened with fear, and she opened her mouth.

She exploded in scarlet flames. Then, so did everyone else in the room.

Mouths open, they writhed helplessly against merciless flames.

Paralyzed with pain, I could do nothing but watch in horror as they boiled to death.

Ungodly ripped from the flaming flesh of innocents and towered to the rafters. Pincers clacked as their six arms attacked.

Fire danced across their patches of exoskeleton harmlessly.

Five men stalked toward them.

Enchanted swords swung in a glowing blur as they carved the ungodly to pieces—the tallest shadow ripped their heads off with his bare hands as flames shot from his fingertips.

I choked on copper as it dribbled out my mouth, and everything spun faster.

Psychogenic dissonance devoured me.

I spat up blood.

Someone bellowed, and shadows fell to their knees around me.

Everything whirled.

Head lolled back like a corpse, I could do nothing but hang helplessly as the shadow who tore the ungodly's heads off carried me against his chest through the maze of halls.

I closed my eyes.

Time twisted.

Chilly air slapped against my skin, and I opened my eyes to see the dark sky.

Malum ripped off his black hood, flames leaping off his head.

I thought I'd seen him angry.

I hadn't.

Molten silver eyes flashed with so much rage I could feel it radiating in waves as Malum snarled inches from my face, "I'm going to kill you for this."

So much for hoping he hadn't realized what he'd seen.

He was fully aware that I'd made a choice.

Watery blood dripped from my eyes as the corner of my lips curled upward in a mocking smirk.

Who was going to tell him?

I was already dead.

CHAPTER 10
ORION
FATE

Orphic (adjective): fascinating, entrancing.

DAY 2, HOUR 20

"Where is she?" I screamed to my mates as we dodged the razor-sharp pincers of an ungodly as we fought in the melee.

Petals drifted across my neck.

I was seconds from losing control.

For the last forty hours, we'd slaughtered every infected we'd come across. Thousands of them.

We were thorough.

Unrelenting.

Exacting.

When there were less than a hundred infected left, we'd chased them through the halls and they'd fled into an expansive room.

The last stronghold.

It appeared to be the compound's living space because there were four stone fireplaces and excessive furniture.

Now smoke filled the windowless space. Velvet chairs and sofas were broken into pieces and scattered about.

Bodies were everywhere, discarded swords lying beside their ripped corpses.

Weapons clashed.

A hair-raising roar echoed. Jax was partially shifted; he had a bear's head and razor-sharp claws. Infected dropped around him as he swiped.

Cobra was covered in writhing shadow snakes, and they were all over the room, biting infected and sending them to their knees, screaming.

Otherworldly wings clattered as the angels hovered on the ceiling and stabbed downward into the fray. They'd ditched their ice swords in favor of the lighter, easier-to-wield enchanted swords.

The room was chaos.

Pieces from the paintings that had once filled every inch of wall space smoldered as they fell like rain.

The dying screamed.

Our plan had been going perfectly until someone had detonated an incendiary device. When the dust had cleared, Arabella was missing.

She had to be nearby, but for some reason, we couldn't find her.

It was maddening.

Our Revered had disappeared.

The tether on my control was fraying precariously, and I couldn't remember why I held myself back from unleashing my voice and slaughtering the world.

Why did I care?

My vocal cords ached to be used.

I chucked a dagger at an ungodly as I dropped to my

knees, and Scorpius swung an enchanted sword where I'd stood. Blood splattered. He sliced two infected clean in half.

Ungodly ripped from their flesh, but Corvus tore their heads off before they could stand tall. Scarlet flames poured off him as he threw the severed heads down onto the red-and-green rug and stomped.

At one point, the rug had been white.

Corvus tipped his head back and growled like a beast. He'd dropped his weapons when we'd realized Arabella had disappeared, and he'd been fighting with his bare hands ever since.

He was no longer a soldier.

He was an Ignis whose Revered was missing—a feral creature.

Arabella had to be nearby because the bond sickness hadn't incapacitated any of us, but we'd searched every corner of the large living space where the fighting was concentrated.

She wasn't beneath the piles of corpses.

We'd checked.

"Where the fuck is she?" I whisper-yelled as we stabbed, lunged, and dodged in unison.

Panic mounted every second she didn't appear.

Cherry blossom petals drifted faster across my collar-bone, and I gritted my teeth as gore splattered across my face.

Five minutes. If we didn't find her in the next five minutes, I was unleashing my powers, and I didn't care if we slaughtered our own soldiers.

They could all die.

"Is Aran with you?" one of the twins shouted as they punched an infected man, stabbed him in the heart, then sliced the emerging ungodly in half.

"No," Scorpius snarled as he spun and kicked. "We can't find her."

The twins stopped moving. Clad in all black, they seemed to disappear into the shadows as the battle raged around them.

"Excuse me," Luka said with vehemence, "where the fuck is *my wife*?"

I was startled by his voice because he never spoke; it was deeper than his twin's.

"She's not your wife yet," Corvus replied harshly. "Arabella is unmated and unbonded." Flames multiplied on his shoulders.

John scoffed as he gutted an infected. "Keep my *wife's* name out of your mouth."

Corvus growled viciously as he grabbed an infected woman's face and snapped her head to the side like he was imagining it was the twins'. She dropped dead. He repeated the motion with the ungodly. Green gore covered his arms.

Flames poured off his fingers and set the rug aflame.

"She has to be nearby," I said to the twins. "Because the bond sickness hasn't set in."

Scorpius dropped his sword and unsheathed serrated daggers.

He stabbed at one of the remaining male soldiers repeatedly but didn't kill him. He knelt close, arms and torso painted red, as the man writhed and screamed beneath him.

He didn't stop.

I watched him mutilate the man with disinterest.

We were unraveling.

Being separated from Arabella was like taking a bullet to the skull. After a lifetime we'd spent searching for her, she wasn't allowed to leave us.

If we didn't find her soon, the ungodly would seem tame

in comparison to what we'd do, because the sun god himself couldn't save the realms from us.

"We've checked the entire room. We don't know where the fuck she can be!" Corvus bellowed with frustration to the twins.

All five of us looked around desperately as we fought.

Even with her clad in black from head to toe, we would recognize Arabella because her long legs and lean muscle definition were uniquely hers. No other woman compared.

She was our Revered.

Our soul.

We'd recognize her with our eyes closed and ears covered.

One of the twins pointed at the hole in the wall. "Is she out in the hall?"

I shook my head. "We looked and didn't see her." I stomped on the exoskeleton of an ungodly and wished this stupid compound didn't have so many hidden rooms and corridors.

Scorpius abruptly stood up straight and buried his dagger in the heart of his victim. He didn't bother to kill the ungodly that sprang from the corpse; instead, he whirled around and stalked toward the far corner of the room.

I killed the ungodly as the four of us followed him.

When he got to the corner of the room, Scorpius pushed his ear up against the brick wall beside the broken paintings.

We waited.

"I can hear her breathing!" he yelled over the fighting. "There must be a different corridor along the perimeter of this side of the room. I think we should—"

Corvus slammed his fists through the bricks, and debris fell from the ceiling as he pummeled through the wall with nothing but brute strength and rage. He slammed his body forward.

The wall exploded, and he stumbled into a dimly lit hall.

We followed.

Scorpius shoved past him and stilled with his mask-covered head cocked to the side as he listened.

We all heard a scream.

Corvus exploded with unbelievable speed, and the rest of us followed close behind.

Up ahead, he turned into a room.

A few seconds later, we followed him inside.

A dozen infected clustered in the corner, hiding, and an enchanted sword pointed toward us, dripping red.

I stilled.

Inhaled.

The copper scent was underlaid with something familiar, an icy scent tinged with power and death. It tasted like adrenaline on my tongue.

It was Arabella's blood.

I opened my mouth to scream as cherry blossoms floated in the air around me. Before I could unleash my voice, the room's inhabitants exploded in red flames.

If I weren't shaking with fear and rage, I would have been amazed that Corvus had unleashed so much fire outside of our powers being activated.

There wasn't time to think.

Ungodly shrieked as they ripped from the flaming corpses, and we launched forward as a group, slaughtering them.

There was movement in my peripheral vision, and my heart stopped beating.

I ran toward the figure.

Crouching low, I screamed as I applied pressure to Arabella's sliced-open abdomen.

No. No. No.

The original plan was not to leave the compound until the last ungodly was slaughtered.

My Ignis lifted Arabella in his arms and sprinted down the halls, faster than he'd ever moved, as if death himself chased us.

We broke protocol and followed behind him.

The battle was almost won anyway.

Our footsteps were thunderous as we sprinted as a group.

Our Revered was our priority.

Finally, we stumbled out of the compound, back into the darkness of the night, and we were in the courtyard.

Fairy lights twinkled in the trees.

Corvus passed Arabella's limp form into my arms, then he gently pulled off her hood.

I pressed a kiss to her icy forehead and cradled her against my chest as I prayed to the sun god.

The others surrounded us.

Blood and gore stained the dusting of snow beneath our feet, then melted into a mess.

Bells tinkled.

Snowflakes drifted softly around us and kissed Arabella's unnaturally pale cheeks.

Corvus ripped off his hood, and his eyes were on fire.

He leaned close so his harsh bronze features were inches from hers, then he snarled harshly, "I'm going to kill you for this."

I stiffened and pulled her closer to my chest protectively.

What was he playing at?

My Protector instincts flared. How dare he speak to our Revered like that? How dare he disrespect her so callously?

It was sacrilegious.

Arabella's lips, which were turning blue from blood loss, curled up into a mocking smirk, and she mouthed, "Go fuck yourself." Her skin was a disturbing shade of gray.

My Ignis smiled, tipped his head back, and bellowed to the night sky.

Flames shot from his mouth like a dragon.

Scorpius grabbed Corvus's flaming shoulders and said, "Get the fuck away from her. What is wrong with you?" He voiced my thoughts as he pulled our Ignis away from our precious Revered.

The twins ripped off their hoods and formed a protective shield with their bodies.

"Are you okay?" one of them whispered to Arabella and stroked her cheek.

She rolled her eyes dramatically. "Clearly, I'm fine." Even bleeding out with a gruesome wound, she was sarcastic.

I would have laughed if my insides weren't curdled with fear.

A dimple appeared on the twin's cheek. It was John, and he poked her nose. "Little Smurf idiot got stabbed."

Arabella struggled in my hold like she was going to fight him.

I tightened my grip as agitation flared sharply in my gut because everyone was acting deranged and she was bleeding out in my arms.

"*We need to get her help!*" I shouted as I backed away from the other men. "Who the fuck has the RJE?" My voice was loud and raw, power sizzling in my veins.

Everyone stopped moving.

I'd entranced them.

Arabella was the only one unaffected; she squirmed against my chest and stared up at me, her wide navy eyes misted with shock. She no longer radiated cold, and her presence felt small in my arms.

I studied every curve and plane of her face.

The jagged scar beneath her eye and the dark circles from exhaustion enhanced the otherworldly nature of her beauty.

She was the only person in all the realms who was completely unaffected by my voice. While I didn't enthrall Corvus and Scorpius, my voice still triggered my mates' powers.

Arabella seemed completely unaffected.

She was perfect—she was also gravely injured.

Unable to help myself, I leaned forward and pressed another kiss to her forehead. "I will never leave your side, ever again," I promised huskily.

Her skin was unnaturally cold beneath my lips.

"I don't forgive you," she breathed out with a harsh rattle.

Snow gathered in the curls that stuck out around her head in a fluffy halo.

I held her tighter against my chest and whispered, "I know, sweetheart. You don't have to."

She winced but pressed her face into my shoulder. Her hand splayed across my chest, and her fingers curled.

Bells tinkled, and snow drifted.

No one else existed in all the realms but the two of us.

Seconds expanded. The ground beneath my boots metaphysically shook as an onslaught of emotions battered me.

Something tender spread between us.

It was the same feeling I had when I'd realized what her name meant.

The science behind soulmates was nebulous because the

unique composition of an individual's soul changed how the bond interacted.

I pressed a soft kiss to her forehead and held her close.

Startling clarity gripped me. It wasn't a coincidence that she was the only person I could speak to freely.

It was fate.

We were destined.

I clutched her against my chest as snow kissed our cheeks and steam rose around our feet.

Fate had brought us together.

The moment broke as the men stalked toward us as the compulsion ended.

"I have an RJE," Corvus said as he answered my original question.

A device whirled.

All four of them lunged toward Arabella at once.

Crack.

I staggered but held both of us upright as I fought off the dizziness of traveling through space.

Shaking my head once, I turned and ran through the quiet forest, down the path. I cut through trees so I could get to the medical barracks quicker.

Throwing myself inside, I laid Arabella down on the first white cot. One of the twins collapsed on his knees by her side and grabbed her hand.

He whispered to her quietly.

Corvus screamed for the doctors. Cherry blossoms floated around my Revered and covered her stomach, like they were trying to heal her.

The doctors gasped as they took in her ruined stomach.

"Enchanted sword wound." A doctor shook her head. "It's too much damage."

An empty bed exploded in flames.

Scorpius was suddenly standing beside the doctor with a dagger pressed to her throat. "Fix her or die."

The doctor's eyes widened with fear.

Arabella tried to say something, but all that came out was a low whimper of pain.

Shock was wearing off, and she was starting to feel her injury. She'd only have a few more minutes before she was screaming in agony.

I clenched my fists.

"Stop it." Luka pulled Scorpius away from the incompetent doctor.

Cherry blossoms formed a whirlwind.

"Don't you know who Aran is?" Luka asked Scorpius, and I realized it was the first time he'd ever looked one of us in the eyes as he spoke. He looked at the three of us like we were pathetic. "She's the *Queen* of the Fae Realm."

We stared back.

Scorpius stabbed the trembling doctor in the thigh and asked, "So?"

The incompetent doctor fell to the ground, screaming.

Luka swore and dragged his hands roughly through his messy dark hair. "Aran can't die without someone ripping out her heart and eating it."

A faint memory of Aran lying in a marble hall explaining fae succession played at the edge of my mind, but I was too stressed to remember it clearly.

"Are you sure?" Corvus sounded unconvinced.

The doctor whimpered, and everyone ignored her.

"Of course he is," John said, darkness glittering around him. "She used to complain about it constantly back at Elite Academy. You'd know that if you ever bothered to listen to her."

Violence ratcheted up.

Tensions sizzled.

The stabbed doctor staggered to her feet and limped through the door that led to the back room of the medical building.

The five of us were locked in a staring contest. Darkness expanded around Luka, and flames leaped higher off Corvus's shoulders.

Another doctor burst through the same door, holding vials of different-colored substances. He hurried to the bed and leaned over Arabella as he brought one to her lips.

The tension broke as everyone whirled toward him.

"What the fuck are you giving her?" Corvus snarled as Luka asked, "What is that?"

Scorpius lunged forward with his knife drawn.

I grabbed my fellow Protector by his neck and yanked him back.

The colorful vials clattered in the doctor's shaking hand. "I-I-It's for p-pain and w-will help her s-s-sleep and heal," he stuttered.

John ripped the glass from his fingers and sniffed it.

He tipped it back and wet his lips, licked at the substance, then nodded and said, "He's not lying."

"*Then what the fuck are you waiting for?*" Corvus bellowed at the doctor. "*Administer it now, she's clearly in pain!*"

Luka snapped, "But do it gently."

I raised my eyebrows because the quiet twin didn't talk to anyone besides John and Arabella; now he was fighting with Corvus and addressing a doctor.

The doctor reached for John's hands, but the twin pulled the vial out of his reach and pressed it to Arabella's gray lips.

Immediately she stopped squirming and whimpering.

Her eyes closed.

A few minutes later, the doctor pushed a clipboard with

hastily sprawled instructions into John's hands and told him to administer her drugs as he ran out of the room.

Pussy.

"You sure she'll heal?" I whispered as my knees gave out at the edge of her cot.

"Yes." John didn't look away from her.

Gradually, my mates and Luka knelt along the bed as our collective panic and aggression decreased until there was nothing but silence and Arabella's strained breaths.

I bowed my head and swore on the ancient House of Malum—on the crest of a fire-breathing dragon, on the tender feeling that had engulfed me when I'd held her against my chest—that she would find shelter with me.

My Revered would find peace in my arms.

It didn't matter that we were champions in the middle of a war. It didn't matter that I was a soulless creature who had hurt her in the past.

Arabella would find sanctuary with me.

Forever.

Bang. The doors to the medical barracks flung open, and dozens of gore-coated soldiers stumbled in.

Doctors swarmed like mosquitos.

The battle was over.

Quiet was replaced by groans of pain as men and women collapsed onto cots. A man was carried in screaming.

White floors turned red, and doctors slipped as they hurried to patients.

Arabella slept through the chaos.

I prayed.

"*Oh my sun god, is she okay?*" Sadie screeched as she fell to her knees beside my Revered's bed.

I glared at her and bemoaned my inability to speak. All

of us bristled as the white-haired woman stared down at *our* woman with wide, worried eyes.

Corvus solved my problem by growling, "Get the fuck away from her. She's *not* yours."

Instead of Sadie obeying, her eyes glowed neon red.

She bared her teeth like a wild animal. A warning growl rattled in her chest as she said, "She's my best friend, so you better fucking watch yourself. I know her better than all of you, and I'll be by her side long after she's done with you."

I narrowed my eyes, and my stomach churned at her words.

"Shit, what happened to her?" Cobra hissed as he staggered over to Sadie. His arm was gushing blood from a stab wound, but he pressed a hand over it and ignored the doctor trying to get him to sit down.

The shifters were a virus.

"Worry about your own people," Scorpius said, his jaw clenched as he traced his fingertips softly over Arabella's arm.

Cobra's pupils narrowed into slits, and his eyes glowed like his mates'. The jewels embedded in his skin turned into writhing black shadow snakes and gave him the appearance of a madman.

What my Revered saw in these animals was beyond my comprehension.

"She issss my people," Cobra hissed angrily at Scorpius, and he took a step closer to the bed like he wanted to fight.

Flames sizzled across Malum's shoulders, and he stood up and blocked Cobra's view of Scorpius and Arabella. The shadow snakes writhed faster across his skin, and flames leaped higher.

On the bed beside us, a man screamed as his nose was stitched back on.

"What happened to Aran?" the posh shifter Xerxes asked as he walked over and stood beside his mates. "Jax and Ascher are getting stitched up but are going to be fine." He stared down at my Revered and furrowed his brow. "Why is Aran not awake?"

John sighed loudly. "For sun god's sake. She took an enchanted sword to the stomach, but she just needs time to recover."

A tense moment passed.

"Are you sure nothing happened to her heart?" Sadie asked with concern, the glow receding from her eyes.

"I'm sure," John snapped at her with annoyance. "We wouldn't be sitting here calmly if something had. Or are you questioning my loyalty to her?"

"Maybe I am?" Sadie snarled.

He glared daggers at her.

A long, tense moment passed.

Finally, Sadie said, "We'll come back later when the men aren't being psychos around her." She tugged her mates away.

Cobra glared back at us with malevolent snake eyes as he let his mate pull him away.

I scowled back.

She was *ours*, not theirs.

They'd learn it soon enough.

CHAPTER 11
ARAN
NIGHTMARES

LOUCH (ADJECTIVE): not reputable or decent.

DAY 4, HOUR 18

"We have destroyed all the infected," I said as I stood at attention in the strategy room—I didn't remember volunteering to speak.

Everything was blurred.

Shadows and shapes bared their teeth and swallowed me whole.

My back was ramrod straight.

Arms behind my back.

Legs wide.

Head bent in deference.

The champions and generals stood beside me, all of us in a neat, obedient line before Dick, who was projected onto the chalkboard. Lothaire and the mysterious cloaked man flanked him on either side.

Lothaire's singular eye was focused on me, and he

nodded as if he was giving me strength. "Are you okay?" he mouthed.

I nodded back discreetly, then focused on Dick.

It felt like someone else was speaking as I continued to give the report. "The battle spilled out into the perimeter, but the foot soldiers secured the valley—to our knowledge, no infected escaped. A map of the realm was retrieved from the battle. It does not contain coordinates, but shows there are three more compounds in the realm. The angels will use it as their guide."

"Good," Dick said casually like we were talking about the weather. "Was there anything else on the map?"

He gestured at the screen, and the projection warped around his wrist and revealed a gold cuff, but when he went still, the skin on his wrist was bare.

Great, now I was seeing things.

"The map? Was there anything else on it?" Dick repeated with a harsher tone, and I realized he was waiting for me to answer.

I squinted.

There was a spot on the map that had been suspicious, but why would the High Court know that? And if they did, why would they ask about it like they didn't have knowledge?

A tension migraine throbbed behind my eyes.

"Yes." I chose my words carefully. "There are strange words written across the settlement located farthest north. It appears to be some type of foreign language."

Dick's expression remained blank as he ordered, "Scan the map on the tablet. We'll have our linguists look into it."

I pointed out, "It might be nothing, but there are *X*s over the mountains outside the valley."

Dick looked annoyed. "An artistic choice most likely. Let's focus on strategizing in *helpful* ways."

Agitation skittered down my spine at his dismissive tone.

"Yes, sir," I said through gritted teeth as I lowered my head and stared at the floor.

Annoyance melted into exhaustion.

"Overall, this is excellent work." Dick's patronizing tone grated on my nerves. "It looks like you're a fourth of the way done with winning the war. Congrats. Focus on eradicating the next three settlements and we will be done with the ungodly. Keep us updated on your progress."

"Yes, sir!" we chorused.

The tablet turned off.

Lothaire frowned just before he disappeared.

Knox, the person who had found the map, carried it over to the tablet and scanned it over to the High Court.

John threw his arm across my shoulder, and I slumped against him grateful for his support.

"Finally, let's all go eat. I'm starving." Sadie rubbed her hands together and led the group out the door as the shifters fell into a protective formation around her.

The thought of food made me sick, but I followed her lead. It was the first time the angels didn't bristle about a grounder telling them what to do.

They followed silently.

Everyone was withdrawn after the battle.

Time distorted.

Fatigue crushed me downward as I slumped at the table and stared at my full plate. My fork was frozen in ice and stuck to it.

The diamond bracelet on my wrist vibrated with warmth, and I barely felt it.

Conversation buzzed like white noise.

Everything was cool-toned, and I drowned in shades of blue-gray, shivering because there was no warmth.

I was a revenant.

All the lines had blurred.

Two days ago, I'd taken an enchanted sword to the stomach. One day ago, I'd woken up from a healing coma with smooth, unblemished skin and an unrelenting urge to cry.

Frost had covered my pillow. Five men had waited in various positions around my bedside.

The twins had hugged me, Malum had glared, and Scorpius had scoffed while Orion had stared at me with unblinking eyes.

I'd ignored the kings.

I still avoided them as I slumped forward at the table.

A woman's sad eyes before she stabbed me had unlocked a new version of the haze.

I curled my arms around my stomach like I was protecting an invisible injury and I inhaled enchanted smoke, but my heart wasn't in it as I twirled my pipe between my numb lips.

Someone swore softly, but I didn't bother to look up.

Dejection was in the air.

Soldiers chatted and ate, but there was a new sullen tension in the cafeteria. Anticipation for war had twisted into gloom, and conversations were more hushed.

People startled easier.

Murdering thousands would do that.

Monsters had that effect.

Before the battle, we'd agreed to give everyone two weeks off to recover before the angels used the map to find the coordinates of the nearest compound.

In the meantime, a combat room was open to practice sparring, the cafeteria was open for meals, and the strategy room was waiting for us.

Just thinking about the windowless room made me sick.

I didn't want to ruminate on the war because I needed time to pretend I wasn't a killer. A part of me recognized there would never be enough time.

Muscles spasmed in my stomach as I remembered I was the last thing people saw before ungodly ripped them apart.

No.

Two weeks wasn't enough.

To my right, Sadie rubbed circles on my back as she chatted with her mates about something.

To my left, John held my hand while Luka had his arm slung across his shoulder, his fingers playing with my curls.

Three points of contact.

Three people tethered me to reality, and without them I'd have floated away.

Across the table, Malum and Orion stared at me while Scorpius clenched his jaw with annoyance. Malum had his arms draped over both his mates protectively.

To test a theory, I held my breath.

Scorpius's upper lip pulled back into a snarl as I watched three minutes pass on the clock.

I gasped for air, and the blind king slumped with relief.

He *was* listening.

Always.

I held my breath and started again because I had nothing better to do than torment men.

Time folded in on itself.

I blinked, and everyone was putting their trays away. The twins took my uneaten meal, and I looked up to find Jinx focused on me.

Black sunglasses blocked her eyes, but I still winced.

She sat with her shoulders back, ramrod straight, and there was something startlingly different about her, but I couldn't put my finger on it. Was she getting taller?

"We need to talk," Jinx said coldly.

I looked down at the tabletop. "Talk."

"As we've discussed, I'm your guardian. I was trying to speak to you during the battle, but our mental connection is —" She paused like she was searching for the right word. "—unreliable."

Jinx's voice in my head.

A monster.

The screams of the dying.

I stopped fighting.

An enchanted blade thrust into my stomach.

I shoved my chair back with a loud scrape. "We'll talk later," I lied and walked away.

A deserter's retreat.

Cowardice was my favorite character trait. At least, that was what Mother had said after she'd kidnapped me from the shifter realm.

I shivered harder as John and Luka slung their arms over my shoulders and led me from the cafeteria, out into the chilly air.

Without their support, I never would have made it back to our barracks.

I would have collapsed among the trees and closed my eyes. I would have laid down on the fog-covered ground and let snow gather atop me. I would have—

I was startled awake by someone shaking my shoulder.

It took me a second to process my surroundings.

It was nighttime, and the room was quiet as everyone slept. I was lying in my bunk bed, tucked under the covers. Wind howled aggressively outside, and it sounded like the flurries had become a snowstorm.

I had no recollection of falling asleep.

"You should eat this. You didn't eat earlier," Malum said

gruffly as he handed me a vegetable sandwich he must have stolen from the cafeteria.

I took it from him mutely.

Did he wake up in the middle of the night to feed me? Strange.

I took a small bite because my stomach was hollow, then I devoured it in three bites like I was ravenous. I couldn't remember the last time I'd eaten.

"Good girl," Malum whispered as I brushed crumbs off my covers, and I stared at him.

"What did you just say to me?" I asked incredulously.

A blush stained his cheeks like he hadn't meant to speak.

The cruel devil who had said how much he hated women could *not* be the same man who was now whispering things about princesses and praising me.

I had to be dreaming.

Snores filled the space as the men slept in the dark bedroom. A faint memory of the twins guiding me into bed played at the back of mind, but it felt like it was someone else's recollection.

Had I been sleepwalking?

Malum and I were the only ones awake, and he loomed over me like a dark god.

I was delirious.

My comforter was covered in frost, and his fingers danced with flames.

"Were you watching me sleep?" I asked slowly as I tried to figure out what was going on. *Why is he feeding me? What's he trying to gain?*

Silence expanded between us, and just when I thought he wasn't going to answer, he said, "It was my turn to stand watch, and you looked hungry."

It took a moment for his words to penetrate.

How does one look hungry in their sleep? Red extended across his bronze cheeks like he could read my mind.

I gaped at him. "Um. Thanks? I'm also pretty sure there are enchanted alarms on all the barracks, so you don't need to stand watch."

He frowned. "I will do what I must in order to protect my mates." With crossed arms, he spread his legs wider.

It was pitch black as the storm raged outside the window.

Insanity was saccharin on the tip of my tongue as the leader of the kings cleared his throat roughly.

He leaned down at the waist, so his head was closer to my bunk.

As if in a trance, I reached up for his neck.

"How did you get this?" I whispered as I traced the pads of my fingers against smooth bronze skin and left a trail of blue ice. It instantly melted, and water dripped between us.

There was a sizzle as my fingers burned from contact with his skin.

It stung, but I didn't pull away.

He moved closer and overwhelmed my space.

Tobacco and whiskey filled my lungs, and the hairs on the back of my neck stood up as goose bumps exploded across my arms.

My subconscious screamed at me to run.

My consciousness screamed at me to punch him in the throat.

My inner demons screamed at me to kill everyone, then myself.

My inner slut screamed at me to sit on his face and suffocate him.

He inched closer.

I pressed my mouth against his lips and jolted because they burned with heat.

He went completely still like he was afraid to move. The fiery king made a rough noise in the back of his throat, and then he moved quickly, pinning me to the bed.

Arousal ignited.

Pain exploded down my spine.

I dragged my nails across the dagger on his neck.

He pinned me to the bed with both my hands above my head.

Hips pressed punishingly against mine as he held me down so I couldn't move. We barely fit on my bed. Where he began, I ended.

We were a tangle of limbs and aggression.

His voice was rough like broken glass and sin as he whispered against my lips, "The neck tattoos appeared after the three of us attempted to complete the bond."

He rolled his hips against me.

Kissed me harder.

I gasped as I realized what he meant.

Images of bare skin on a black silk bed—Orion between Malum and Scorpius as the three men devoured one another with groans of pleasure and sweat-soaked skin—had me holding my breath.

The temperature spiked between us.

Embers fell off his flaming shoulders and melted as they touched my chilled skin.

"Oh," I gasped eruditely.

He rolled his hips again, and my eyes rolled back in my head from the pleasure. Agony danced across my back.

One hand held my hands above my head while his other hand palmed my ass. He swore against my lips, "Fuck, Arabella, you're going to be the death of me."

I pushed my hips hard against his length.

"I'm going to ruin you," he whispered as he kissed me

harder. His lips trailed down my jaw, then lapped at the column of my throat.

He sucked on the sensitive skin, and my stomach twisted with need.

It was too much.

His teeth trailed across my neck.

I gasped as I realized he was purposely marking me. Desire increased, and agony tore my back apart.

It was too much.

I panted and pushed him away.

He took a step back and put his hands in the air like he was making a show of acting harmless. Wiping the back of his hand across his swollen lips, he smirked down at me with male satisfaction.

His pants strained forward obscenely.

My stomach twisted as white-hot pain splintered down my spine.

I swallowed a whimper.

Silver eyes narrowed. He stared at my lips with a feral expression and asked, "Any other questions?" He tried to sound casual, but his voice was thick with lust. "Everything doesn't need to be a fight between us. We want to help you. I want to help you—you're *my* Revered."

He stared at me possessively.

My eye twitched, and doom was corrosive in my veins.

That damned word again.

I was nothing but an object to them, a fixture of importance separate from any individuality.

There was no Aran.

Only *her*.

His perfect Revered that didn't exist.

Their divine obsession.

"That's okay." I cleared my throat and pulled the covers over me protectively. "I don't want your help."

He took another step forward and crouched so he was hunched and half leaning over my bed.

"That's fine," he said, and the corners of his mouth curled up into a forced smile. "We'll do everything we can to protect you and make sure you're okay."

His words said one thing, but the tension in his posture said another.

Shadows stretched between us.

The energy slowly shifted between us, and I squirmed as his expression darkened.

"You can go back to bed now." I itched the back of my neck. "No need to stand watch."

He didn't move.

Was he mad that I'd pushed him away? Since my back still strummed with pain, I didn't have a choice.

Awkward tension lengthened between us.

He kept smiling down at me, but a muscle on the underside of his jaw ticked like he was grinding his teeth. Veins stuck out across his forearms as he clenched his hands into fists.

I scoffed as I realized what was happening.

He was pretending to be harmless, and it was killing him, but I could sense the truth—inside he was seething because once again I'd refused to be his Revered.

"Um, I think I'll step outside to get some fresh air." I glanced behind him at the door and pulled myself out of bed.

The room was suffocating with just the two of us awake.

I needed space.

Moving past him, I was determined to throw myself out into the cold and scream on all fours until warm steam burned away the heinous memories that festered inside my skull like parasitic monsters that ripped people apart and—

"No." Malum's arm shot out. He grabbed my bicep so I couldn't move.

Even through my sweatshirt I was hyperaware of the burning heat emanating off his wide fingers.

More embers fell off him and hissed as they touched the exposed skin on my neck and hands.

His touch was scalding.

I was frozen.

My gaze drifted downward, and I gulped as I saw his impressive size was still straining against his pants.

Need mixed with fury between us.

Pain shivered down my spine, and I yanked backward. "Let me go," I demanded, too delirious from lust and exhaustion to play his games.

I was confused.

The villain wasn't supposed to ooze sex appeal; your enemy wasn't supposed to pin you to the bed and ravish you.

He flexed his fingers, and I couldn't move an inch.

I opened my mouth to scream.

Yet again, his mouth covered mine. He kissed me with such ferocity that my knees gave out.

His grip became unbearably painful, and air left my lungs as he yanked me close and whispered darkly, "I want answers. I *know* what I saw in that room."

Pleasure mixed with pain as I gasped and struggled to catch my bearings. His heady tobacco scent wasn't helping.

My head spun from secondary smoke inhalation and delirium.

I was high on him.

Silver eyes hardened into unfeeling chips of steel, and

there was no softness left in his expression. "I know what you did," he snarled cruelly.

His lips were swollen, and flames danced across his shoulders.

He looked like he couldn't decide between ravaging and murdering me.

The funny (concerning) part was that I also couldn't decide which one I preferred.

We had to stop meeting like this.

One thing was obvious: he'd just been pretending to be a gentle, nice guy when he'd blushed and given me the sandwich. He'd started the altercation with a false smile and a relaxed posture, but somewhere along the way, he'd dropped his mask.

Now his face was contorted with fury.

This was the *real* him.

I kicked my legs and arms out as hard as I could, fighting against his grip, but after a few minutes of struggling, I was panting heavily, and he hadn't moved an inch. He squeezed my arm tighter and scowled.

Bronze features—too perfect to ever be called ugly, and too harsh to ever be called traditionally handsome—lowered inches from my face.

Breath whistled through his clenched teeth.

We were chest to chest, and my neck hurt as I stared up into his eyes. "Why did you do it?" he demanded.

It took every ounce of control I possessed not to flinch under his intense scrutiny.

"Do what?" My face scrunched up with feigned confusion.

I was nothing but an imbecile; the mask was too easy to don.

"Don't play games with me—it's not cute." He loomed

closer, and steel flashed. "I know exactly what I saw. You did it on purpose." Red flames sizzled across his arms.

Harsh features glowed in the fire.

I stayed silent.

He scowled and spat, "Why?" White teeth gnashed, and his canines were ever so slightly pointed at the end.

He was more devil than man.

I stared back blankly with deadened eyes. "I have no idea what you're talking about." My voice was monotone and bleak, empty like my soul.

He shook me back and forth harshly. "Tell me." His voice rose. "Caring about your well-being is *sheer* torment when you care so little about yourself."

Fire flared hotter between us and charred the edges of my nerves.

"No one ever asked you to care," I said through gritted teeth. "So save yourself the trouble and *don't.*"

He laughed with malice, an angry, dark sound. "Unfortunately for both of us, that's not how it works—*you are my soul.* Do you think I have any control over my feelings? My obsession with you?"

He pressed his hips against me as if to prove a point.

Desire pooled in my stomach, and I ignored it.

I scoffed and rolled my eyes so hard they hurt. "Please, everyone has choices." I made a mocking face. "If I upset you so much, then just *ignore me.*"

"You think I could just ignore you?" Furious scarlet flames shot out of his mouth and warmed my face. "You *think* I could just walk the fuck away from you, Arabella?"

I shrugged. "Yeah."

He made a frustrated noise and said, "You're more of a *fool* than I could've ever imagined."

I stood on my tiptoes so our faces hovered inches apart. "And you're a spiteful psychopath—leave me the fuck alone."

He smiled, and it was pure evil. "No, I don't think I will."

The grip on my arm tightened, and my humerus creaked like it was seconds from snapping.

A whimper escaped before I could stop it.

Bedding rustled, and someone swore.

There was a blur in my periphery, and then Scorpius and Orion joined us in the middle of the room. Unlike Malum, they were fully clothed. Orion's eyes locked on where Malum was gripping my arm tightly, then he took in our swollen lips and messy hair.

Finally, he stared at my neck.

From his expression, Malum had left his marks on me.

Orion whispered to Scorpius, and their faces contorted from sleepy to enraged.

"Don't touch her like that," Scorpius said as he yanked Malum away from me by the back of his neck.

Malum allowed himself to be pulled away without a fight, but his eyes were full of insidious promises.

He was going to rip away my secrets.

Tear me to pieces.

Ravage me.

He wasn't going to let this go.

Backing away from the three kings, keeping my front to them at all times like they were wild animals, I collapsed back onto my bunk even though I didn't want to sleep.

"I'm going to bed," I announced.

Awkward silence stretched among the four of us.

"We can help you shower like we did before," Scorpius offered quietly.

I pulled the comforter over my body.

"Um, that's okay," I said awkwardly.

Orion whispered, and I was startled at how close he was. "We'll take care of you, sweetheart, we promise. Corvus just lost control of himself—he'll be better."

Sure, and I'm mentally stable.

The scent of chocolate-covered raspberries was deliciously sweet, and I held my breath.

Finally, he stepped away.

"You *will* be mine, Arabella," Malum promised harshly across the room, then grunted as someone hit him.

I closed my eyes tight and breathed erratically because he knew my secrets; he'd seen me let myself get stabbed. The other men would freak out if they realized, and they'd smother me.

For some reason, he hadn't told them yet. My heart skipped a beat as I realized he'd voluntarily kept my secret.

Malum was protecting me. It was almost…sweet.

He'd also kissed me like he was trying to consume me, again. He kissed like it was a war he was determined to win. *Did he fuck the same way?*

I squeezed my eyes shut and tried to stop thinking about fire, whiskey, and sin.

My wrists tingled where he'd pinned them above my head.

Heat unfurled inside me, and pain streaked down my spine as I clenched my legs together.

I needed to concentrate on something off-putting and weird.

It was an emergency.

Desperate to stop my traitorous body's reaction, I pictured Sadie trying to dance seductively in the fae realm. I hadn't even known someone could move their limbs in two different directions like that at the same time.

The little pinpricks of pain streaking down my spine slowly faded away.

However, it was hard to concentrate on Sadie's dancing (convulsions). The memory of Malum's razor-sharp eyes as he promised not to leave me alone played on repeat through my mind.

There was clearly only one solution.

I had to have sex with him, then I'd have to kill him. Praying-mantis-style. Dagger down, ass up.

It was the only way.

I ignored the arguing kings and, with disturbing swiftness, fell asleep—the nightmares came quickly.

CHAPTER 12

CORVUS MALUM
CONNECTIONS

IGNIFY (VERB): to form into fire.

DAY 7, HOUR 3

My nightmares usually consisted of flames and failing my mates, of red fire pouring from my skin while I screamed without relief.

There was a recurring theme to my dreams.

In some of them, I had all three of my mates around me, but I couldn't find my Revered. I used to dream about a faceless male cowering somewhere in need of protection. Now I dreamed about a fierce woman with eyes like ice who didn't want my protection.

I knew something was very wrong because this dream was not like the rest.

I knew in my gut that I was trapped in someone else's body, experiencing their memories.

The person was lying partially naked on a marble floor. Ornate frescoes decorated the walls, and the high ceiling seemed to go on forever. Everything flickered in shades of gray as if the person's vision filtered out warm colors.

There were no windows.

No escape.

They—the person whose body I was inside—shivered uncontrollably.

Somehow, I was aware of the person's emotions, but could still have separate thoughts.

It was overwhelming and disorienting.

Eight men stood in a circle around them in matching uniforms, and for some reason, I recognized the insignia as that of the fae guard. I knew, without reason, that I was in the grand basement of the fae palace.

The guards stepped closer, caging the person in so there was nowhere to go.

For a second, I was distracted by the delicate pale arms that trembled as they held them up because they were so different from my dark, bronze muscled limbs.

The waves of terror streaking through them were wholly unfamiliar.

I'd never experience fear like this.

A guard reached out and slammed the toe of his thick black boot into the person's side, and they gasped at the sharp sting. Their fragile frame curled up on the marble floor. Their joints ached with growing pains.

They were all gangly limbs and bones.

The person was young.

Scared.

Weak.

Their anxiety swelled as they dragged fragile forearms across the floor and tried to hoist themselves up.

A guard slammed a boot down on their spine, and they collapsed.

A high-pitched whimper escaped their lips.

Indignation flared in my chest because my gut was telling me the person being kicked was young. These men were pathetic cowards bullying a child.

Pressure burned behind their eyes, but no tears fell.

Their bravery impressed me.

Few children could be surrounded by so much adult cruelty and hold themselves together, and the vitriol wafting off the guards was staggering.

They *loathed* this child.

Another kick sent them sprawling back into a guard's leg, but instead of crying, the child gritted their teeth and tried to stand up. They didn't complain or break down even as blind terror was coursing through them.

They were resilient.

Brave.

Shivers racked through their unclothed frame, and their teeth chattered.

The experience was bizarre because I'd never been cold a day in my life. Yet this child was plagued with bone-freezing chills.

No one else in the room appeared to be cold.

Suddenly, all the guards took a big step back and opened the circle wider. There was more space around them to flee, and it should have been a good thing, but the child started to hyperventilate.

Something was very wrong.

They were paralyzed with noxious panic.

A distant part of me recognized I could escape this nightmare if I wanted to; all I had to do was wake myself up.

Curiosity had me consciously trying to stay asleep.

I wanted to know what in the sun-god-damned realms was going on. I wanted to know who these people were.

It felt important.

High heels tapped loudly against marble, and a woman approached in a long gossamer dress composed of rare silk webs. She was stunningly beautiful with an unusual coloring —blue hair and eyes.

The child's terror peaked.

My heart plummeted.

The woman's voice was frosty as she said, "Your tutors have told me you were slacking in your lesson today. Is that true?"

There was something off about the woman's expression, like she was just mimicking emotions.

Fear seized the child, and they tried to crawl away.

They needed to escape.

It was a life-or-death situation.

A soldier's boot slammed down across the child's back and halted their progress. A crack echoed in the cavernous space, signaling something had broken.

Air left the child's fragile lungs in a loud oomph, and they whimpered on the floor.

The guards laughed.

I wanted to rip their spines. From the child's thoughts, they were innocent. Young. Helpless. They didn't understand why this was happening to them.

The fae guards were monsters, and the child viewed the woman as the worst of them all. Even with pain radiating from the broken bone in their back, the child was more afraid of the beautiful woman.

Their every thought was consumed with escaping her.

The child stuttered desperately, "I-I-I just f-forgot one l-l-line from a thousand-page book. I'm not slacking, Mother." The voice was soft and feminine, and I jolted as I realized I was in the body of a young girl.

The sinking sensation became a plummet, and rage burned brighter inside me.

"*Lies!*" the woman screamed, and her pleasant expression dropped. Mania shone in her wide, glassy eyes as she smiled wider.

The girl reeled back and begged, "No, Mother. I promise I'll be better. Please don't. I promise. Please listen to——"

The woman snapped her fingers.

Blue flames everywhere.

Agony like I'd never experienced decimated the girl's body, and it was so intense that her broken back cracked as it bowed. Mouth opened wide, she screamed silently as mind-numbing, paralyzing pain racked through her.

It was heinous.

Obscene.

She wanted to die.

I wanted to kill for her.

The flames stopped, and the girl threw up all over the floor as her muscles twitched in the aftermath. Embarrassment flooded through her as she realized she'd soiled herself.

The guards wrinkled their noses with disgust, and she groaned in shame.

Why won't any of them help me? What did I do to deserve this? Her thoughts were despondent.

I wanted to smash the guards and woman to pieces; I wanted to make them suffer like they made this defenseless girl suffer.

They deserved to die.

At times like this, I was glad for my abilities because it would be too easy for my mates and I to hunt them down. I'd snap their puny necks with my bare hands.

It would be much easier than the efforts they were exerting to torment a child.

Consciousness pulled me away from the child's form, but I forced myself to stay in the memory and not wake up.

I wanted to memorize faces.

I wanted names.

The cruel woman clucked her tongue and knelt next to the girl's convulsing frame. "We've been over this, darling— you're powerless, pathetic, and an embarrassment to my name. You will suffer until you learn."

She snapped her fingers.

Blue flames.

Silent screams.

Unfathomable torment.

The torture stopped, and the woman gloated down at the girl. "The palace aides told me you freed those monstrous birds from their gilded cages." Her smile contorted into a frown. "Your maid told me you defended a filthy villager child that was caught stealing." Her frown deepened. "And that was just from this week. Do you see why I must do this?"

The girl shook her head. "S- S-Sorry. I won't. I promise. I swear. I'll stop."

She snapped her fingers.

The world burned blue.

The blue flames stopped, and as the girl coughed and shivered on the cold marble floor, I started to put the pieces together.

The woman's unique blue hair and familiar otherworldly beauty, the fae palace surrounded by fae guards, the girl being tortured by her mother.

It was obvious, but I desperately wanted to be mistaken.

I needed to be.

The woman snapped her fingers, and yet again the girl suffered in shades of blue. Her world was a cruel hell, and she knew only torment.

Her slight frame felt like it was breaking at the edges because she was too young to withstand such torture. Few adults could.

Again.

The agony stopped.

The woman grabbed the girl's chin, and as she leaned close, she smelled like corrosive acid.

She whispered, "You'll *never* amount to anything if you keep being so softhearted. Nothing good comes from being weak." Her eyes were unfocused. "That's what they want you to believe. They want you to be tethered to righteous morality and *neutered* like a dog with a fucking handler—they're wrong. These realms will destroy you if you give an inch. So much power in your ancestry—yet you produce nothing? Not even a single shard of ice. At your age, I could move *mountains*."

The woman paused, then spat, "You disgust me, Arabella."

Horror engulfed me.

The girl zoned out as the mother ranted; she was used to her senseless prattling during torture.

"We'll continue these lessons every night until you learn." The woman smirked, and Arabella dropped her forehead to the floor.

Every night. Horror seized me.

My gut feeling had been correct—I was experiencing Arabella's memories. I was living through her torture.

The child on the ground was my mate.

She was helpless.

Tortured nightly.

I could tell from her thoughts that there was not a single soul in the realm who had protected her from her mother.

The fae guards had kicked my mate.

They'd broken her back.

Sneered at her as she convulsed with agony for hours, naked.

My Revered had suffered in unimaginable ways, and we'd failed her more than we ever knew.

Unholy rage pierced the veil of sleep as I was thrown out of the sickening memory. I sat up in my bed, panting.

The bedroom was quiet, and the clock read three a.m.

My body burned with heat, and even in the darkness, colors were richer. The grayish-blue filter was gone from my vision.

The strange emptiness I'd felt inside her chest was replaced with an overwhelming need for control.

Immediate regret filled me as I remembered how I'd treated her. How I'd lost control of my temper and yelled at her, just like her mother—I'd been afraid for her safety, but it was no excuse. I was disgusted with myself.

A whimper echoed in the sleeping room.

In a blur, I flung myself at the lower bunk on the opposite side of the room and knelt before her.

It took me a second to realize Scorpius and Orion crouched beside me.

I turned to my mates with confusion and asked, "Did you experie—"

"Yes," Scorpius cut me off.

The silence among us was fraught with angst and regret as we processed what we all knew.

We knelt together in disbelief.

Disciples at her altar.

Since we'd all been affected, it was obvious what was happening—the bond sickness had connected us to her memories. It was punishing us like we deserved.

"No, Mother, please," Arabella whispered in her sleep as

she tossed and turned before us. Her forehead glistened with sweat, and her covers were a mess. She slapped her arm back and forth like she was trying to fight off an invisible assailant.

I ordered, "Wake up," as Orion shook her gently and Scorpius patted her face.

She whimpered louder.

Then she opened her mouth, bowed her back, and silently screamed.

Helplessness churned in my gut. I hated that I knew exactly what torment she was experiencing.

"Please," I begged as my mates tried frantically to wake her.

Nothing worked.

She continued to thrash about.

Suffer.

We couldn't wake her, but I couldn't stand by and do nothing. Flames exploded across my shoulders, and red blurred my vision.

They had desecrated my Revered. I needed vengeance, or I was going to burn the war camp to the ground and murder everyone within it. Embers fell around me as I turned to my mates.

"We need to make this right," I said roughly. "I refuse to do nothing."

"I agree." Scorpius cracked his knuckles. "We need to go now, or I cannot be held responsible for my actions."

The eye tattooed on his neck shot wide open. It stared down at Arabella's thrashing form.

I nodded in agreement, flames crackling hotter across my shoulders.

"One of us has to watch over her," Orion whispered. "I'll stay." He caressed her sweaty blue curls as she thrashed about.

"Then let's go." I grabbed Scorpius's arm to guide him and stalked from the barracks.

We ran through the snowy forest. It was eerie at night. The once steaming ground was covered in a thin layer of ice and snow slammed against us from all directions.

The white contrasted with the vibrant green and rich brown conifer trees.

It was nothing like the shades of blue and gray that had painted Arabella's vision.

What was wrong with her sight? What was that crushing sense of emptiness she felt?

I couldn't breathe as another terrible thought struck me. Did Arabella still experience the world this way? Had we made the emptiness worse?

We'd failed our Revered in every possible way.

For a second, I stopped running and tilted my head back to the storm.

I inhaled.

It smelled like winter and rage.

It smelled like *her*.

The fire crawling beneath my skin intensified like it recognized her presence in the ice. Flames multiplied on my shoulders. The urge to unleash my powers spiked dramatically.

Sun god, I'm ruined for her.

When we got to the strategy room, I threw open the door with a bang and unlocked the desk's drawer. Then I grabbed the RJE device Lothaire had given us before the war started.

The world whirred.

Crack.

We disappeared.

Only one thing was on our minds.

Vengeance.

CHAPTER 13
ARAN
ALONE

TENEBROUS (ADJECTIVE): causing gloom.

DAY 8, HOUR 14

Mouth open on a silent scream, I jolted awake and sat up straight.

I cracked my forehead against wood.

Sun god help the idiot who had designed the cramped bunk beds, because I was going to hunt them down.

"Oof, that sucks." Orion was sprawled out on his bunk across the room, reading a book.

We were alone.

I rubbed at my forehead and winced. The clock on the wall showed I'd slept late into the day.

Seeing the question in my eyes, Orion smirked and said, "The twins and demons are bringing you back food from the cafeteria. It's just the two of us." He winked seductively. "Wanna hang?"

I flopped back onto my covers. "Yeah—*myself.*"

Orion laughed loudly, and I startled as I realized he'd

been speaking to me at full volume. His voice was as beautiful as his face.

Life wasn't fair.

"Where are your mates?" I asked as I threw myself out of bed and avoided thinking about warm brown eyes, long lashes, plush pink lips, and a sinful voice.

"They're doing some important king business, don't worry," he said.

Malum's words from last night came back to me. Orion had earned his cherry blossoms with open-mouthed kisses and moans of pleasure. I closed my eyes and tried to rub away the feeling of warm lips devouring me.

Turning around, I walked into a wall of muscle and jumped. My mouth watered at the divine scent of chocolate raspberries.

Orion stared down at me with a strange intensity. He'd moved silently across the room with impossible speed.

His full lips gave him a perpetual pout.

The memory of how soft his lips had felt when he'd kissed me at Elite Academy played through my mind. He kissed differently from Malum. Less rough, but equally passionate.

I licked my lips and swayed closer to him.

A sharp bolt of pain slammed down my spine and brought me back to reality.

Wondrous, I was becoming a pervert like the men.

I staggered away.

"Seriously. Are you okay?" he asked at full volume as he reached for me.

I flinched and kept backing away from him.

"Obviously—I'm clearly thriving," I said drolly instead of admitting I kept making out with my mortal enemy and I was beginning to suspect that I wanted to bone both him and Malum at the same time.

I grimaced as I made my bed just to give myself something to do.

One day, you were a woman with hopes and dreams, and the next, you were fantasizing about sitting on two men's faces just to shut them up.

Awkwardness stretched between us.

"Do you want to talk about it?" he asked.

I swallowed manic laughter. "Hard no."

His scent spiked sweeter as he moved closer to me, and I covered my mouth. Head spinning from too many hours of sleep, I staggered into the cramped bathroom and slammed the door shut, then locked it for good measure.

I turned on the water and collapsed into the tub.

Scalding-hot water burned my flesh, and I pretended not to notice that it reminded me of Malum's kisses.

There was screwed, and then there was *screwed*. I was the latter.

Pink blotches covered my limbs.

Wet curls were plastered across my face.

I laid my head back.

Orion hadn't told me where Malum and Scorpius were, but I pictured them walking hand in hand on a date while they gave each other kisses and talked shit about me.

Was I being rational? No. Did that matter at the moment because I was spiraling? Also no.

I lay in the tub under the shower spray like a frigid corpse who was not sexually attracted to her enemies.

Arms crossed over my chest.

Legs straight.

Mouth sewn shut.

The Necklace of Death hot against my chest.

Ice coated my fingers, then receded in the hot water.

For a second, I hallucinated there was snow in the shower. White flakes flurried down, then dissipated in the scalding steam.

A layer of thick cobalt ice coated my feet where they stuck out of the water.

What in the sun god is wrong with me?

When I'd discovered I was an angel, I'd pictured soaring over mountains and brandishing ice swords. I'd imagined poise and frosty control.

I had never pictured *this*.

The ice coating my feet traveled across the porcelain tub and welded us together.

"Are you all right in there?" Orion shouted through the door. His lyrical voice cracked, and he said softly, "Please tell me you're doing okay."

"Do you think I'm part angel, part Abominable Snowman?" I asked, slightly hysterical.

This was my final straw.

"What?" he asked with confusion through the door.

"I read about it in a book," I said. "It's this big beastly creature that lives in the ice and snow with thunder thighs and sharp teeth and claws and—uh, a freak," I finished lamely.

There was a long pause.

"I know what it's like to be a freak," he said softly through the door.

My heart twisted at the pain in his voice.

"You aren't one—don't say that," I said fiercely.

I yawned loudly. It seemed impossible that I could be so tired when I'd slept for so long. Panicking over becoming a snowman did that to a woman.

My eyes drifted closed.

"It's okay," Orion replied. "The first time I enchanted someone with my voice, I was four years old…" His voice was mellow as he told me stories about his childhood.

I listened with my eyes closed, imagining a cherub little boy with golden skin and white-blond hair crying himself to sleep because he was forbidden from talking to anyone.

My heart hurt as he revealed his parents had given him away to an all-boys home because they'd thought he was defective. Strength and power were the ultimate tenets of devil life, and those viewed as different were discarded.

He talked about living with the other foster boys on an expansive farm. How he'd loved visiting the village's farmers market.

I struggled to make sense of the world he described.

I'd pictured the devil realm as a dreary, miserable city filled with gangs and violence, but what he described sounded provincial and rural. It was a place of quiet living, apart from extreme tenets regarding strength and personhood.

His voice calmed the panic in my chest.

He talked about how being with Corvus and Scorpius had saved him.

How Corvus secretly had a soft side you would never believe unless you saw him in his home. How Scorpius could make pain feel greater than pleasure ever could.

My stomach flipped, and a whimper escaped my lips.

Orion changed topics, and he talked about the euphoric feeling of unleashing his powers with his mates. He said it felt divine but also like torment because their mating bond wasn't complete.

There was a painful knot in his chest that wound tighter when they unleashed their abilities. When they lost all awareness, it felt wrong, like they were being punished for not having their fourth.

I listened intently.

What he described was so foreign I couldn't even imagine it. To have so much power that it felt like euphoria—it sounded like a fairy tale.

Then Orion randomly asked softly, "What's with Luka?"

I frowned. "What do you mean?"

"Uh." He cleared his throat. "Why's he always so quiet? I've noticed that he seems—intense."

The tone of his voice was weird, and I couldn't place it.

"John's hinted that he's been through a lot," I said. "He's a very protective, intense guy." I smiled. "But he's secretly a softie." I thought about all the times he'd helped me during training, and we hadn't even known each other.

Orion was silent.

"Why do you ask?"

He cleared his throat. "Just wondering. I've noticed him watching me sometimes, and I was wondering if that was something he usually does?"

His words startled me. "No, it's not—he usually only looks at me and John. Sometimes I don't think he knows other people exist."

Orion made a noise in the back of his throat. "Interesting."

I smiled to myself. "He also has wicked-cool tattoos and a piercing somewhere you'd never expect."

"Really?" Orion asked, the interest clear in his voice.

Grinning, I launched into a detailed account of every fine-line tattoo that covered Luka's chest.

As I talked, the ice on my toes didn't seem like such a big deal.

After a while of objectifying Luka, I asked more ques-

tions about Orion's childhood, and he launched into a captivating tale of survival.

Yet again I drifted off to sleep, but this time in the shower
to the sound of an enchanting voice.

The nightmares stayed away.

I dreamed of grassy pastures, rolling hills, cherry blossoms floating on a warm summer breeze, and Orion smiling
as he talked to me.

CHAPTER 14
ARAN
PARTY

REVERIE (NOUN): the condition of being lost in thought.

DAY 9, HOUR 19

"A safe place for the soldiers to unwind."

That was what Lothaire had called Elite Academy last week. The unspoken *I'm doing this for you, my daughter* had hung in the air between us.

Yesterday, he'd burst into our sleeping barracks and dumped RJE devices onto the floor. "In recognition of your sacrifices, I procured these for you and your soldiers. Your old room and the academy's servants are yours to use. Thank you for your service."

He'd ruffled my blue curls and whispered, "You're doing great."

Then he'd RJE'd away, and I'd gaped at the place where he'd stood.

One day, a man's hitting you with a baton and the next he's trying to be a cool dad.

Life comes at you fast.

Now we were back partying in our bedroom at Elite Academy, and it didn't feel like a safe place.

It felt wild.

Muted red light, so dark it was almost black, filtered through the stained-glass windows and cast shadows over the dancers.

I wanted to scream with grief over the war, and I would have, but…

I couldn't feel my face.

I also couldn't feel my back or my limbs.

Or the crushing existential despair that was squeezing my —wait, never mind, that was still present.

I danced as the party raged around me.

My hands waved in the air, diamond bracelet glittering for all to see, as my hips rolled against the masses of sweaty flesh. The floor beneath my feet was covered in black ice and sent some partygoers falling to the ground.

I bared my teeth with satisfaction as another student fell.

We were all just carnal beasts looking for our next fix.

A few feet away, Ghost kissed a burley male student, who liked to make homophobic and misogynistic comments, on the lips, and he fell to the ground, convulsing and foaming at the mouth.

I gave Ghost a high five as he floated past. His incorporeal hand went through me, and I shivered.

We loved an ally.

Apparently, he was not constrained to the library, because he glided around the party, sending students into comas.

Tears filled my eyes.

I'd missed Ghost so much, and things just weren't the same without him around because no one traumatized people like he did.

He had a rare gift.

Demon brew coursed through my veins as bodies gyrated around me, and instead of crying, I did what I did best in life.

Drugs.

Sun god bless the demon culture; they were the true silent heroes of the realm for helping us all get so gloriously wasted.

I saluted Zenith, who was across the room, grinding on Vegar.

Zenith scowled back at me, and I blew him a kiss.

He rolled his eyes, but I could tell from his acerbic expression that he secretly loved the attention.

Bodies shifted in the packed room and blocked my view of the demons.

I tipped my head back and smoked.

Rolling my body to the beat, I held up my hand, and five fingers waved in and out of focus. *Five.* It had been five days since we'd slaughtered an entire compound full of people.

Now the party (funeral) raged in our old bedroom with enchanted music, soldiers, naked students, drugs, sex, and alcohol.

The PTSD wasn't included.

I brought my own.

"Fuck you," I snarled at no one in particular as faces blurred around me. The singer crooned on the speakers, and I exhaled a cloud of smoke.

"You tell them," Sadie shouted over the music. "You get 'em, girl."

She moved against me, gyrating her hips and swinging her arms in what most parts of the realm called "having an episode."

I chuckled to myself as I remember how thinking about her dancing had saved me from my attraction to Malum.

In the present, in what was supposed to be a seductive move, she spread her arms wide and jumped into a split.

Shockingly her legs locked a few feet from the floor.

She screamed in pain and fell over.

"I think I pulled my crotch," she moaned pitifully.

Between gasps of laughter, I said, "You know, I picture you dancing when I'm trying *not* to be turned on."

She smacked at my hands as I tried to help her up. "Please, we both know it's the opposite."

"I'm not joking," I said, laughing uncontrollably as she struggled to stand.

She lowered her voice and leaned close to me as she half shimmied, half twitched. "Whatever you say, sweet stuff."

I pushed her away. "That is *exactly* what I was talking about. It's just weird."

"Sun god," she groaned. "You don't need to be a bitch because you find me sexy. A lot of people do."

She tried to wink, but both her eyes closed at the same time.

She blinked furiously.

"Clearly," I said dryly, "that's exactly what's happening here."

The music changed to a faster beat, and she suddenly grabbed my arms and spun us both around.

Unlike all the uncoordinated students and soldiers who kept slipping, Sadie didn't hate the patch of ice that had spread beneath my feet; she tipped her head back and laughed as she spun us both faster on it.

A thought struck me. She'd grown up in the cold shifter realm and was at home with ice and snow.

Maybe that was why she was at home with me?

My heart swelled with emotions I couldn't afford to feel, so I tipped my head back and lowered my shoulders, swung my arms back and forth as I smoked five pipes at once.

Five.

It had been five days since five people from the Legionnaire Games had been slaughtered in the battle. One angel and one assassin inside the building, two leviathans and one devil outside in the snow as they fought against the ungodly that tried to escape.

All their corpses were unidentifiable.

I didn't even know the names of the angel and assassin, but I'd fought beside them as the ungodly ripped them apart.

I knew how they'd died.

"Okay, Aran, I see you. Go off." Sadie rolled her body against me as I tipped my head backward further.

"Hit it. Hit it. Hit it," she shouted encouragingly as I swung my arms and legs back and forth and squatted low.

I rocked faster.

Smoked harder.

Seventeen was the total number of soldiers we'd lost in the battle, because twelve foot soldiers had died securing the perimeter. There were five odd numbers between five and seventeen.

So many fives.

I grabbed a bottle of demon brew from a student's hands and tipped it back. Drank until it was empty, then chucked it against the far wall.

It exploded, and students yelped.

Sadie cheered.

The number 5555 was an enchanted one that stood for change.

They'd changed all right. Living to dead.

I wheezed, and my chest tingled.

"Here, sweetie," Sadie said as she pressed another pipe between my crammed lips. "Have another smoke. This will help."

I inhaled the drugs until my lungs felt like they were disintegrating inside my sternum.

She was right.

It helped.

I loved her so much; she always knew what I needed.

She pulled me close and whispered into my ear, "We should pretend to have sex in the shower again sometime."

Never mind—she knew nothing.

"What?" I stopped dancing.

She snickered. "Scorpius told me the other day that he would make you come harder than I ever could."

I pulled back and gaped at her. "He did not."

"Yep." She popped the *p* loudly. "Then he told me my stroke game was weak." She smirked as she shimmied her hips. "I told him I was better at giving head because I was a girl and knew what felt best."

I choked on smoke. "You did not say that."

She grinned. "Oh, I did. He was so pissed—you should have seen it. Poor guy stabbed himself in the thigh with a pen. Can we please do it again? I think your men would actually have aneurysms."

"They're not *my* men," I said reflexively.

She rolled her hips and winked. "Suuuuure, whatever you say. And I don't shift into a saber-toothed tiger and enslave people with my blood."

I rolled my eyes, and we resumed dancing.

"Fine," I said a few moments later and drawled seductively, "You can fake fuck me again."

She squealed and pulled me close. "You will not regret this decision."

I laughed because I definitely would, and we rocked together in the flailing mass of sweaty limbs and hormones.

Everything was a jumbled mess.

Students were on their knees.

Soldiers pressed against the walls with their heads tipped back.

Sounds of pleasure echoed.

Pincers scraped.

Exoskeletons crunched.

High-pitched chittering sounded.

Eighty-three was the number of soldiers left in our army, and you couldn't divide it by five.

It was all disturbing.

Horse cawed with agitation as he flapped above the heads of the partygoers. His tail and wings were covered in long trailing feathers, and his neck was longer.

He stopped flying and perched on my shoulder, nuzzling his beak against the side of my head.

I leaned my head back to try to make the dark thoughts fall out.

I tipped backward, but they stayed inside my head.

Regrettable.

Sadie caught me before I crashed to the floor, then spun me around the room like we were at a fancy ball on a spacious dance floor.

Plot twist, we weren't.

We crashed into bodies, and drinks sloshed everywhere as people swore.

I couldn't help but laugh as Sadie grinned like a maniac and spun me faster in the crowd. She slammed me into a student like a battering ram, and he crashed to the floor.

It was the most fun I'd had in weeks.

My elbow cracked against someone's nose, and blood

sprayed like diamonds. Sadie's cheeks were rosy, lips glossy, as she twirled with me.

We laughed uncontrollably.

This was the feminine experience.

We slammed into someone, and they hit the ground with a thud. Horse cawed in his face, then settled on Ghost's shoulder.

They haunted the party together.

Goals.

"What the fuck are you two doing?" the student we'd just bowled over spat from the floor. "I'm a royal student, and I don't recognize you, which means you're filthy commoners." He lumbered unsteadily to his feet.

What a delightful man.

"Spinning sexily," Sadie said in a duh voice as she flipped her white hair over her shoulder and made an obscene gesture with her hands.

I put my hand over my mouth to hide my laughter.

Sadie grinned over at me, clearly proud that she was making me laugh, and gyrated her hips to the music.

The man said something else, but we ignored him as we danced.

In my peripheral vision, he lunged toward us. "You little commoners think you can—"

"Is this man bothering you?" Cobra appeared out of nowhere and blocked the man.

He stared down at Sadie with an intense expression as the jewels embedded in his skin glinted prettily in the dimly lit party.

She chuckled. "Nooooope."

"Go away, snake man," I slurred and chucked three of my pipes at him like daggers.

They bounced off his chest and fell to the floor.

Snake eyes glowed in the darkness as Cobra said, "I didn't ask for your opinion." Slit pupils flickered as he faced me, and he arched his brow. "I see you're struggling like usual. How predictable."

I studied my fingernails. "I've always thought it fascinating that snakes have brains the size of peanuts. It must be difficult being such a—" I wrinkled my nose. "—dimwit."

Cobra smiled back meanly. "Interesting talk coming from the girl who was crying an hour ago while chugging demon brew."

"How dare you," I gasped. "I had something in my eye. Also, at least my pupils aren't lobotomized."

His eyes twinkled. "How is therapy going? Are you still sad?"

"No." I laughed falsely. "I'm cured."

Cobra spread his arms wide and blocked the student who was still trying to charge at us as he proclaimed, "It's a miracle. Especially after you let yourself get stabbed just a few days ago. Good to see you're doing better."

I stumbled, and Sadie righted me.

How did he know? Had Malum talked to him? No, the king thought he was above the shifters; no way he would have told them something so personal.

It must be a lucky guess.

Recovering my composure, I relaxed my posture and smiled. "Awww, thanks for your concern," I said condescendingly. "Also, don't worry, I'll keep your secret. Sadie's told me all about your *little* problem in the bedroom?"

"What did I say?" Sadie whispered in my ear. "I don't remember."

Sun god bless her.

The student we knocked over tried to push past Cobra,

but this time, the snake shifter said, "You just threatened two of the champions in the war."

The man paled, and his eyes widened as he realized who we were. He bowed respectively. "I didn't know, forgive me."

Cobra slammed his foot down. "You're not forgiven." Bones crunched, and the student went down with a scream.

A dark corridor.

Glowing blue swords.

A bear roaring.

Infected dying.

High-pitched chittering.

A woman screaming.

I tripped and looked down.

It was a body.

CRACK.

"Snap out of it." Cobra slapped me across the face, and the party (funeral) came back into focus.

I touched my lip, and my finger came back red. The cold liquid hardened into ice.

"Thanks," I said sincerely.

"Don't mention it." He grunted and stepped away. "Seriously, never talk to me again. Better yet, forget I exist."

"Who are you?" I asked with feigned confusion.

A slow smile curled his lips as he pulled Sadie to his side, tucking her under his shoulder protectively.

He looked at something behind me and pulled his mate into the crowd. Before the dancing bodies swallowed them, Cobra winked.

I cocked my head in confusion.

His meaning was clear a second later when long fingers grabbed my cheeks and pulled my face to the side.

The hand was freezing.

Harsh.

Unrelenting.

A tongue licked across my lower lip wantonly, and I was just depressed enough to enjoy it. I trembled.

"Why is my Revered bleeding?" Scorpius asked menacingly as he shook my head back and forth. "I heard a slap, is that what this is from? Who do I need to kill?"

He breathed roughly, and warm air puffed against the side of my face.

The blind king stood flush against me. He curled his body around mine like a dragon hoarding its treasure.

I'd noticed that he was doing it more often.

Shielding me with his flesh.

"It's not blood," I drawled, my cheeks pressed against his fingers as I forced my lips into a smile. "I'm just overflowing with existential dread, practically bursting at the seams."

He didn't release my face.

Instead, he rubbed his wide chest against my back and purred, "Seriously, who am I killing?"

I leaned back against him and swayed.

"No one." I sighed. "I slapped myself because I was trying to feel something. Sadly, it didn't work. I'll make sure to use a shovel next time."

Warm breath fanned against the side of my face, and for a long moment, we swayed to the music in a toxic imitation of dancing.

One began where the other ended.

"You're a shit liar, Arabella," he said harshly in my ear.

I slammed my elbow back into his sternum. "My name is not Arabella. It's Aran."

Instead of letting me go like I'd planned, Scorpius moaned and jerked his hips against my ass.

Hardness pressed against me.

He curled his one hand around my face so his fingernails

pressed against my skin in five pinpricks of pain. He palmed my core with his other hand.

Fire exploded down my spine.

I whimpered.

"If you wanted it rough, you just had to ask." His hips swayed against me faster, in time with the music. He clutched my pussy through my sweatpants like it belonged to him.

Arousal pooled inside my stomach.

Male and female students shot me dirty glares, and it took me a second to remember that everyone at the academy had Stockholm syndrome over the kings.

They were all deranged.

Not me.

Nope, I had my head screwed on straight and a crystal-clear understanding that the three of them were psychopaths.

In fact, I was so intelligent that I was letting one of them publicly fondle me. Slay (in the sexual sense).

I sucked on my remaining three pipes.

Desire flamed hotter.

"The problem is," I whispered as I melted back against Scorpius, "I fucking hate you."

His grip on my core tightened. Fingers massaging.

I shuddered.

My hips jerked against his hold.

Scorpius nuzzled the side of my face and breathed harshly into my ear. Goose bumps exploded across my skin, and I shivered violently.

"Don't worry, Arabella, I forgive you for your cruel words." He tightened his hands and a spasm fluttered through me.

I pressed my thighs together and said weakly, "Release me."

"But you don't want me to." He laughed, and the sound was filthy.

My voice dripped with frost. "But I'm telling you to, and you're not listening. Some *Protector* you are."

He released me like I'd burned him. He stepped away, and his expression was dark. "I'll always protect you. Don't you dare question that."

I scoffed.

Ignored the wetness between my legs.

"You tortured me when I was a man *and* when I was a woman. Turns out you're an equal opportunist piece of shit. How progressive." I clapped mockingly, and manic chuckles burst from my throat. "Also, you are literally the opposite of a Protector. You're a cruel, insecure bully."

It was just *so* funny.

I sucked harder on my pipes, and everything became a little hazy.

Scorpius remained in harsh focus.

Shadows filled hollow cheeks, cheekbones glinted razor-sharp, unseeing, milky white eyes narrowed, and full lips curled back.

Something new flashed across his features, and his mask cracked. "What do you need from me?" His teeth clicked as he gnashed them. "How do I fix how terrible we've been? I understand now how horrible the things are that you've gone through." He choked on the last word like he couldn't say anything more.

What did he mean?

Why does he now understand?

"You can't," I whispered with confusion. "It's too far gone."

He flexed his hands.

Tilted his head to the side and slowly fell to his knees.

"What are you doing?" I gaped down at him. "Stand up." I pulled at his wide shoulders.

"No, Arabella." Scorpius's voice was harsh, and he remained kneeling in the crowd of bodies.

Students and soldiers stopped dancing to stare.

Why was a king on his knees?

Confusion was written on all our faces as the sado-masochist bowed his head submissively. The posture was wrong on him. Foreign.

"Please forgive me, Arabella Alis Egan," he spoke loudly so everyone could hear.

The weight of everyone's attention was smothering.

I gritted my teeth. "Get up." I tugged at his shoulders desperately.

"No."

"I'm not joking, Scorpius. Stop this at once."

He bowed lower and announced, "You've been wronged in despicable ways, and I have also wronged you. I vow to be your servant. From this day forward, let it be known that I am not a king of the sun god. I serve only you. I'm your hound."

I stumbled back and covered my mouth, half expecting the sun god to strike him down for his blasphemy. Everyone knew the kings lived to serve him. That was their lives' purpose, and they never shut up about it.

Women and men oohed and aahed in the crowd.

My breath came out in frosty puffs.

"She's so lucky," someone whispered next to me, and a person replied, "I'd kill to have him on his knees for me."

They giggled.

"You don't mean that." I took another step back.

His voice took on its familiar sneer as he said, "I've never meant anything more in my miserable existence. Let me serve you. Please."

There was a fresh round of swooning in the crowd.

I rubbed at my eyes, half convinced I was hallucinating because of excessive drug use.

"Um, okay?" I scratched at the back of my neck.

The crowd parted as Orion and Malum stepped forward to flank their mate. Looming shadows of death, they fell to their knees beside him.

All three of them bowed their heads to me and said in unison, "From here on out, we will be known as your hounds."

Someone swooned in the crowd, and there was a smattering of applause and wolf whistles.

I was going to be sick.

"I don't get why they're so obsessed with her?" a different girl whispered cattily from behind me.

"They'll tire of her eventually. It's just for show," someone replied, and they burst into laughter.

They spoke my fears aloud.

I pressed my palms into my eyes and took another step back. Could they not give me one party to rot in depression by myself?

"I've always been more of a cat person," I mumbled under my breath as I looked around for Sadie, desperate for my friend to distract me from whatever the hell was going on in front of me.

Men were messy.

Each day, I became a bigger advocate for mandatory male imprisonment at birth.

"You belong to us," Malum said harshly, then his cheeks turned scarlet like he was embarrassed for voicing his true thoughts.

Case in point.

He couldn't even pretend to be contrite while prostrating himself before me in a crowd.

I inhaled, tipped my head back, and scoffed in disbelief, "You're out of your minds if you think I'll forgive you."

Bright flames exploded across his shoulders, and he lifted his head, molten silver pinning me in place as fury contorted his features.

The crowd fell over themselves as they put more space between themselves and the volatile king who was known for losing his temper.

Orion grimaced. He looked up with pleading eyes like he was apologizing because his mates couldn't pretend to play nice.

"Do you want me to crawl for you?" Malum asked loudly, and his deep, baritone voice made it hard to breathe.

Another person swooned.

The Academy seemed to have a passing-out problem.

Malum crawled forward toward me, harshly handsome features appeared insidious in the room's dark shadows.

He tried to look repentant.

He looked savage.

I subconsciously rubbed at my neck as I remembered how he'd dragged his teeth across my sensitive skin.

The floor vibrated with music.

I pulled three pipes from my lips and blew out as I tried not to look at the man crawling across the room toward me. "I'm yours. I'm your hound," he said as he got closer. "Forgive me—please."

I choked.

Somehow he'd managed to make an apology sound like a command.

They were on their knees before their *Revered*; Malum was crawling toward *her*.

Not me.

He was trying to manipulate my womanly disposition by groveling.

The worst part was it was working.

I girded my loins and reminded myself that my most feminine quality was that I was pure evil.

It forced out a dark chuckle as I glared down at the flaming king who knelt at my feet. "You are all delusional."

Turning my back to them, I pushed through the gaping crowd toward the two men who'd been standing against the wall behind me all night, silently observing as I'd danced with Sadie and sparred with her mate.

Their presence was a constant comfort.

Their energy was different because they wanted *Aran*.

Not Arabella.

Not a Revered.

John rolled his eyes at my expression, but he flashed his dimples and licked his lips as I sauntered forward and wrapped my arms around his neck. Luka pulled his gaze away from where Orion knelt, and focused the full weight of his attention on me.

"Should we give them a show?" I asked him.

He tried to look disinterested but failed spectacularly. "Are you sure you want us and not Sadie? You've been rubbing all over her all night," he asked petulantly.

"Aw, are you jealous, sweetheart?" I asked back.

"It depends." He wrapped his arms around my waist and pulled me flush against his hips. "Does it turn you on?"

He winked, and I laughed. "Maybe."

Luka played with a curl and asked, "Are you feeling okay?"

"Like today or in general?" I squinted.

He arched a dark brow. "How are you doing right now?"

"Horrible." I smiled up at his concerned expression as the room spun around me.

He frowned and massaged the back of my head. "I don't think we should—"

"Fuck me in front of the kings until I feel better," I demanded, loud enough for the devils to hear.

The crowd broke into murmurs.

"What the fuck are all of you standing around looking at?" Malum asked the crowd, and the dancing resumed.

John pulled me closer and tsked as he shook his head. "Are you trying to use us to get to the kings? Am I nothing but a hunk of meat to you?"

"Nah." I winked. "You've also got some gravy."

He threw his head back with laughter. "Are you hitting on me, Aran? Is this your attempt at flirting?"

"It depends." I rolled the pipes between my lips. "Is it working?"

"Yes," John said at the same time Luka whispered, "Fuck me. You can't say things like that."

"Why?" I asked, genuinely confused.

Luka leaned forward and whispered against the shell of my ear, "Because I'll take you up on it. Aran, I'll make you scream our names so loudly that everyone will know who you belong to."

CHAPTER 15
LUKA
PARTY

BELAMOUR (NOUN): one who is loved.

DAY 9, HOUR 21

Aran was pressed flush against me, and I inhaled her wintry scent, dry ice exploding across my senses.

Music boomed from enchanted speakers and the room glowed with bright scarlet light.

The crush of bodies rocked around us.

We trapped her between us; John pressed flush against her back as I claimed her front.

My skin buzzed, but this time, the compulsion wasn't telling me to keep her close and protect her. It was telling me to own her.

Mark her as mine.

Consume her.

Do depraved things to her.

Corrupt her.

Show her just what it meant to be the fiancée of an antisocial man with an attachment disorder.

I wanted Aran's skin to tingle with pleasure like mine crawled with need. I wanted her to know my torment and understand what it meant that we owned each other.

When she'd accepted our betrothal jewelry, she'd agreed to tie her souls to ours.

Irrevocably.

Aran gazed up at me in the dark, her hooded eyes rimmed with dark bruises. My girl was tired and struggling with handling the weight of the war.

I wanted to shield her from all suffering.

I wanted to help her forget.

Cupping her face tenderly, I traced my thumb across her scar. The half crescent adorned the top of her cheek and enhanced her fragile beauty.

Warm breath tingled across my wrist as she leaned into my hand.

Melted against me.

She was an island of softness and trust in a harsh, jagged room of killers.

Loud music and gyrating hips. The scent of sweat and sex. Drugs consumed with desperation. Soldiers tried to forget.

She was different from all the men and women in this cursed castle.

I'd recognized her uniqueness the first day I'd met her, when she'd broken through my barriers. She wore it in her eyes, clear as day.

Aran was empathetic.

Terribly so.

In realms full of immortal beings where ruthlessness and cunning were admired above all else, she defied the norms.

Aran broke the equation of an individual's power directly correlating with their callousness.

Case in point, I didn't care about anyone but my twin, and the kings only cared about one another. The demons were consumed with themselves, and the angels thought they were the superior race. The shifters kept a close familial circle and distrusted outsiders.

We were all perfect soldiers because we killed others easily.

Slaughter or survive because immortality was a long time to live under another's thumb.

Yet despite it all, Aran Alis Egan was compassionate and struggled to hurt others even though she was born with a crown and power in her veins.

How could one woman be so fierce, yet so caring?

The duality of man incarnate.

I stroked her chilled skin, and sooty eyelashes fluttered against the pad of my thumb.

Need burned in my lower gut.

Everything narrowed until all I could see was hooded dark blue eyes, wild blue curls, smoke curling from plush pink lips as Aran stared up at me like I was her savior.

Awareness exploded across my skin.

Because I wanted nothing more than to be her champion.

A tortured woman like her needed a tortured man like me; like Sisyphus, we were bound to suffer. Together.

Diamonds sparkled on her wrist, and the jewel of death hung heavy across her chest.

I was touching her.

She was at my mercy.

At last.

Since the party had started hours ago, John and I had stood against the wall, watching as she flirted with Sadie.

And even though I didn't have an issue with the woman

like my twin did—since she made Aran happy, that was all that mattered to me—it had still been frustrating to watch without touching. Claiming. Defiling.

Alas, she smiled differently when Sadie was around, so we'd stayed back in the shadows. Watched with amusement as they'd flung themselves through the crowd like battering rams.

They'd danced wantonly and drunk heavily. Taken random drugs from strangers with mischievous grins.

She'd been carefree.

Different.

She'd only sunk once into the darkness, but Cobra had slapped her and brought her back to reality. By the time John and I had realized what had happened, the snake shifter had disappeared into the crowd and the kings had arrived.

We would punish him later.

For now, I held her in my arms.

I pressed a soft kiss to her forehead, and her icy scent was like adrenaline straight to the veins.

My lips tingled from the innocent touch.

Electricity sparked between us.

Aran's mouth curled up into a smirk, and she whispered huskily, "Fuck me in front of the kings, pretty please." She batted her eyelashes.

Blood rushed south at the thought of taking her so publicly.

The idea of Orion watching was an added bonus.

Lately, I'd noticed how his dark eyes were always fixated on my Aran. He'd bite his pouty lips like he was dreaming of devouring her. I understood exactly how he felt.

It was intriguing to see someone else fixate on her with the same obsession.

The strangest part of it all was that I'd noticed he existed.

Now his long lashes fluttered as he stared at Aran with undisguised hunger. His gaze flitted in the space between our lips.

I liked knowing he watched.

I liked knowing he was just as obsessed, but she was mine.

I smirked and cupped her precious face with both my hands, trailing my thumbs across her cheekbones as I cradled her before me.

"You don't have to beg, love," I said softly.

She inhaled sharply and relaxed into my touch. She let me hold her up. Own her.

I whispered into her halo of curls, "But I like the way you melt for me."

A soft moan escaped her lush lips, and it was the sweetest ambrosia after a lifetime of starvation.

"This is your only warning." My voice was rough as I pushed myself flush against her. "I'm not going to hold back because we're in public."

Navy eyes widened as her lips made an *o* of surprise, then she smiled shyly and mumbled, "That's fine."

I couldn't stop my smirk.

It was time to show her just how attached I could be.

CHAPTER 16

ARAN

PARTY

AMATIVE (ADJECTIVE): strongly moved by love and especially sexual love.

DAY 9, HOUR 21

Luka pulled the pipes from my lips and pressed them into his mouth. He tipped his head back and inhaled with his eyes closed. The lines of his neck strained, and he shivered.

I gulped.

He tipped his head back forward and licked frost off the pipes like he was savoring my taste.

Students and soldiers moved around us in a mass of flailing limbs. The shadowy darkness of the room wrapped around.

We were blanketed in darkness.

Desire flamed between us.

Courage burned my sternum, and with the room warped in slow motion, I fell to my knees.

Before.

Luka.

His eyes were chips of obsidian, and he tracked my every movement like he was obsessed with me.

He always watched and touched me like he couldn't get enough. When I was around the twins, I felt cared for.

With Luka, I felt cherished. Special.

He sucked on my pipes, the vapor from drugs curling around him as his fingers tangled in my hair and he looked down at me ardently.

My knees dug into the hard floor.

His pupils were blown wide, swallowing his irises, and he radiated strength. I was powerless before him.

A worshipper on the steps of the sun god's chapel.

Luka didn't tell me to stop; instead, he slowly unzipped his cargo pants and widened his stance with smoke above his head like a crown.

Colors swirled in my peripheral vision as demon brew pulsed through me.

My head spun with giddiness.

Drugs in my blood, lust in my veins.

I laughed as someone bumped into me from behind. The crush of bodies swarmed around us, and we were swallowed by the dancing mess.

Everything was surreal.

I still couldn't feel my face.

Not an ounce of pain streaked across my back because I was floating; I'd entered into a higher plane of existence.

I was incorporeal.

The haze wrapped around me in shades of seductive black.

Luka pulled himself free from his pants and rubbed himself leisurely against my mouth, cold metal and velvet heat.

I stared up with wide eyes up as he stroked his pierced dick across my lips. He groaned deeply.

Obsidian eyes were hooded and his muscles tensed.

He was seconds away from losing control.

A sense of power rushed over me, and I slowly opened my mouth, leaned forward, and took him in.

Cold metal on my tongue.

The music switched, and the floor vibrated to the bass as people jumped around us with their hands in the air.

I lapped at the tip with my tongue and flicked his piercing back and forth. Teased him slowly.

Sweat dripped down the side of his face.

For a second, I imagined a black glittering cape hanging off his shoulders, but I blinked and it disappeared.

Pulling back, I licked wantonly at his head like it was a lollipop. His Adam's apple bobbed as he swallowed thickly.

Long graceful fingers reached down and gripped my chin in a punishing grip. He held my face immobile so I couldn't move as his dark eyes flashed.

Pleasure coiled in my gut.

The moment was so intense that it left me lightheaded.

Surrealism morphed into hyperrealism as every hair on my body stood at attention.

I tingled down to the tips of my toes.

Nothing could ever compare.

Hands tangled in my curls and powerful legs pressed against my back as John straddled me from behind.

The intensity crescendoed as it reached new heights.

Luka held my face in his grip with his dick between my lips, and John held my curls in his fists as he pressed my face forward.

I was trapped.

I was flying.

The twins towered above me on either side.

The party raged around us as bodies danced and the floor vibrated beneath my knees. There was nowhere else I'd rather be.

They moved in tandem and pulled my face to the left so I was no longer looking up at Luka.

There was a wet pop as I released him from my mouth.

For a second, I stared into the crowd, confused about what they were doing.

Then I realized.

My core pulsed, and I pressed my knees together.

The kings had stood up.

They were unmoving, disturbingly still in the middle of the dancing crowd, as they fixated on where I knelt between the twins. Red flames leaped across Malum's shoulders and were reflected in silver eyes. Orion whispered in Scorpius's ear, his pretty features contorted with anger. The blind king was grinding his teeth together with his hands fisted.

Cherry blossoms swirled. A dagger glinted like it was solid. A third eye blinked.

The kings were close to losing all control.

They were murderous.

Good. Satisfaction was heady and warm in my chest as I remembered all the times the kings had fucked in this very room while I watched on dispassionately. They could proclaim their devotion to me as much as they wanted, but it didn't change the past.

Karma was a bitch.

And so was I.

Without saying a word, the twins turned my head away from the kings.

Luka dragged his thumb across my lower lip slowly as he

pulled my chin down, then he leaned his hips forward and pressed velvet-wrapped steel against my tongue.

I gagged around his length.

He pressed himself deeper.

John massaged my scalp as he fisted my curls tightly and pressed my head forward.

I inhaled roughly through my nose as I was speared between them.

Someone bumped into John as they danced, and all three of us rocked, but they didn't release me.

"You're taking me so well, my love," Luka said roughly as he thrust in deep, languid strokes, then groaned under his breath, "Fuck me."

I flushed with pleasure.

Hardness pressed against the back of my head as John stepped closer and pinned me.

Drool dripped out of my mouth and trickled down my chin.

"We belong to each other, Aran," John said roughly as he used my curls to bob my head up and down faster on his twin's dick.

I tried to nod, but I couldn't move my head.

Students and soldiers stared down at me with envy on their faces as they danced near us. They watched us with lust-glazed eyes like they were imagining taking my place.

I let their attention wash over me in a wave of smug satisfaction.

They could look, but they would never get to touch. The twins were mine.

Luka stared down at me with rapture on his face. "I didn't exist until you came into my life; there was no purpose or meaning to the monotony. Now I burn with life because I live for you. Every breath I take is yours. You are the totality of my essence. I survive by your mercy."

I swallowed, and he groaned.

It was the most I'd ever heard him say at once.

Callused fingers squeezed my chin as he thrust deeper. "You're doing beautifully, my love. So perfect."

I floated on his praise.

Then he thrust deeper and stilled. John pushed forward as Luka pulled me close and jerked against my face as he spilled himself down my throat.

It was intimate.

Overwhelming.

He pulled himself out my mouth, and he spilled down my chin. I coughed, and he pulled me to my feet, then he claimed my mouth with his.

The kiss was depraved.

I exhaled as I collapsed against his chest in a boneless heap.

In one smooth motion, John picked me up and cradled me tightly against his chest.

"Are you okay, Aran?" he asked.

I shivered at how intensely he said my name, and nodded sleepily. The room spun, and my head buzzed.

I closed my eyes.

An RJE device whirled.

Time folded, and I gladly let it go because the twins would take care of me.

I sighed with contentment.

Water blanketed me in a hot spray, and the twins were pressed flush against me in the narrow shower. We were back at our barracks.

John shampooed my hair, and Luka cleaned my body.

I tried to help, but my arms were too heavy.

"Relax, love," Luka commanded. "Let us take care of you." His eyes were softer obsidian as he scrubbed every inch of me with painstaking attention.

I relaxed, boneless between them.

"For once, the queen has nothing to say," John said playfully as he massaged my scalp. "It's sad that all it took was a public blow job." He tsked, like he was disappointed in me.

"I'll still kill you," I mumbled, then moaned as he dug deeper into my scalp.

He laughed. "You can try, little Smurf. You can try."

Time melted.

A towel was wrapped around my body as another dried my hair.

Fuzzy socks were pulled onto my feet, and oversized sweatpants that didn't belong to me were pulled up my hips. I smiled as an oversized sweatshirt enveloped me in heat. Sandalwood and musk wafted from it deliciously.

"Duck your head, love," Luka whispered, and I squinted with confusion as I climbed into my bed. It was all hard planes and warm skin, and there was barely any room.

"Shh, settle down and lie on me," John whispered in my ear as I lay spread atop him. "I refuse to sleep apart another night."

"But Luka?" I asked sleepily.

"Right here, love." Luka's hand tangled in my hair, and I opened my eyes. He was sitting on the floor and was leaning against the low bunk bed so he could touch me.

I furrowed my brow and asked him sleepily, "Are you comfortable?"

Luka whispered, "There's nowhere else I'd rather be."

I fell asleep with John wrapped around me and Luka's fingers buried tightly in my curls.

That night, a small piece of ice in my chest thawed.

CHAPTER 17
JINX
OPPRESSION

DRACONIAN (ADJECTIVE): cruel, severe.

DAY 9, HOUR 20: AN HOUR EARLIER

The shifters left for Elite Academy, and Warren went to get food from the cafeteria.

I finally had the room to myself, and the silence was blissful.

Until it wasn't.

Knock. Knock. Someone was outside.

I stilled.

The door was enchanted to permit inhabitants entry—only an outsider would knock.

Apprehension prickled down my spine as I realized the party had created the perfect opportunity to get me alone. It might have been planned for that very purpose.

Sweat broke out across my forehead.

It was a good plan.

Sun god forbid my family members miss an opportunity to drink themselves into oblivion. Technically, I was twenty-five, but since they were under the misconception that I was a decade younger, I was left out. They'd *know* I'd be left behind.

Knock-knock-knock—knock.

The pattern was familiar.

Instantly, I felt sick to my stomach.

I was still waiting on a prosthetic for my leg and could barely maneuver around, let alone face who was at the door.

I cursed my family for putting me in this situation. If any of them bothered to use their critical thinking skills, then maybe I wouldn't be left to shoulder dark consequences, but alas, they were oblivious, insensible, incognizant, and I was cornered.

Sitting on my lower bunk with a heavy tome spread across my lap, I debated the best course of action.

"I know you're in there," an ominous voice said.

With a deep, steadying breath, I closed *The Ancient Art of War and Manipulating Those Around You* and tucked it under my pillow.

I was on the bottom bunk, but it still took effort to roll myself out of bed without falling over. Grabbing onto the bedpost, I jumped on one leg.

My remaining knee was stiff and uncomfortable.

Apparently having my leg burned completely off wasn't enough trauma, because new growing pains were making my joints perpetually achy. The lovely benefits of being a species who went through puberty in under a year.

I grimaced.

The door was only a few feet away, but it might as well have been miles.

Cursing the High Court for not getting me a prosthetic by now, I hopped forward awkwardly with my arms outstretched. They said they were acquiring one, but every time we asked, they acted weird about it. It had to be an intimidation tactic.

A foot away, I crashed onto the floor.

I crawled awkwardly on my elbows, then grabbed the doorknob and hoisted myself up. Foreboding washed over me as I opened the door.

Frigid air pooled into the room in a flurry of snowflakes and malfeasance.

"Hello, Jinx," Dick said coldly as he brushed past me and entered the space like he belonged, which made sense because a corrupt oligarch was most at home in the suffering of others.

Cold from outside wafted in.

I hung off the door and said a quote often attributed to Plato, "The price of apathy toward public affairs is to be ruled by evil men."

Dick smirked. "True."

We sized each other up as snow and ice dripped off his shoulders.

I white-knuckled the doorknob and said crisply, "Let's disregard the false niceties and get to the point of this visit."

The man who controlled us kept smirking at me and said nothing. Another purposeful intimidation tactic.

Our battle of wills persisted.

We'd both shed our masks because there was no use for subterfuge between us. We both knew the worst of each other.

Dick stood up straighter and dropped his mask. Pale skin glowed with health and ruddy fixtures became more sculpted as he said, "I forgot how much you see through me." He gritted his teeth. "It's quite refreshing." An obvious lie.

I pocketed my sunglasses and let him see his death in my eyes.

He had the audacity to bare his teeth with mirth.

Dick was part of the handful of people who were naturally immune to my abilities.

I wouldn't call them powers, because that word was synonymous with something mighty and impressive, something with the potential to give something to society.

My abilities were Machiavellian in their cruelty.

They only took.

Violently.

Dick wrinkled his nose as he looked around the messy room.

My family were savages, and I was used to it. To expect anything better of them was an act of futility. So I didn't.

"What do you want?" I held my chin up high, unwilling to cow before him like he wanted me to.

A horrible smile curled the edges of his lips. "I see you've begun puberty." He stared down at me.

It wasn't a question, so I didn't respond.

I waited.

Sunset blanketed the room in an eerie lavender glow, and everything the sunlight touched sparkled. There was something off about the extreme beauty of the realm, and it put my teeth on edge.

I had a bad feeling we'd discover something sinister in the glimmering landscape.

It wasn't a matter of if.

It was a matter of when.

Moving quicker than my eyes could track, Dick grabbed my wrist in a punishing grip and squeezed. The pressure was overwhelming, and my bones creaked.

I screamed.

Something snapped.

I cried out louder as unwelcome tears streamed down my

cheeks because unlike everyone else in my family, I was physically pathetic. No amount of mental prowess could make up for the fact that my body was flimsy.

Breakable.

Dick exploited it mercilessly.

I fell hard onto my knee and collapsed forward, my arm twisted in his grip at a horrible angle as snot ran down my nose.

I sobbed pathetically.

Dick wrenched and twisted it further.

"P-P-P-Please," I blubbered pathetically as spots danced in my vision. A horrible sense of helplessness consumed me.

Click.

Metal fell to the floor, and I followed its trajectory. He released me, and I smashed face forward, unable to stop myself in time.

Blood splattered across my shattered nose as I faceplanted onto the chilled concrete floor.

Long moments passed.

I wheezed before my jailer.

"Stand up," Dick ordered, voice tight with annoyance like he found me deplorable.

It took a few fumbling tries, but finally I pulled myself off the ground using the doorknob, back pressed against it as I put as much space between us as I could.

Watery hiccups racked my slight frame.

"Stop acting so pathetic," he spat with disgust as he glared at me like I'd disappointed him.

I covered my mouth, but the hiccups didn't stop.

Copper, snot, and tears pooled across my hands as I trembled. A pitiful mess.

How easy it was to break me.

Shame cornered me. *The ability to suffer is a small matter—*

weak women and even slaves can achieve mastery in that. Nietzsche's sexist observation was so much crueler because it applied so perfectly to me.

How easily I suffered.

It made me feel miniscule.

I was nothing like Aran.

The disgust that choked me as my knee shook and I gagged on blood was almost worse than the pain in the first place. I hated the sight of blood because it made me woozy.

Another weakness.

Spots slowly receded from my vision, and a noise of shock escaped me as I stared down at the innocuous gold cuff sitting on the floor between us.

I knew from experience that a similar cuff was hidden by enchantments on his own wrist.

"W-W-Why?" I asked shakily as I stared at the invisible metal still heavy on my other wrist.

The sense of foreboding increased.

I wasn't fool enough to believe it was an act of goodwill.

After I'd used my voice and frozen the worthless shifter who'd kidnapped us back in the beast realm, Dick had increased the number of cuffs from one to two.

He'd neutered me completely.

Sun god forbid I defend myself from attack.

His expression was bored as he pocketed the removed cuff and walked toward my cowering form, then his face twisted with cruelty. "Let me make this very clear, little girl."

I bristled with indignation because we both knew I was a woman.

It was a mortifying ordeal to be at his mercy.

Dick's voice was hard as steel. "Make no mistake, your abilities are still mostly constrained. If you try anything—I will *personally* eliminate you. Your worth only extends as far as you allow yourself to be used, understood?" His voice cracked like a whip, and I jumped.

"Yes," I said through gritted teeth as I lifted my head and pretended to be stronger than I was.

His expression changed to boredom, and he said clinically, "Seventeen men and women have already been killed in this war. The numbers are unfortunate, and our projections of the war efforts are not pretty. We've calculated that all able bodies will be necessary to defeat the ungodly—you're included in that number."

I waited.

Tears and snot still running down my face.

He smirked.

"Are you not able-bodied?" he asked mockingly as he stared at the space where my leg used to be.

I fisted my hands and didn't rise to his bait.

Instead I said slowly, "My species is banned from the High Court realms. If I use my *other* abilities, I will be executed. I'm not ignorant of my situation."

"In peacetime, yes." He smiled condescendingly. "This is war, and the High Court has made an exception on your behalf. Just like we did once before."

I wrapped one arm around my stomach protectively. "I didn't want to."

Instinctually I shielded my organs from a predator that wanted to disembowel me.

He tipped his head back and roared with laughter.

"We both know you're always the aggressor." His expression flatlined. "Don't we?"

"How do I know this isn't a trick to get me arrested?" I enunciated each word as I tried to steady my jumbled thoughts. It was next to impossible with the pain radiating through my face from my broken nose.

His face was a mask. "You don't."

A long moment passed as neither of us spoke.

"Is that all?" I asked haughtily.

We kept staring at each other, and the longer he stood above me, the more I wanted to scream.

He smirked and said, "The High Court will be unable to procure you a prosthetic or hover chair, now—or in the future."

A ringing echoed in my ears.

"Excuse me?" The room swayed around me. "How am I supposed to get around, let alone *fight*?"

He tipped his head back and laughed. "You have to keep the monsters neutered. Otherwise, they'll turn on you." He smirked. "We both know you'll be fine."

Fingernails digging into the concrete wall, I gestured with my head for him to leave.

Time expanded.

He didn't go.

Muted orange light glowed around Dick, and his features hardened. "You'll still be punished nightly to ensure your compliance. If you attempt to use your abilities outside of battle, I'll be alerted and you will be eliminated. If you attempt in any way to overthrow the High Court or work against our objectives—you'll be eliminated."

Silence stretched.

Again he smirked. "Am I clear?

"Crystal."

He rubbed his hands together as he turned to leave. "Glad we could have this chat. Like usual, if you tell anyone about this situation, you and everyone you care for will be tortured beyond recognition."

He stared into my eyes like he was trying to read my mind.

Inside my head was a vast black lake, and if he tried to step a toe inside the waters, he'd drown.

A part of me wanted him to try.

Breaking eye contact, he shook his head and said, "You're the only person in centuries who has dared to challenge me." He smirked like he knew something I didn't, like he was complimenting me on my strength.

Blood poured down my nose as my nails scraped against concrete.

I didn't feel strong.

I felt like broken glass, shattered across the floor.

Dick opened the door.

"Wait," I blurted out, and he stopped but didn't turn to look at me as frigid air wafted into the room.

For a split second, his side profile changed into something marble-esque. He looked like a familiar statue.

Dick's ruddy features returned, and I blinked rapidly.

Snowflakes blasted against my skin as the room's temperature dropped further.

"Why take one cuff off now?" I asked. "Why not wait until there are fewer soldiers? Why do this now? What do you know about the war?"

Dick left without another word, and the door swung closed.

Outside, I glimpsed a towering figure in a dark cloak. Their blue eyes glowed like lightning and were staring directly at me. They always accompanied him.

The door slammed shut.

I slid down onto the floor. For a long moment, I lay panting as shock permeated my bones. The silence surrounded me.

Cradling my throbbing face, I acknowledged that Nietzsche would be satisfied.

The abyss had gazed back into me.

And it hurt.

Warren started when he returned a few minutes later and found me dejectedly sprawled out.

He swore and fell to his knees as he snarled, "They can't keep fucking hurting you like this. We have to tell the others."

He knew I was tortured at night and sometimes people paid me a visit, but he didn't know it was Dick. He didn't know the cloaked figure was usually present. He didn't know anything that mattered.

Secrets stood between my life and his death.

Because of what I was, everyone I knew was at risk.

"No," I said as he wiped blood off my face with a wet washcloth. "We'll tell them I tripped and fell."

The shifter frowned, but he didn't argue as he carried me back to my bed. He gently put down a sandwich from the cafeteria.

"Thanks. You're a good friend." I stared down at my covers and cradled my wrist.

Warren sighed as he climbed up into his bunk above mine. "What are we going to do?"

"What we always do." I gingerly reopened my book with one hand and started reading. "Survive."

CHAPTER 18
ARAN
TRAINING

MATUTINE (ADJECTIVE): rising in or just before the dawn.

DAY 10, HOUR 5

"Wake up. It's time to train."

I cracked open an eyelid to find Malum shaking my shoulder. Excessive drug use at the party last night made my skin feel clammy.

My head throbbed.

The bronze king glared down at me, silver eyes glinting eerily in the darkness. Scorpius and Orion flanked him on either side.

The clock on the wall read 5:00 a.m.

We'd returned home from the party at 4:00 a.m.—I was going to kill them.

Who did this to a person?

"No." I turned over. "Go away." Closing my eyes, I burrowed deeper into the warmth.

A hangover pounded through my skull and made me regret ever trying to find a will to live.

Fingers tangled in my curls and pulled as Malum whispered fiercely, "It's crucial to the war effort that we master our powers. Every day we waste could be another soldier's death. The High Court is waiting for us to be able to perform."

I rolled my eyes. "You just want to force me to mate. Don't act like it's any other reason."

There was an awkward pause.

Malum dragged his hands over his face like he was tired. "I don't care about that—"

"Please," I said sarcastically.

Who did he think he was fooling?

He sighed loudly and, sounding defeated, said, "I just want you to be safe and…well. If that means you won't bond —so be it. But we still need to try to master our powers. One thing I won't do is put you in needless danger."

I took a moment to let his words sink in.

Then I shrugged.

"If it's just about training, then let the soldiers die," I mumbled. "I hope the ungodly win." I squeezed my eyes tight and wished everyone around me would stop trying so hard to save everyone else.

Every man for themself was my life motto.

I'd always said this.

"You don't mean that." Malum's voice was rough from sleep, and I shivered.

"I really do."

The covers were ripped away, and I shrieked with horror as the cold became crippling.

"Shut the fuck up," Zenith shouted sleepily from across the room.

I whispered, "Sorry," as I grabbed the covers back from his hands. Frost marks covered the fabric where I grabbed, and I repositioned the blankets so the ice wouldn't touch my skin.

The warmth from the bed was a harsh contrast to the freezing air.

I shivered miserably.

Malum whispered back angrily, "So you're fine with the ungodly murdering our soldiers because you wanted to sleep? Or you're fine with us unleashing our powers and killing them anyway?"

"Both," I mumbled.

"Just wake up," Scorpius said tiredly, like he didn't want to have this conversation. "Please."

I buried my face in the warm body laying beneath me. "I hate you three so much," I mumbled. "But especially Malum."

"I know," Malum said darkly. "Let's go."

I groaned.

Once again, I wished I weren't such a good person, because it was hard being so sun-god-damned magnanimous. I should get an award for how much I gave to others. It was exhausting being the backbone of society.

Also why was everyone so obsessed with me?

With a hangover pounding in my skull, I pushed myself out of John's warm embrace and stumbled over Luka's sleeping figure sprawled partially on the floor and leaning against the lower bunk so he could be close to us.

The twins mumbled in their sleep.

"I'll be back." I ruffled their messy hair and gave them both a smacking kiss on the forehead. Icy blue outlines of my lips lingered on their foreheads, and I admired my work.

"Bye, love," Luka murmured, and my heart hurt because he was just so adorable all rumpled on the floor with his arms wrapped around his twin.

Cuteness aggression made me want to bite him.

Malum swore, and I was 99 percent sure he purposely tripped over Luka and kicked him in the stomach.

"Don't hurt him," I snarled. Normal aggression made me want to stab him.

The kings made noises of annoyance.

I scoffed back at them as I fumbled through my drawer and got dressed.

So much for them prostrating themselves before me and swearing to be my hounds. Watching them pretend to be remorseful was giving me whiplash.

So much for Malum crawling.

It was like they could only pretend to be meek and repentant for a few hours before they overloaded with aggression.

I zipped up my jacket and shivered as I followed the harbingers of doom out into the chilly morning where an ice storm raged. Another gray day.

Being mated to them was proof that sexuality was not a choice.

As we left the sleeping barracks, instead of walking ahead of me like I expected, Malum fell into step behind me. Scorpius and Orion flanked my sides.

"With all due respect," I whispered to them, "which by the way, is none—why do we have to train at the ass crack of dawn?"

They didn't respond.

As we walked through the snowy forest further away from the camp, Orion kept looking down at me with a strange expression.

It almost looked like pity.

I shifted back and forth uncomfortably as I shivered because whoever had decided that our uniforms didn't need gloves deserved to be shot.

Repeatedly.

Scorpius grabbed my right hand.

"I'm warming you up." He gave no other explanation.

Orion grabbed my other hand and held tight.

It was nice to hold hands.

Comforting.

That was how I found myself walking for miles through a quiet, snowy forest holding hands with my enemies.

I tried to swing my arm dramatically and skip to make fun of them, but they flexed and I couldn't move my arms an inch.

"Boring," I mumbled.

Only once did the kings try to make small talk, and it wasn't what I ever would have expected. Orion mumbled something about Luka putting on quite a show, and Scorpius asked me if John had always had such a side to him.

I gaped at them in disbelief, unsure how to handle the fact that they were intrigued by the Princes.

Malum just grunted, like he was used to their antics.

Then I ruined the small talk by bringing up how Luka's piercing felt in my mouth. Apparently, *that* was too far. All the men glared at me (they were jealous of how good I was at sucking dick).

As we left the valley and climbed up one of the towering mountains, we were able to speak at full volume. The wind howled with so much force that our voices didn't carry up in the higher elevation.

As the air thinned, I got more annoyed that I'd left the comfort of my bed. The weather mimicked my mood. Tiny snowflakes transformed into thick, wet flakes and the snow-covered dirt was replaced with icy rocks.

I slipped on black ice.

Arms flailing, I tipped forward toward the edge.

Malum grabbed me and barked, "Be careful." Orion and Scorpius also scrambled to hold my arms.

They pulled me to safety and let me go.

Silver eyes narrowed. "You need to watch where you're going. Do you ever pay attention? What is wrong with you?"

I closed my eyes. *Three. Five. Seven. Nine. Eleven. Thirteen.*

Nope, counting didn't work.

I whirled on him. "How about you watch where *you're* going, Mitch?"

"Don't call me that." Flames exploded across his arms, and I leaned toward the warmth. His sleeves must have been fireproof, because his clothes didn't melt away.

"Then don't act like a Mitch and I won't," I countered.

He glowered. "Well, don't almost fall off the mountain like an idiot, and I won't act that way."

"Maybe I wanted to fall off," I countered.

Silver eyes sharpened into steel. "Try it and see what happens."

I gasped with fake outrage. "Are you threatening me?"

"Maybe I am." Flames climbed up his head. "What are you going to do about it?"

I pointed at his chest. "Don't you dare tempt me."

"You're all talk." He smirked cruelly.

"Move it along," Scorpius ordered as he grabbed Malum by the back of the neck and dragged him up the side of the mountain. Orion motioned for me to walk forward like a gentleman, and we resumed our hike.

Malum shot dirty glares back at me over his shoulder.

I mimed snapping his neck.

His eyes widened, and it was my turn to smirk.

"Watch out, baby girl," I mouthed, and he shook his head like I disturbed him.

Mission accomplished. Slay (in the celebratory sense).

Thirty minutes later, huffing on thin air, I asked, "Why again do we have to go so far away to train?"

"For the tenth time," Scorpius said impatiently, "so we don't accidentally hypnotize our fellow soldiers and murder them. We don't know exactly how far Orion's voice projects, but in our experience, it travels much further than normal sound."

I sighed and kept climbing. "Well, I'm willing to risk it."

"We know," Orion said loudly.

Scorpius and Malum stopped moving on the side of the mountain. They were entranced. Frozen. Eyes glazed over.

"That shut them up," I snickered, and Orion narrowed his eyes like I was ridiculous, but I didn't miss the way the corner of his mouth turned up.

We had a secret.

It was nice to have something over the other kings, something only the two of us knew.

Unfortunately, they reanimated a second later and resumed climbing up the mountainside, none the wiser that Orion had temporarily frozen them with his voice.

Finally, after what felt like an eternity, Malum stopped climbing and pointed at a low boulder. "Here will work."

Sun god help whoever had to purchase property with him, if this was the extent of his judgment.

"Oh yes," I said sarcastically. "Thank the sun god we've found *this* rock in particular." I patted the top. "I like the poop-brown color."

We were halfway up the side of the jagged cliff face surrounded by nothing but snow and icy wind.

The visibility was shit.

Malum snarled, "That is not funny."

Scorpius snickered, and I pointed at him with satisfaction. Malum looked like he was having an aneurysm.

"You sure about that?" I asked as I kicked a rock, and it tumbled off the mountain's sheer cliff face. I admired the steep incline; you could *really* do some damage if you fell off. All your bones would be easily broken.

"Oooh, I'm going to fall." I flailed my arms and pretended to stumble.

Faster than my eyes could track, Malum grabbed me around the waist and threw us both away from the edge.

I landed on top of him.

For a long moment, we lay in stunned silence.

"You're an idiot. It was just a *joke*," I said haughtily as Orion and Scorpius yanked me to my feet.

Malum exploded into angry scarlet flames as he stood. His expression was pure violence.

"Sadie would have laughed," I pointed out as I pursed my lips and rubbed my hands together. They were frozen solid.

Men truly had no sense of humor.

"Don't mention that *whore* in front of us," Scorpius sneered.

I gaped at him. Sadie wasn't exaggerating when she'd said the men were *still* jealous of her for having fake shower sex with me.

"Oh my sun god," I exclaimed. "Is it hard?"

The three of them straightened and looked around for danger. "Is what hard?"

"Being so stupid?" I asked at the same time Scorpius asked, "My cock?"

I ignored him.

Flames sizzled as they shot higher off Malum's arms, and I smirked with triumph. It was too easy to rile him up. I might have even called it a hobby.

Their ire was even more satisfying because they thought I

was their precious Revered. They were all, *you're our mate, we'll kill everyone and cherish you forever.* They were *so* into me.

It was so cringy.

I pitied them.

They couldn't handle me—few could. I had the body of a large bird, mind of a lunatic, and personality of a divorced middle-aged woman with a shopping addiction.

I was perfect.

"Deep breaths," Scorpius barked at Malum and grabbed his neck in a tight grip.

I covered my mouth to hide my laughter, and Orion looked over at me with exasperation.

"Is Mitch seriously going to kill us all right now with his fire?" I asked between gasps.

Somehow I'd gone from sleeping in the warm embrace of John to being halfway up a mountainside while Malum struggled not to burn us all to death.

Emotionally, this was too much for me.

Delirium was setting in. Also, I was 99 percent sure I was still intoxicated.

No one responded, because they were too busy trying to help Malum get control of himself.

To help the situation, I pointed at the flaming king and said, "You need therapy."

A muscle in Malum's jaw ticked, and when he spoke, flames shot out of his mouth. "We are *literally* in therapy with you." He roared and painted the cold air in shades of scarlet.

I grimaced.

Some people didn't get sarcasm.

I sat down on the ugly boulder and blew into my cupped hands. "How long is this going to take?" Tucking my pipe between my lips, I closed my eyes with relief as I inhaled drugs. "Can we hurry this up? I want to go back and cuddle the twins."

Malum screamed out more fire.

"You sound like a dying cow," I said as I held my arms out to get some of the warmth from his fire. I exhaled with relief as I defrosted. At least he was good for something.

Malum fell to his knees, still screaming, and the scene was reminiscent of when he'd lost control on the shore of Elite Academy. Back then I'd been concerned about him and had stepped in to help.

That was before he'd chosen me for the last competition.

Now, I didn't care.

I studied my abused nails and made a mental list of products. *Cuticle softener wasn't a need; it was a must. A clear coat would do me wonders, and what did a woman have to do around here to get some vanilla-scented lotion?*

My fictional lover would have given me a basket with nail care on the *first day* of being in this hostile environment.

A good man would protect my cuticles.

I grimaced as I looked at the kings—these weren't good men.

Flames burned hotter as they rolled off Malum and his mates tried desperately to calm him down.

At least I had Sadie because she would definitely have a miniature spa day with me. She was always down.

"Are you even listening to me? What did I just say?" Malum asked loudly, and I realized he'd been speaking.

I gnawed on my lower lip and narrowed my eyes.

"*Yes?*" I asked slowly.

Malum chucked a boulder—different from *the* boulder—off the side of the mountain and screamed louder. Scorpius tackled him and started whispering frantically in his ear.

Orion stared at me and mouthed, "Are you doing okay?"

His eyes were haunted, and I had a strange feeling he wanted to ask me something else but didn't know how to say it.

I was going to ask what he meant, but Malum bellowed and slammed his fist into another rock. It shattered into pieces, and when he stood up, his knuckles were swollen and coated in blood.

The memory of when I'd thrown myself fruitlessly at the wall haunted me.

How come it was the men who had all the power? How come I was just the stupid, useless Revered that needed to be taken care of and stop their murderous rampages?

I wanted to punch rocks and smash them.

I wanted to rampage.

Sun god, the *things* I would do to people with that type of strength.

I rubbed at my temples and announced, "I'm bringing this up to Dr. Palmer next session. Frankly, your flames are giving me a migraine. Can you turn it down?"

I wasn't kidding.

The bright flames were blinding on my corneas, and a headache throbbed more intensely.

I closed my eyes.

"You're hurting her!" Scorpius shouted, then whispered into his ear, "You know what…" His voice dropped lower, and I couldn't hear.

"Know what?" I asked.

No one answered.

Malum's flames slowly extinguished, and he looked dejected, sitting on the ground with his head cradled in his hands. Scorpius rubbed his back while Orion patted his head.

I would have felt bad.

But I didn't.

What could I say—bitches were harsh like that. For context, I was bitches.

"Break's over team." I clapped my hands. "Let's hurry this up."

Malum stumbled to his feet, and all three kings turned their attention toward me.

I took a step back.

Their expressions were mournful.

I glanced behind my shoulder to see if they were looking at someone else, because the energy radiating off them put my teeth on edge. Apparently giving the twins a blow job in front of them had broken their spirits.

If I'd known that was all it would take, I would have done it sooner.

Sun god, I hadn't known oral sex was such a big deal to them.

"So how do we want to do this?" I asked.

"Take off your coat and shirt," Scorpius ordered.

I rolled my eyes and spat at his feet. "You're a pig."

"What did I say about spitting?" he asked in a mocking, cruel voice, and all of a sudden, I was struggling to breathe.

He stalked across the rocks and leaned close to me. "I said—that I'd spit in your pretty little mouth if you ever spat at me again."

His breath mixed with snowflakes and fanned against the side of my face. "Did you forget, Arabella? Or are you purposefully being a brat?"

I forgot how to swallow.

"Um?" I asked eloquently.

He arched his brow and sneered, "Open up."

My jaw unhinged, and his eyes widened with surprise,

then I snapped it closed. "You gotta be quick," I taunted—opening and closing it repeatedly.

He looked down at me with pity.

Yep, I was 100 percent still intoxicated.

Scorpius rolled his milky eyes and took a step back. Apparently, I'd killed the mood. *Oh darn.*

He explained, "You need to reveal your wings. That's why you need to take off your clothes."

"Fine." I ripped off my coat and pulled my long-sleeved thermal over my head so I was in nothing but a sports bra. The Necklace of Death and diamond bracelet were warm against my skin even though they were exposed to the elements.

The kings stared at me hungrily.

Their hooded eyes were locked on my sports-bra-covered chest, and I looked down.

I crossed my arms over my chest. It wasn't like I was well endowed in that department, so I didn't understand why they were acting obsessed.

Instead of wondering about the inner workings of deranged men, I took a deep breath and focused on unused muscles.

Appendages exploded from my back.

Blue crystal feathers clattered together in my peripheral vision, and I twisted my torso back and forth, making them shimmer in the sunlight.

They were stunning.

The beauty lost its appeal ten seconds later as I panted and struggled to stand up straight under their weight. The wings were heavy, and it felt like someone had tied boulders to my shoulder blades.

I leaned forward to stop myself from tipping backward.

Sweat dripped uncomfortably down my sides from the strain even though it was freezing.

"Now what?" I asked.

Molten silver eyes melted me where I stood. "Now you stop us." Malum nodded to his mates.

Orion opened his mouth.

And we walked together into hell.

CHAPTER 19
ARAN
DEVILS UNLEASHED

IGNEOUS (ADJECTIVE): of, relating to, or resembling fire.

DAY 10, HOUR 10

Click. Click. Click.

The gold hardware on the kings' ears levitated upward and separated into shards. Three gold crowns floated above their heads.

Snow whipped around them in a frenzy as the icy wind shrieked. The storm picked up, and the sky darkened.

Rocks groaned under the onslaught.

I bent my knees and leaned further forward as I tried to alleviate the weight on my back muscles. A part of me was shocked that we were really doing this right now. No preamble.

The wind and ice slammed against me, and I cursed the mercurial weather.

Silver, brown, and milky white eyes darkened to black, and talons lengthened on their hands, eerily similar to the serrated ice talons I'd donned when I killed my mother.

Gore in my mouth, blood dripping down my chin, Mother howling as I consumed her heart and stole her crown.

Malum's baritone voice dragged me out of the memories as he proclaimed, "As the Ignis from the illustrious House of Malum, I invoke the power of my mates."

He pulled the silver dagger from his throat and said, "As the crowned King of the Sun God, I invoke the power of my mates."

"Venimus! We came," Orion sang loudly as he triggered the sequence that unleashed their powers. The three of them went unnaturally still. They became mindless.

My eyes widened at the sheer beauty of his voice.

A petal slapped against my face as cherry blossoms mixed with snow in a swirling vortex of white.

It was magnificent.

It was terrifying.

Scorpius proclaimed, "Vidimus. We saw," and the eye tattoo on his neck blinked open. It stared straight at me. His blind eyes glowed, and he turned his head like he was searching for people.

"Vicimus. We conquered," Malum finished as flames poured off him.

My thighs trembled, and I put my hands on my knees to keep myself upright. Crystal feathers clattered against the rocks as my wings drooped.

I wanted to lie down.

Flames tumbled off Malum faster, like the air was kerosene, and somehow the frozen mountainside caught fire.

It should have been impossible.

Somehow the kings' power broke the laws of thermo-dynamics.

I gnawed on my lip as I stared at the three men who were in a trance.

It hit me like a punch to the gut that this was an astronomically stupid idea.

How was I supposed to do anything to stop them?

Ice radiated around me, but whenever I tried to channel it into something different, nothing happened. It was like I was an inanimate frozen object, incapable of anything but misery.

No, I was not having a pity party.

It was called being aware of your limitations.

My knees knocked together, and it took everything I had not to sprawl down under the weight of my wings.

"Stop it," I said and pointed my icy hands at the fire. Immediately I felt like a fool because nothing happened.

If anything, the warmth felt delicious, and I wanted more of it. Why would I try to put out the fire that was warming the chill from my bones? I wanted to flame it brighter.

"Stop the fire," I repeated lamely to the kings and envisioned ice exploding from my fingertips toward the devils like it had when I'd fallen atop Jinx and stopped them.

At least, that was how I imagined it happening. It wasn't clear to me how I'd stopped them.

I gnawed on my lip as the flames expanded across the mountainside.

Swearing under my breath, I visualized putting out the fire. My stomach twisted with apprehension.

No ice exploded off my hands toward the scarlet inferno.

If anything, frost receded from my fingers as the air warmed around me. I thawed and basked in the inferno.

I clapped my hands loudly and tried a different approach. "Snap out of it."

The kings remained mindless beings of fire and death. The very unwell part of me was jealous. It would be nice if I could sink into a mindless craze and stop worrying about my actions.

Shockingly, they did not stop.

No one could say I hadn't tried.

The mountain became uncomfortably warm as scarlet flames expanded in every direction. They leaped high into the air and formed a wall of fire.

I squinted against the brightness while I inhaled the heat greedily.

The kings were shadowy outlines, untouched in the middle of an inferno. Tools of death waiting to be deployed.

For a split second, I had the horrible sense that I was the one supposed to be doing something, and it didn't feel like it had to do with stopping them. It felt like they were working an enchantment over me and lulling me into a trance.

What else could be the fire's purpose?

There were no enemies around, and it was just the four of us up in the thin air of the mountains with snow and rocks all around.

My eyelids fluttered shut.

I was unbelievably tired, and the flames called to me. They melted me in the most intoxicating way.

The fractured, icy bits of my soul thawed.

The Necklace of Death and diamond bracelet warmed and vibrated until my skin buzzed.

It was heavenly.

Bending forward so I could get closer to the raging fire, I enjoyed the delicious warmth as it chased away the invasive chill that was always present in my bones.

I wanted to curl up like a cat and bask in the inferno.

I wanted to lie on a bed of ashes for eternity.

It was pure relief after years of being plagued by chattering teeth and goose bumps.

After a lifetime of ice, I finally knew what genuine warmth felt like.

It was everything.

I wanted more because it was so much better than I could have ever imagined.

My legs gave out, and I fell to my knees. The rocks were toasty against my chilled flesh, and I pressed myself into the ground.

Everything became hazy in the best way.

The heat intensified, and I sighed with relief as my lungs thawed.

I closed my heavy lids and drifted off.

Into.

Blissful.

Sleep.

"Wake up!"

Someone bellowed down at me, and I batted at them. "Shut up," I mumbled as I tried to sink back into the warm darkness.

It was divine.

"She's fine." A different person sighed with relief, and I shivered as cold battered my face.

"No, she's clearly not fucking fine."

There was a smacking noise and what sounded like a fight.

"I *am* fine," I said sleepily as I curled tighter into a ball and mourned the exquisite warmth because, yet again, everything was uncomfortably cold.

"More heat," I begged.

There was silence.

Then someone broke into laughter. "Hear that, Corvus. She wants *more* heat. Sun god fucking damn it, I can't do this."

"Arabella, wake up right now," Malum ordered as he yanked me to my feet.

I narrowed my eyes at the angry devil snarling in my face and immediately wished I was sleeping again.

"What?" I asked petulantly.

Scorpius filled my vision, and his jaw was tight with anger. "Why did the three of us just snap out of our powers to find *twelve hours* had passed and you were sleeping peacefully in the middle of a fucking fire?"

My eyes shot open as memories rushed back. The blizzard had stopped, and the night was cold and still. More stars were visible than in the valley because we were halfway up the mountain.

I stumbled out of Malum's embrace.

My wings had retracted, and the awful weight was gone. In its wake, energy strummed through me.

I felt better than I had in a long time.

Alert.

Strangely healthy.

I felt limber, and the pervasive cold was gone.

It felt like I'd come out of a monthlong coma with a new lease on life. For the first time in forever, I didn't feel a crushing emptiness.

I was satisfied.

"Wow," I said slowly because the once snow-covered rocks were now scorched black as far as the eye could see in every direction, as if a fire had raged for hours.

"Once we unleashed our powers, what did you do?" Malum's deep voice snapped me out of my thoughts.

He glowered at me, a dark god in a barren wasteland of

scorched earth and anger. Snow whipped angrily back and forth.

Silver eyes narrowed. "Tell me you used one of your wings to stab me or that you tried to counter my fire with ice. Because that's what we *expected* you to do."

All three of the kings were standing uncomfortably close as they waited for me to speak.

I kicked a rock, ducked my head, and mumbled, "I was going to get to that." My cheeks burned with embarrassment, and I couldn't look at them.

I had no idea why I'd fallen asleep instead of trying to stop them.

It was bizarre, even for me.

A rough sound escaped Malum's throat, and Scorpius sneered, "Please tell us. What part of the stopping us did you get to?"

I ripped a flap of skin off my lower lip.

Threw it to the rocks.

I lifted my nails to gouge harder, but Orion grabbed my wrist and brought it to my side, his long lashes fluttering as he looked down at me with concern.

"You're upsetting her," he whispered. "Take a step back. Give her some space."

Shockingly, Malum and Scorpius obeyed.

"Here, let's get you dressed," Orion mouthed as he grabbed my undershirt and pulled it over my head.

Still reeling from my own strange behavior, I stood still and let him dress me. He zipped up my coat and brushed snow out of my hair.

"There," he whispered. "Are you feeling warmer?"

I nodded stupidly.

He smiled down at me, and a new warmth prickled in my chest. "I took a nap in the heat," I blurted out.

There was a long pause as they processed what I'd said.

A muscle in Malum's jaw ticked, and he opened his mouth. I turned my head to the side to avoid his censure, but my eyes widened.

Rocks were scorched black miles down the mountainside and stopped inches from the valley.

Holy sun god.

Sadie. Jinx.

They'd almost been murdered because of my idiocy.

Emotion and energy burst through my veins, and I vibrated from the onslaught.

Malum said, "What do you—"

I didn't catch the rest of his sentence because I darted down the side of the mountain, intent on getting back to camp.

Boots pounded against rocks as they sprinted after me.

Malum bellowed at the top of his lungs, "What the fuck do you mean? You took a *nap?*"

"*I don't know!*" I yelled over my shoulder as I ran faster. "*I got really tired.*"

"*Excuse me?*" Malum's voice was so deep that the hair on the back of my neck stood up. He didn't like my answer.

Neither did I.

Scorpius swore. "You're going to be the death of us."

"*I don't know what came over me,*" I shouted into the night as I kept running. "*It was weird.*"

"Do you think this is a joke?" Malum's voice was closer. "Do you think all this is a bloody fucking lark? Do you know what's at stake—*I was really worried about you!*"

I sprinted with all my might.

Pretended not to hear him.

Nothing was funny.

It was all falling apart around me.

Crumbling.

Memories of Orion chasing me down a marble corridor played in my mind as black boots slammed against icy rocks, and I slid forward.

My arms pumped.

I threw myself down the side of the mountain, half sliding, half sprinting as fast as I could with my heart hammering in my chest. I was going insane.

The storm picked up.

My muscles were warm and ready to be used, and I exploded forward with unbridled adrenaline.

Adrenaline pumped through my veins.

Snow whipped my face, and my eyes watered from the frozen air.

For the first time since we'd started to train together, I outran the kings back to the camp.

For hours, they couldn't catch me because fear was truly the best motivator.

But I wasn't running from them.

I was running from myself.

CHAPTER 20
CORVUS MALUM
THERAPY

RIPOSTE (NOUN): a retaliatory verbal reply.

DAY 11, HOUR 5

"So how did the last week of—" Dr. Palmer looked down at her clipboards like she was reading off something prepared by the High Court "—training and battle go?"

I shifted, and my thigh bumped against Arabella's.

Rain splattered against the window, and it was gray outside.

At the beginning of the session, I'd made sure to take the spot next to her on the couch. We were pressed flush against one another because there wasn't enough room for all four of us.

There was a patch of frost beneath her feet on the carpet, and as I shifted my foot closer, the ice melted into water.

I needed her next to me.

Lately my control on my fire was tenuous at best, and it wanted to explode from me and burn the world.

Whenever I was around Arabella, the urges intensified. But the pain was nothing compared to the memory of her begging on a palace floor while she was tortured.

The threadbare couch creaked as I spread my legs wider and reassured myself that my Revered was okay. If anyone wanted to torture her, they'd have to go through me.

Arabella mumbled something under her breath about manspreading and wanting to stab me.

I pretended not to hear her.

Cracking my knuckles, I focused on the severe-looking therapist instead of releasing my flames and demanding that Arabella tell me every single wrong that had been done to her.

Eventually I'd discover it all.

In the meantime, I was making a list.

Dr. Palmer cleared her throat and peered at us over her thin spectacles.

No one spoke.

This session was the worst one yet because she kept asking us to recap our last week.

I would rather die.

In summary, our Revered had allowed herself to get stabbed in battle and had almost bled out, she'd had sex with the twins in front of us at a party, we'd scorched the side of a mountain, she'd run away from us and straight into the arms of the twins, and we were no closer to mastering our abilities.

It had been the worst week of my life.

Easily.

Dr. Palmer sighed with exasperation, then squinted at her clipboard. "It says here you successfully defeated the ungodly at the first battle. Tell me about it. Did anything especially traumatizing happen?"

Arabella choked.

I patted her back and glared at the therapist. "Get her water. Now."

Dr. Palmer frowned but handed over a cup of water.

Arabella gulped it down while I rubbed soothing circles on her back and tried not to tangle my fingers in her blue curls.

She didn't pull away.

My fingers clenched as I remembered a slur was carved into her skin. I forced my hands wide and kept rubbing.

The arm on the other side of the couch went up in flames.

Scorpius muttered something derogatory under his breath as he smacked out the flames with his sleeves, and Orion tried to peer past me to look at our Revered.

I draped my right arm over his shoulder, and he snuggled against me. He turned his face so he could stare at her.

Water splashed over the rim of the water cup and fell as snowflakes onto her clothes as she took a sip.

A noise of distress rumbled in my chest.

Everyone turned to stare at me, and I ignored them. Lifting my chin high, I concentrated on keeping the flames contained to my skin.

"Aran, from your reaction"—Dr. Palmer looked at her shaking hands pointedly—"it seems that something did happen in the battle. Let's talk about it."

Her trembling intensified, and the water in the cup turned to ice.

My upper lip pulled back. How dare she ask such intrusive questions of my Revered?

Only I could pester her about her choices.

This random woman had no right to distress her.

Scarlet shooting off my fingertips, I leaned back and draped my arm over the cushion behind Arabella as I fantasized about Dr. Palmer's expression when she went up in flames.

I felt significantly better.

Maybe therapy was working?

"Please, Aran?" Dr. Palmer looked at her expectantly.

There was a long pause. "Fine—I'll tell you. "

I glanced down at her in surprise.

It never failed to shock me, having a woman for a Revered. No one would accuse Arabella of being weak, especially after her performance in the Legionnaire Games, but she was clearly more empathetic than the three of us.

She was a composite of contradictions: kind and playful, sad and morose, a victim and an aggressor, tenacious and merciless.

I wanted to crawl under her skin and learn every nuance.

My fingers curled around a turquoise curl that stuck out from her messy hair and hung over the edge of the couch.

Arabella was also shockingly pretty.

Her arching cheekbones and lush lips haunted me. Dark lashes fluttered over wide navy eyes that were rimmed in dark circles and highlighted with a slashing scar. Sleek muscles tapered into curves.

"Something did happen in the battle," she whispered, and Dr. Palmer clicked her pen in anticipation.

Arabella wet her lower lip, and I swallowed a groan, unable to tear my eyes away from her.

Now that I had gotten used to the idea, I was more than content with the House of Malum having its first female Revered. It was not a sign of weakness but rather showcased how strong we were because we would take care of her.

Our Revered was someone softer and kinder who needed Protectors and a powerful Ignis to shield her.

It made sense.

Before us the realms had not been kind to her.

Now she had us, and we would not be kind to the realms on her behalf.

Sure we'd fucked up badly at Elite Academy and we still had to make it up to her. There was a reason the sun god only chose devils for his kings. Unlike angels, we couldn't be constrained. When we wanted something, we didn't stop until we got it.

Period.

Going forward, we would shield Arabella like no mate had ever been shielded before. We hadn't been lying when we'd called ourselves her hounds.

We were hers to use.

She just didn't know what that meant yet, but she would.

Cherry-red lips parted. Arabella nodded like she was fortifying herself, then blurted in one breath,

"I-got-stabbed-in-the-stomach-with-an-enchanted-sword-and-would-have-died-but-didn't-because-I'm-the-fae-queen-and-can-only-die-by-having-my-heart-ripped-out-and-eaten-like-I-did-to-my-mother-which-is-weird-because-actually-I'm-an-angel-so-I-don't-understand-how-I-can-be-queen."

Arabella collapsed back like it had physically hurt her to speak, and she waited for a response.

Preoccupied with what she'd revealed, she didn't notice she'd slumped against my side.

I noticed.

Dr. Palmer's eyes widened.

I tucked my arm around Arabella's side protectively and glared at the therapist, daring her to say something upsetting.

I didn't like what she'd done, but I didn't want her to have to relive it.

My left hand rested against Arabella's forearm, and cold wafted off her sweatshirt. Her skin must be freezing if I could feel the chill through her clothes, especially since it was uncomfortably warm in the cramped office.

Lately ice trailed behind her wherever she went, and I didn't like it. None of the other angels radiated cold like my Revered did, and I was worried something was wrong.

When we'd first arrived at the war camp, Jinx informed us that Arabella's mother was renowned for her power. It had driven her to madness and the angel governing body refused to grant her wings.

Needing to do something to help, I tucked Arabella closer to me as I created a small fire in my right palm, then laid my flaming hand on her lap.

Subconsciously, she huddled closer to me and the flame.

With Orion leaning against my right and Arabella pressed against my left, I felt like I was flying.

I reached over and grabbed Scorpius's shoulder so all three of them were touching me.

Instantly, I relaxed.

I was an Ignis taking care of his mates.

I was warming my Revered.

It was a dream that a month ago I'd thought would never come true.

Dr. Palmer scribbled furiously on her clipboard, then glared over her spectacles. "Do you feel like you've been processing getting stabbed and almost dying? Have you been thinking about this traumatic event a lot?"

I gnashed my teeth.

Dr. Palmer ignored me.

Arabella pulled out her pipe, inhaled smoke, and said hoarsely, "I feel the same as always." An opaque crow settled onto her shoulder.

"And how do you normally feel?" Dr. Palmer asked.

Arabella scoffed. "Empty."

I jolted, Orion made a sad noise, and Scorpius muttered something harshly as all three of us remembered the hollow sensation in her memory.

Did she still feel that way?

I wanted to scream.

Her crow cawed, and my eyes widened; while she'd sobbed on the palace floor, her mother had accused her of setting monstrous birds free from their gilded cages. Was that why she kept the bird as her companion?

I tucked her tighter against my side, and she scooted closer.

My heart soared.

My eyes burned with pressure.

"Could you expand on the emptiness you feel? Try to put it into more words." Dr. Palmer scribbled aggressively on her clipboard.

"It feels like I'm missing something."

"And when did this start?"

"I woke up one day at fourteen years old, and the world was colored in shades of dark blue and gray." Arabella stared off into the distance like she was somewhere else. "It was freezing cold. I remember it vividly because for the first time in my life, living felt like a chore."

Dr. Palmer furrowed her brow and stopped writing. "You mean you *felt* like the world was colored in shades of dark blue and gray."

"No, the colors changed." Arabella shook her head.

"Well, to start, you need to recognize that you just felt that way." Dr. Palmer waved her pen. "The colors weren't actually different."

"Yes, they were," Orion whispered.

Everyone turned to him.

"What did you say?" Dr. Palmer asked.

I scoffed. "She said the colors were different, so they were. Ask something else," I spoke harshly to end the conversation because we couldn't let Aran know we were in her memories.

She would want to stop the connection.

We were desperate to link ourselves to her.

Any way we could.

Dr. Palmer bristled but looked at Arabella and changed the subject. "How is your relationship coming along with your mates? Do you trust one another more after the battle?"

"No," Arabella said at the same time we answered in unison, "Yes."

Arabella whipped her head toward us. "What are you talking about?" Navy eyes narrowed. "You three have done nothing to earn my trust."

Scorpius scoffed loudly.

Arabella gritted her teeth and asked condescendingly, "Do you have something you want to say, Scorp?"

"Yeah, I do." Scorpius laughed cruelly. "We fell to our knees in front of hundreds of witnesses and proclaimed ourselves your hounds. We promised to serve you and not the sun god, and you have the audacity to say we've done nothing."

"Lie." Arabella laughed louder. "There were sixty people. Max."

Scorpius let out a string of expletives, and Dr. Palmer snapped, "Control your mouth in my office."

Everyone ignored her.

Scorpius continued with exasperation, "Corvus even *crawled* for you."

My gut twisted at the reminder.

She acted like it meant nothing to her.

"What else do you want us to do for you?" I looked down

at my Revered. "Do you want us to watch you suck off the twins and say nothing about it? Because we've done that—we haven't even brought it up?"

"Excuse me. Suck who off?" Dr. Palmer asked with confusion.

Scorpius muttered something about John holding her head as he adjusted his pants.

I rolled my eyes; his new obsession with the human was entertaining.

Poor John.

Arabella jabbed her finger into my chest. "Wow, you couldn't just let it go? You *had* to bring it up. Sun god, I knew the three of you couldn't be mature."

"*You had his cock down your throat, what do you want us to do?*" Scorpius's face turned red, and he gesticulated wildly. "*Congratulate you?*"

Arabella bared her teeth at him. "Maybe it would be nice to have a little support and not be slut shamed for owning my sexuality. Sun god knows it's been hard enough for me after what I've been through."

"Sweetheart," Orion whispered. "Of course we support your sexuality." He reached across me and grabbed her hand. "I thought it was hot."

She held his hand back and smiled. "Thank you. That means a lot."

I gaped at my Protector. "You cannot support her *sucking off* the twins?"

"Technically, I only sucked off Luka," Arabella pointed out.

Orion nodded. "I support *her*. Not her actions." He shrugged and whispered, "You have to admit it was —intense."

I glared, not him too.

What was happening with my mates and the twins? Couldn't they see that they were stealing our Revered from us?

"No," I said. "What it was—*was horrifying!*"

Fire buzzed beneath my skin, and the urge to burn the world intensified because now I couldn't stop remembering my Revered gazing lovingly up at another man, who had his dick down her throat.

A piece of the carpet went up in flames.

Everyone ignored it.

"*What the hell is going on?*" Dr. Palmer shouted. "*Someone explain. Now.*"

Arabella didn't take her eyes off me as she snapped, "I gave Luka a blow job at a party last week while the three of them watched, and John pulled my hair during it." She clapped. "Case closed."

I glared right back at her.

Dr. Palmer put down her pen. "I'm not paid enough for this."

"Are they paying you?" Arabella furrowed her brow. "Wait a second—is the High Court paying us for fighting in the war?"

"Stop talking." Dr. Palmer clicked her pen. "None of you speak."

Arabella made a noise of annoyance but slumped back into the couch, and I pulled her back against my side.

She moved both her hands to hover over my still-flaming palm.

More warmth fluttered in my chest because my Revered might be mad at me, but she still needed my warmth.

She *needed* me.

I'd never been more grateful for my abilities.

"Since the High Court thinks it's crucial that you mate

and come into your full powers for the war effort—and they've tasked me with the impossible job of helping you— here's what we're going to do." Dr. Palmer smoothed her hands over her already slick bun. Then she grabbed a stack of small books off the table next to her and handed one out to each of us.

"This is an enchanted truth journal. In order to avoid species rights violations, the High Court gives them to inmates incarcerated at the Olympus realm's maximum-security prison. It is supposed to help unfeeling sociopaths build relationships." She glared at us. "I think they would be beneficial for you four."

Arabella crossed her arms. "Are you calling us—"

"Yes," Dr. Palmer said.

Arabella slumped petulantly, and I couldn't stop my chuckle because she was so adorable sometimes.

Dr. Palmer forged ahead. "Your answer to the prompt will appear in one another's journals. That way you can discuss back and forth the implications of your answer and build a connection."

Arabella made a sound of disbelief.

"I understand your doubts." Dr. Palmer stared at me as she spoke. "At the very least, it should begin a discourse among the four of you, which it seems like you need. Communication is the key to forging any type of connection."

"Sounds like a pseudoscience," Scorpius muttered under his breath loud enough for everyone to hear.

The doctor turned purple.

I patted the book on my lap. "We'll take them."

Dr. Palmer narrowed her eyes. "This is not up for debate. All four of you will answer the prompts whenever you have free time." Her tone was clipped with annoyance. "The pen is enchanted to only write down the truth."

She looked down at the books pointedly.

None of us touched them.

Dr. Palmer frowned. "Also, I'm mandated to inform you that if you try to use the pen as a weapon, it is enchanted to electrocute you."

It took a second for her words to process.

Arabella opened her book. "Cool," she said as she stabbed the pen into my thigh.

She was electrocuted.

I lunged and grabbed her twitching form, just barely saving her from falling off the couch. I gaped down at the woman in my arms.

I'd never met anyone so reckless.

Keeping her safe was near impossible. *Sun god, she's a hazard to herself.*

"She just stabbed Corvus," Orion whispered with horror, and Scorpius barked with laughter.

After painfully long minutes where I worried over the physical but mostly mental health of my Revered, she stopped twitching and grinned.

"That was sick." Her curls stood up around her head as they crackled with electricity.

I snatched the pen out of Arabella's hand, and a shock leaped where our fingers touched. "Don't be a brat," I ordered.

She smirked, and for a second, her gaze caught on my lips. Her pupils expanded, and lust sparked between us.

Abruptly she winced and jolted.

Strange.

Blood trickled down my leg and pride welled in my chest at the force of her stab. I liked that she wasn't a weak, simpering fool; it was extremely attractive how strong she was.

Scorpius couldn't stop laughing, and Orion grinned over at her.

Dr. Palmer's mouth was wide open. The alarm went off, signaling the end of the session, but she didn't react. She seemed stunned by Arabella's violence.

We RJE'd away before she could come to her senses.

Entering our barracks, I stared down at the book in my hands labeled, "Journal to Help Facilitate Relations among the Criminally Insane," and my spirits soared.

CHAPTER 21
JOURNAL PROMPT #1
TRUTH JOURNAL TO HELP FACILITATE RELATIONS AMONG THE CRIMINALLY INSANE

What does a toxic relationship look like to you? How does this relationship make you feel?

ARAN ALIS EGAN

This is fucking stupid, but I can't sleep, so I'm going to write in this to make it clear how much I hate you.

A toxic "relationship" (this is not a relationship) is whatever I have right now with you three, in case it was not obvious enough.

You're the worst people I have ever met in my life. You're unfeeling bullies who hurt others for fun. You need help.

Just thinking about the three of you makes me feel murderous. Other than that, right now I feel nothing but a mountain of nihilism with a smidgeon of self-deprecation.

Side note: Sun god, these pens have a serious truth enchantment. I couldn't have put it better if I tried.

Corvus Malum

Thank you, Arabella, for taking this seriously.

I will also share my thoughts so we can repair our relationship (you're right, this is not a simple, pathetic "relationship," you are my soulmate, which means I would die and kill just to make you smile).

A toxic relationship to me means Arabella, Scorpius, and Orion are all dead. I failed them. I attend their funeral and am so overcome with grief that my flames explode around me and I murder hundreds of thousands of people.

Afterward I walk through the carnage feeling nothing, not even remorse, because my mates are gone, and that is all that matters. I am alone.

Aran Alis Egan

My name is <u>ARAN</u>, not Arabella, you flaming jerk.

Corvus Malum

You are not masquerading as a male anymore. Stop being childish. Arabella is a gorgeous name. ~~You are also the most gorgeous woman I have ever seen in my life.~~

I didn't mean to say that.

Aran Alis Egan:

You're so obsessed with me that it's insane (HAHA, it's the truth). Also, remember when I stabbed you earlier with the pen?

I want to stab you every time you call me the wrong name. It fills me with joy (still the truth, take that!).

Corvus Malum

If you hurt yourself again, I will put you over my knee, Arabella. But I'll let you hurt me any way you need to, as long as you don't hurt yourself.

That is unacceptable.

~~I can't stop thinking about how gorgeous and murderous you are.~~

Also, you missed.

Aran Alis Egan

ERROR

This is an automated enchanted message that the owner of this journal's pen is out of their immediate vicinity. They are not ignoring you, don't panic. The High Court wants you to remember, you are enough and criminal insanity does not define you.

Corvus Malum:

Don't throw your pen across the room like a brat or I'll treat you like one. ~~I fantasize about painting your ass red, and I need to cover you in my cum.~~

Orion Malum

Oooh, are we playing a game where we only talk through the journals?

This is fun.

Nice aim, baby. Don't worry, I'll bring your pen back over to you.

Also, in a toxic relationship I can't talk to my mate or share anything with them. They don't acknowledge me when I am trying to communicate with them. They don't let me watch over them as they sleep. They don't like that I want to own them like a treasure and consume them.

I feel lonely and abandoned.

That is why my relationship with Corvus and Scorpius is not toxic. They always listen to me. That is why I'm enraptured with you Arabella, you fit in with the three of us perfectly.

Aran Alis Egan

Thanks for the pen, Orion. Some people are chivalrous gentlemen unlike other people (<u>MALUM</u>), who are dramatic and misogynistic.

Also, side note, is that why I've been having weird dreams about a figure watching over me?

I thought Malum was the only one who did that?

Corvus Malum

I like to stand watch for everyone's protection. It is my job as Ignis. As my Revered, you should love it.

I noticed you didn't call me ugly like you so often do when you run that mouth. Perhaps because it's a lie, my gorgeous girl.

Aran Alis Egan

You're ugsome, unkind, unruly, and unwell.

. . .

Corvus Malum

You can't write ugly while describing me, can you?

Aran Alis Egan:

Ugsome is a synonym for ugly.

Corvus Malum

Then use it in a sentence, gorgeous. Ugsome also means offensive, which is how you meant it. ~~I like arguing with you. Intellectually you stimulate me, in every sense of the word.~~

Aran Alis Egan

You are utilitarian. UGH FUCK THIS SHIT. ~~I also like arguing with you. The fact that you aren't stupid is attractive.~~

Corvus Malum

~~I'm hard right now.~~ Everyone, please ignore that.

Aran Alis Egan

You did <u>not</u> just say that.

Orion Malum

Holy sun god, I can't believe you said that Corvus.

I'm glad your sensitive side is finally coming out for Arabella.

Also, to answer your earlier question, I don't stand watch

like my Ignis. I stalk. It's different. I need to watch you breathe, or I can't breathe myself. I'm obsessive compulsive about other people, but I've never fixated on anyone like I have you, sweetheart. You're much more fun to watch than Corvus and Scorpius. ~~I also like to watch Luka.~~

Sometimes my fixation can turn violent, and I feel terrible for chasing you down the hall in Elite Academy. My urges overcame me, and I lost myself in obsessing over you.

I am truly so sorry.

I never want to be a source of fear for you.

I want to be your home.

Sorry guys, it's the truth. She smells better, and is prettier, and is captivating, and vicious, and stunning, and is everything I've ever wanted in a mate. I want to kill for her.

So. Badly.

Corvus Malum

~~My feelings are slightly hurt, Orion, but I understand what you're saying about obsessing. I can't stop thinking about our Revered. She consumes every second of my thoughts.~~

These journals must be broken.

Aran Alis Egan

Aw, Malum, your feelings are hurt? Poor baby girl.

Thank you, Orion, for saying sorry. It means a lot. I like that you obsess over me because sometimes I find myself obsessing over you too. Also, I think it's so adorable that you like Luka. Um, I mean, you're cool.

. . .

Orion Malum

Sweetheart, that's everything I've ever wanted to hear. I love that I can speak aloud to you, and you listen. I love that you aren't scared of my devotion. I will never stop apologizing for chasing you. Sun god, I'm blushing right now. I'm not ashamed of what I'm saying.

Please don't tell Luka how I feel.

Corvus Malum

~~Seeing you two get along gets me so fucking hard. My hand is in my pants right now. I fantasize about both of you in bed. You're both so pretty.~~

THESE JOURNALS ARE BROKEN.

Scorpius Malum

I was wondering why my journal kept vibrating. Did you guys know it was enchanted to include braille?

Of course that deranged therapist wouldn't let me get out of this shit show.

Since I fucking have to, a relationship is toxic if they don't like pain and they're a fucking pussy and only want pleasure. I would feel nothing but embarrassment for them because they were a weak, mindless sheep.

Corvus, I am slightly embarrassed to call you my Ignis right now. Control yourself, you're coming across as a pervert. I love the idea of hurting, or being hurt, by all three of you during sex. It makes my toes curl.

Also, I wouldn't mind stabbing John.

Aran Alis Egan

Wait, are all of you named Malum? I'm confused. I thought Mitch was the only one named Malum.

Also, I'm laughing so hard right now I can't breathe. John is going to hate that.

Orion Malum

Scorpius and I are members of the noble House of Malum through matehood. Mitch is the only heir of the noble House of Malum. Any other questions, sweetheart? I love talking to you and would rather stay up all night writing in these journals than go to sleep if it means I get to communicate with you.

My love language is obsession.

What is yours, sweetheart?

Corvus Malum

~~My love language is touch. Thanks for asking, Orion. It's part of the reason my abilities drive me insane. I also love words of affirmation.~~

I'm moving to a different realm.

Scorpius Malum

Mitch. I'm cackling. I'll cuddle you more, you little flaming softie. You just had to ask. Also, my love language is pain. Obviously.

Aran Alis Egan

My love language is quality time.

That is why I love the twins so much. They are always

there to support me in big and small ways. It is healthy and fills me with comfort when everything else inside me feels very dark.

Also, we know you're cackling, Scorpius. Everyone can hear you, and Zenith just told you to shut up. Listen to him or we're all going to have nightmares.

I'm going to stick with Mitch from now on, for accuracy.

Orion Malum

It hurts me to hear you say that about the twins. It makes me realize how much we've failed you. Whatever you need, baby, we will give it to you going forward. We support you. Just to be clear, we will never hurt you for fun, never ever again.

Pinky promise.

Also, I'll scalp Zenith if he gives you more nightmares, sweetheart. No one hurts my woman and lives. I promise. Don't worry about anything.

We'll protect you.

Scorpius Malum

I can't agree to not hurting her for fun. Pain can be very pleasurable if done right. I want to tie you up and stick a… no, I'm not saying that.

Also, Arabella tell Zenith that if he tells me to shut up one more time, he's getting stabbed.

Aran Alis Egan

Tell him yourself, coward. Or just make Mitch do it, since he's the scariest with his fire and is supposed to be a leader. ~~Sometimes I find myself attracted to how ferocious he is.~~

These books are broken.

Corvus Malum

Scorpius, how did you stop yourself from writing?

~~I'm fisting my dick and squeezing thinking about all three of you beneath me.~~

Please don't read that.

Aran Alis Egan

You're so obsessed with us. ~~It turns me on, the thought of you being turned on.~~

Orion Malum

I'm also turned on right now, but I'm glad I have more self-control than Mitch. I am also slightly embarrassed for him right now.

Mitch, tell Zenith to stop telling Scorpius to stop laughing. Our Revered is scared of him giving us all nightmares, and it infuriates me. Do something before I kill him.

Aran Alis Egan

Oh my sun god, Mitch, I can't believe you actually said something!

Zenith's just brandished an ink dagger, and I think he's going to throw it at Mitch for talking back.

. . .

Scorpius Malum

Their swords aren't made of ink. They're made of nightmares.

Orion, leave the killing to me if it comes to that. I want someone writhing in pain beneath me, although no amount of pain has truly satisfied me lately because I want Arabella beneath me.

Unlike Mitch, I am not ashamed of the truth.

Aran Alis Egan

Damn. Zenith threw the dagger. No one is hurting anyone on my behalf. It stresses me out. Please don't.

Orion Malum

Mitch, are you okay? That's the second time you've been stabbed today. Also, of course, sweetheart, I will kill them secretly so you do not worry.

Anything so my girl doesn't stress.

Scorpius Malum:

Fuck, I'm jealous. What's your secret, Mitch? Arabella, will you stab me?

Aran Alis Egan:

No. No one is killing anyone on my behalf, with my knowledge OR in secret.

I might stab you. It sounds fun.

. . .

Scorpius Malum

You're perfect.

Corvus Malum

~~Too late.~~ I hate when you call me Mitch.

Aran Alis Egan

What does too late mean? Were you referring to hurting people in secret??????? Also, don't be sad, baby girl. (hahaha)

Orion Malum

Poor Mitchy needs a kissy. I do love you so much, Mitch, and I hope this name does not hurt your feelings too bad.

Scorpius Malum

His love language is touch. I'm going to crawl down and cover him in kisses.

Corvus Malum

~~Please come touch me, Scorpius. I am so hard just thinking about it.~~ Sun god, please make it stop.

Aran Alis Egan

AWWWWWWWWW. ~~A part of me loves that you are being vulnerable. I like this side to you.~~ LIES.

.   .   .

Orion Malum

It's okay, Mitch, I'd come sleep on top of you tonight, but I need to watch Arabella, so I can't. Try to take some deep breaths.

Scorpius Malum

Do you need me to hurt you, Mitchy? I'll give you love bites.

Corvus Malum

You have five seconds to get down here or I'm crawling up the bunks.

Orion Malum

Listening to you two make out right now is driving me insane.

Aran Alis Egan

Same.

CHAPTER 22
ARAN
MORE FAILURE

ALIFEROUS (ADJECTIVE): having wings.

DAY 12, HOUR 11

"Bend your knees and pinch your shoulder blades together."
Knox pulled his shoulders back and shook his wings to
demonstrate. "Your power comes from your wings. First, you
must learn to fly. Once you've mastered your wings, then
you'll be able to use the energy of your feathers to create an
ice sword. However—flying is the crucial first step."

His crystalline feathers were so pale they were almost
silver and were streaked in black. They clattered loudly in the
quiet forest.

Knox bent his knees, flared his wings wide, then flapped
downward with a whoosh as he said, "Without flying, we are
nothing."

He hovered a few feet off the forest floor.

Snow whirled around his levitating body and the frosted
forest floor. Gray branches clattered together on a chilly
breeze that carried the scent of pine.

The wintry forest was eerie with no animal life.

It was steeped in shadows.

Tones of blue-gray distorted my vision even worse than usual, and a preternatural chill froze my bones from the inside out.

I shivered uncontrollably as Knox hovered gracefully among the trees.

His shoulder-length brown hair defied gravity; it floated around the crown of his head like a halo as the rapid beat of his wings created wind.

His face was ethereal.

Contorted in pure bliss.

One black and one yellow eye were opened wide and staring up at the sky as if he'd found his life's purpose and there was nowhere else he'd rather be, nothing he'd rather do.

He was built to fly.

I'd never known such rapture.

The angel captain folded his wings against his back and dropped to his feet. He smirked at me.

Sadie clapped loudly in the silence, and I glared over at the traitor.

Rina put her pointer finger to her red lips in an exaggerated shushing motion.

Sadie made an obscene gesture back, and Cobra smirked down at her. Jax rubbed at his face like he was exhausted, while Ascher and Xerxes stood behind Sadie, making similar gestures in solidarity.

No one would ever say they didn't support their mate.

The twins sat on the ground in front of the shifters, watching me silently. I made eye contact with John, and he gave me a thumbs-up.

Scorpius was the only king present, and he'd announced

that Orion and Malum had to do "secret High Court business."

He'd sounded angry that he hadn't been included with his mates and had been left behind to babysit me.

A part of me was upset that two of the kings had disappeared again.

The blue-tinted forest darkened to gray.

All pigment disappeared.

The cold intensified.

The kings were keeping secrets and lying.

"Now you try." Knox pointed at me as he demonstrated the motion with his shoulders.

I took a deep breath even though I knew it was pointless. I'd already tried and failed plenty of times.

Standing up straight, I tried to ignore the crushing weight that pulled my spine toward the ground as sweat streaked down the sides of my face and dripped off my chin.

Wild curls were itchy where they stuck to my neck and forehead.

Discomfort radiated down my spine.

Bent knees shaking, I flared my wings wide, flexed my arms, and pushed my shoulder muscles downward with every ounce of strength I possessed.

My muscles strained, and I grunted through gritted teeth. Groaning, I tried to replicate Knox's smooth flapping.

Unfamiliar appendages ached with pain.

My wings flapped like they were in molasses.

Time morphed and expanded until each second lasted an eternity.

I didn't fly.

Again.

Mother would have loved this moment, too bad I ate her heart.

Back buckling under the weight of my wings, I gave up and rested my hands on my knees, gasping loudly while cold air whistled through my teeth and burned my gums. I tasted copper in my mouth even though there was no blood.

My teeth ached from inhaling harshly.

Freezing temperatures were a miserable bitch.

"Good job. You're doing it." Sadie clapped loudly, and I shot her a glare because I clearly was *not* doing it.

She stopped clapping when she saw my facial expression. "I swear I saw you hover a few inches." Her face was earnest and shone with pride.

"Did I really?" I asked doubtfully.

She crossed her arms over her chest and made the symbol of the sun god with her fingers. "I swear on Cobra's life that I saw you rise off the ground."

"Excuse me?" Cobra hissed.

Across the clearing, Zenith mouthed, "No, you didn't fly. You suck," while Vegar gave me a thumbs-up.

I exhaled exhaustion.

"I promise you flew!" Sadie said aggressively and glared at the other people in the forest, daring them to contradict her.

"I hope so," I mumbled as I concentrated on not passing out as I asphyxiated on air. Fatigue and zero progress after hours of effort were killing me.

It was like running in place.

Banging my fractured skull against a brick wall.

Being trapped at Elite Academy.

Fighting in a battle against monsters.

Killing when I wanted to rest.

"She's lying to try to make you feel better," Jinx's voice rang inside my mind. *"Nothing happened."*

Her voice cleared the haze.

It sounded like she was speaking directly into my ear. Each word was crystal clear and nothing like the fuzzy connection that had cut out in the middle of battle.

I stopped spiraling and glared over at her, nearly falling over from my sudden movement. The unfamiliar weight distribution pulled me lower into a hunch.

I gasped out clouds of water vapor.

Hyperventilated.

Jinx leaned against a tree next to Scorpius, who clenched her elbow in a tight grip and made sure she didn't fall over. Since Warren was currently in ferret form, wrapped around her neck, it seemed the king had taken his place.

She had a black cast on her wrist. She said she broke it tripping while trying to maneuver into bed.

Annoyance flared in my gut. What was taking the prosthetic so long? The High Court couldn't be this incompetent.

Black sunglasses hid Jinx's face as she watched me with a bored expression. Standing next to the tall devil, she almost came up to his shoulders. She no longer looked like a small child.

Had she always had curves?

She was definitely getting taller.

"How old are you again?" I asked in my head, forgetting to be annoyed that I hadn't made any progress with flying. *"You don't look fourteen."*

Jinx's voice echoed crisply through my skull. *"I'm older than you."*

I scoffed aloud. "Good one."

"What?" Knox's mismatched eyes focused on me. "Who are you talking to?"

"A crazy bitch," I mumbled as I turned back to the angel.

In my peripheral vision, Jinx and Scorpius shared a smirk. When had they become friends? I sensed danger.

"Try again," Knox said encouragingly as he showed me how to push my shoulders back. Now that I had earned my wings, the angel captain was nothing but pleasant and positive.

In fact, he made it a point to be nice to everyone in the camp.

His attitude differed vastly from how he'd acted during the Legionnaire Games, and contrasted with the haughty arrogance of the rest of the angels.

They used the term *grounders* frequently.

They sneered when we gave them instructions.

Case in point, Rina huffed loudly at Knox's proclamation, and she flopped back against a tree with annoyance. The men and women angels around her did the same.

They grumbled and shuffled with boredom.

Glared at me with disgust.

I hated to say it, but I got where they were coming from. It seemed like the gods had made a mistake naming the shifter and academy legions as champions.

We were chaotic, unorganized, and prone to falling apart. Not the best candidates for leading a war.

I wouldn't want to listen to me either.

But the angels could fly.

They were majestic and elegant, full of confidence, and seemingly unfazed by the ungodly's violence.

Meanwhile, I still hadn't stopped spiraling.

Arthur made a comment under his breath, and a female angel laughed beside him.

I ignored them and focused on Knox's encouraging smile. Whatever his reason was for suddenly acting nice, it didn't matter to me. If he wanted to pretend to respect us, then I'd take it.

I pushed my hands off my knees and staggered into a standing position.

Thighs trembling, pain screaming across my shoulder blades, I lifted the wings high at my sides.

Blue-white crystals clattered.

Flexing with everything I had, I gritted my teeth.

Closed my eyes.

Focused on moving the new heavy appendages quickly and pretended it wasn't like trying to sprint straight up a cliff.

Sweat poured down my face.

I yelled through gritted teeth and strained with everything I had, hands fisted as pressure pounded in my skull from the force of my concentration.

My combat boots sank deeper into the snow as my wings pulled me downward instead of upward.

Cartilage and feathers chained me to the dirt.

Tied me down.

The temperature dropped, and when I opened my bulging eyes, the shades of gray had become shades of black. Emptiness expanded into a chasm within my chest.

"You are nothing but a failure." Mother straddled my writhing form. Blue flames tortured me as I screamed in pain.

I'd failed as a fae, and now I failed as an angel.

Pressure intensified behind my eyes, and liquid dripped down my cheeks, thicker than tears.

"That's enough. She's had enough training for today. Everyone, leave." Luka's voice cracked like a whip through the forest, and his tone brimmed with violence.

For the first time, Rina had nothing to say.

"Pull your wings in, Aran," John said in my ear.

I hadn't seen him approach.

He grabbed my arms and used his strength to tug me up

while he wiped his fingers across my cheekbones. They came back stained with blood.

At least, that was what I assumed the black substance was. My vision wasn't picking up most of the color spectrum.

Shadows coalesced around me.

I choked, unable to draw the frigid air into my lungs.

"Pull your wings in. Now," John ordered in an uncharacteristically angry tone.

I complied.

The crushing weight became manageable, and suddenly the chains pulling me to the ground disappeared.

I felt bizarrely light, like I could float away as a shaky trembling permeated through my muscles.

"Whoa, steady." John wrapped his arms around me.

He grinned down at me with his dimples on full display. His dark eyes twinkled as he took in my questioning expressions and pulled me flush against him.

Pinpricks of pain raced down my spine.

I loved his smile.

"Yes." John grinned. "I pretended to get mad to make you obey. Reverse psychology. I'm a genius."

"You're an idiot," I huffed as I leaned into his embrace, relieved in ways I couldn't put into words.

There were two constants in the realms: John was good-natured, and I was depressed.

It was who we were.

Intrinsically.

Two halves of a whole.

His arms wrapped around me squeezed punishingly, and I relaxed for the first time in hours.

He mumbled into my hair, "Let's get you inside and warm."

"I think we can still work—"

Knox was cut off by Scorpius shoving him in the chest and sneering menacingly, "She needs to rest."

Knox's black and yellow eyes flashed with violence.

They squared up to each other, equally matched in height and muscle, warriors bristling with barely constrained energy.

The forest appeared darker.

Sinister.

Abruptly, Knox's features smoothed out, and he held his hands up in the universal gesture of surrender. "Of course, I meant no offense. My mistake. I didn't realize we had been going at it for hours." He stepped around Scorpius and looked at me. "Don't get discouraged. Most people earn their wings when they're younger and have spent their entire lives preparing to fly. We'll figure it out."

He smiled.

Too late, I was way past discouragement. We were entering manic breakdown territory.

Everything is going to work out great. Just have positive thoughts and keep trying. Blah. Blah. Blah.

I'd show him how *positively* deranged I could be.

John stepped forward and blocked me as I flipped off Knox with both my hands. The angel missed the gesture.

I punched him in the gut. "Move out of my way."

He punched me back, with far less force, then the forest blurred as he swung me over his shoulder like a sack of potatoes.

I was too tired to stop him.

"To the bunk beds." He pointed an imaginary sword dramatically and ran down the path.

"You're so fucking stupid," I said between laughs. "I hope the ungodly kill us all for being loud."

The world tipped again, and I shrieked.

Head swinging upside down, it took me a moment to process that John held my ankles in his hands with his biceps extended above his head.

He held me upside down behind his back so I was perpendicular to the ground.

Since we were almost the same height, my head was close to the ground and enveloped in warm steam.

I shrieked and tried to kick free. "Put me down right now, you idiot."

"Nope." John ran forward awkwardly as I pushed against his calves.

"I'm going to trip you," I threatened.

He flexed and straightened his hands so I was hanging higher off the ground.

In this ridiculous position, he ran past the rest of the group, who were *walking* on the path like normal individuals.

Sadie slapped my ass as we passed.

John almost tripped at the loud crack and then said in his most serious tone, "Touch my wife's ass again and I'll remove your hand."

"What did you just sssssay to her?" Cobra hissed.

Before we could die via snake, Luka appeared out of nowhere and blocked us protectively. There was a loud *shhhhk* that signaled Xerxes had pulled out his knives, and suddenly Orion was standing beside Luka creating a wall.

"Later, suckers!" John shouted as he continued running down the path.

Sadie yelled after us, "I fucked her first!"

John stumbled but caught himself and resumed running awkwardly with me hanging behind him.

"Be fucking quiet and stop breaking protocol," Rina snarled angrily, and Sadie replied, "That wasn't very quiet of you."

They were getting far behind us, and I barely made out Rina saying some choice swear words that were mixed with the words *grounder* and *idiot*.

Abruptly, we burst into our barracks, and John dumped me.

I was lying in an undignified heap on the floor of our room. Out of breath from laughing and general exhaustion, I could do nothing but lay immobile and gasp.

John grinned down at me proudly. "That was fun."

I kicked him in the back of the knee, and he crashed down beside me.

"You're so stupid," I said. "I don't know why I put up with you."

Before I could catch my bearings, he was straddling me as he smothered me with a pillow that he'd somehow procured.

"Be silent, witch," he said dramatically as he pressed harder and actually asphyxiated me.

I kneed him in the balls and threw him off.

He moaned as he rolled over, cupping his junk like a wuss.

I ripped the pillow away from him and slammed it down into his face as hard as I could. There was a crunch because I'd accidentally made the fabric icy.

I grinned with satisfaction.

"She's killing me. Someone help!" he wailed dramatically.

I hit him harder.

The crunch was louder.

"What the actual fuck is wrong with you people?" Zenith snarled from where he was lying on Vegar's bunk, and from the way the covers moved, he was also lying on top of Vegar.

At this point, all the demons did was nap and yell at us.

Frankly, I respected their lifestyle.

"So much." I staggered to my feet and held my hand out to help John up, but instead of taking my offering, he kicked out at my shins, and I slammed down on top of him with an oof.

The wind was knocked out of my lungs.

While I was momentarily distracted, two hands wrapped around my throat.

Darkness twinkled around John as he winked down at me. "I win. Take that. Now who's the idiot?"

I flipped him off as he crushed my trachea with his fingers.

He waggled his eyebrows like he wasn't strangling me to death. I slammed my hips upward with all my force, and pushed him off.

A flash of black streaked across the air.

John's eyes widened, and suddenly he was moving much quicker. In a split second, he rolled on top of me protectively and tugged us across the floor.

Clang.

A black dagger, made of nightmares, lay on the ground right where we'd been fighting.

"Did you just try to stab them?" Luka asked with anger, chest heaving as he stood silhouetted in the doorway, snow and ice wafting around him.

Scorpius stood behind him, plush upper lip contorted into a scowl. "Did you say 'stab'?" he asked menacingly.

The violence ratcheted up.

"To be fair"—John offered to help me up—"we deserved it."

I ignored his hand and stood up, then shoved at his chest. "Maybe lay off choking so aggressively? What is wrong with you?"

John shoved me back with so much strength that I flew across the room and slammed onto my bunk bed.

He stalked after me and leaned forward. His voice dropped an octave, and he grinned. "But I liked that my fingerprints are on your neck."

He winked.

"What the fuck? Be gentle with her." Luka grabbed his twin and pulled him back from me.

I gaped at John as he was dragged across the room by his twin, and I tried to process his words.

He shimmied his hips and winked in his brother's arms, dimples on full display as he licked his lips.

His dark eyes twinkled with mirth.

Outrage turned to gratitude in my chest as I realized what had just happened.

Once again, John had acted so ridiculously that he'd successfully distracted me when I was spiraling.

Scorpius pushed past John, bumping against him with his entire body as he passed, then he glowered down at me. "I wanted to ask you something." He clenched his teeth, and a muscle ticked in the sharp edge of his jawline. "Can we talk?"

His cut cheekbones were stark against his hollowed cheeks.

There were dark-purple smudges underneath his eyes.

The man before me looked exhausted, and my gut told me his change in demeanor had nothing do with war against the ungodly. Scorpius was a self-proclaimed sado-masochist and wasn't someone to balk at something as trivial as murder.

No.

It wasn't the war; it was something else.

His jaw clenched tighter, and he tapped his foot with impatience as he waited for me to respond.

I sat silently and stared up at him blankly as I purposefully said nothing just to piss him off.

He clenched his jaw tighter.

Pride filled me because it was nice to set goals and achieve them, especially when those goals were tormenting men.

I rubbed my eyes, trying to process the fact that John had purposefully left red marks on my throat while we play wrestled, and now Scorpius was asking for permission to speak.

Men were bizarre creatures.

"Shoot." I leaned back on my covers with my arm behind my head, legs spread wide like the fuck boy I used to pretend to be. Casual and unbothered, with the confidence of someone who'd achieved greatness while doing nothing.

It was empowering being delusional.

"I'm manspreading, just so you know," I said, just so he could get the full picture.

Scorpius's dark eyebrows contrasted with his pale complexion as they lifted. "Okay?" he asked with confusion, then shook his head and said forcefully, "I know you're exhausted after training, so"—he gritted his teeth together—"*please* let me wash you in the shower."

He said "please" like it was a filthy word.

"Why?" I asked, genuinely confused.

He pulled at the neck of his sweatshirt like he was dying from discomfort.

"I'm your Protector," he said with a sneer that insinuated I was stupid for asking.

"False—you're just a rude asshole."

White teeth flashed as he bared them at me, then his

expression smoothed over like he was forcing himself to appear unthreatening.

He failed.

"I want to show you that I meant what I said about serving you. I want to be your hound. I want to—" He swallowed thickly. "—have a relationship with you."

"And I want to fly," I said dryly. "Get to the point."

His sneer returned, and he snapped, "You're literally a fucking angel."

"But"—I popped the *B* obnoxiously—"I can't fly."

Scorpius exhaled loudly, and it sounded like he was screaming through his nose. I slumped back on my bed and rolled my eyes.

Instead of walking away like I expected, Scorpius smiled, and it transformed the harsh edges of his face into a breathtaking work of art. "I would like to have some quality time between the two of us. Is that okay with you?"

For a second, I was speechless.

I'd never seen the cruel king smile before, and holy sun god, his face was a weapon of mass destruction.

Pain streaked across my back, and my breath hitched.

He frowned and narrowed his eyes.

I whispered, "No."

He scowled darkly and clenched his hands into fists, and the dark circles under his eyes seemed to expand.

"No," I explained with another heavy sigh. "You do not get to spend quality time with me, because I still hate you."

His scowl deepened, and he opened his mouth.

"However," I cut him off, "you can spend quality time with me because it will probably piss off Malum."

He would be *so* angry if I let Scorpius shower with me when he wasn't around. I could practically feel the heat from his meltdown.

The blind devil kept looming over me, but he unclenched his hands and quirked an eyebrow.

I opened my mouth to say something derogatory about his mates—because I never missed an opportunity to talk shit about my enemies—but he grabbed my wrist and I forgot what I was going to say.

Without saying another word, he tugged me out of bed toward the small bathroom and pulled us both inside before I could change my mind.

"Don't do anything I wouldn't do!" John yelled cheekily, and we both ignored him. "Let us know if you want help. We're happy to join."

Scorpius mumbled under his breath, "We'll get to that later."

I stumbled. He really was becoming obsessed with John.

"Speak for yourself," Luka muttered as the door closed with a loud click.

Suddenly, I was trapped.

With the king who liked pain.

CHAPTER 23

SCORPIUS

SHOWERS

Cordolium (noun): heartfelt grief.

DAY 11, HOUR 12

"While we're in the shower, I'm in charge," Arabella said.

She was adorable.

And delusional.

I quirked my eyebrow and crossed my arms over my chest as I mockingly waited for her directives. Then I remembered I was trying to appear nonthreatening, and I softened my features, relaxed my posture.

Earlier her breathing had changed like she was in pain, and my stomach had plummeted because just being in my presence had hurt her. I didn't want that.

I inhaled deeply. Her icy scent filled the small bathroom.

She was pure adrenaline to the veins.

Muscles flexing, senses heightened, I forced myself to keep my arms at my side. Fingers relaxed.

Listening to her wrestle with John had triggered something inside me.

They were both so noisy.

So playful.

I wanted them both.

I'd start with Arabella.

Cold wafted off her, and goose bumps prickled my skin from her proximity.

The bathroom was pathetically small, and just standing in front of the shower meant we were chest to chest, mere inches between us.

She breathed unsteadily, and her breath puffed against the exposed skin on my neck.

I held back a moan.

"So. Now that we're in here, we're going to…" Arabella trailed off like she wasn't exactly sure what she wanted to command of me.

I swallowed down a mocking laugh because I knew exactly what she needed.

She needed to be cared for.

Looked after.

Pampered.

"Um," she said awkwardly as she struggled to come up with an idea.

It took every ounce of control I possessed to appear receptive to directions.

It was the least I could do.

Ever since I'd learned that Arabella had been tortured as a child, a sick sense of guilt twisted my stomach. I woke up nauseous and went to bed feeling weak. It permeated every second of my day.

Just like myself, my Revered had suffered at the hands of others when she was too young to defend herself.

Yet I'd called her pampered. Weak. I'd tormented her and added to her distress.

I'd been a fool.

My chest ached with regret.

If Arabella was ever going to accept me as her Protector, I needed to build a relationship with her, which would only happen if I came across as nonthreatening.

I forced my shoulders to relax and tried to look approachable.

My lips curled up in a welcoming smile.

Corvus always grouched about how stupid John was with his "fucking dimples and constant smiles." Most likely because Orion said Arabella liked to comment on how much she liked John's jokes and smile.

Fucking John.

There was something intriguing about a grown man making jokes and acting so idiotic all the time. He was just so *nice*.

But if he was the type of man my Revered preferred, then that was exactly who I would be for her. Just because I wasn't nice didn't mean I couldn't pretend I was.

My plan was simple.

Effective.

Failure was not an option.

"What's wrong with you?" Arabella asked me with concern. "Do you need to use the bathroom? Should I leave? Why are you standing like that?"

She moved toward the door.

Frustration welled. I stepped in front of her and blocked her exit. "I'm fine, say your demands," I snarled, annoyed that she was misinterpreting my relaxed demeanor.

Could she not tell I was pretending to be a nice guy? What was wrong with her?

She scoffed. "No need to get all huffy."

I opened my mouth to retort, but my teeth clicked as I shut my lips, and I breathed deeply.

I would wait patiently like a normal, nice man would.

For her, I would pretend.

"Why are you making that face?" she asked incredulously, then whispered, "Are you having stomach pain? Sometimes I also get it after a battle. Don't worry, I think it's normal."

I gaped down at her with disbelief.

She continued rambling, "It's probably just an ulcer from worry. I read somewhere that loads of people get them, especially during violent times in history with lots of upheaval."

A headache throbbed against my temple as I struggled to come up with a response to her inane statements.

What would a nice guy say in this situation?

"Do you need me to get you medicine for your stomach?" I asked slowly as I pulled my lips up into an approachable smile.

"No need to snarl at me." She made a disgruntled noise. "I was just saying."

I wanted to scream with frustration because I wasn't snarling, I was fucking smiling.

Why can't she tell the difference?

Stepping forward, I used my larger size to surround her.

Frost burned my tongue, and my heart thudded erratically in my sternum. My skin tingled with the urge to wrap my fingers around her cold flesh and dig my nails into her skin.

I needed to mark her as mine.

I wanted to hurt her until she cried with pleasure.

I wanted to show her how much I cared.

I wanted *her*. Period.

Lately, everything had been dull and unexciting. The ungodly were predictable, and the infected were pathetic.

Everything was dissatisfying.

Boring.

Everything except for the woman who was standing before me, trapped in three cubic feet of space by her own voluntary will.

I used my larger size to press her against the wall.

"Back off!" she yelled abruptly, and the side of her hand slammed into my trachea.

I stumbled back, unprepared for her outburst of violence.

Goose bumps exploded down my back, and I shivered from the ecstasy of her touch.

My throat throbbed with pain, and it felt delicious.

I licked my lips.

The skin on my neck burned where her icy fingers had touched. I pressed my hands against it and marveled at the difference in temperature where she'd made contact.

Adjusting myself in my sweatpants, I took a deep breath as I tried to figure out how to proceed.

Should I pin her against the wall and ravish her? Beg her to punch me in the throat again? Dig my nails into her throat as punishment until her blood coated both of us?

So many fucking options.

I was paralyzed by indecision, so turned on that I couldn't think rationally.

She sighed and repeated, "This is what we're going to do." There was a creak as she turned the shower nozzle, then the sound of rushing water. "We're going to get into the fucking shower."

I gulped.

Pressing my fingers harder against my neck, I tried not to

jerk my hips as I remembered the blissful pain that had rocked through me when she'd punched me.

Then I remembered I was pretending to be someone I wasn't.

I was pretending to be a nice guy.

It wasn't an exact science, but I was pretty sure John didn't get turned on from throat punches and fantasize about digging his nails into Arabella's skin and making her bleed.

I forced my hands away from my neck and said slowly, "I'll wash and pamper you in the shower. I'll take care of you."

It wasn't a complete lie, since I did want to care for my Revered.

The problem was my standard of care was probably very different from what a normal man would imagine. It involved daggers, wax, screams of pleasure, and moans of pain.

I reached down for the edge of my sweatshirt and began to tug it off.

"No." Arabella pulled the fabric back down and stopped me. "Don't take your clothes off."

Bemusedly, I waited for her instructions.

A long moment passed awkwardly between us, like she was waiting for me to fight her and didn't know what to do with the fact that I'd obeyed her command.

I smiled softly and waited.

She exhaled heavily like I was being difficult. "We're going to both get into the shower, and we're going to talk to each other. Fully clothed."

"Why would we do that?"

"Because I like to think in the shower, and this way we can clear the air between us," she said sassily. "I don't believe we've ever just sat and talked to each other."

"We can do that unclothed," I pointed out.

Her teeth ground together, and her breath hitched unevenly as she said, "Either get in and shut up, or be a pervert like Malum and leave. It's your call."

I arched my brow at the venom in her voice.

Women made no sense, and I'd never understand them. Their logic was unsettling. Unfortunately, a nice guy would not point that out.

Shrugging, I pulled back the shower curtain and stepped in.

The scalding water immediately soaked through my clothes, and the warm fabric hung heavy off my frame. It was unpleasant but easily ignored.

I sat down, folding my long limbs awkwardly in the narrow tub, and waited for further instructions.

"What are you doing?" Arabella asked with confusion.

I scrunched my knees up and parted my legs as wide as possible to make room for her in the cramped space. "I'm doing what you said."

"Exactly!" She sounded genuinely disturbed. "Why are you listening to me?"

I rolled my eyes at the insinuation that I would never obey her.

She was absolutely correct.

Still, it was rude to point it out so obnoxiously. She was making it fucking hard to be the nice guy that she apparently preferred.

"Are you going to get in or not?" I asked slowly as I tried not to bite her head off.

Nonchalance was extremely difficult to portray because my throat still burned where she'd punched me and I was painfully erect.

But I did it.

For her.

Anything for Arabella.

There was a long moment of silence, then an exhale and the flutter of the shower curtain as she climbed into the tub and joined me.

My sweatpants became uncomfortably tight.

Water sprayed down and splattered across the both of us, mixing our scents as her legs brushed against mine as she positioned herself.

I swallowed down a moan.

It didn't matter that we were both clothed; the knowledge that her skin was so close to mine was enough to make me groan with awareness.

Breathing heavily through my nose, I tried to maintain a calm facade. Unfortunately, that meant I inhaled more of her intoxicating scent.

Blood rushed south.

My head spun with dizziness.

This was torment. *Why in the realms would I agree to sit in a fucking tiny space with my fated soulmate? A space where people usually got naked.*

I was an idiot.

Soapy skin and moans of pleasure filled my imagination. I tipped my head back, squeezed my eyes shut, and prayed to the sun god for self-control.

Also, why had I thought it was a good idea to approach her when my mates were gone?

I should have forced Orion to stay and helped Corvus—sun god knew it had been fucking rewarding last time I'd gone—but Orion hadn't wanted to miss out on the fun and I'd agreed to be the one to stay back.

My control was waning.

"So." She thudded her head against the shower wall.

"What should we discuss?"

I barely stopped myself from snapping at her not to hurt herself.

Only I got to do that, not her.

She didn't know how to make the pain enjoyable. She needed a teacher; she needed me.

I shrugged as I tried to think of what a nice guy would want to talk about.

After a long pause, I finally settled on, "How are you feeling?"

Arabella burst out in laughter.

Annoyingly long minutes passed where she cackled to herself like a maniac. Finally, she gasped and said, "I've been better. How about you?"

She laughed harder, clearly mocking my attempts at pleasantries.

She was begging to be punished.

I harrumphed and said, "I was trying to be nice. You don't need to be fucking rude about it." I grimaced as I realized what I was doing.

Forcing my muscles to relax, I tried to look apologetic and nonthreatening.

"What is wrong with your face?" she asked. "Your expression is weird."

I clenched my jaw as water poured over me, overstimulating my arousal-heightened nerves.

That was it.

I was done with the games.

"Really, can't you fucking see I'm trying to be a nice guy for you?" I snapped as I glared at her. "Since that's all you seem to want in a man, I'd think you'd be a little more appreciative of my efforts—sun god, could you be any more difficult?"

Arabella scoffed, then replied with venom, "I never told you to be a nice guy. News flash, I already know you're not nice, so don't pretend to be something you're not. It's pathetic and frankly, creepy."

I ground my teeth together. "You're the pathetic one who has us sitting here fully clothed in the shower like idiots."

"Well, you're the pathetic one who listened to me."

"Well, you're the pathetic one for making me so obsessed with you."

"That doesn't even make sense."

"Why are you so difficult?" I shook my head in exasperation. "Why do you have to make everything so fucking hard? Can't you just be all weak and simpering or whatever a woman is supposed to be like?"

"You sexist piece of shit," she said through gritted teeth. "Why can't you be all gallant and chivalrous like a man is supposed to be?"

"Gallantry is for foolish men." I laughed cruelly at the idea of simpering about.

She laughed back louder. "And weakness is for foolish women."

I opened my mouth to argue but snapped it closed because she had a point. Neither of us fit into any gender stereotypes.

"So where does that leave us?" I asked slowly as I trailed my fingers across the cracked edge of the tub and counted the seconds between her breaths.

She didn't breathe for five seconds, then her breath expelled in a whoosh. "It leaves me sitting in the tub with an ass." She mumbled under her breath, "And you wonder why I don't want to be your mate."

I scowled.

Fisted my hands and tried not to growl with frustration.

Within five minutes of trying to be nice, I'd ruined everything between us.

Again.

"I just want to be your Protector," I said dejectedly.

Her breathing hitched, and I fixated on the soft whooshing noise amid the thundering water.

She sounded upset. Was I making her sad? Was she frowning? Sun god, I wished Orion were here to whisper her every facial expression.

I felt lost.

Pathetic.

Unable to be anything but the broken blind man who couldn't control his vitriol. The man who liked pain when everyone yearned for pleasure. Even my Revered didn't understand me.

It was my turn to gasp.

Unable to breathe.

Icy fingers grabbed my hand and squeezed. I fixated on the sensation. Every molecule was highly attuned to where we were touching.

"You don't need to panic," Arabella said softly. "I know you aren't a nice guy. I don't need you to pretend to be someone you're not."

I exhaled shakily.

"There's no pressure." She squeezed my hand encouragingly. "We're just sitting here talking, even if it means we argue, although I'm tired of arguing. Why don't you tell me about yourself."

The tingling sensation in my hand intensified, and my arm went numb.

Shock held me still as I tried to process that she was voluntarily touching me and acting like I hadn't ruined everything.

I inhaled the steam, warm water, and my Revered's icy scent.

"It's difficult," I blurted out before I'd gathered my thoughts. "Being the weak, blind guy who's mad at the world."

Pressure burned behind my eyes, and I cursed myself for speaking so rashly. *What the fuck was I doing*? She deserved a strong Protector, not a pathetic, broken man who doubted himself.

I opened my mouth to take it back, but her nails dug into my skin.

"Don't try to take it back," she said forcefully.

My jaw snapped closed.

She squeezed me, "I want to know the real you, not whatever stupid Protector you need to be." She scoffed. "What's the point of all the bullshit we've been through and survived if we don't even know each other?"

The warm water sprayed between us, and I frowned at the melancholy in her voice.

"I'm tired too," she whispered dejectedly. "If you're the blind, mean guy, then I'm the depressed bitch who can't be what anyone wants her to be."

I curled my fingers around her hand.

"You're not a bitch," I whispered.

"And you're not the weak, blind guy."

I dug my nails into her skin, like I did for Corvus when he was spiraling. I squeezed to let her know I wasn't letting her go.

"We're quite the pair," she laughed hollowly. "The angel who can't fly and the assassin who can't see."

"I don't need to see to kill," I said honestly. "And you just haven't learned to fly yet."

She made a noise of disagreement under her breath but didn't argue.

Silence expanded between us.

"What was it like growing up under the mad fae queen?" I blurted out, then sighed with relief when she didn't try to pull her hand away.

It felt wrong that I'd lived through her heinous memories but had no idea what her current perspective was on anything.

How had we never asked her about her past?

Just when I thought she wasn't going to answer, she whispered, "I think it broke me. Permanently."

My heart twisted in my sternum, and a volcano of rage engulfed me.

Long minutes passed before I could speak. Since she was being so honest, I said, "I used to not like pain. But in the devil realm, the weak males are culled. There's no such thing as a blind devil because any who make it to adolescence are killed off in the brutal school systems."

My words hung between us.

She didn't gasp or give false platitudes like I expected. She squeezed my hand with hers like she was telling me she understood.

After all, with how she'd grown up, she probably did.

I didn't need to explain to her how cruel childhood could be.

There was something about the cramped tub and scalding water that made it easy to bare my soul.

I spoke words I'd never revealed to another person, not even my mates.

"I don't know exactly when it happened. All I know is that one day after a beating, I licked the blood off my lips and reveled in the pain. I found myself craving the violence and dreaming about hurting them back. I wasn't born a monster—I became one."

The intoxicating icy scent intensified.

Emotions swirled between us.

She whispered back, "I hated my mother, but I never wanted to kill her, and I find myself thinking about her constantly. She was horrible, but I still don't know how to cope with what I've done. What I've become."

The rage intensified inside me, and I scowled.

"You did what you had to do," I said harshly. "You survived, that's all you did. You've become who you needed to be to live in a cruel world. It's something to be proud of—not something to be ashamed of."

Water sputtered off her lips.

She squeezed my hand like we were tethered together. "Then that applies to you too," she whispered. "You survived despite the bigotry of the devil realm. If I'm not broken—then neither are you."

I dug my nails harder into her skin and nodded.

"I agree." My voice was hoarse as I struggled to process the influx of unfamiliar emotions filling my chest. The power she held over me was insane, and I was drowning in her. Gladly.

She shook our hands up and down. "It's nice to meet you, Scorpius."

"Same, Arabella." My voice cracked.

Her breath caught as she inhaled, but she didn't reprimand me for using her given name.

The unfamiliar emotion tripled in my chest, and it was like sunshine straight to the soul.

Something fragile burned between us.

It was delicate and new. It was everything.

It felt like hope.

CHAPTER 24
ARAN
STEAM

ALGOPHILIA (NOUN): a morbid pleasure in the pain either of oneself or of others.

DAY 11, HOUR 20

Scorpius and I sat across from each other in the narrow tub.

When I'd told Scorpius to sit down fully clothed, I'd assumed he'd scoff and tell me to go fuck myself.

I'd thought he'd only wanted to play Protector and Revered, and I'd assumed if he did stay, that he'd leave after a few minutes. At most, I'd thought we'd talk through some things, spend thirty minutes going over our issues, then resume snarling at each other.

I'd been wrong.

Eight hours later, we still sat across from each other.

Neither of us wanted to leave.

Talking to Scorpius was one of the most intimate things I'd ever experienced. Our legs touched because we were both too tall to fit, but it wasn't sexual.

Both our voices were scratchy from overuse.

I could tell from the way he clenched his jaw that he was worried I was going to try and leave.

He worried for naught.

Neither of us wanted the moment to end.

Scorpius broke the lull in our conversation and said, "It does something to you, never being able to see or understand the colors that everyone seems so in love with. It's less about the sights themselves and more about feeling disconnected from everyone. Feeling different."

He tipped his head back and showcased his cut jaw.

The eye tattooed across his neck glowed.

He whispered, "I've always felt disconnected from others. Trapped by their perceptions of me and the world."

I sighed as I rested my head against the wall.

"I know what you mean," I said after a weighty pause. "Obviously, not about the lack of sight, but I know the feeling of the walls closing in around you—invisible parameters crushing you while everyone lives freely."

Scorpius glowered like he was suddenly enraged.

Unable to understand his change in demeanor, I kept explaining. "Others decide they know you. They label you a weak princess. A powerless fae. An incapable angel." I trailed off, lost in memories as I whispered, "A whore."

He clenched his fists and said darkly, "People act like they understand, but they don't. They form their opinions and judge you. Nothing you do will change who they've decided you are." He snapped his fingers. "The blind one is weak." He snapped again. "Destroy the weak."

I studied the mold that trailed across the ceiling and tried not to think about a fae palace dripping in gold and filled with pain.

I fingered the Necklace of Death. It warmed like it was trying to fill the hole inside my chest.

My voice sounded far away as I spoke. "And they never change. No matter how much you show them differently. They trap you so you can never escape. Some confines have no freedom."

"All you can do is suffer," Scorpius said hoarsely. "Endure."

"And just the act of enduring is an act of strength," I said.

He narrowed his eyes. "Maybe hurting them is the only freedom available."

His perspective was fitting.

It didn't make it any less brutal.

I countered, "Or maybe just surviving is the solution. Maybe you don't have to hurt them, because just existing to defy their expectations enrages them. You don't need to inflict the pain—you need to free yourself from them." I nodded wistfully. "The dream is to build a life that is so satisfying, you forget the hell ever existed."

He smirked at me. "Says the woman who ate her mother's heart."

"I never wanted to kill her," I whispered.

"You did what you had to do to survive," he said gruffly. "You took your vengeance. It's impressive—you should be proud."

"But I didn't mean to. Sadie was in danger, and I had to do something because I couldn't lose her. I wouldn't survive a life without her."

Scorpius's smirk fell.

Intense emotions vibrated between us.

"I'd rather not kill others," I blurted out awkwardly. "Mother was a monster, and I don't want to be like her. I don't want to perpetuate terror like she did. It's exhausting."

Scorpius's frown deepened, the dark circles under his eyes appearing more purple under the fluorescent bulb.

"I'll kill them for you," he said casually, like he was talking about the weather.

I squinted at him. "I just said I don't want them to die."

"No." A muscle in his jaw ticked. "You said you didn't want to *be a murderer*. They don't deserve to live for trapping you, and you don't deserve to worry about becoming like your mother. The solution is simple: I'll kill them."

"You better not," I warned him.

"Don't worry." He smirked, and it was vicious. "I won't tell you when I do."

"How is that supposed to make me feel better?"

"Because I'm killing your enemies for you," he said.

"It's not that simple," I argued. "It's a morality issue. Can't you see that?"

He bared his teeth. "I can't see anything."

"Har, har. Hilarious." I rolled my eyes. "Do you seriously have no ability to understand the ethical dilemma of murdering other people? Does it not plague you?"

His grin was alarming. "No." Long pale fingers reached forward and wrapped around my wrist. "You know I'm going to do terrible things for you, right?" he asked slowly.

I winced. "Please don't."

"Too late." He yanked me forward. "Can we talk like this more often?"

"Yes," I said automatically. "I'd really like that."

I sprawled across his chest. His skin was feverish compared to mine, and steam sizzled where we connected.

"You're so perfect," he whispered, then he slammed his lips against mine.

His fingernails dug into the side of my face as he kissed me like he was trying to devour me.

Pain exploded down my back, and I ignored it.

His teeth bit down on my lower lip, and copper flooded my mouth. "Mine," Scorpius said.

Half-dazed with pleasure and pain, I pulled my head back, and between gasps, I countered, "I don't belong to anyone."

He pinned me against the tub. Pushed my sweatshirt up and dragged his nails down the sensitive skin on my sides.

I trembled with desire.

My head swam. Pain made me lightheaded. I was going to pass out, but I didn't want it to end.

He tweaked my nipples, and my back arched.

A door slammed.

Metal scraped against metal as the shower curtain was ripped open to reveal two towering men who barely fit in the narrow bathroom.

I pulled myself away from Scorpius and slumped on the other side of the tub gasping for air. Bergamot and musk tingled across my lips.

"What in the holy fucking sun god is going on in here?" Malum scowled down at us. Orion stood beside him with wide eyes and a thoughtful expression on his face.

"We're fully clothed," I said as I awkwardly tried to climb over Scorpius's limbs and get out of the tub.

The blind king reached out and grabbed me. He didn't let me move.

"You dared to let him touch you without us present?" Malum asked angrily, flames dancing atop his shaved head as he glared at us with disgust like we'd been caught cheating.

I choked.

Scorpius's voice was razor-sharp. "I've told you before

not to speak to her like that. Get fucking control of yourself or get out."

Malum turned and slammed his fist into the bathroom mirror. "What else happened between the two of you while we were gone? It sure as shit didn't look like nothing." He gestated wildly.

Both he and Orion were covered head to toe in streaks of vibrant red.

"You don't have any visible wounds," I said slowly. "Where have you been? Whose blood are you covered in?"

Malum smirked, and Orion's eyes filled with guilt.

"Whose blood is that?" I repeated.

Malum countered, "What have you and Scorpius been doing for the last eight hours?"

"We were fucking." I climbed out of the tub and elbowed past the kings. "It was filthy, and I came five times."

Malum made a sound that was somewhere between a dying cow and a screaming goat.

"Actually," I tossed over my shoulder. "Ten times."

Malum whimpered.

Orion reached for me, and I skirted around him pointedly, then slammed the bathroom door closed behind me. Malum bellowed on the other side.

"Why do you keep antagonizing him?" Vegar asked, and Zenith shot him a glare like he wasn't supposed to speak to me.

They were sitting on the floor playing a card game, and the twins were asleep in their beds.

I shrugged. "Because he deserves it."

The demons nodded like my answer was acceptable and said, "Good work."

I saluted them and climbed into my bunk.

Sleep claimed me quickly.

That night, I dreamed of a handsome, blind devil with a voice like sin, whose nails dug into my skin as he ravished me. He whispered huskily in my ear and promised to kill for me.

In my dream, I thanked him.

CHAPTER 25
ARAN
WAR

AMOK (ADJECTIVE): possessed with or motivated by a murderous or violently uncontrollable frenzy.

DAY 14, HOUR 7

Last night, the scouting angels had returned with the coordinates for another ungodly settlement.

Today, we went to war.

Snow fell in thick chunks as we marched through the quiet forest.

"I'm going to steal Scorpius and Orion from you," I whispered to Malum, just to terrorize him.

He scoffed beside me. "Please, we both know any relationship with them means you're one step closer to being mine."

"You're delusional," I whispered as I discreetly inhaled his tobacco whiskey scent.

A vein pulsed on his forehead.

He leaned down, and his breath was hot against my ear.

"Stop pretending with the twins. It's pathetic—we both know you belong to me."

My hands curled into fists. "That's my future *husbands* you're talking about." He was so high-handed that it was infuriating.

Flames whooshed as they jumped off his arms. "Stop fucking saying that," he said darkly. "They will *never* have that title."

I rolled my pipe between my lips. "Are you sure about that?" I drawled.

His jaw clenched. "Yes."

I shivered as the storm picked up. "I wouldn't bet on it," I whispered. The twins walked in front of me and formed a protective wall. Darkness shimmered around them.

Malum's voice was rough like broken glass. "I would."

I narrowed my eyes at the twins' darkness. It seemed to form a shape on their heads, but I couldn't discern the object.

"What would you bet?" I asked mindlessly.

Malum answered immediately, "My soul."

We walked the rest of the way in silence.

I unraveled at the seams.

The battle raged.

The world devolved into shades of black and pain.

Smoke.

Screams.

Pleas.

Women and men bellowed as we murdered them.

A bear shifter roared, and the sound reverberated menacingly down the dark corridor.

Demons swung swords made of nightmares.

Crystal wings clattered as the angels hovered along the ceiling and struck from above.

Pincers slashed desperately. Hands grabbed helplessly.

An enchanted blade sliced through an ungodly carapace.

Red poured from flesh.

Green gore splattered.

This settlement was like the last. It was a maze of dark, twisting corridors, false walls, and sprawling rooms where the battles spilled into.

These infected also had enchanted swords. Little good it did them.

We hunted them through the halls.

The Necklace of Death pulsed with energy against my chest bone like a heartbeat.

I tripped as a body slammed against me.

John grabbed my arm and pulled me off the wall that I didn't remember leaning against.

"Focus, Arabella!" Malum shouted harshly. "Don't you dare lose us again."

I fought numbly.

Jinx's voice garbled in the back of my skull.

The twins flanked my front, and the kings flanked my back.

I spun and thrust, dodged a flying projectile, stabbed, decapitated, slaughtered. I did it all and felt nothing.

Time warped around me.

It was quiet.

My chest heaved from exertion. I was drenched with sweat and covered in disturbing substances.

The battle was over.

"Do you need help standing?" Scorpius asked.

"No." My voice was hoarse, and my lungs ached like I'd run for miles.

Sadie limped over and patted my back.

"Good work," Malum announced to the soldiers. "Let's stay together, exit the structure, and convene with our troops on the perimeters to make sure no ungodly escaped."

I blinked, and I was laying in my bunk.

A sheen of ice covered me, and I couldn't move.

I was frozen.

PART THREE
ECCEDENTESIAST

"Is it better to out-monster the monster or to be quietly devoured?"

—Nietzsche

CHAPTER 26
ARAN
FUNERALS

SEPULCHRE (NOUN): a place of burial; tomb.

DAY 18, HOUR 19

The funeral processed in the war camp's forest.

An enchanted camera flashed.

A line of witches stood off to the side and hummed a dark melody. Runes glowed on their skin. The ban on silence was temporarily lifted because an expensive timed enchantment had created a sound boundary.

Dick, Lothaire, and the cloaked man stood off to the side and watched with solemn faces.

Lyla performed the ceremony a few feet in front of us.

The rest of the soldiers stood apart.

Up close, the runes on Lyla's skin shone with a much brighter light than the runes on the other witches. Lyla practically glowed like a star, while the rest were muted. She pulsed with power.

The left side of my face prickled under the weight of

Lothaire's attention. Unlike everyone else, he wasn't watching Lyla perform the ceremony.

His jagged scar pulled tight as he frowned.

He stared at me.

"Keep up the good work," he mouthed silently.

I nodded back and tried to appear stronger than I was.

The witches hummed louder, their voices dropping to an eerily deep octave that no other creature could replicate.

Lyla spun a ball of energy between her hands.

The glow emanating off her intensified.

The High Court had returned to help us mourn. At least, that was the excuse they'd given when they RJE'd into the camp after we'd given our progress update on the last battle.

Sharp light blinded my corneas as another camera flashed.

They'd brought journalists with them from across the realms.

The funeral was a PR stunt.

Branches clattered in the frozen wind.

An enchanted broadcasting stone hovered high above our heads. Dick stooped like he was overcome with grief.

My stomach churned at his fake display.

He didn't care about soldiers.

The High Court only cared about themselves. They cared about their image and how the public perceived them.

The witches hummed. A camera shuttered and dots danced in my vision.

Snow fell softly, and the steaming dirt created the illusion of fog. The setting sun cast the pines in ominous shadows.

Lyla waved her arms and spun. Her green hair defied gravity as it lifted around her head, and the energy of the universe strummed around her in a display meant to inspire the viewers across the realms.

It was disturbing.

A witch hit a high note, and another hummed baritone. The sounds coalesced. Another camera flashed.

Fifty-nine soldiers stood behind me in the forest, as Lyla performed a silent funeral ceremony for the deceased.

Fifty-nine. An iniquitous number, indivisible by anything but itself and one.

It was an abomination.

We'd started the second battle with eighty-three soldiers. The strategy had been the same. To limit casualties, only the strongest had fought within the settlement, and the rest of the soldiers had secured the perimeter.

There'd been no deaths among the academy, shifter, angel, and assassin legions. Twenty of us had entered the infected settlement, and twenty of us had emerged.

We'd been unaware that dozens of ungodly were flooding out of a back entrance and trying to escape into the mountains.

Four leviathans and one devil had perished, which left only one devil in the legion. He was inconsolable.

He wasn't the only one.

Nineteen other soldiers had died holding the perimeter.

They'd given their lives and successfully stopped the ungodly from disappearing into the mountains. It was a small consolation.

We'd started with one hundred. Forty-one dead after two battles, and we had two more left; it didn't take a mathematician to recognize that we were doomed.

So.

Many.

Dead.

In front of me, runes glowed across Lyla's dark skin as she raised her hands above her head, palms together, in the gesticulation of eternal energy flowing through the universe. It was the ancient sign of death, symbolic of how a soul lifted above a body and rose into the valley of the sun god.

The weight of eyes prickled across the back of my neck as soldiers watched me.

I stood apart from the rest.

The High Court had requested that I partake in the ceremony to help raise morale and demonstrate leadership.

Their request had come in the form of an order.

Dick had pulled me aside in the strategy room and said I was a symbol of hope across the realms.

Apparently, it was widely known and accepted that the fae queen had manifested both fae and angel abilities. Her power was the stuff of legends.

The problem was she didn't exist. It was all a ruse.

The headlines apparently loved that the fae queen was best friends with a powerful shifter from the beast realm.

Dick pulled me aside earlier and told me that I united the realms like no one ever had before.

Now in the snowy forest, Lyla extended her arms forward so her pressed-together palms were pointed directly at my heart and the energy of the dead was directed toward my soul.

The witch stared at me.

I stared down at the steaming dirt.

She pulled her hands apart and turned over her palms.

Something tugged inside my chest and expanded, then sizzled into nothingness like I was leaking from the inside.

Lyla's eyes widened, and she took a step away from me. She opened her mouth like fate itself was going to ask me a question, but no sound escaped her lips. Instead, she lowered her glowing arms to her sides and stood perfectly still.

She glanced over at Dick, and then back to me, like she

wanted to tell me something but couldn't because he was present.

Her expression was horrified.

Ice dripped off my fingers.

Finally, the ceremony ended. An RJE device swirled as Dick, Lothaire, the cloaked man, Lyla, the other witches, and the journalist all disappeared.

Branches rustled.

It was eerily quiet in the aftermath of the humming.

The snow picked up and the sky darkened.

The realm's weather was unpredictable, and blizzards arrived with no warning.

My teeth chattered.

The soldiers realized the funeral service was over, and they hurried back to their barracks. No one wanted to linger in a storm.

Suddenly, I felt death's familiar presence lingering in the shadows of the towering pines. He was still haunting me.

He'd appeared when I was a child. The world had flat-lined into shades of gray, and I'd woken up with an unnatural chill and an emptiness in my soul.

Death stalked me.

"You're catastrophizing. It's not death that makes you feel empty." Jinx's voice was loud and crisp in my head.

I stumbled with surprise and barely kept myself upright. Snow gathered on my eyelashes, and my eyes burned from the icy wind as I looked around the forest. Jax carried Jinx on his back as they walked down the path away from me.

The blizzard intensified.

"Then what makes me feel this way?" I asked back tiredly.

Silence.

"Take a deep breath." Scorpius stepped forward from the

shadows. "It might feel like you're trapped, but you're not. I promise."

"How do you know?" I asked.

He held out his hand. "Because you're not alone anymore."

I reached forward and took the lifeline. Calloused fingers grounded me.

The numbness receded.

"Thank you," I whispered up at the blind king as we walked together down the snowy path.

"Anytime, Aran."

CHAPTER 27
ARAN
SHOPPING

BETISE (NOUN): an act of foolishness or stupidity.

DAY 20, HOUR 7

I hadn't slept since the funeral, and exhaustion had transformed me into a jittery mess of adrenaline.

Slumped over in the cafeteria, face hovering inches above my full plate, my breath came out as a frosty puff.

My food froze.

I was suffering from sleep deprivation.

"Have a bite of my fruit," John said as he pushed a non-frozen mango toward me and rubbed my back comfortingly.

"Thanks," I said as I took it from him.

Luka's fingers tangled in my long curls, and he scooted his chair closer, so our legs were pressed together. He didn't comment, just grabbed more of my hair like he was holding on for dear life.

Malum glared at me across the table.

I leaned over and gave John a soft kiss on the cheeks. "Thanks again," I whispered. "For looking after me."

He smiled tenderly back and said, "Of course. No need to thank me."

I turned back to the table and naturally, Malum was on fire.

Scarlet flames danced across his wide bronze shoulders.

I leaned forward and enjoyed the heat.

Scorpius ran his tongue over his lips, and Orion stared at me with wide, unblinking eyes. Luka's fingers twisted around more curls, and John gave me another soft kiss on the cheek.

I smiled at Malum.

His eyes flashed as he glared at where the twins were touching me.

"You have soup on your face." I pointed my frozen spoon at him.

He frowned and wiped at his cheek.

"Got ya," I chortled.

His expression promised unspeakable pain. I smiled and ate my mango. He stabbed his knife through his meat like he had a vendetta against it.

"Why are you so agitated?" I asked with feigned innocence.

His knife snapped in his hand. "You seem to let everyone kiss you these days."

I stilled. "Are you calling me a whore?"

"Of course not," he said. "Just making an observation."

"Well, don't," I said with a fake smile. "Men should be seen, not heard. Remember that."

Cobalt ice crawled across the table toward him and coated his plate. He brought a flaming fist down over the ice and it melted with a sizzle.

"I'll keep that in mind," Malum said darkly.

I replied with falsetto sweetness, "Make you sure you do."

"Oh, I will."

"Good."

"Perfect."

"Marvelous."

"Stupendous."

"Extraordinary."

Malum didn't say anything, and I flipped him off with both hands. "I won, suck on that."

Flames shot higher into the air and the temperature at the table increased.

"What's happening right now?" John asked with confusion.

Scorpius replied, "Honestly, I don't want to know."

John chuckled. "That makes two of us."

"Are you laughing at me?" Scorpius's expression twisted with anger.

"What?" John looked around. "Why would you think that?"

Scorpius slapped the table and plates rattled. "Answer the question!"

John jumped in his chair. "Um, I-I—"

"I'm just messing with you." Scorpius smirked and leaned back in his chair with his arms behind his head, biceps flexed.

John looked at me for support.

"Men," I mouthed as I shrugged.

He frowned back.

Across the table, Malum continued to burn like a malfunctioning flame thrower. Orion shared a long-suffering look with Luka, and John discreetly checked out Scorpius's impressively sculpted arms.

Suddenly, I was the most normal person at the table.

I went to take a sip of my water, but a block of ice hit my face. *Oops.*

Okay, maybe we all had our quirks.

"Are you ready?" Sadie yelled across the room, and I welcomed the distraction from all the testosterone in the air.

She sauntered over from the table where her mates were still eating.

I narrowed my eyes at her. "What are you talking about?"

The remaining soldiers trickled out the door, and the cafeteria was mostly empty.

Sadie smacked the back of my head. Hard.

"Hey, what was that for?" I rubbed at the back of my most likely concussed head. She'd definitely used her cat strength, because it felt like getting bludgeoned by a chair.

I twisted around to glare at my best friend.

Sadie smirked. "I just wanted to hit you."

I tried to punch her in the tit, but she dodged.

She waggled her eyebrows up and down. "All right, my beautiful, perfect ray of sunshine." She clapped her hands together. "As your best friend, I've decided that we're going shopping to take your mind off of—" She waved her hand casually in the air as she looked for a noun, then settled on, "—things."

"You're not her best friend," John said.

Malum burned hotter. "She's not *your* anything," he said fiercely. "She's mine."

"Ours," Scorpius corrected, and Orion nodded.

Luka's fingers tangled deeper in my curls.

Sadie and I ignored the men as we stared at each other.

A smile spread across my lips, "that's the smartest thing you've ever said."

"Also, can we get our nails done?" Sadie asked.

"Obviously." I smiled wider. "It's like I've always said, give me healthy cuticles or give me death."

She nodded with a serious expression. "You have always said that. I really respect that about you."

We high-fived each other.

Cobra sauntered over and asked, "When are we going to the mall?"

Sadie frowned up at him. "Do you think you're any fun to shop with? Last time we went, you spent six hours in a weapons store and refused to look at a single piece of clothing—then you shot the store clerk because he wouldn't give you a discount."

Cobra's eyes flashed. "False. I got the gun for ninety percent off."

"Because you *shot* the man in his private area," Sadie argued.

"Are you surprised by his behavior?" I looked at Cobra's black sweatsuit and shuddered. "Look how he dresses. It's disturbing."

"What the fuck does my sweatshirt have to do with anything?" Cobra looked down at himself. "We're wearing the same issued clothes."

I studied my nails. "There's a huge difference between me and you. I do not wear these rags by *choice*. Also, I'd like to use this time to bring up that I've always thought you dressed hideously."

Luckily, Jax was walking over because he grabbed Cobra as he lunged at me.

"Perfect." Sadie did a little dance. "I already have the RJE device ready to go. We can go to the beast realm shops that we loved before. Mitch is the one who gave me the idea earlier, so everyone is cool with it."

"Really?" I struggled to process what was happening. "Mitch wanted to go shopping? And he told *you*?"

I've entered into an alternate dimension.

Sadie played with her white hair and said, "Technically, Mitch said *you* would want to go shopping. But he asked me to bring it up to the group without saying it was his idea."

"My name is not Mitch," Mitch said as he slammed his cup down on the table.

"Don't you dare raise your voice at her," Xerxes said as he walked over with Ascher. He withdrew his knives and death glared at the leader of the kings.

"Let's go. We can talk shit about the kings and the patriarchy as we try on shoes." Sadie grabbed my arm and tried to pull me out of my seat.

Key word being "tried."

I had at least fifty pounds of muscle on her, and it was frankly disturbing how weak she was. I made a mental note to make her do more push-ups again.

"Do you want us to come with you?" Luka offered, then broke into a coughing fit.

I startled as I realized he had dark circles under his eyes that rivaled Scorpius's. He'd been talking to me through the sleepless nights, which meant he also was extremely sleep-deprived.

Guilt gnawed at my stomach.

"No, if I go shopping, you two need to sleep. I've been keeping you up for days. Use it as a chance to rest—please." I pushed the unruly curls off Luka's forehead and gave him a gentle kiss on the cheek.

Malum growled like a wild animal.

Luka stared at me like he was trying to read my mind, then nodded. "I'll miss you," he whispered.

I gave him a shy smile. "Same."

Malum made a gagging noise and Orion hit him.

"I would argue, but frankly, I'm dead on my feet," John said grudgingly as he continued to rub my back in soothing circles. He pulled my hair to the side and gave me a kiss on the back of my neck. "I want all the details when you get back."

I melted into his embrace. "Of course," I promised.

"Yay, let's do this!" Sadie punched me in the side. I struggled to breathe.

Across the table, Jinx made the sign of the devil.

I blew her a kiss as we RJE'd away.

"Just so you know, sir—most men get a clear coat of gloss," the nail technician said to Malum. She winked and leaned into his personal space.

"Don't care," he said gruffly as he looked over at me. "I want the one called 'destined nights.'" He held up the navy bottle that he'd spent almost an hour searching for. "It's the color of Arabella's eyes."

The woman made a breathy noise. "You're so devoted. What a lucky woman." She fluttered her eyelashes up at him.

"You're embarrassing me," I mouthed across the room at him.

He smirked wickedly, then settled back into the enchanted massage chair that the five of us were sitting in. We were all getting mani-pedis done at the same time.

Me, Sadie, Malum, Orion, and Scorpius.

Sadie's mates had wandered off to look at weapons, and I'd encouraged the kings to go with them, since only one of them needed to stay with me, but they'd all refused to leave.

Which was why shifter nail technicians, both men and women, were currently twittering over the devils. For each devil, two people were massaging their legs, while another did their nails.

Meanwhile, Sadie and I each only had one worker.

Apparently, we were not impressive enough to be fawned over. *Disappointing.*

You'd think the shifters had never seen a seven-foot-tall flaming man before?

A male technician grabbed Scorpius's bicep and squeezed like he was checking out his strength. The blind devil frowned and furrowed his brow like he was trying to figure out if that was a normal part of a mani-pedi.

I snorted and flopped back in my chair.

Closing my eyes, I grimaced as the woman attacked the thick calluses on my feet. She kept mumbling under her breath about disgusting blisters and smacking my foot with a brush like I was a wild animal.

I debated asking her to stop hitting me but couldn't find the courage.

"What are you getting done?" I asked Sadie, as I tried to distract myself from the torture happening between my toes.

"Something understated and classy."

"Smart choice," I said.

An hour later, I admired my glossy-short black nails. They were perfect for battle.

"What do you think?" Sadie waved four-inch-long rhine-stone-covered acrylic nails through the air.

"Cute," I said. "Good thing we're not fighting in a war."

She narrowed her eyes. "I can't tell if you're being sarcastic or not."

"Think about it." I patted her head and walked away towards where the men were seated.

"Wait, Aran!" Sadie called after me. "I can't tie my shoelaces with my nails."

I ignored her and glared down at the kings, all three of

which were still getting their legs massaged an hour later. Sadie and I had gotten ours for fifteen minutes.

"Really?" I asked with exasperation as I stared down at the atrocity that was Malum's feet. "First, why are your toes so freakishly large? Second, what in the realms made you do that?"

He oozed male satisfaction.

A woman squealed behind me as she looked at his toes, and then there was a thud as if she'd fallen out of her chair.

He had the audacity to wink.

I prayed for patience.

"What do you think?" he asked gruffly.

I stared at the man who had voluntarily gotten "Arabella" spelled out across eight of his toenails. It was white letters on top of dark blue polish. He also had snowflakes on his pinky toes.

"That is stalkerish and creepy," I finally said.

He admired his feet. "I like them."

Exasperated, I turned to the other kings. "We all match," Orion whispered with a smirk as he wiggled his glossy black nails.

Scorpius snapped, "Do mine look good? Someone tell me." He sounded gruff, but he curled his fingers self-consciously, like he was embarrassed that he couldn't see for himself.

"They look good," Orion and I reassured him at the same time.

"Thanks." He sighed with relief.

I leaned over and patted his arm. "Seriously, they look great. I really like black on you. I think it's your color."

He grunted and dragged his hands through his matching hair. A small smile curled the edges of his lips.

"Getting your name was more impressive," Malum announced confidently.

Everyone ignored him.

A few minutes later—after I'd tipped my nail technician generously and thanked her again for her amazing service, tied Sadie's shoelaces for her, and redone her ponytail because she couldn't—we left the salon.

"Wait," a woman called after us, and we stopped in the middle of the mall.

She blushed prettily and held out a slip of paper for Malum, then she turned and ran back into the salon.

All five of us gathered around the slip.

It was a drawing of a stick-figure on fire, inside a heart. A house address was written below the picture in big loopy handwriting and said, "Visit me anytime you want."

I pointed at it. "I like how she drew the eyes looking in two-different directions. She really captured your manic energy."

"She's so real for that," Sadie said.

Malum frowned. "I'm sure that was an error."

"I don't know," Orion whispered. "It seems pretty accurate to me."

Scorpius laughed.

Sadie pulled me down to her level and growled into my ear, "If he goes, I can kill him for you. I can make it clean. No evidence. Easy—only fourteen small payments, subject to twenty-percent interest."

I rolled my eyes and yanked away from her.

"If I was going to kill someone, I'd do it myself," I said. "Also, I can't believe you wouldn't do it for free. We're supposed to be best friends."

She scoffed and blew on her ridiculous nails. "Please, I've got to make a living somehow."

I rolled my eyes at her antics.

There was a burning sound, and we pulled away from each other.

The paper went up in flames between Malum's fingers, and he smirked at me like he'd proven something.

"Damn it," Sadie swore. "There goes my business."

"You're canceled," I said to her, then I turned to Malum. "And you're still not forgiven."

He bared his teeth, navy fingernails dancing with fire. "But I will be, and then you'll be mine."

"Ours," Scorpius corrected as he gripped Malum by the back of his neck. "She'll be *ours*."

"Ours," Orion whispered in agreement.

Sadie nodded. "She's *our* special Aran."

The men scowled at her.

I walked away.

CHAPTER 28

ARAN

MORE SHOPPING

ANHEDONIA (NOUN): a psychological condition characterized by inability to experience pleasure in normally pleasurable acts.

DAY 20, HOUR 9

"You can't come in here," I hissed as the kings slipped inside the cloth curtains of the narrow dressing room.

I was half-naked, clothed only in my bra and the miniskirt I was trying on.

Silver eyes hardened to steel. "You're never allowed to wear that in public." Malum trailed his eyes across my body, like he was devouring me with his gaze.

My heart rate increased.

I put my hands on my hips and whispered furiously, "Get out. This is *highly* inappropriate."

Scorpius glided forward and grabbed my waist with both his hands. "Shhhh," he whispered. "Let me feel." He dragged his hands upward across my abs.

Things were escalating.

Pain streaked across my back, and I swallowed a whimper.

I meant to push him away.

I meant to stand my ground.

Scorpius's long, elegant fingers trailed mercilessly up to my chest. He pushed my bra up and made a harsh noise as he cupped my chest with his hands.

My knees knocked together, and my head spun with pleasure.

Orion moved closer.

So did Malum.

The three kings crowded me against the ice covered mirror.

I shivered.

Scorpius plucked at my nipples as Orion claimed my mouth in a fierce kiss.

I drowned in whiskey, tobacco, chocolate-covered raspberries, bergamot, and musk.

They were intoxicating.

"Don't be cold," Malum whispered as he dragged flaming hands gently over my body. "I got you."

The three men devoured me.

It was overwhelming.

Overstimulating.

Pain and pleasure rose to impossible heights.

Scorpius muttered, "I just need a taste," then he leaned forward and took my nipple into his mouth. As he scraped his teeth against my sensitive flesh, I whimpered into Orion's openmouthed kisses.

Malum tangled his fingers in my curls and yanked my head back, so my spine was arched.

Orion didn't break the kiss; his lips were soft, and his tongue was merciless.

As the men worshipped me, I reached out blindly.

My hands grabbed Malum's hardness, and I stroked him through his sweatpants. I could barely get my hand around him. His heat burned through the fabric, and I squeezed.

Scorpius laved at my chest.

Malum whispered against the shell of my ear, "Good fucking girl." He nipped at my sensitive flesh and ordered, "Stroke me harder."

My vision warped with pleasure, and everything became heady.

An unfamiliar warmth spread through my chest.

My skin tingled.

There were noises nearby as people entered the changing room, and Malum whispered in my ear, "You better be quiet, or you'll get us in trouble."

"Do you need help in there?" a female attendant called outside my curtain.

Malum whispered, "You better answer her."

Orion stopped kissing me, and his hands dragged up my thigh and pushed my panties to the side.

Orion stroked across my clit as Scorpius sucked on my nipple.

"Answer," Malum ordered.

"N-N-No," I stuttered breathlessly. "I'm good."

"Okay, let me know if you need help," the woman called as she walked away. Scorpius sucked harder, and Orion put his hand over my mouth.

I moaned against his fingers.

Scorpius pulled away and moved to the side so his mates could have access to my body.

Malum's hardness jerked against my hand, and then he pulled away to tug down his sweatpants. Orion's pupils were blown wide as he kept one hand over my mouth and took

Malum's impressive girth in his other. He guided it toward me.

Malum cupped my pussy and spread me wide. "Fuck, you're dripping." His voice was an octave deeper.

Orion dragged the head of Malum's obscene cock teasingly through my heat.

Slowly.

I forgot how to breathe.

Sun god, I wanted him inside me.

As my pleasure reached new heights, the pain streaking down my spine became unbearable.

The agony brought clarity. I remembered that being intimate with the kings would complete the soul bond. We'd be mated for life.

Not like this.

My knees gave out, and I shoved at the men. "Please stop," I begged as I grimaced and pushed them away.

The kings immediately staggered back.

"Are you okay?" Orion whispered with concern. Malum's silver eyes were wide and frantic as he tucked himself away. Scorpius scrunched his face with worry.

"I'm fine." I smoothed down my skirt and struggled to catch my breath. "I don't want to bond, not like this…in a dressing room."

Malum blushed as he rubbed the back of his neck. "That wasn't what we were doing."

I arched my brow at him and tried to look classy as I stuffed my boobs back into my bra. "Then what were you doing?"

I tried not to glance below his belt.

"We just wanted a moment alone with you," Orion whispered. "It's rare that all three of us are together with free time."

"Some moment," I whispered as I tried to get control of myself.

I was flustered.

"Things escalated unexpectedly," Scorpius conceded as he reached into Orion's pants and adjusted his dick for him.

The quiet king jerked his hips and groaned roughly.

Scorpius licked his lips and pumped him before he pulled away and licked precum off his fingers.

"Fuck, don't do that," Malum groaned as he fisted himself. "You three are going to be the death of me."

I bit down on my inner cheek and tore my gaze away from the disheveled kings. They were incredibly tempting, but the pain pulsing down my spine was like a bucket of cold water.

"We can revisit this conversation later." I pushed against the men.

It was like shoving a brick wall.

"Get out," I hissed. "I don't want to get in trouble."

My stomach clenched at the memory of what we'd almost done, and I felt faint from arousal.

Malum looked unimpressed. "If anyone gives you trouble, we'll kill them. Don't worry about that."

"Get out!" I shoved him with all my might.

"We're going, relax," he said as he straightened his clothes and raked a hand over his shaved head.

When I was alone, I collapsed against the wall and closed my eyes as I rode out the pain still shooting down my spine.

I stretched and jogged in place.

Finally, I worked up the courage to leave.

I found the men a few minutes later browsing through the department store.

My face flushed when I saw them.

I couldn't believe what we'd almost just done.

"Are you okay, sweetheart?" Orion mouthed, lashes fluttering with concern. "Do you need us to get you water?"

A soft melody played throughout the store.

"I'm good," I said with a confidence I didn't feel as I smiled at him reassuringly.

He gave me a soft smile back.

Silver eyes narrowed with exasperation, and Malum ruined the nice moment. "You are clearly not well. You had some sort of panic attack five seconds ago. You seemed to be in pain." His voice was rougher than usual and tinged with concern. "What happened?"

I scowled up at him. "Nothing, I just realized I didn't want to mate in a *public* dressing room."

It wasn't a lie, after all.

"That's not the full truth." Scorpius's concerned expression turned hostile, and he took a step closer. The harsh planes of his face scrunched up. "Her breathing was suddenly choppy, like she was in agony—something happened back there. Are you injured?"

Scorpius and Malum immediately patted me down like they were searching for hidden wounds.

"I'm fine," I said with feigned calmness as I extracted myself from the men. "You have nothing to worry about."

My smile was so fake it hurt.

The kings didn't look convinced.

I gave them a thumbs-up.

Malum frowned harder.

"Done acting like a little bitch?" Cobra asked as he walked past with his arms full of leather jackets. Jax shook his head in exasperation as he followed behind his shifter mates.

Grateful for the distraction, I called after Cobra, "You'll look like a clown in those jackets."

"Um, so how can we help you shop?" Malum asked as he walked up behind us, and it took me a second to process what he'd said. "We want to help you feel better," he repeated, softer this time like he was embarrassed the shifters were listening. His bronze cheekbones flushed.

Cobra said something rude under his breath, and Jax looked at the king with pity. Meanwhile, Ascher and Xerxes were arguing over who would look better in a pair of jeans.

The upscale department store gleamed with marble and fancy finishings. It was sprawling with sections for every type of clothing imaginable. Neon signs hung in the air, showcasing high-fashion shifter models.

There were a handful of shoppers and fancy-dressed salesclerks, who stared at the towering kings with open interest, but for the most part, the store was empty.

I shrugged. "Fine, you can hold my clothes for me," I said to Malum.

Instead of blanching like I expected, he nodded with a serious expression and sidled closer as I handed him my mini skirt that he'd been defiling a few minutes earlier.

"We'll also help," Orion whispered, as he and Scorpius moved closer.

Sadie held up a jean jacket with rhinestones. "Is this cute?" Her nails were so long that she struggled to hold the hanger.

Closing my eyes, I prayed for inner peace and mental strength. Then I turned to my best friend and said, "Do you want the truth?"

She nodded with a big smile.

I ripped it from her hands, put it back on the rack, and hissed under my breath, "Stop being so tacky. If it has rhinestones on it, it's an automatic no." I pulled her down the aisle. "Try to search for high-quality fabrics and *real* diamonds. We are *high-quality* women."

"Are we really?" Sadie asked with narrowed eyes.

I pursed my lips. "Not if you purchase that jacket."

Sadie nodded with a big smile.

I might not be feeling my best (my back still hurt), but that didn't mean I was going to purchase tacky clothes.

Some things were sacred.

I had a reputation.

Two hours later, the kings had their hands full of shoe boxes, miniskirts, and a fluffy white sweatshirt I couldn't wait to wear.

Sadie and I had decided at the beginning of the trip that we'd focus on purchasing necessities.

She held up a third sparkly real-diamond thong with a silver *S* that sat over the butt crack. "Do I need this?"

I sucked on my pipe and exhaled a cloud of smoke. "What do you think?"

She shrugged. She was helpless without me.

"*Obviously*," I drawled in an imitation of Jinx. "It has real diamonds and silk."

She squealed with delight and placed the thong on top of the sheer dress and thigh-high boots Jax was carrying for her. Necessities meant slutty clothes made from quality fabrics that we could wear to get absolutely obliterated in for the next party at Elite Academy.

I wanted men to look at me and be *disturbed* by how hot I looked.

I wanted men to be *scared* of how much of a slut I was.

That was the goal.

"Do they have an *A*?" I asked, and Sadie nodded as she picked up a matching thong for me and placed it on top of Malum's full arms.

"How about an *M*?"

She handed it to me, and I held the tiny scrap of fabric up to the light. "Malum, how big do you think your butt crack is? Thirty-two inches?"

There was a sizzling noise as the fabric caught fire.

"Absolutely not," he said harshly.

I stared at the eviscerated fabric in disbelief. "You're paying for that."

"Fine," Malum said as he pulled me away from the table.

"Also, you never answered the question." I held my hands up in front of my face. "This long?" I pulled them apart. "Tell me when to stop."

He stared at me in silence.

My mouth dropped open. "That big? That can't be healthy."

If his silver eyes could have killed me, I'd have been dead.

"You're a menace when you shop," he said as he pulled me away from the nipple tassel section.

I put my hand over my heart. "Thank you."

He dragged me towards the checkout counter where the rest of our group was headed.

Orion placed a black hoodie with a skull on top of Malum's full arms, then draped his arm across my shoulder. He radiated warmth, and my mouth watered for chocolate-dipped raspberries.

He pressed a quick kiss to my temple and pain shot down my still sensitive spine.

I jolted.

Orion released me. Scorpius stopped petting a fuzzy coat, and his head snapped in my direction. "Why did you make a pained noise?"

"Uh, I didn't." I shuffled closer to Sadie for protection.

Unfortunately, that meant I was closer to Cobra. He was

wearing a new floor length leather jacket and jewel-rimmed sunglasses even though we were inside.

"You look ridiculous," I said.

He bared his dagger-sharp canines and hissed like a snake.

"Cute," I drawled as we all moved to the check out.

"Oh wow, are you the don's son?" The man at the checkout counter tittered as Jax dumped the pile of Sadie's clothes down.

Cobra's smirk turned into a frown as he glared at the worker. "No."

The jewels embedded in his skin flashed into shadow snakes, and he radiated aggression as he threatened, "Don't look at any of us."

Cobra lunged forward threateningly, and the worker gulped as he stared at the counter and stuttered, "O-O-Of course, sir. We p-p-pride ourselves on the utmost discretion for our high-quality shoppers."

Sadie chuckled and leaned over to me. "That's us." She wiggled her eyebrows at me.

Who was going to tell her?

After all the shifter's clothes purchases were wrapped up in tissue paper, Xerxes sauntered forward and pressed his thumb to the screen to pay.

The screen lit up, and his net worth was displayed. There were eight zeros.

Show-off.

The worker got flustered when he saw how rich Xerxes was and gave him his business card and a free cologne. Xerxes graciously took the card and smiled at the man. Since he'd grown up in the upper crust of shifter society, he was used to people fawning over his wealth.

Finally, when my clothes were wrapped up, I leaned forward to place my thumb on the enchanted pad.

Flaming fingers grabbed my forearm and stopped me.

"I got this," Malum said he pressed his down.

I rolled my eyes and blew out a cloud of smoke. "Whatever." Scorpius and Orion stood next to me, smirking like they had a secret, and I made a point of ignoring them.

"S-S-Sir," the worker stuttered, and Malum shifted to the side.

Thirteen zeros filled the screen, and more were listed, but they were cut off by the edge of the monitor.

The worker gaped up at Malum with wide eyes like he was in the presence of a god, and I scoffed as the kings smirked. Nothing upset me more than seeing a male filled with confidence.

As we walked out of the store, Malum's rough voice whispered in my ear, "The House of Malum is ancient and illustrious. Are you sure you don't want to be our mate? We can go back to the dressing room right now."

I blew smoke into his face and rolled my eyes. "Your money means nothing to me. I have my own."

Surprisingly, it wasn't Malum who responded. Orion whispered in my other ear, "Whatever you need to tell yourself, sweetheart." His tone turned seductive. "Just imagine how much shopping you could do."

Scorpius took the bags from my hands and smirked.

I inhaled smoke angrily as the three pompous, apparently filthy-rich devil kings escorted me through the mall. They thought they'd proven something with their little display.

Too bad for them, I was not swayed by the hollowness of materialism. Okay, only a little. Fine, I had a shopping addiction.

Sue me, I liked cute clothes.

There were worse things in the world. For example, I could have a drug addiction. I stared down at the pipe in my hand. *Never mind.*

As we walked through the mall, I fantasized about all the cute new outfits I could wear.

It was going great, until I saw the wall.

My vision blurred.

I forgot how to breathe.

CHAPTER 29

CORVUS MALUM
PUBLIC DEVOTION

ACEDIA (NOUN): apathy, boredom.

DAY 20, HOUR 16

She stood unnaturally still. Pale skin was flushed a sickly gray.

Mesmerizing navy eyes were wide with horror as she gaped at the enchanted billboard that listed the High Court news. The floor beneath her feet was shiny with black ice.

The temperature in the mall plummeted.

Shifters moved around her, unaware.

Women and men—arms overflowing with shopping bags —chatted and laughed as they stopped to read the billboard, then moved on to make more useless purchases.

Clad in all black, Arabella was an immovable force among sheep. She was different from them all.

Harder.

Colder.

Stronger.

She was so frustrating that I wanted to strangle her; she

was also so beautiful that I wanted to burn the world for daring to hurt her, myself included.

I couldn't stop thinking about how she'd melted beneath the three of us in the dressing room. She'd played with my cock like it was hers. *It was.*

Sun god, I wanted to do depraved things to her.

Flushing with heat, I focused on thinking about Dick and Lothaire naked until my erection deflated.

My mind wondered to what Arabella had written in the truth journal. She thought our relationship was toxic, which meant my Revered hated being around me.

The aching hollowness in my chest expanded.

I could feel her slipping through my fingers.

She shared glances with my mates and seemed to open up to them, but with me, she was a blizzard.

Unrelentingly frozen.

My worst fears had come true. I'd found my Revered, and she hated me, and I had no one to blame but myself.

"Move," I snapped at a male shifter who walked in front of me and blocked my view of Arabella.

The man stuttered with outrage, and I shoved him aside.

He glanced up at my face, and his scorned expression morphed into fear. He hurried away into the crowded mall, running like he was on fire.

I scoffed.

I'd give him something to really run from.

"Don't torment the pathetic shifters," Scorpius drawled in my ear as his fingers wrapped around the back of my neck and squeezed.

Orion walked up to my other side and whispered, "Do you think she's going to forgive us?"

He stared at our Revered with wide, unblinking eyes. Unlike Scorpius, he probably hadn't noticed the shifter that

I'd shoved to the ground, because he was solely focused on Arabella at all times.

I took a deep, calming breath and drew strength from my Protectors.

All of us were together.

We still had a chance to fix this.

She'd just been writhing beneath us and moaning with pleasure.

"Yes," I said with a confidence I didn't feel and dropped the pile of bags for them to carry.

Cracking my neck back and forth like I was getting loose for battle, I slowly approached Arabella. I stood beside her, facing forward. We were about a foot apart.

Minutes passed.

Neither of us spoke.

With painstaking slowness, I sidled closer.

Inch by inch.

She shivered and subconsciously swayed toward my warmth. A soft sigh of relief released through her parted lips, and I couldn't hold back my smirk. Smugness filled the chasm in my chest.

I was serving my Revered.

I fought the urge to release my flames and scorch the mall to the ground. It would fill me with joy to burn all the useless shifters just to give her warmth. My fingertips tingled as flames danced and the urge to explode mounted.

I smiled as I imagined how good it would feel, scarlet pouring onto the marble floors. I bared my teeth as a shifter swore and stumbled away from me. Exhilaration filled me.

She would never forgive you.

My smile dropped.

The flames extinguished.

As the mall buzzed around us, I stood silently beside my

Revered and studied the scrolling neon words like I hadn't worked with the High Court on each sentence.

"Why?" Arabella whispered so quietly that I almost missed it.

I turned and stared at her side profile.

My Revered was breathtaking and fragile, and I would protect her from everyone who dared to harm her.

Her voice rose as she asked, "Why does it say that the Queen of the Fae is being courted by three handsome fae who have pledged to serve as her hounds, and why is there a picture of the three of you?"

She turned to glare at me, and her eyes were a shade of blue that was so fierce it was hard to maintain eye contact.

I held her gaze and took a step closer.

Using my size to overwhelm her personal space, I said, "Because we're your hounds and we're here to serve."

She tilted her head back. "You aren't fae."

"Neither are you, *Your Majesty*."

Her face scrunched. "Explain yourself. Why would you have this drivel published? What game are you playing?"

She stared up at me like I was manipulating her, and my hackles rose at the assumption that I was doing anything but protecting her. It was unacceptable that she was doubting my competency as her Ignis.

"There's a reason nobody knows the full truth about angels and devils." I shook my head. She was too smart to act this dumb.

Her eyes widened as she remembered those closest to the sun god were mostly hidden from the masses.

True power was unexpected.

How better to serve your god than to walk among the realms overpowered and overlooked?

I thumped my chest. "Now everyone in the fae realm

knows their queen has protectors. They will hesitate before they come for you."

Her lush lips parted, and she looked so angry it was adorable.

Lately words like *cute* and *sweet* were filtering into my internal vocabulary. There was something about her rage that amused me.

It was the reason I'd listened to that idiot Sadie and gotten Arabella's name written across my toes. She'd blushed prettily and sputtered when she'd saw what I'd done.

For a split second, before she'd rebuilt her shields, she'd looked at me with softness.

I'd do anything for that expression.

I uncrossed my arms and tried to sound calm. "I didn't lie. I'm your hound, and now everyone knows it. We'll stand in front of you as shields and serve you, in this war and beyond. We won't let anyone hurt you—ever."

She exhaled a cloud of smoke. "That's exactly why we'll never work."

"Excuse me?"

She grimaced. "You keep missing the point—I don't need anyone to protect me."

"It is fundamentally our role to protect you," I said with agitation. "You don't understand our culture."

"I got you a cinnamon pretzel." Sadie pushed past me and handed a sugary monstrosity to Arabella. "I couldn't remember if you ate butter, so I told them to not use it. Also, Cobra tried to take a bite, but I stabbed him with a plastic knife."

My Revered smiled at her idiotic whore of a friend and took the stupid pretzel like it was a priceless gift.

"Can we buy matching diamond push-up bras?" Sadie asked as she hugged her. "I was thinking it would raise our morale in battle if we knew we had them beneath our outfits."

"They're uniforms, not outfits," I corrected her idiotic ramblings.

"Or we could both free ball it," Sadie continued like I hadn't spoken. "Pro is we'll feel very empowered joining the free the nipple campaign. Con is that it might hurt if we get punched in the chest."

Instead of pushing Sadie away and telling her to stop her moronic drivel, Arabella's face lit up like she'd stepped in sunshine. "Amazing ideas. Great battle strategizing."

There it was.

My Revered's softness.

The problem was it wasn't for me. Sadie preened and tugged my Revered away from me. "Let's go to another store."

I imagined setting her white hair up in flames.

Arabella looked back at me, and her smile fell. "You don't understand *my* culture. I don't need shields. I just want friends who stand by my side." She turned her back to me and walked away.

I exhaled flames and the hollowness in my chest expanded.

If that was what she needed, I would show her I could be that man. Even if it killed me.

CHAPTER 30
ARAN
NECKLACE OF DEATH

DISCONSOLATE (ADJECTIVE): dejected, downcast.

DAY 22, HOUR 3

The men snored loudly in the dark room.

As per usual, their testosterone-addled brains, overinflated senses of self-worth, and general delusion allowed them to sleep peacefully after a long day of disturbing everyone in public.

I was not so lucky.

Because of them, I'd seen things I could never forget.

At the mall, Malum had picked out a pair of expensive skull earrings and put them in his ears, which normally would not be concerning.

However, normal people had their ears pierced *before* they tried on earrings.

He hadn't.

The jeweler had gaped in horror as Malum waved his painted nails and grinned in the mirror. He'd said that he'd take the skulls while blood rolled down the sides of his neck.

Then Scorpius had sniffed the air creepily and sauntered over. He'd fingered the bloody jewels in his mate's ears and had immediately demanded a pair for himself, then he'd stabbed them through his lobes in solidarity. And since all men were lunatics, Orion didn't want to be left out, so he'd also pierced himself with a pair.

At this point, I'd had to walk away from them out of sheer embarrassment.

Now, lying in the bedroom, I shuddered thinking about how they were still wearing the bloody earrings.

The worst part—skull earrings and painted nails looked good on them. The accessories went well with their tattoos.

Sun god I'm screwed.

Snores echoed as I tossed and turned.

A blizzard raged outside. Wind howled and rattled the window and door, while snow somehow slipped through cracks and drifted inside.

Flurries swirled inside the room, and the flakes gathered on my face.

The men slept peacefully.

I shivered.

Wide awake.

Luka's arm was hanging over the edge of the bunk above, and my right hand was reaching up, tangled in his grasp. My fingers tingled from loss of circulation, but I had no urge to pull my hand away.

I had bigger problems.

The jewel of death pulsed against my chest like a heartbeat intensifying.

The vibrations increased like the stone was trying to burrow underneath my skin and crawl into the emptiness that plagued me. I wrapped my left hand around the unnaturally warm stone.

My fingers buzzed from the force, and my forearm twitched.

Something was happening.

Maybe the Necklace of Death was trying to live up to its name and kill me?

Light suddenly exploded from the necklace.

I squinted as the new brightness burned my eyes.

The wooden bunk above my head was illuminated.

My breathing was loud and strangled as ice spread from my fingertips. It crawled across the bottom of the bunk that hung close to my head and coated it in a blue sheen.

Someone snored loudly across the room, and it startled me. I swallowed a scream.

My nerves were electrocuted from stress, and the cavernous hole inside my soul was expanding to consume my existence.

The jewel vibrated against my heart, and then there was an odd snapping sensation inside my sternum. Snowflakes swirled.

Everything went dark.

CHAPTER 31

JOHN

CURSED

PORTENTOUS (ADJECTIVE): being a grave or serious matter.

DAY 22, HOUR 3

I sat up in my bunk, heaving, with my hands placed over my heart like I was trying to keep it from falling out of my chest.

Unfamiliar panic filled my bones.

The darkness of the bedroom was stifling, and I must have been hallucinating, because snow drifted through the air.

The pressure inside my chest was unbearable.

I patted against my sternum like I was putting out a fire, half expecting to feel ravaged flesh, but my skin was warm and unblemished.

The pulsing sensation continued.

Were we under attack? Were the Fates themselves tearing me apart from within for failing to do my duty to the realm like Uncle always warned they might?

If so, I had no regrets.

Even with my chest tearing apart in pain, I knew I'd do

nothing differently. There was no other choice I'd ever have made. I would always choose Aran and Luka before any duty.

I'd do nothing differently.

Legs jackknifing, I collapsed back onto my covers, writhing in pain, clawing at my heart as the agony ate me apart from the inside. The bunk bed jostled violently beneath me.

I wanted to make sure Luka and Aran were okay, but I couldn't do anything but lie paralyzed. I twitched like I was electrocuted.

The pressure mounted until tears dripped out of the corners of my eyes.

My thoughts were scattered and jagged, and it was impossible to understand where I began, and where the pain ended. We were one.

One thought penetrated the blinding agony—*I never got to tell Aran I love her.*

CHAPTER 32
LUKA
BONDS

CIMMERIAN (ADJECTIVE): very dark or gloomy.

DAY 22, HOUR 3

My eyes shot open.

Instantly I knew something was very wrong.

A window must have been open because snow was falling inside. Cold wetness coated my cheeks, and there was a fine layer of white dust across my pillow.

I was lying on my stomach with my arm hanging over the bed, but Aran was not holding my hand like usual. Her fingers were limp in my grasp. Ice froze us together.

I opened my mouth to call her name, and I meant to shake her hand to wake her.

Nothing happened because I couldn't move.

I was paralyzed.

A vibrating sensation pulsed inside my chest, and it felt like I was being stabbed with a serrated blade. It felt like my heart was being carved out.

The bunk shook harshly beneath me.

My mouth opened on a silent scream as agony tore through my insides. It took a moment to process that the bed rocking was coming from above.

Twin intuition filled me, and I knew without a doubt that John was not well. I needed to get to my younger brother.

I needed to save him.

As a young child, I'd promised myself that I would never stand by and watch him get hurt. I would sacrifice every bone in my body to protect him.

Body taught with unimaginable torment, I shattered the ice and released Aran's hand.

I slowly turned myself over and stared up at the twitching bunk. Horror filled me as I realized Aran hadn't made a noise of disgruntlement like she always did when I stopped holding her hand.

John twitched violently above me.

Aran's bed below me was eerily quiet. Too quiet.

The pain intensified to another level, and my back arched as an invisible force dug my heart from my chest.

The only two people I lived for were suffering inches apart from me.

I was paralyzed.

Unable to help them.

Useless.

There was a snapping sensation as the agony in my chest crescendoed.

The bunk above my head went still.

Darkness blurred my vision, and I clawed desperately against unconsciousness, but it mercilessly pulled me under. There was nothing left of me as everything went black, just a peculiar sensation inside my chest.

A staggering barrenness.

I felt dead.

CHAPTER 33

ARAN
FALLING TO PIECES

APRICITY (NOUN): the warmth of sun in winter.

DAY 22, HOUR 8

I woke up to lilac morning light clutching the Necklace of Death.

My first thought—*I'm going to learn how to fly today.*

A strange dream about falling snow, vibrations, and glowing light teased the edges of my consciousness, but it drifted away into nothingness.

I shrugged it off.

Sadly, hallucinations were not uncommon with my lifestyle.

Once as a child, I'd had a string of dreams that I'd been abducted and probed by an alien creature from a faraway realm. Mother had slapped me when I'd told her.

There were two types of people in the world: those who were probed, and those who judged those who were probed. The latter were all secretly jealous that no one had abducted them.

My eyes struggled to adjust to the morning light.

I groaned and rolled out of bed.

Since I had no other plans for the days (other than annoy Malum), I might as well get some flying practice in.

There were wings in my shoulders and angel blood in my veins, and I was going to get airborne if it was the last thing I did. If not for myself, then I would do it to spite Mother.

It was time to succeed.

"I'm going to practice flying behind the barracks. I want to do this alone." I announced to the room.

Malum paused his one-handed push-ups. "Don't go too far. I don't want to see you hurt." His voice was extra gravelly in the morning, and I shivered at its deepness. Silver skulls twinkled in his ears, and he didn't have socks on, so my name was on full display.

He'd 100 percent done it on purpose.

I flipped him off with both hands, just for fun.

He winked. "Don't tempt me."

I put my hands down as I realized what he meant.

Ugh, he was infuriating.

John and Luka groaned loudly as they woke up, and I smiled because they were not morning people. I was also not a morning person—or a night person, or a day person.

"Wait," Scorpius said as he emerged from the bathroom in a cloud of steam, a white towel hanging dangerously low on his hips. Orion followed behind him, similarly unclothed, toweling his blond hair.

They'd been showering together.

There wasn't enough oxygen in the room, and I didn't know where to look.

Scorpius smirked, and my eyes trailed downward.

He looked like he was carved from white marble. His

Adonis belt glistened with water, and his dark hair was wet and messy around his face.

The two of them sauntered past me. Cherry blossoms fluttered down Orion's golden biceps, and Scorpius's neck tattoo opened, pupil expanding as it stared directly at me.

Their tattoos were much more brightly colored than I'd ever remembered.

I'd always though Orion's flowers were a pale shade, closer to white. Now they were such a rich pink that they practically glowed against his golden skin.

He was mesmerizing to look at.

They both were.

I forgot what I was doing.

What was my name?

How old was I?

The pain streaking down my back turned into fireworks.

"Distracted, Aran?" John asked in a teasing tone, and his voice brought me back to reality.

My face warmed as I realized I'd been gaping at the half-naked kings like an idiot.

I wasn't mad about objectifying them because I was a staunch supporter of bullying men. Everyone knew this. It was just a little embarrassing that my entire legion had just witnessed me ogle my enemies.

At least the twins were also checking them out.

"We got these for you," Scorpius said as he dug into one of the mall bags beside his bed. His towel dipped dangerously low, and my blood pressure soared.

He stood up and handed me fuzzy black mittens.

"Wear them if you're going outside," Scorpius said, his tone somewhere between an order and a plea.

I stared at the gloves, dumbfounded.

"Here." Orion gently tugged them onto my hands. My

fingers were engulfed in warmth as my stomach filled with butterflies.

I turned my hands over.

"Ara" was written in tiny gold script across the wrist.

My throat was dry, and I forgot how to swallow as I looked at it with confusion.

"Why Ara?" I asked. "Did the embroiderer make a mistake?"

"No," Orion whispered, the words like honey on his tongue. "It wasn't a mistake."

Malum looked up from the floor with confusion. "Wait, it wasn't an error?" Scorpius narrowed his eyes.

I stared at Orion and waited for an explanation.

None came.

"You'll figure it out," he whispered as he took a step closer.

Bergamot and chocolate filled my nose, and pain streaked down my spine.

Orion's golden abdominal muscles rippled as he stretched his hands above his head, and Scorpius's chiseled chest expanded as he breathed deeply.

What were we talking about?

I wet my lips twice and croaked out, "Uh, okay."

Scorpius took a step closer. "You're welcome for the gloves, Arabella." His voice had a cruel tilt to it, like was really saying "get on your knees."

His cheekbones glinted like cut diamonds.

Suddenly, I liked my men mean.

"Um, th-thanks?" I stuttered.

"Of course, sweetheart," Orion whispered with wide eyes as Scorpius smiled like I'd made him proud. Together they were exquisite. Divine.

The bursts of pain down my back ratcheted up to

another level as I admired the nude men and my fuzzy black mittens.

"I picked out the color," Malum grumbled mid-push-up.

"No one cares." I tried to flip him off, but the mitten made it look like I was waving.

I put my hand down with defeat and purposefully avoided making eye contact, or ab contact, with anyone. I announced to the room with determination, "I'm going to stay close and practice in the woods so the bond sickness doesn't act up, but I want to do this alone—anyone who interrupts will get punched in the throat. I'll be back when I've learned to fly."

Zenith drawled from his bunk bed, "So—never?"

I glared at the demon. "That was hurtful and unnecessary."

"Oh darn." He rolled over in his bed.

I stalked out into the light snowfall. Muttering about stupid men, I stomped around the side of the barracks to a space where the towering pines would conceal me.

The morning was overwhelmingly bright.

I tipped my head back and gaped. They sky had changed overnight from gray to a glittering lavender.

It was stunning.

Green pine needles coated in ice sparkled like emeralds in the overcast sky. Lilac colors refracted through the snowy forest.

I basked in the colors.

Then I frowned.

It was *too* stunning. *Was this what the realm had always looked like? Was my vision that bad? Why had it changed overnight?*

My skull ached as I thought about.

I shook my head and concentrated on the task at hand—

I was going to prove Zenith wrong. The change in my vision was a problem for another day.

There were wings on my back.

I was an angel.

It was time to fly.

That was what was important.

With newfound determination, and cute fluffy mittens on my hands, I took off my coat and thermal shirt. Folding them neatly in a pile, I ignored the goose bumps that exploded across my exposed skin as I flexed my thighs.

For once, the cold was barely noticeable.

The day felt mild.

I bent down.

Crystals clattered and air whooshed as I splayed my wings.

Cartilage and bones snapped deliciously as I shook the unused appendages and gritted my teeth.

Ignoring their heavy weight, I bent my head low and remembered Knox's instructions. I flexed my back muscles. My boots sank into the warm dirt, and steam heated my ankles as my upper body shivered.

Everything faded away as I concentrated on the will coursing through me.

I *was* going to fly.

My wings spread wide, and I flexed my back muscles as I pushed upward with everything I had.

Nothing happened, but I didn't let it deter me.

I was going to be smart about this.

My wings disappeared as I pulled them back inside me, and I rolled my neck, stretching and trying to loosen up. I wasn't going to exhaust myself needlessly.

After I mentally and physically recovered, I withdrew my heavy wings and tried again.

I had this.

Hours later, I collapsed onto my knees with exhaustion and heaved. The cartilage in my wings felt frozen stiff, and it hurt to retract them.

I'd leave them out, just for a few more moments.

My heart pounded erratically, and my breath was loud and uneven as I choked on the snow-drenched air.

Of course, since I was cursed with misfortune, a few minutes into practicing, the blizzard conditions had returned.

A storm had raged continually since.

Now the snow slammed against me in a punishing blur, and my teeth chattered uncontrollably. Visibility was nonexistent.

The world was a vortex of white and gray.

I was bone tired.

I'd never felt so cold.

Crystal wings clattered together as their heavy weight tipped me forward, and I sprawled face first into the pile of snow that had accumulated on the frozen ground where I'd been standing.

The morning light through the clouds was long gone, and the forest was frozen with extreme cold. The blizzard had kicked up a notch.

It was a whiteout.

Sun god, I hated the realm's temperamental weather.

I turned my neck awkwardly to the side and looked up at the towering pines. They'd frozen completely solid in the storm and were covered in white. Disturbingly sharp icicles hung menacingly off their branches.

Were the trees dead?

Was I dead?

My curls were uncomfortably stiff, plastered against my neck and back. They'd frozen solid with sweat.

I wasn't sure how much time had passed.

Did time even exist?

Delirium and existential dread clouded my thoughts. *Never a good sign.*

Gums burning from breathing harshly in the cold wind, I tasted copper on my tongue and moaned pitifully into the snowbank beneath me. Snowflakes sprayed.

I tried to push myself up.

I searched for the determination that had spurned me forward, but it was gone. There was nothing left to give.

For hours, I'd heaved as I spread my wings wide and flexed unused shoulder muscles. For hours—I'd failed.

My feet never left the ground.

At one point, I was so demoralized I jumped up just so I could pretend that I'd flown an inch. My wings were so heavy I'd stumbled and slammed into a tree.

A humbling experience.

It would have been disheartening if I hadn't already hit rock bottom. Good thing I was already there.

At least my fingers were warm.

The mittens worked amazingly. They were clearly enchanted because the temperature inside them had increased as I'd gotten colder.

Toasty-warm fingers felt like such a luxury, especially since I was lying half-dead in a snowbank. A part of me recognized I should try to move, and there was something crucial I needed to do.

But my thoughts were sluggish.

The snow seemed to fall in slow motion. The storm was pretty, in a violent, terrifying sort of way.

Exhaustion melted into sleepiness. I just wanted to curl up and embrace the stillness.

Crystals clattered as the wind gusted.

The longer I lay in the snow, the more moving seemed like a ridiculous endeavor. Snow was soft and pillowy. It had a nice cushion.

I closed my eyes, content to take a nap.

Time passed.

"You idiot!" Malum shouted with agitation. He said more things, but I purposefully stopped listening as soon as I heard his voice.

"Pull your wings in." John's dark eyes were wide with concern as he knelt in the snow. "Pull your wings in right now, Aran, or I swear to the sun god I will spank you."

I grinned up at him.

Postexhaustion endorphins made me see double. Two of his heads blurred in front of me—one of them had dimples, and the other didn't.

The head without dimples grabbed my cheeks forcefully and ordered, "Pull your wings in now." His sentence was short and clipped like he was vibrating with rage. "Do this now or I'm never letting you out of my sight ever again." He reminded me of a man I'd once known named Luka.

John shook me and yelled, "*Retract your wings!*"

I focused on my cramped shoulder blades. There was a pulling sensation, then the heavy crushing weight disappeared. I sighed. My lungs expanded greedily.

I blinked.

The frowning man carried me while John held my hand.

Malum stalked beside us, scowling. "You gave yourself fucking frostbite." Flames shot from his mouth.

"You look like a dragon," I pointed out helpfully.

Silver eyes became molten with rage.

I blinked.

Time warped.

I was lying in a tub, and hot water poured over me from above. John was lying beneath me, and Luka was kneeling off to the side, scowling as he leaned over and wiped my face with a hot washcloth.

He gently scraped off layers of ice.

The cloth was deliciously warm, even hotter than the warm water.

Luka pulled back and held up the cloth to Malum's flaming hands, and shades of scarlet danced off bronze fingers.

For a second, I was hypnotized by the richness of the color. I'd never seen anything so vibrant. Even Malum's skin had warm undertones that I'd never picked up on before.

Everything became hazy as the tub heated.

Steam sizzled off my skin as water melted ice, and I sighed. It was surprisingly unpainful. I craved the warmth.

"I'm so angry with you," Malum said. "You're lucky Scorpius and Orion had to go take care of some business today." His voice strummed with anger as he knelt next to the tub. "I know my mates, and if they saw you like this— they'd also be furious about you hurting yourself. Especially Scorpius."

Darkness expanded around Luka, and he made a harsh noise in the back of his throat. "Careful how you speak to her," he threatened.

Malum continued like he was unbothered by Luka's threats. "Lucky for you, I'm so fucking angry that I can't stand to be around you right now because I'll burn this realm to the ground."

As if to punctuate his point, he stormed out of the bathroom.

John's hands traced up and down my forearms comfortingly, and I focused on the soothing motion.

I fell asleep.

I woke up and two menacing shadows towered over my bed.

"Malum said he found you frozen in a snowbank, half-dead from exhaustion." Scorpius leaned forward and invaded the narrow space of my bunk.

Orion stood behind him, and his brown eyes were narrowed into slits.

Silver skulls glinted in both their ears like bad omens.

I'd never seen them so angry.

"Leave me alone, I'm tired."

Spicy bergamot and burned chocolate filled my senses. Their scents were harsher than usual.

The bunk bed above me rattled as the twins shifted in their sleep.

White teeth glinted as Scorpius bared his teeth. His voice was deadly as he said, "We'll talk about this in the shower. You *will* explain yourself."

"You're delusional."

"Don't test me, Arabella," Scorpius sneered, and Orion scowled in agreement. "I'm not as civilized as I pretend to be."

The men who'd been opening up to me were gone. Had they ever existed?

They shifted and came into focus.

I blinked in horror.

They were covered head to toe in streaks of blood.

Was this a nightmare? Was I imagining them?

"Let's go. Get up and get in the shower. You have ten seconds, or you'll be punished," Scorpius ordered.

I stared at him in disbelief.

The scent of copper intensified in the air, like a dark omen.

"Is this a joke?" I asked groggily. "Are you real?"

Scorpius's blind eyes widened with mania. He bared his teeth. "Do you want to find out how much I'm not joking?"

I was 98 percent sure that they were figments of my exhausted imagination.

I pushed my covers aside and rolled out of bed. I groaned softly.

The two kings towered above me like angry gods.

Scorpius smirked viciously as they walked together to the bathroom and waited for me.

"Crawl for us," Scorpius snarled. Orion stood silently next to him.

Definitely a nightmare.

"Fuck you," I whispered.

Scorpius smiled cruelly. "That can be arranged. Crawl. Now."

I purposefully didn't move.

Long minutes passed as we glared at each other, neither budging.

Slowly, I inched forward across the hard floor.

Finally, I stopped at their feet.

They whispered something that sounded remorseful, but my ears had whited out and I wasn't listening.

I punched out both of their knees, and they slammed to the ground beside me.

"Fuck you both," I gloated. My plan had worked.

I waited for them to retaliate.

Their expressions were oddly emotional for nightmares.

I tried to stand up, but my arms trembled from the strain. Hands gently grabbed beneath my armpits.

They pulled me up.

Well, this was a confusing nightmare.

Scorpius carried me into the bathroom, and Orion started running the shower.

Moments later, fully clothed, the three of us were squeezed together in the small shower.

"Tell us everything that happened today. Please," Orion whispered as he pressed himself flush against my back.

Pressure twisted in my sternum because dreams were usually disconnected from the day's events.

Holy sun god—was this real?

CHAPTER 34
ORION
SHOWER DEVOTIONS

ALGID (ADJECTIVE): having a low or subnormal temperature.

DAY 23, HOUR 4

Arabella was pressed between us in the warm shower.

All three of us were fully clothed. She was limp, unable to hold herself up of her own volition.

There was something inherently wrong with her surrender. It made me ill.

We'd mistreated her.

Yet again.

All three of us rocked back and forth under the spray, and I wasn't the only one trembling. Scorpius shook as he held our Revered, her cheek pressed against his chest, long lashes fanning over pale skin.

The scar underneath her eye was puckered and red.

A visible testament to how much we'd already failed her. The most important person in our lives, the person we were born to protect, and we couldn't stop hurting her.

We'd grown up expecting a male mate to be the center of

our worlds. Someone who towered over everyone like the rest of us. Someone who was mean and cruel, who bottled up their emotions and expressed themselves through violence.

Our Revered was supposed to be like us.

We'd all assumed he would be the submissive to our dominance, a man who wanted to kneel before us so we could shield him from harm.

Most Revereds wanted to be sheltered. Their nature was the perfect balance that fit within the Ignis and Protectors' powerful urges to shelter them.

But we weren't a normal devil house.

We were the ancient House of Malum.

We were the right hand of a raging god with more power inside us than the devil culture had seen in eons.

It made sense that our Revered would subvert power dynamics.

"So, this isn't a dream?" Arabella asked with confusion, and my stomach nose-dived.

I wished it were.

I wished we could take back what we'd done.

"No," Scorpius whispered shakily. "It's real."

She exhaled. "You're the worst grovelers in the history of grovelers."

"We're trying," Scorpius said softly, "but we know."

"I'd hate to see what *not* trying looked like." She chuckled. "You'd probably just bash me over the head with a shovel."

Both Scorpius and I recoiled at her graphic words.

"*Never*," Scorpius snarled, and I nodded in agreement.

"So where do we go from here?" she whispered like she thought we could still move past this.

She was a woman who'd grown up facing horrifying violence. She didn't cower from us. She didn't submit.

Arabella embraced suffering to the point of recklessness.

It was who she was.

I tangled my shaking fingers in her unruly curls and breathed in her icy scent. She smelled like a blizzard at midnight and holding her was akin to walking through a quiet, snowy forest under starlight.

Scorpius traced trembling fingers across her dark brows, his jaw clenched and neck muscles twitched like he was holding back a scream.

We were soaked to the bones and our clothes were heavy. Pink water pooled at our feet.

Minutes turned into an hour.

No one spoke.

Arabella's eyes stayed closed, but her lashes fluttered, and she rocked back and forth from time to time like she was thinking. Her mouth was pursed, but no words came out.

We held one another.

Desperately.

Nothing among us but regret.

Our history was barbed wire wrapped around our necks strangling all of us, and for the first time in my painful life, I was hit with an overwhelming urge to cry. Suddenly all I could think about was Arabella's definition of toxic in the truth journals.

She'd said it was what we had.

The twins would never lose control like we just had.

Scorpius pressed her harder between us. My back was pushed against the shower wall, faucet digging into my spine, and I couldn't find the energy to care.

I breathed raggedly as my fellow Protector pressed us against the wall with all his might like he was trying to make us burrow under his skin.

He was making it clear that he was never letting us go.

I leaned forward so my head rested next to hers, and I pressed my face into Scorpius's bicep. A noise of contentment sounded in her throat, and she nuzzled against me.

I sighed with relief at the contact.

It was outrageous that we'd ever thought I was a Revered.

The woman between us was our purpose.

I wanted to stare at her, watch her every second of the day, and burn her existence into my corneas until I knew nothing else.

"I'm so sorry." Shaky words whispered across my lips before I realized what I was doing. Water splattered off my lips as I spoke.

Scorpius pressed us harder against the shower wall.

Dark lashes fluttered, and electric-blue eyes stared through me. "I know," Arabella whispered back like she, too, couldn't speak aloud.

I tightened my fingers in her wet curls.

Scorpius made a noise like a pained animal, and his trembling intensified. His voice was hoarse as he rasped, "I'm sorry for speaking to you like that. You should never crawl for us. Not after everything that's happened. Never again. We should crawl for you."

A heavy sigh escaped Arabella's lips.

Long painful seconds passed.

She whispered very quietly, "How about everyone stops crawling?"

I released her hair and wrapped my arms around my mates in a hug. "You're right, we shouldn't play games with each other. What's growing between all of us is precious, and it deserves to be treated as such—*you* deserve better."

She sniffed.

I promised, "We will never speak to you like that again, sweetheart. You mean too much to us."

Scorpius nodded and the three of us shifted. "I saw that you…" He trailed off like he couldn't speak. Tipping his head down in shame, he said, "I saw that you were trembling with exhaustion, and I didn't help you. I watched you crawl and did nothing."

His entire body convulsed.

Arabella whispered, "I thought it was a dream."

I squeezed my arms with all my might and tried to hold all three of us together before we shattered into irreparable pieces.

We were fragile, jagged edges and broken promises.

For people brimming with power and strength, we all shared one thing in common: we were terrifyingly flawed.

"Prove it to me," she said. "Please prove that you care. Prove that this isn't all some toxic power trip."

Scorpius pressed my back painfully against the tile wall.

I squeezed us together until I lost circulation in my fingertips and my muscles ached from exertion.

We squeezed her between our arms.

"We're your hounds to command," I whispered reverently, the words a prayer across my lips. "We have no purpose other than to serve you. I promise."

"I don't want that." Her voice cracked. "I want to be *more* than your Revered. I want to be a *person* to you. I'll never be your perfect, ideal mate. I'll never be him."

Scorpius staggered back and pulled away at her purposeful use of the male gender.

My stomach dropped to my feet, and I swayed like I was going to collapse. She wrapped her arms around me and kept me from falling.

"We don't want a male devil," Scorpius rasped loudly. "I-

I used to think I wanted one, but I was a fool—I don't want anyone but you. You're the only person I've ever sat in a shower with fully clothed for hours talking. You're the only person I don't like seeing in pain."

She squeezed me tighter, fingers pulling my sweatshirt taut as she clung to me.

Scorpius pulled the wet hair off her nape and softly kissed the exposed skin. "You're the only person I've ever wanted, Arabella," he said fiercely like he was proving something.

She exhaled against my chest.

Her heart raced with such force that it pounded against my sternum, and I could feel it through our clothes.

"You're the only person I've ever spoken to without fear," I whispered down to her. "And you always listen. You see me for who I really am, and I want to provide that same solace to you. I want to be *your* person because *you are* mine. No one can ever compare, and you deserve to be treated like the treasure you are."

She sighed loudly. "You know, you guys aren't as hopeless as you think you are. You're different from the fronts you present to the rest of the world. Even Malum."

Scorpius wrapped his arms around both of us and resumed pinning us against the wall of the shower. "We don't deserve you," he said.

I agreed, "No, we don't."

Time slipped around us under the warm spray.

No more words were spoken.

There was nothing left to be said because words couldn't fix our mistakes. Only we could.

CHAPTER 35

Aran
STRATEGY

Dreich (adjective): dreary.

DAY 25, HOUR 16

"What is wrong with you people?" Rina asked, her pretty features contorted in a sneer as she leaned against the desk.

No one answered her.

The strategy room was colder than usual, and the small lamp that illuminated the space glowed golden. The red rug that covered the room was reminiscent of freshly spilled blood. I'd never noticed its intense hue.

Jinx and I stood on one end of the blackboard, and Malum stood at the other. The kings had found crutches for Jinx at the shifter mall.

Although, "found" was a generous term because they'd dragged a shifter with a broken leg into an alcove, punched him in the stomach, and forcibly stolen his crutches.

Jax had scowled at their methods, Cobra had patted Malum on the back and taken the crutches with a grin, while

Ascher and Xerxes had bemoaned that they should have thought of attacking an injured person sooner.

Men.

The kings had smirked at me like they'd proven something.

They weren't smirking anymore.

None of us were.

Four angels crowded around the table, frowning. Rina was their ringleader. The two angels that were best at navigating were away finding the next location.

A headache throbbed in my temples.

The shifters sat with the rest of our legion in the leather chairs and watched the conflict awkwardly.

John was sitting next to Scorpius, and Luka was sitting next to Orion. All four of them were whispering among themselves like they were friends.

When did that happen?

Rina made a loud noise of agitation, and I grudgingly turned my attention back to the irate angels.

At first, the others had tried to step in and stop the angels from yelling at us, but ice swords had materialized, and Jinx had ordered everyone but the angels to sit down.

Violence still buzzed in the air, and everyone stared at one another with distrust.

I was too tired for this bullshit.

I felt like the twins looked—their olive skin had an ashen hue, and their eyes were ringed in dark circles. *Were they sick?*

Worry turned my stomach.

I made a mental note to ask them about it later. They were always taking care of me, but who was taking care of them?

Rina made another sound of annoyance.

As champions, we technically outranked them, but the

High Court made it clear that we had to make decisions together, and the lines of leadership were blurry. I'd thought the war structure made sense.

I'd been a fool.

Rina slapped her palms on the table for emphasis. Her voice went up a decibel as she said, "We need to find a solution. We can't fight like this." The angels nodded behind her like they were all in agreement.

Knox stood behind them with his arms crossed, but even he nodded in agreement.

Everything out of the angels' mouths was garbage. A child's fairy tale. Their emotional breakdown was useless in the grand scheme of war strategy.

They'd lost their minds.

If I'd wanted to make dumb decisions, I'd have asked Sadie for strategy advice. I loved her with all my heart, but the woman made bizarre choices in the heat of the moment.

She'd *voluntarily* mated to Cobra.

Enough said.

Rina let out a pitchy laugh and tapped her foot.

Beside me Jinx let out a long rattling sigh, and I agreed with the sentiment. Across the board, richly colored flames danced along Malum's shaved head, and chalk snapped between his fingers.

Forty-one soldiers had not died fighting against the ungodly for the angels to have a crisis of consciousness. Only fifty-nine of us were left standing between the realms and the destruction of civilization as we knew it.

If I was going to be forced to lead a war, I wasn't going to make stupid decisions to pander to emotional people.

I'd lost too much of myself to stop now.

Sweat dripped down my temple, and my skin tightened as it froze. I scrubbed at the side of my face to wipe it away.

Neither Jinx nor Malum had responded to Rina's inane statement. Everyone was waiting for someone to take charge.

I swallowed down a scream because I wasn't paid enough for this—actually, I wasn't sure I was being paid at all.

Why was I doing this?

Inhaling enchanted smoke, I blew out my emotional support Horse. He settled onto my shoulder with a soft caw, and his long smoke feathers whispered against my skin.

His neck was longer and plumage more dramatic than ever before, which was strange because every time I conjured him, I imagined the same bird.

He was changing.

I would have been interested in solving the puzzle of his evolution if my cortisol levels weren't spiking through the roof. I mindlessly petted the crow on my shoulder and focused on the mess in front of me.

Rina's scowl darkened as she waited with growing impatience.

"I don't understand your position," I said slowly, enunciating each word to make sure my tone was moderate and noninflammatory.

My lips curled up in a soft smile.

I gave off nonconfrontational, peaceful vibes.

Rina put her hands on her hips and shouted, "*We refuse to fight like we've been*! There has to be another way. We need to work on finding a cure for the infected. There are thousands of innocent people in these compounds."

It felt like I was falling.

Rina's voice rose as she continued, "I refuse to put myself in a position where I have to harm this many civilians. Come up with a new strategy."

She waved her fingers like she was shooing me.

Jinx muttered something scathing under her breath, and I held myself back from leaping across the table.

You know what we needed to bring back?

Scalping.

How self-absorbed were the angels? Did they think I wasn't haunted every second of my life with the screams of the dying?

"Do it," Sadie mouthed at me from her seat in the front row like she could read my mind.

I closed my eyes and inhaled. I was the champion of the gods in a war and I was going to be mature and respectful.

"Thank you for sharing your opinion," I said, overenunciating each word.

"It's also wrong," Knox said righteously from the back of the group. "We can't afford to make mistakes and murder innocent civilians. There could be far-reaching repercussions for the High Court. We need to come up with a new strategy. Is anyone working on a cure?"

My eye twitched.

Knox crossed his arms over his chest and stated, "We need a change of plans."

The pounding in my temple intensified, and ice glistened as it spread from my fingertips and streaked across the chalkboard behind me.

Jinx pushed her dark sunglasses harshly up the bridge of her nose. "Do your heads hurt?"

"What?" Rina snapped.

Jinx scowled. "All of you were clearly dropped on your heads as children, so I'm asking. Do your heads hurt?"

It took a moment for her words to penetrate.

The room erupted.

Sadie and Scorpius laughed, Malum grinned, Rina started screaming, and one of the male angels kicked a folding chair, while Knox yelled something about disrespect and shouldered his way to the front of the group.

Crack.

The chaos stopped, and everyone gaped at me.

My hand stung from where I'd slapped Knox across the face.

His jaw dropped open as he touched the red fingerprints that were already visible across his cheek.

"That's my girl." Sadie clapped loudly and pumped her fist.

Her support was not appreciated.

Rina snarled. "How fucking dare you touch him? He is one hundred times the angel you'll ever be," she spat. "You can't even fly."

The snowbank.

Straining for hours.

Failing.

Malum let out an unholy noise and moved like he was going to hit Rina. I grimaced and flung myself in front of him to stop him. "Whatever," I said, "she's not wrong."

"I'm going to kill her," Scorpius promised as he stood up. Orion pulled him back down.

"Why did you do that?" Knox asked as he fingered his cheek.

Malum shifted in front of me and blocked my view of the angels. Flames leaped across his skin protectively. Whiskey and tobacco tingled across my senses.

"Why?" Knox asked again.

My gut told me saying, *because I've wanted to hit one of you ever since the Legionnaire Games* probably wasn't the best move.

"I didn't mean to," I said weakly. "Adrenaline overwhelmed me, and I acted before I could think."

There was a long moment where I tensed and prepared to fight to the death.

Knox said crisply, "It's fine. Let's move on. You've been suffering of late because of your overwhelming failures to fly. I forgive you."

Pompous prick.

"Don't talk to her with that tone." Flames leaped higher off Malum's shoulders, and he cracked his neck back and forth menacingly. "Your legion can focus on the oldest and largest infected during battles. Everyone else will handle the rest."

I gritted my teeth and nodded in agreement.

"However," Jinx said, "questions about a *cure* should be directed to the High Court." She pointed toward the enchanted tablet on the table. "The *organization* that is making all of us fight in this war. Save your ire for the people who deserve it."

The angels sulked but didn't say anything. They slunk to the back of the room.

Jinx, Malum, and I turned back to our strategy board and started over.

With no windows to filter light, there was no sense of time.

We projected weapons onto the board and rough renderings of the compounds we'd plundered. We wrote down our numbers and estimated the number of ungodly waiting for us in the third location. We counted how many soldiers on average were lost guarding the perimeters and where we needed them positioned.

At one point, Jinx created a math equation that calculated the odds of finding a cure for the infected.

Chalk symbols and letters covered every inch of the chalkboard.

Malum and I updated the equation where she made mistakes, and all three of us solved it for quality control.

We all got the same result.

There was a .07 percent chance of finding a cure, assuming the High Court was already working on one, and a 342 percent greater chance the ungodly would murder millions if they expanded into other realms and infected people.

Jinx smirked condescendingly and turned around, brandishing her chalk to the room. "This is why your position is idiotic," she spat at the angels.

No one responded.

I rubbed grit out of my tired eyes.

Everyone was asleep.

Jinx hobbled over and smacked her crutch against Rina and Knox until they woke up. "See why your idea was asinine." She pointed at the board.

The angels squinted sleepily at the board with confusion. "What are we looking at?" Knox asked as Rina said, "I just see letters and symbols. What is this?"

Jinx let out a small scream of frustration and hobbled back to the board while Malum shook his head like he too was disgusted with their mathematical incompetence.

The angels went back to sleep.

I grimaced at Jinx. Poor girl had forgotten for a second that other people were genuinely simpleminded and useless. She'd learn with age.

Either I was hallucinating, or she didn't look like a child anymore. She looked like a teenager.

Her limbs were long and lanky like she was going through puberty, and her face had lost baby fat.

"How old are you again?" I asked.

Jinx ignored me as she stared at our equation. "I don't

have time for this. We need a plan if the angels refuse to fight because they're cowards."

I winced.

We sounded like monsters.

They weren't wrong for not wanting to kill the innocent infected; sun god, neither did I. However, this was war.

Suddenly, I didn't feel so good about our position. Maybe we should do something to try to save—

"No." Jinx cut me off like could read my mind, which she very well might be able to. "*No*. We know the facts and the numbers. If we're going to win this war, we can't worry about the fate of the few in the face of real, assured destruction."

I tried to nod in agreement, but my neck muscles cramped.

My chest knotted with regret.

"She's right," Malum said as he tapped the tablet and flipped through the different projections. "We've thought through every angle and calculated the odds. We need to stay level-headed and not be swayed with emotion. The three of us are effective strategists because we make decisions based on hard facts."

Silver eyes looked melancholic.

The chalk in my fingers froze solid and dropped. It shattered across the floor in thousands of little pieces. For the first time, I noticed the similarities between Malum and me.

The heartlessness.

The learned cruelty.

We adapted and survived.

He looked at me and whispered, "We're different because of our analytical abilities. We recognize that this is war. We understand the stakes."

I exhaled.

"Here." Malum walked across the room and dragged over the angel's tea cart. He looked ridiculous wheeling the little silver trays filled with flower-shaped cakes.

He sat down in one of three leather chairs and gestured to Jinx and me.

"Um," I said awkwardly as I stared at a chair, then back at him.

Pink stained his cheeks as he cleared his throat and waited. A yawn climbed up my throat as I sat in his offered chair.

"Thanks," I said.

His blush intensified. "Anything for you."

All three of us sat.

He leaned toward me, and I pretended not to notice navy painted nails twisted a curl that had come free from my bun.

He casually played with my hair.

My spine hurt.

Jinx reached for the cups, and Malum stopped her.

"I got it," he said gruffly, then held a flaming finger under the kettle to warm it.

When he was satisfied with the temperature of the water, he packed strainers with tea leaves and placed them over each of our cups. He took painstaking care pouring the liquid.

It felt like a fever dream.

After he was satisfied with the state of our tea, he grabbed little plates and piled them high with cucumber sandwiches and cakes.

Pink became scarlet as his blush deepened under my scrutiny.

"You both need to eat more," he said as he pushed the overflowing plates in front of Jinx and me.

Jinx nodded and attacked the food.

I sat rigidly and stared at the leader of the kings.

The corner of his mouth quirked up into a lopsided smile.

I forgot how to breathe, my stomach pinched, and pain tingled down my spine.

In the back of the room, a demon snored and John moaned something in his sleep.

Malum held up a cucumber sandwich, laughably small compared to the size of his hands, and it took me a second to realize what he was waiting for.

I touched my sandwich to his. "Cheers."

"To winning this war," he whispered as a scarlet flush spread down his neck. "We can do this."

"Hopefully," I said tiredly.

He shook his head. "I have a good feeling. Did I ever tell you about how we became kings?"

"No," I said, shocked that the recalcitrant man who literally *breathed fire* was opening up to me.

"Trust me, our odds were *way* worse back then," he said.

Then to my utter astonishment, he launched into an unbelievable tale about how they'd fought for days with no weapons. They'd only had their fists, one another, and the power in their veins.

What he described was the bloodiest, most gruesome tournament known to man.

I felt sick to my stomach listening to how they'd been hunted through the woods when they were still teenagers.

Malum spoke about enduring torture like it was nothing.

He talked about how he'd learned to rely on Scorpius's advanced hearing for tracking, and how Orion's enthralling voice had saved them an infinite number of times.

Then he talked about how he'd unleashed his flames on the other competitors.

The rules banned full use of mate powers, so they hunted down the other competitors like animals and killed them. One by one, Malum lit them on fire.

It was a savage, gruesome tale.

It was awe-inspiring.

When he was done explaining how they'd survived, half-beaten for weeks with barely any food and water, he picked up his tea and took a sip.

Jinx and I blinked at him.

"Does that give you—nightmares?" I asked cautiously, unable to reconcile how someone could survive such an ordeal and still function.

Malum shrugged and rubbed at his chest. "No. Physical pain is not what I'm afraid of. It's never been my weakness."

A strange sensation unfurled around my heart.

I understood. A broken bone would heal and bruised skin would recover because the violence of a blow was temporary.

It was mental pain that crushed you relentlessly into smithereens.

You didn't heal overnight.

It was a long-festering suffering that persisted as long as the conditions that fostered it remained, and sometimes long after they'd gone.

Mental pain lingered.

It would take an insane life change—I'd have to live in a peaceful realm that was fully sheltered from violence and war —before I'd even hope to recover.

I'd take a punch to the face over the feelings of emptiness any day.

"I know exactly what you mean," I whispered as I stared at Malum like I was seeing him for the first time.

The tea in his hand shook.

He stared back at me with haunted silver eyes, and it felt like I was staring into a mirror.

"Someday, both of us will feel whole," he whispered. "The mental pain will lessen—it has to." His voice cracked like he was trying to reassure himself.

Before I could think through what I was doing, I reached forward and laid my hand across his. "I agree. We're going to heal," I said with conviction. "I have a good feeling about us." The truth of my words strummed through me.

Then, because bronze cheekbones still blushed pink as he stared at me, I added, "Thank you for sharing your past. I enjoy talking to you—not as enemies."

Pink became scarlet.

His fingers trembled and tea spilled. He wiped at the mess as he cleared his throat. "It's nice, getting to know each other." He cleared his throat. "Let's do it more often."

"It's a plan," I said and a strange warmth zinged in my chest.

There was something about this disheveled, blushing version of the fire king that brought down all my defenses.

There was an extreme vulnerability about him. He hid it behind bluster because he was afraid of getting hurt.

We were both emotionally damaged and afraid.

"Okay, let's keep working." Jinx clicked a pen and opened her notebook, and I jerked because I'd forgotten she was here.

Warm, callused bronze fingers laid across mine.

His touch was tender.

Pain zipped down my spine. In the back of the room, John made a noise in his sleep.

"Thanks for listening to me, *Aran*," Malum whispered.

I forgot how to breathe.

My proper name on his lips felt more intimate than a kiss.

Something shifted between us.

"Thanks for sharing." I gave him a small smile.

His eyes crinkled as he grinned.

We beamed at each other.

His warm thumb traced back and forth over the top of my hand. Ice melted off my skin.

"You're so screwed." Jinx's voice echoed inside my head, and it was my turn to flush as I pretended not to hear her.

We worked together for another fourteen hours.

And the entire time, his hand never left mine.

CHAPTER 36
ARAN
FLAGELLATION

ECCEDENTESIAST (NOUN): someone who hides their pain behind a smile.

DAY 25, HOUR 22

"Pretend to kiss me," Sadie shouted up at me as we swayed on the dance floor at Elite Academy. Her breath stank of demon brew, and she'd spent the last hour alternating between drunkenly laughing and sobbing.

Her outburst wasn't surprising. Frankly, I'd be worried if she *weren't* crying.

She kissed me sloppily on the cheek, and I grimaced.

Not because it was gross.

I grimaced because I couldn't feel where her lips touched my skin because my face was numb from excessive substance abuse.

Students, and a noticeably smaller number of soldiers, crushed around us in our old bedroom as speakers boomed. A gothic beat strummed eerily through the air, and the floor vibrated beneath us.

Vibrant red light filtered through the windows and made everything glow scarlet.

Once again, I shivered because I'd always thought the light at Elite Academy was a much darker shade.

I had a bad feeling the color had always been this rich.

I knew my vision had changed when I was younger, but I never realized it was to this extent.

Why had it changed back? That was also the question.

So many questions.

Still, no answers.

We'd finished strategizing, and after another day had passed with nothing to do but sleep and lightly exercise, we'd started going insane.

We were having another party for morale.

The angels were expected to return soon. We had days until we fought the ungodly again. Maybe a week if we got lucky.

Mental health recovery was very important to me.

That was why I was doing drugs.

Jinx had said there was no logical reason to party, but she hadn't slaughtered thousands of men and women as they screamed for mercy and then watched as monsters erupted from them. Her boots didn't stick as she walked.

So, what did she know?

War did things to a person.

We *needed* this.

I swayed to the music, arms wrapped around Sadie's shoulders, multiple cigarettes and pipes hanging from my lips as I drowned myself in smoke.

It curled around my face like a mask.

Sadie grabbed my shoulders and yanked me closer.

"Hear me out!" She stood on her tiptoes and yelled, but her words were barely audible over the booming music.

"Let's scrap the shower sex plan. Why don't we just make your men jealous—right now?"

She pulled back, mouth upturned in a manic smile as she wiggled her eyebrows.

Her ruby eyes sparkled with excitement. Golden skin was flushed as she practically vibrated with energy.

Now that I could see the full color spectrum, I was awe struck by how gorgeous my best friend was.

She seized my face with her hands and pulled me lower to her level. "Please, just kiss me—and maybe hump me a little. It will be so worth it! I promise."

The partygoers nearest to us looked over.

I flipped them off.

Stunning ruby eyes twinkled up at me.

Before I knew it, my platonic best friend—who was mated to three ferocious shifter men, and a creep named Cobra—buried her one hand in my curls, yanked my head down to her vertically challenged level, ripped the multiple pipes out of my lips, and slapped her hand over my mouth.

It took me a second to comprehend the nuance of what was occurring.

Sadie was making out with her own hand.

Over my mouth.

Aggressively.

I tried to pull away, because I wanted to pick up my pipes before someone stepped on them, but she yanked my curls. She tugged harder. Her ridiculous nails were tangled, and she couldn't get them free.

I narrowed my eyes.

Hers were closed like she was in the middle of a passionate embrace. She opened her mouth wantonly and licked across her palm like she was licking a lollipop.

Music spun around us.

Bodies danced.

As Sadie fake kissed me harder, her hand tightened across my face and obstructed my nose.

I suffocated.

I tried to pull away, and she tugged on my hair again.

Her kiss was rough and—what was with all the hair pulling? She bit down violently on her own palm, and I jolted at her aggression, glad it wasn't my lips.

I hated to say it, but we were not sexually compatible.

Her interest in Cobra was making a lot more sense.

I suffocated. I'd had enough. Sacrificing a chunk of my scalp, I yanked away from her and slapped her hand away.

She slapped me back and tried to plug my nose. Her talons barely missed my eyes and stabbed the sides of my nose.

I hadn't realized her nails were hot pink. I'd thought they were a neutral color.

They were a *look*.

After five minutes of wrestling, I used my height and strength to pin both her arms behind her back.

"Calm down. Stop it," I warned her as she struggled.

She giggled. "How was that?" She wiggled her eyebrows and beamed like she was proud of herself.

"Literally—*horrible*." I grimaced. "What the hell was with the biting? Are you a wild animal? What possibly made you think that I would want to be *bitten* aggressively in a sexual situation?"

She looked at me with shock and said, "*Wait*—I thought everyone was into biting?"

I prayed to the sun god for mental strength.

This was what happened when you let your best friend mate with shifter men. I was an awful friend for getting kidnapped and leaving her alone in the beast realm.

I frowned. "Normal people *don't* bite others. Not like that. You were really chomping. Be honest with me right now—are you doing that during sex?"

Her face turned bright red.

She mumbled, "Some people like it."

"Why are you actually a cat?" I tried to sound scolding but ruined it by playing with her long white hair.

She smiled as I released her arms and pulled me close. "Why are you such a silly little angel goose?"

"I'm not a goose." I shrugged sadly as we swayed back and forth. "I can't fly."

She smacked me. "I swear on my life, you hovered off the ground for a second."

"Thank the sun god," I drawled sarcastically. "Every girl dreams of hovering an inch over the ground. How exhilarating."

She took the lead and spun me around.

The sweaty partygoers punching the air and gyrating their hips melted into nothingness as we spun together in the middle of it all.

Red eyes narrowed. "One of these days, you're going to fly *so freaking high,* and I'm going to be watching, cheering you on and telling all the stupid grounders, that's my best friend. She's an angel, and you're all *wingless peasants.*"

I laughed at how ridiculous she was.

Lately Sadie had started using the angel's derogatory term for nonwinged folks, which was slightly concerning because she also didn't have wings. The logic wasn't there, but the sentiment was nice, so I was choosing to ignore it.

The loud music thumped faster and dancers fist-bumped the air.

We swayed slowly.

"I like your skirt," I said.

She beamed. "I like yours too. You look perfect tonight."

"You look perfecter."

We were just two classy women wearing lace bralettes and tiny black miniskirts. Matching initialed crystal thongs stuck out the tops of our skirts and elevated our looks.

Her bralette was bubblegum pink and mine black.

We'd gotten ready together, and Sadie had covered her eyes in pink sparkles that made the red of her eyes look like blood. Pink lip gloss also complemented her gold skin.

She'd convinced me to wear makeup, so I'd agreed.

Feeling fun and flirty, I'd swiped black mascara across my eyelids and under my eyes, so it looked like I'd been punched in the face.

I called it—racoon eyes.

I thought lipstick might have been too much, so I'd left that off. I didn't want to overwhelm everyone with my beauty.

When we'd stepped out of the bathroom, both our legions had been waiting for us—a long second passed as they took in our exposed thongs.

Cobra had hissed something, but Jax had pulled him away before we could try to translate it, and Malum had burst into flames and ordered me to change.

John had flashed his dimple and given me a fist bump. "I like the eyes."

That was why he was still my favorite.

Now, as I swayed back and forth with my best friend, I smiled because I felt the black makeup drip down my cheeks like tears, which was exactly the look I was going for.

"I love you," Sadie said with a rosy smile as she pulled me close.

My voice was hoarse from smoke inhalation as I replied, "I love you too."

"Someday this is going to be all over. We're going to go somewhere warm and sleep under the stars together. We'll have picnics and frolic," she whispered.

I nodded. "It sounds amazing."

I didn't point out that it sounded too good to be true.

The fae realm wanted to fight to the death for my crown, and the beast realm was a rainy, dreary place.

Such a picturesque place didn't exist.

Not for us.

"We'll find it," she whispered like she could read my thoughts. "I promise."

She wrapped her four-fingered hand behind the back of my neck and slowly pulled me closer. Then, with a roll of her hips, she placed her hand over my mouth and gently tugged me down to her level.

"How's this?" she whispered as she gently made out with the hand covering my mouth.

"Better," I mumbled as we pretended to make out, much softer this time.

Someone wolf whistled loudly, and a man yelled, "Holy sun god, isn't that Aran making out with the shifter legion girl?"

I grimaced.

How hard was it to remember the name Sadie?

My best friend kissed me harder like she couldn't help herself.

Personally, I thought she was acting crazy, but I just let it happen because we all had our breakdowns.

Seconds later, I was hugging empty air.

The crowd had parted around us.

"How fucking dare you touch our Revered?" Scorpius's tone was deadly.

John and Luka had pulled Sadie away from me, Malum

was on fire, Scorpius was trembling with rage, and Orion's eyes were wide, pupils dilated as he stared at Sadie like he was fantasizing about hurting her.

Sadie was smiling like she'd won a war.

"You have one ssssecond to remove your handsssss from my mate before one of my ssssnakes bites you," Cobra hissed as he sauntered forward.

John swore and leaped away from Sadie. A shadow snake darted across his skin.

Cobra flashed pointed canines. "One."

"What's going on here?" Jax asked calmly as he joined the growing group of testosterone-laden idiots. Xerxes flanked him with daggers drawn, and Ascher cracked his tattooed knuckles.

I sighed heavily because I wasn't high enough for this.

"Does anyone have any demon brew?" I asked tiredly.

"Really?" Malum asked. The rug was on fire beneath him.

Luka nodded and handed me a bottle of demon brew. The twins settled in behind me, both tangling their fingers in my curls like they needed contact.

I relaxed back against them and chugged.

Intoxicants filled my bloodstream.

"What happened?" Jax repeated as the kings and the rest of his male mates bristled with aggression.

Sadie winked at me.

I chugged faster. Demon brew dribbled down my chin and mixed with the black makeup.

"I *heard* your mate," Scorpius spat with disgust. "Making out with *our* Arabella."

My stomach flipped over at the use of "our," and pain streaked down my back. I tipped the bottle and took a long swig because I wasn't intoxicated enough if I could still feel things.

The twins tugged on my curls like they were upset.

The song switched, and the new beat was more frenzied. The partygoers shrieked with excitement as they recognized it.

"Are you kidding me?" Cobra hissed out. "Of all the people in the realmsssss, you wanted to kisssss her? What issss wrong with you?"

The anger exploded hot and fast. I slammed the bottle onto the ground, and it shattered. "What's that supposed to mean?" I glared at Cobra. "She kisses you? Clearly her standards aren't that high."

Flames leaped higher on the carpet.

"You admit to kissing her?" Fire exploded from Malum's mouth, and his silver eyes glinted with mania. "I can't fucking do this."

I shrugged. "Then don't." I took a step forward, but his arm shot out quicker than I could follow and slammed me back.

"There's glass on the floor," he said through gritted teeth. "You could get hurt."

"I know, I put it there," I drawled. "Stop trying to protect me."

Silver became steel, and he growled, "Stop kissing this pathetic woman who is not your mate. We've forgiven you for the twins—but this is *too far*!"

"Since when have you forgiven me for the twins?" I asked.

"Everyone, calm down," Scorpius snarled, sounding very uncalm himself.

He tried to step between us, but Malum breathed fire in his direction, and he stumbled back.

Ice crackled across my fingers, and the rug turned slippery beneath my feet. It expanded and extinguished some of the flames.

We glared at each other.

"We promised we wouldn't be like this," Orion whispered as he stared at me and grabbed Malum's shoulder.

"I didn't promise anything," Malum said grouchily.

I tipped my head back and laughed. "I knew it—I *knew* you crawling and promising to be my hound was all a ruse. I knew the news story in the beast realm was just as *fake* as you —it's all for show—you don't mean any of it."

I didn't dare mention how he'd opened up about his past. It hurt too much to say.

Malum's bronze skin darkened in the shadows of the party. A dagger glinted on his neck.

What had I honestly expected from a man who had "we conquered" tattooed on his skin?

White teeth contrasted with bronzed skin. "I meant *every fucking word* about serving you. I'll fall to my knees a million times if it means you'll forgive me."

The music pounded between us.

With his eyes locked on mine, he suddenly slammed down to his knees. He was wearing only black training shorts from his workout earlier, and the rug was covered in broken glass.

Blood pooled beneath him.

I took a step back.

He smirked cruelly, like he still had the upper hand while impaling himself. "I will *kneel* on glass for you every day if that's what you need to believe me. I'm serious about you, Arabella, but I will not stand by as you have a relationship with—*that woman*. She already took your virginity. She will *not* take you from me too."

My jaw unhinged.

He picked up a piece of glass and slammed his palm down on it. "Is this what you want?"

"Stop it!" I begged.

"Do you want all of us to kneel?" Orion whispered as he and Scorpius moved like they were going to mimic Malum.

"Don't!" Surprisingly, Luka also leaned forward like he was going to stop the quiet king from hurting himself.

I shook my head.

There was too much bloodshed.

Too much war.

Too much violence.

"Um," Sadie said awkwardly as she rubbed the back of her neck. "I think we should be honest. Honestly, I thought it was like the funniest thing ever, but now it's feeling a tiny bit concerning. Side note—aren't you guys in group therapy? It doesn't seem to be working."

"How do you stand to be around this imbecile?" Scorpius asked with genuine confusion.

John mumbled, "Finally someone said it."

"Hey, don't call her that." I rubbed tiredly at my eyes. My fingers came away coated in black.

Symbolic.

Malum eyed a jagged shard like he was thinking about using it.

"Don't you dare," I warned.

"*It was fake!*" Sadie blurted. "I was just making out with my hand, also—we faked it in the shower. We've never had sex." She shrugged. "Honestly, the thought makes me feel a little queasy because Aran is my best friend and sometimes romantic relationships end and the thought of ruining what we have is *horrible*."

I grimaced because my friend was a rambler when she was stressed.

"Excuse me?" Cobra hissed. "Romantic relationshipsssss with me do *not* end. Ever."

Sadie pursed her lips and smiled at him like he wasn't creepy.

Before I could point out how weird he was, John pulled my head to the side and grabbed my cheeks.

His dark eyes were imploring as he said, "Tell me it's true. You've never had sex with her?"

I rolled my eyes. "I've never even kissed her. She's my friend, nothing more."

John smiled, dimples on display, and he patted my cheeks. "That's my girl."

I flushed.

He winked and released me.

"What a relief," Malum said calmly as he got to his feet. His bronze legs were streaked in red, and shards glinted in his skin.

I pointed at him. "What is *wrong* with you? Why would you do that?"

Pink stained his cheeks, and he had the audacity to shrug like it was nothing.

"We're going to the medical barracks. Now." I grabbed Malum's wrist. Our skin sizzled as ice melted against heat.

I shivered, but it wasn't from the cold.

Pain exploded down my back.

John grunted as he grabbed my arm, and the rest of the men gathered around me as we RJE'd from the party.

I blinked, and we were back in the forest.

Malum burst into laughter and leaned forward to kiss my forehead.

I yanked away and stomped down the path to get a doctor.

Snow fell around us and the chilly air felt pleasant after the heat from the party.

"I like your outfit," Malum called after me.

I shook my head and didn't look back.

Men.

CHAPTER 37

JOURNAL PROMPT #2

TRUTH JOURNAL TO HELP FACILITATE
RELATIONS AMONG THE CRIMINALLY
INSANE

**If you were in love, how would you communicate
your feelings to your partner?**

Corvus Malum

Since we're all lying awake in bed (I can hear you
muttering insults under your breath, Arabella) and we've had
an illuminating night, I thought it would be a good time to
answer the second prompt.

I'm also a little intoxicated and want to talk to my mates.

Love is a weak, pitiful emotion that doesn't apply to
devils. Since I'm an Ignis, I'll answer this question as it
applies to my fated Protectors and Revered. I'd communicate
my feelings by protecting them with my fire and killing for
them. I'd touch them constantly because I crave physical
contact.

I will do everything I can to keep you safe, Arabella, even
if you hate me for it.

Aran Alis Egan

~~Thank you, Mitch, for sharing your feelings. That was very brave of you.~~

This is supposed to be hypothetical, and once again you're making it weird.

I would hang out with my <u>hypothetical lover</u> all day and talk to them. I would wrestle them and tell them inappropriate jokes. We'd nap beneath a tree and laze the day away. I would trust them and tell them everything that bothered me. We would be inseparable and close.

They would taste like freedom and would be handsome and strong and would burn the world for me and would get turned on just from looking at me and would be... I forgot where I was going with this.

Side note: If this is about helping prisoners, why is everything so romantic? Are they trying to make them fall in love? Do you guys think Dr. Palmer has a prison pen pal she writes to? Do you think they have sex? How does that work? Do they do it through the bars?

I'm still drunk. Please ignore what I'm saying.

Corvus Malum

You've never wrestled with me.

~~My feelings are hurt, and I am struggling to not burn my bed into ashes at the thought of you not caring for me.~~

I do not think the doctor has a lover.

She is a frigid bitch.

Aran Alis Egan

You're sexist Mitch. But seriously screw your misogyny.

I hope Dr. Palmer has a beautiful lover who worships her and is inspired by her strong personality.

They're probably making love as we speak.

Corvus Malum

The woman is a bitch.

Every time you call me a misogynist, I want to scream flames. Yes, I used to hate women because my mother abandoned me, said nothing about my abilities, and let me murder my family as a baby. I thought women were weak, manipulative creatures because that was the only experience I'd had with female devils growing up.

It's become clear these last few months that I was wrong.

I opened up to you in the strategy room, and it meant something to be able to share my past with you. You looked at me like you understood exactly how I felt.

Arabella, you're one of the strongest, most infuriating people I've ever met. I do not think less of you because you're a woman. Jinx is also highly competent, and I respect her.

Even your short, loudmouth, stupid, idiotic friend is not really that bad. I will refrain from killing her because she has never had sex with you.

~~After Scorpius heard you kissing her, I was planning on staging an accident next battle and murdering her because I can't stand for you to choose her over us. I knew I needed to get rid of her if you were ever going to be our mate.~~

Please ignore this part. I am very concerned what you will think when you read it.

The important part is, I respect women more since I met you.

Aran Alis Egan

YOU WERE GOING TO MURDER SADIE, MY BEST FRIEND, OVER A PRANK KISS??? WHAT THE FUCKING SUN GOD IS WRONG WITH YOU??? WHO DOES THAT???

I also loved talking to you in the strategy room.

Sometimes I wonder if we're not as different as we seem…but I am still furious about Sadie.

Corvus Malum

~~I still might kill her if she ever touches you.~~

The important part is that I am not going to murder her anymore.

Let's talk more in the future. I want to know all about your past.

Aran Alis Egan

HOLY FUCKING SUN GOD, YOU STILL MIGHT KILL HER!?!?

ERROR

This is an automated enchanted message that the owner of this journal's pen is out of their immediate vicinity. They are not ignoring you, don't panic . The High Court wants you to remember, you are enough and criminal insanity does not define you.

Orion Malum

Don't stab him with the pen, sweetheart. You'll hurt

yourself. If you knee him in the balls, that will hurt him the most. Once when we were kids, a horse kicked him in the dick, and he cried. It was the funniest thing I've ever seen.

I would show my mate affection by watching them every second of every day.

I will stalk all of you for eternity.

Scorpius Malum

Corvus, stop wrestling with Arabella and let her kick you in the balls.

Also, if you set this bunk on fire, so help me sun god, I will stab you with the butcher knife I stole from the kitchen. Do not test me, I sleep with it under my pillow.

In regard to this prompt, I would communicate my feelings to my mates by hurting them in a pleasurable way. I would dig my nails into their skin until they bled, to show them how much I care. I would make them scream with pleasure as I drove my cock inside them.

I will not cross out what I said, because unlike some people, I stand by my words.

Aran Alis Egan

Thank you, Mitch, for letting me kick you in the balls. However, if you hurt one hair on Sadie's perfect head, I will disembowel you in your sleep. You better beware because you are on thin ice with me.

Scorpius, you can't say things like that! What if Dr. Palmer is reading this? Oh my sun god, what if she is sharing what we write with her prison pen pal as we speak?

Weirdly, Scorpius, I do not hate the idea of you hurting me because I know you would never really *hurt* me. It's confusing because I don't like pain. I've had enough of it to last a lifetime. But for some reason, your violence intrigues me.

Corvus Malum

~~I am hard after wrestling with you. Your kick was weak and didn't hurt. Please come back and wrestle some more. I am desperate for affection. Lately Scorpius and Orion are mad at me for being rude to you, and they are not touching me as much. It hurts my feelings.~~

Scorpius Malum

Come on, man, not again.

Orion Malum

What do you think of my answer? No one has responded to me.

Aran Alis Egan

I like that you are always watching, Orion.

Although sometimes it is a little creepy when you don't blink for hours. I really liked talking to you and Scorpius in the shower. ~~Also, it turns me on the thought of you two showering together.~~

Whatever, I can't help it, you're both handsome.

Orion Malum

You're so perfect. I want to part your pretty pussy like I did back at Elite Academy.

I want to feast on you for hours. I want you to sit on my face while Corvus, Scorpius, or Luka fucks me. I want to fall asleep with my tongue inside you and wake up and keep eating you out. I want to take my cock and paint—

ERROR

More than four sexually explicit messages have been detected in a row.

This is an automated enchanted message reminder that your messages are being monitored by an administrator. We are aware that therapy journals can elicit strong emotional reactions and want them to be a safe space for you to share your thoughts. If you are comfortable having your explicit thoughts read by others, please proceed. Otherwise, have caution.

Orion Malum

I am not afraid to share that I want to paint all four of your faces with my cum. You all are mine. I can't wait to fuck all three of you, and maybe Luka if he's interested.

Do you think he'd ever be interested in someone like me?

Aran Alis Egan

DR. PALMER, ARE YOU HERE RIGHT NOW? ARE YOU LISTENING?????

Please let me know if you are partaking in a torrid romance with a prisoner. This is very important to me. Pleeeeaaaase answer if you are reading. I just want you to know that I support you and everything you do. I hope your lover treats you like you deserve.

Us women gotta stick together.

Scorpius, I'll pay you a small fortune from the fae palace's coffers if you get Mitch on his knees and cum on his face.

Also, yes, I know for a fact Luka is interested.

Corvus Malum

I was not aware that these journals are being monitored. This is a grave invasion of privacy.

Do you know who you are messing with? We are the devil kings from the ancient, illustrious House of Malum. We will make you suffer if you dare speak a word of this to anyone else. ~~I am embarrassed because I have spoken from the heart in this journal~~.

Orion, if you try it, I will set us both on fire, so help me sun god. The only person I'll kneel for is Arabella.

Scorpius Malum

I agree with my Ignis.

Whoever is reading these messages better beware because I will hunt you down and slowly remove your flesh. Do you know how it feels to have your skin removed from your skull? Don't worry, you'll find out soon enough. Count your fucking days because I will find you.

Please, all three of you and John will be on your knees before me. John doesn't know it yet, but he's going to be mine. Don't worry, I'll make it good for everyone.

. . .

Aran Alis Egan

Don't you dare threaten Dr. Palmer, she is a beautiful woman with a beautiful lover who is trying to help us. It's not her fault that she has an off-putting demeanor and bad interpersonal skills.

What matters is that she is trying her hardest, and that is so special to see. People just don't try anymore.

She's an inspiration to us all.

Are we having an earthquake or am I just drunk? What is the earthquake procedure...stab Mitch and run?

Also, I think Mitch would look pretty on his knees with a blush staining his cheeks. He's always blushing around me for some reason. I'll pay you a fortune Scorpius if you get him to kneel in front of you.

Scorpius Malum

Deal, but I don't want money. I'll trade for sexual favors.

Aran Alis Egan

Hmmm, I don't think so. I only support male prostitution. Sorry.

Corvus Malum

I do not blush. I have a manly reddening of the face caused by overheating because I am enchanted by your presence.

Why does the truth journal always make me write the most embarrassing things?

I think mine is broken. I demand a new one.

Please, Scorpius, you'll be on your knees before me. We

both know it will just take a little pain and you'll be begging me for it.

Aran Alis Egan

Which one of us do you think will be the best at sucking cock?

My money's on Orion because his lips are so pretty. ~~I want to kiss them.~~

Corvus Malum

Arabella.

Scorpius Malum

Arabella, then John.

Orion Malum

Arabella.

This is a fun game.

Which one of us do you think Scorpius is going to hurt the worst during sex?

I think it will be Corvus.

Aran Alis Egan

Mitch or John.

Scorpius Malum

I agree, it's a close one between those two.

. . .

Corvus Malum

What is wrong with the three of you? I am the Ignis in this matehood. That means I am the one who is supposed to dominate everyone.

~~But a part of me is tired of always being angry, and I will do whatever it takes to pleasure my mates even if that means~~

Aran Alis Egan:

I'm on the edge of my seat. Finish the sentence, Mitch. What are you going to do for us?

Orion Malum

Sweetheart, you agreeing that you're our mate makes this the best night of my entire life.

Also, yes, Mitch, tell us how you're going to get on your pretty little knees for all of us and stick out your tongue and take it.

Scorpius Malum

Mitchy poo, I'm going to tie you up with ropes until you sob and beg for it. You do make the prettiest noises.

However, Arabella's little breathy moans are my favorite.

Corvus Malum

I agree, Arabella makes the best sounds.

Also, please stop calling me Mitch. It hurts my feelings.

You know what, I will not be ashamed for having

emotions. I am a grown man with wants and needs. I've read that since Ignises are in touch with the soul flames of others, they feel things more deeply. That is all that is happening here.

Aran Alis Egan

Awwwwww. Mitchy, that was sweet.

Scorpius Malum

Mitch, I'd let you sleep with me, but these bunk beds are extremely uncomfortable and we wouldn't fit together.

We can sleep on the floor if you really need it? On a scale from one to ten, how likely are you to lose control tonight?

Ten being you burn the entire valley to ash.

Orion Malum:

I like this sensitive side to you, Mitch.

While it has made me respect you less as a warrior, it has made me respect you more as my mate.

Corvus Malum

I'm not going to burn anything tonight! I'm fine!

~~I just might cry a little in my sleep.~~

Orion Malum

I wish we could all fit in a bunk with you, Mitch. I miss sleeping together. It sucks having to sleep apart.

.   .   .

Aran Alis Egan

Mitch, how do you feel about the fact that Scorpius and Orion keep calling you fat?

Also, don't cry, baby girl.

Corvus Malum

This is not funny. Why do you keep calling me a girl?

I'm a grown man with an above-average-sized cock. My girth is immense, but I am not fat. You are all jealous of my muscles.

Aran Alis Egan

Whatever you say, baby girl.

~~I am jealous of your strength, I wish I could destroy rocks with a punch.~~

Corvus Malum

Wait, Arabella, are you joking with me? You said in the beginning that you would show your love for someone by joking with them, and you always call me ridiculous names that you think are funny.

Holy sun god. Are you in love with me, Arabella?

I'm very pleased.

Also, your muscles are perfect.

Orion Malum

Mitch does have an amazing cock. I can't wait for when we can finally all mate together.

. . .

Aran Alis Egan

WHAT. That is not exactly what the situation is unfolding to be.

Corvus Malum

Can't say no, can you? All of a sudden I'm a huge fan of these journals.

Scorpius Malum

Wow, Arabella, I can't believe you think it's hot that Mitch is being so embarrassingly emotional.

Is this what women want out of a man? Do you want me to start saying weird and off-putting things like Mitch?

Corvus Malum

Watch it, Scorpius.

Orion Malum

I think it's sweet that Arabella likes Mitch now that she knows he is secretly pathetic.

Corvus Malum

Are you both for real right now? Have you no loyalty????

Aran Alis Egan

I'm going to sleep. Everyone, forget everything that has been said tonight. Sweet dreams.

Corvus Malum

I will remember this night for the rest of my life.

Orion Malum

You know I'm just joking with you, my sweet Corvus— mostly. Sleep well, the loves of my life.

Scorpius Malum

Sleep tight.

I have somehow both gained and lost a lot of respect for my Ignis.

Corvus Malum

I am still taller and larger than you, and I can hurt you. ~~But I would never because you mean too much to me.~~

Scorpius Malum

Please, I'm longer where it counts. Also, I will hurt you, and I will enjoy it. Sweet dreams, baby girl.

Corvus Malum

Only Arabella gets to call me that.

. . .

Orion Malum

Guys, I really like that we are opening up to one another like this. I want to get something off my chest.

Corvus Malum

Please share. I'd love to know.

Scorpius Malum

Please don't. Tonight has already been traumatic enough.

Orion Malum

I went through a phase where I jacked off watching my mates sleep at night.

Corvus Malum

Thank you for being vulnerable with us.

Scorpius Malum

Excuse me?

Scorpius Malum

No. We are not doing this with these journals. This is supposed to make us closer to Arabella, not for you two to be weird.

. . .

Orion Malum

Also.

I am still in that phase.

Corvus Malum

Wow. I am feeling a lot of emotions right now.

Scorpius Malum

????? I'm burning this book. Neither of you are allowed to talk to me tomorrow. I need space.

Orion Malum

I'm doing it right now.

Scorpius Malum

GO TO BED RIGHT NOW AND STOP WRITING OR SO HELP ME SUN GOD I WILL STAB YOU BOTH!

Corvus Malum

~~I'm turned on.~~

Orion Malum

Same. Love you all.

CHAPTER 38
LUKA
TWIN REVELATIONS

Psychomachy (noun): a conflict of the soul.

DAY 28, HOUR 6

I woke up hyperventilating as a crushing emptiness expanded in my chest. Dark-gray light filtered through the single-pane window of the barracks, and I rubbed at my eyes to clear the fog.

Muted colors remained.

Snores echoed as the rest of the legion slept, and I gasped for air on the narrow bunk as my chest collapsed.

Disintegrated.

The chasm inside my sternum made it hard to move, think, or live. What was once vibrant and colorful was now faded and cold.

The empty feeling had arrived a few days ago. I'd woken up heaving from forgotten nightmares, and it had felt like a piece of my soul was missing.

The new abyss pervaded every moment of my existence.

It wouldn't leave.

My hand was hanging over the bed holding Aran's.

I leaned over the edge and took in her peaceful expression. Slowly, with my heart screaming at me to stop, I disentangled our grip.

As soon as her fingers left mine, the feeling of wrongness intensified exponentially. Lately, contact with Aran was the only thing that kept the emptiness at bay.

Minutes passed as I sprawled back on my bed and felt miserable.

Sick of wallowing, I crawled out of my bed and hauled myself up to my twin's bunk. I acted on instinct.

I laid on top of John and hugged him tight to me.

We barely fit together on the narrow bunk, but I didn't care, because the worst part of the emptiness was that I wasn't the only one affected.

I'd promised to protect my younger brother.

Yet we were both suffering.

Neither of us spoke as I held him tight to me. He'd been lying awake in the bed when I'd climbed up, dark eyes glossed over with pain as he, too, struggled with the yawning chasm.

"We need to figure this out today," I whispered. "It's time."

John turned his head to look at me. Expression grim, he nodded.

Yesterday, we'd snuck away to the medical barracks under the guise of getting food, and the doctors had performed dozens of enchanted diagnostics.

They'd found nothing.

There were no more options left.

We couldn't continue to suffer like this and fight effectively, so there was only one thing left for us to do.

Moving as silent as the spirit of Hesychia—the personification of quiet—we dressed for battle in our all-black uniforms with heavy combat boots. John stretched as he dressed like he was preparing for war.

We placed our prepared note on top of the dresser. We'd kept it vague and short. It stated that we'd return as soon as we could.

John dragged a hand through his messy hair. The circles under his eyes were gray, and his olive skin had an unnatural pallor that matched my own.

We were both sick.

"I hate leaving her," John whispered as we stood over Aran's sleeping form. He pressed a gentle kiss to her forehead and traced his fingertip over her scar.

I whispered, "Same." Nauseousness made my stomach roll. Separation was unacceptable, even if it was temporary.

The chasm in my chest continued to radiate pain.

We had no choice.

I ripped my gaze away from Aran and forced my feet to walk toward the door. If I let myself get closer to her, then I'd never leave. I'd curl myself around her like a cat and breathe in her wintry scent. I'd close my eyes and pretend everything was fine as I clung to her like an addict with his fix.

Sunlight reflected across the small room in streaks of unnatural gray.

I made a harsh gesture toward the door, and John sighed loudly, the noise desperate and broken. He tangled a blue curl around his finger and gave it a soft kiss. He released her slowly.

Incorporeal clouds of regret and unease hung around us as together we slipped out of the warm, enchanted room, and into the snowy forest.

The air was freezing.

I barely noticed.

I was too busy drowning in cool tones. The world was shades of bland. The once vibrant green needles of the conifers was now a sickly gray, and what was once a rich brown bark was now a sullen, bleached white.

Even the snowflakes were muted.

They no longer glinted as they fell and reflected sparkles from the sky in prisms of colors. They swallowed the sunlight.

Consumed it.

John stared at me with intensity. His dark-brown eyes now appeared black. He asked, "Are you sure about this?"

"I'm not sure of anything anymore," I said honestly, and John grimaced in agreement.

He gave me a curt nod, and I didn't wait for him to change his mind.

I released the darkness I always held in check.

Gray snowflakes disappeared into the void and the forest grew quieter as if it sensed the disturbance.

Shimmering black expanded before me as I let my power flow. The dark coalesced into something wider.

Taller.

The fabric of reality trembled, as it always did when it was introduced to a new form of matter. Our power wasn't solid, gaseous, or liquid, and it didn't buzz like enchanted technology.

It was silent.

The absence of matter within the presence of a realm's force.

I tipped my head back and let it flow. It was like taking a deep breath after drowning. Using my mind's eye, I shaped the darkness into a floating rectangle that was about the dimensions of a door.

It hovered over the steaming ground in front of us, glittering and black. It was a state of high energy.

Cold air filled my lungs, and snowflakes gathered on my lashes, reminding me of the woman we were leaving behind.

We had to do this.

For her.

For all of us.

"Let's go," I said. "Hopefully we can get answers before anyone realizes we're gone."

John dragged his hands over his eyes tiredly as he half stumbled, half threw himself into the darkness.

He disappeared.

Branches scraped together, as the storm picked up. My hair whipped around my head as frost burned my cheeks.

It was blizzard conditions.

For a second, I hallucinated that the realm was sentient. The storm was *alive*.

I threw myself through the doorway—I walked across realms.

RJE was our preferred form of travel, but this was an emergency, and we needed an audience with the king immediately. Entering directly into his domain was the best way to get his attention. He would recognize our presence immediately.

John was waiting for me on the other side. He brushed snow off his shoulders as I pulled the darkness back inside.

The door disappeared like it had never existed.

"Let's go, I don't want to linger," John grumbled as he stalked down the cavernous path that we were both intimately familiar with.

Monsters roared, rocks vibrated, and pebbles fell as the cavern shook. We both ignored the noise.

We were used to it.

My eyes adjusted to the new dim lighting. Hellfire glinted off the silver bars that lined both sides of the path.

I followed my twin deeper into the most dangerous prison in all the realms. I smirked as another monster roared.

Its existence was widely believed to be a myth. People were stupid.

The boogeyman was real, and so was the prison that housed him.

The king ran the prison, and in some ways, he *was* the prison because his powers were inexplicably tied to it.

Since we were his heirs, our powers were also tied to it.

John ran his fingers along the stalactite that hung from the ceiling like he was greeting an old friend, and the rocks vibrated with pleasure.

As we walked down the winding caverns—thousands of feet beneath the realm's surface—my twin stood taller.

Power clung to him.

He was stronger now that he was within the source of his abilities.

We both were.

We turned a corner, and a Minotaur prisoner threw himself at the bars next to John, opened his maw, and screamed bloody murder.

My twin turned to him and smiled.

Dimples flashing, he tsked at the beast that had murdered thousands.

The Minotaur went wild.

I rolled my eyes at my brother's antics. Since we were little boys and had discovered our heritage, he loved to taunt the prisoners, and they hated him for it.

I was indifferent.

Per usual.

John's steps took on a swagger as more prisoners threw

themselves at the bars as he walked past. They screamed, roared, and shrieked at him but flinched when he turned toward them, and scuttled back into the darkness.

If it weren't for his youth and dimples, he could be mistaken for the king. His darkness formed a glittering cape that hung off his shoulders.

A dark crown jutted off his head.

Similarly, the heavy weight of a cape settled on my shoulders, and I adjusted the crown that dug into my head.

The Princes of Darkness had returned to their land.

Rocks shifted beneath my feet like they were trying to touch me through my boots. The jagged path became smooth before us as the rubble reshaped itself. The rocks were always trying to impress.

"Thank you," I said as touched a boulder on the side wall.

It warmed and shivered.

I felt the cavern sigh with pleasure, then the energy shifted into pure excitement.

As if a switch had been flipped, the prisoners went dead silent and fell to their knees. They bowed their heads.

"My sons, to what do I owe this delightful visit?" The king's voice boomed. He stood under arching stalactites, hellfire casting shadows across his velvet robes, as he smiled at us.

Dark hair, dark eyes, olive skin.

Power rolled off him.

We were his mirror images. The blood of the royal family overwhelmed any other heritage we might have had. Which made sense because our mother had been a layperson. A human who'd secretly traded goods in both realms.

She'd left pregnant on a trading trip and had never

returned. The king hadn't known of our existence until Lothaire rescued us and brought us to him.

We'd gone from mortals to princes overnight.

Both had their challenges.

The king smiled with happiness in a cavernous prison dripping with stalactites, power, and fear.

His voice echoed. "No one expected the Princes of Darkness to visit the underworld anytime soon. I must say, I'm ecstatic. You've made your old man very happy."

He walked toward John slowly, then threw his arms around my twin in a punishing hug. As they embraced, he nodded at me over his shoulder.

I nodded back, and he didn't try to touch me.

I'd set my boundaries years prior, and the king respected them.

"We have a problem, Father," John said softly as he was clapped on the back.

The king straightened.

His dark eyes flashed as he glanced around at the kneeling prisoners. "Not here. Let's go to the castle and discuss."

He grabbed our arms.

Glittering black power—a derivation of our own—wrapped around us, and we were transported into a white marble foyer. Servants bustled around, and the familiar scents of marble and olives hung heavy in the air.

The ceiling was arched and lined with colonnades.

Olive trees filled the corners of the room.

A stately woman swept into the room and shouted boisterously, "For once, the oracle was correct. My favorite nephews have returned. Blessed be the day."

John smiled as she hugged him. "We're your only nephews, so we better be the favorites."

She pulled away and slapped me on the shoulder aggressively.

Our aunt was one of the queens who ruled Olympus and she'd never liked boundaries.

I pulled away, but the corners of my mouth lifted into a grin as she fussed over us like we were children.

"Nonsense. I'm sure someone has produced another child by now." She winked, and the king shook his head at her antics.

The royal blood was renowned for being too powerful to procreate.

They'd lived too long.

Immortality was both a curse and penance.

Before our mother, no woman had been strong enough to bear a child of our family's legacy. The embryos killed the mothers, and consequently themselves.

We were the king's miracle children.

We were his secret.

"Hades, prepare their room," the queen boomed authoritatively as she smacked John's wide bicep and tsked. "They're withering away. The boys clearly need to eat. They don't look well."

She snapped her fingers at the king.

"Yes, Athena," the king said, then he grumbled under his breath about meddling women and went off to find a servant.

Aunt's smile fell as he disappeared down the hall, and she turned to us. "Now that Hades is gone, tell me, boys. Honestly. What's going on? You don't look well, and I can feel your energy. It is disturbed."

"We're not sure." I rubbed at my sternum. The emptiness was a tangible chasm.

Her frown deepened. "Now that you're back at Olympus,

we can figure this out." She leaned forward and gave us both kisses on the cheek.

I withstood her touch because I knew she needed it.

With a dramatic flourish of her gown, she led us down the hall where the king had disappeared. Toward the kitchens.

Her heels clacked loudly across the white marble floors.

Servants ran out from the wings to polish the floor behind us as we walked, and I ignored the bustle of the palace like I always did.

"What have you boys done?" she asked, her eyes filling with fear. "I gave you the jewels because you said you were in love. Yet you come back appearing wan and depleted. Did she reject your advances?"

"She accepted," John said, and his voice cracked like just thinking about Aran being realms away was killing him.

It made sense.

It was killing me.

"That's not our problem. Something else has gone wrong," I said as she led us deeper into the castle.

She stopped walking abruptly, and all three of us halted.

Her olive-toned skin leeched of color, and she looked like she'd seen a Minotaur. Her eyes were unfocused, and she grabbed at her emerald necklace. "I think I know what's wrong," she said cryptically. "It's the enchanted jewels."

John's eyes widened.

Her fear was contagious.

"What do you mean?" I demanded as I pulled my twin behind me, a reflexive protective instinct I'd never grown out of. "What did you do?" I shouted, my skin crawling with worry.

Her head snapped in my direction. "It's not what I've done—it's what's been done to her."

CHAPTER 39
ARAN
TWISTED BONDS

ONEIROMANCY (NOUN): divination by means of astrology.

DAY 28, HOUR 6

I was trapped in the most insidious of nightmares—memories.

Three guards dragged me down the gilded halls toward the ornate cellar. Mother waited, tapping her foot with a frown on her face. I was fourteen years old, and we'd been playing this game for years.

You would think she'd have grown bored with it by now. Apparently, torturing your daughter never lost its appeal.

Mother's blue eyes widened with excitement as the guards threw me to the ground. Knees and elbows smacked painfully against hard marble. I bit down on my lower lip and said nothing.

Lay still.

There were a few rules I'd learned during these nights.

If you were quiet, the torture didn't last as long. If you acted repentant and weak, the torture didn't last as long. If you bowed your head respectfully, the torture didn't last as long.

The golden rule, never cry.

If I cried, then she'd light me on fire until dawn.

As a result, my eyes were perpetually bone dry, my heart was a shriveled hole inside my chest, and blue was my least favorite color.

My breath was unnaturally loud in my ears as dozens of guards watched from the perimeter of the room. They no longer stood in a small circle around me. They lined the large space and watched with blasé expressions.

A demoralizing tactic Mother loved to use.

She filled a room with guards to make it clear that I could never escape. You were outnumbered and trapped. It also added an element of shame that heightened the experience.

Mother was mad, but she was a great strategist.

Her voice echoed off the ornate walls as she said, "Your tutors have informed me that you glare and whisper petulantly under your breath. Have you forgotten your obedience lessons, daughter? A pathetic weakling like you has no right to address her betters—if you'd *bother* to show a little initiative and develop abilities, your behavior would be acceptable." She shook her head. "The *things* I could do at your age. You can't even imagine."

Her condescending smile widened as she crouched down next to me.

White teeth gleamed.

The fine details of her eyelashes and pores of her skin came into focus as she leaned close.

A distant part of me knew this was a dream.

But it felt so real.

She crouched before me.

Her red lips pursed like she was sad, and she ran freezing fingers across my forehead, then she smiled.

The world exploded in blue flames.

For a split second, my senses were so overloaded with pain signals that I felt nothing.

Cobalt fire danced across my skin.

It was almost beautiful.

My neurons resumed firing, and I arched my back with such force it cracked loudly. I screamed silently as blue devoured every edge of my existence. There was no end and no beginning, only pain. Time stretched. Every second lasted an infinity.

Mother crouched next to me with a mocking smile.

I was lower than an animal.

I was less than an object.

I was already dead.

The flames stopped, but I kept convulsing.

"Do you think she learned her lesson?" Mother asked loudly as she looked around the room at the guards.

No one moved.

"What do you think?" Her voice was laced with steel.

A familiar earth fae named Roy stepped forward. He was an older man and one of Mother's favorite guards. "She has not learned her lesson, Your Excellence." His dyed green beard quivered as he sneered in my direction.

Of course, because my life was an endless march of suffering, Roy had hated me since birth and used every opportunity to get me in trouble. I'd never done anything to him.

A monster screamed inside my head.

It wanted Roy's blood.

Since Mother's back was turned to me, I forced my trembling lips into a condescending smile and mouthed, "You're a pathetic waste of space."

His expression turned murderous.

I *used* to never do anything to him. Now, I taunted him every chance I could.

What was he going to do, tattle and have Mother torture me?

Too late.

"She's a petulant brat," Roy spat. "Make her pay until she learns how to be obedient."

I smiled at him with my teeth and mouthed, "You're a pathetic bitch."

He grabbed the hilt of his sword.

Mother nodded, then whirled around, and I lowered my gaze respectfully—hooded eyes, blank expression, subservient posture.

Roy exuded smug satisfaction as Mother snapped her fingers.

I kept my eyes locked on his as the world writhed in shades of hellacious blue. I let him see his death in my gaze as my back arched and palms slapped against the marble.

For hours, there was nothing but the pain.

A door slammed shut.

Consciousness wrenched me violently out of the nightmare. I was in a bunk bed.

The wood above my head was covered in a thin sheet of cobalt.

Sweat poured down my face and froze as it dripped onto my neck. I shivered violently.

Nine, eighteen, twenty-seven, thirty-six, forty-five, fifty-four, sixty-three, seventy-two, eighty-one, ninety, ninety-nine. Counting by my favorite odd number didn't help.

Sparkling lavender morning light filled the room.

Ten years later and the fae palace still felt like yesterday.

I was too old to be this young.

The barrack door opened, and someone entered from the outside. The steps came toward me.

"Do you want to talk about it?" Malum's voice had an odd tilt to it.

I sat up.

Bronze features were tight with rage, and scarlet flames danced off his shoulders to a violent beat. Silver eyes were hard as steel, and his jaw ticked like he was holding himself from saying something.

"T-Talk—" My teeth chattered, and I took a second to compose myself. "Talk about what?"

His knuckles cracked as he fisted his hands, and the dagger glinted on his neck as he swallowed thickly.

He took a step back from my bed.

I waited.

He remained silent and furious.

"Talk about what?" I repeated.

His face contorted with malice. "Talk about whatever has you freaking out right now. I don't know." He crossed his arms. "You tell me. Did you have a bad dream?"

"No, I actually had a pleasant dream," I said sarcastically. "It was super beautiful. Lots of sunshine and rainbows."

"You have nothing you want to tell me?" he asked slowly.

"Nope." I popped the *p* and studied my black nails.

Scarlet flames traveled up his shoulders and engulfed his head.

Why is he so angry? He couldn't know about my dream.

"Tell me what you dreamed of right now, Arabella!" he exploded, and I jumped at his sudden aggressiveness.

"Uh," I said. "I already told you. I dreamed of nothing."

"No." His voice was dangerous like whiskey, broken glass,

and freshly spilled blood. "You lied and said you had a fucking good dream. So tell me the truth."

"I'm not lying," I lied.

"You are clearly lying, tell me the truth!" Malum barked out.

A headache throbbed in my left temple.

This was bizarre behavior, even for him.

"What have I said about yelling in the morning?" Zenith snarled as he sat up on his bunk.

"I'm not yelling!" Malum shouted back.

I peered around uneasily. Orion and Scorpius were missing. I peered over the edge of my bed and looked up. The twins were also gone.

They'd all left and hadn't thought to tell me where they were going.

My stomach twisted, and my heart sank.

Ice crackled between my fingers, and my hands turned cobalt blue like I was wearing gloves.

"Tell me the truth." He bent over so we were eye level with each other.

I deadpanned, "I already did."

"I know you're lying."

"No, you don't."

"Yes." Flames trailed out of the corners of his eyes. "I do."

Creepy.

I pointed at him. "You have a little fire on your face."

He made a harsh noise and scarlet engulfed his head completely.

"There he is." I sighed as I inched closer to the warmth. It felt divine.

Flames shot from his mouth as he yelled, "You're the most infuriating woman!"

"Aren't you supposed to be wooing me?" I asked with genuine confusion. "If you keep this up, you're going to be single forever."

"I'm not single." Fire shot toward the ceiling. "I HAVE A MATE, AND SHE IS IN FRONT OF ME, LYING HER ASS OFF!"

His face was flushed with passion, and he heaved like he'd been running.

I blinked. "That was a lot. Simmer down."

He took a deep breath.

Silver eyes glowed as the flames receded from his head.

"Caring for you is *killing* me," he said. Without warning he grabbed the back of my neck and slammed our mouths together.

It wasn't a nice kiss.

It was brutal.

Vicious.

"Imagine how hating you feels," I said against his lips as we fought each other with kisses.

Malum wrapped his mammoth hand around my throat and slammed me down against my bed. His grip was tight. He towered over me like a vengeful creature from a foreign realm. Like a devil.

He was disturbingly handsome.

Pain streaked down my spine.

As he held me pinned, he said, "You're the most infuriating, insolent Revered in all of history. You're going to be the death of me."

"Good," I rasped out as I struggled to breathe.

His grip loosened, and he stroked his thumbs across my sensitive skin tenderly as I regulated my breathing.

"Are you okay?" he asked gruffly, pink staining his cheeks like he was embarrassed that he'd lost control.

"Peachy," I said sarcastically.

"Want me to kiss it better?" he quipped, and I smacked him with my pillow. He laughed darkly and sauntered away.

I flopped backward onto my bed, put my pillow over my face, and tried to smother myself.

The skin on my throat burned with heat.

The worst part.

I wanted more.

CHAPTER 40
ARAN
WARPED SOULS

ADUST (ADJECTIVE): burnt or scorched.

DAY 28, HOUR 14

A few hours later, I stood on a mountainside with the bane of my existence as a blizzard raged. Snow whipped in a frenzy, and sheets of ice slammed against us mercilessly.

The twins, Orion, and Scorpius had all disappeared without a word and left me alone with the blight on womankind who had choked me this morning like he owned my body.

The problem was I hadn't hated it.

I'd spent the entire trip up the mountain daydreaming of Malum holding me down as he did wicked things with his mouth.

"Okay," Malum said as he cracked his neck back and forth like he was preparing for battle. "So—I'm going to release my flames, and you need to try to stop me with your ice. Can you do that?"

I didn't reply.

Stupid questions didn't deserve answers.

I inhaled enchanted smoke and exhaled Horse. He circled and spun in the snowy air above my head.

Up on the mountainside, visibility was at an all-time low as the wind whipped angrily through the basin. The sky was dark with cloud cover.

Only idiots would venture up a mountain in a blizzard, and here we stood because of Malum.

It made sense.

He stretched his flaming arms out wide. "I'll take your lack of response as a yes—let's do this. Are you sure you don't want to use your wings? Knox says they are the source of your power."

I gave him a death glare. "I'm sure."

There was a 0 percent chance I was taking off my coat and exposing my wings in the middle of a blizzard.

Knox kept saying that our power generated from our wings, but Mother had lit me on fire nightly and she didn't have them. He could shove his bad advice where the sun didn't shine.

My fingers curled in my warm mittens.

After our morning fight (Malum had an episode and I watched), he ranted on and on about responsibility and the importance of making progress.

Then he'd dragged me up the side of a mountain.

"Like I said earlier," he said, like he thought talking about it more would change something, "I think it will be helpful for you to use your powers against my flames without all of us being present—I think we were trying too much at once. Let's start small."

I glared at him as my teeth chattered together.

Starting small would have been me trying to put out a fireplace while warm and cozy indoors.

"Okay, I'm going to release my fire—get ready." He bent his knees and took a step away from me. "I don't think it should be that much because the other men aren't present."

Flames roared as he exploded.

I was not ready.

Scarlet fire hissed as it fought against the blizzard. The wind sent red shooting out in all directions like a sadistic flamethrower.

I put my hands forward to get a little warmth.

It felt delicious.

If only I had some marshmallows and chocolate; suddenly I was craving s'mores.

"Try to stop me now!" Malum bellowed as he waved his arms. Ice melted around him, and the rocks in his vicinity caught fire.

Sucking on my pipe, I tried to figure out the best way to kill him while exerting the least amount of energy.

I patted my pockets.

I didn't have a gun.

Regrettable.

Flames leaped higher off him. "*Give it your best shot!*"

Raising my hands before me, I imagined the ice that always dripped from my fingers crawled toward the flames and put them out.

Nothing happened.

Snow mixed with fire and the elements roared.

Malum tipped his head back and screamed out fire.

There was no doubt in my mind, *he* was the dragon of the House of Malum.

I pulled off my warm mittens and stuck them into my pockets. My bare fingers were immediately covered in a sheen of ice that had nothing to do with the weather. I pointed them toward Malum.

Scarlet leaped off him, toward me, like solar flares on a sun.

The ice thawed off my fingers.

I put my hands under my armpits.

Hopping up and down to warm myself, I yelled, "It's not working!"

Exhaustion weighed down my bones, and my eyelids felt too heavy for my face. The urge to curl up under the flames and sleep was overwhelming.

Not again.

"Stab me with your feather, that worked before!" Malum yelled as his flames shot toward me with increasing frequency.

He took a step forward.

I basked in his warmth.

He gestured toward his stomach, and I realized he was showing where I should stab him.

My stomach pinched at the thought of purposefully making him bleed. That, or something I'd eaten wasn't sitting right.

I scowled. "Knox said our feathers are precious! I'm not wasting one on stabbing you."

Malum made an aggressive hand gesture that seemed to indicate annoyance, but it was hard to tell because his face was engulfed in fire so I couldn't see his expression. "I've seen you make ice claws, use that!"

"Fine," I said.

Snow gathered on my lashes and made it hard to see. Somewhere far above in the howling gray, Horse cawed out encouragement.

I once again extended my hands like an idiot.

Mother had never done something so idiotic.

A wild thought struck me, and I snapped my fingers like

she always had and pictured Malum writhing in pain.

I waited.

Nothing happened.

Honestly, in retrospect, it was probably for the best that I didn't have torture powers (I was a little disappointed).

I focused on ice claws, and within seconds, cobalt serrated edges extended from my fingers.

I admired them but frowned as I pulled them closer because the ice dug into the edges of my nails. Blood dripped down my hand. Holy fucking sun god. I scoffed in disbelief. Now I knew why my cuticles were so ruined.

How embarrassing.

"Do something!" Malum roared. "What are you staring at?"

"You really think stabbing you with these will help?" I waved the serrated edges around doubtfully.

A streak of scarlet arched toward me. The heat almost touched my cheek. I smiled because it felt nice.

I took a step toward the inferno.

Malum stumbled back. "Wait. Don't come near me. My flames might hurt you—I don't have control right now!"

I gaped at him as I waved my ice claws. "*You just realized this?*"

He took another step back. "Don't come closer. Put your claws away. The idea was shit—just try to use your powers from a distance."

For a second, I debated listening to him, then I remembered I didn't listen to men.

I smirked and took a big step toward him.

Seven feet of flaming male trembled at my proximity, and walked backward like I was poisonous.

I did what any woman would do if they were trapped on

the side of a mountain with the man who'd used to bully them—I ran forward, cackling.

A noise that suspiciously sounded like a squeal escaped from Malum as he ran away. "Don't come close, I don't want to hurt you!"

Of course, I ran faster.

Snow and flames whipped around us.

I hadn't had this much fun in years. Horse flew beside me like he was also giving chase.

"Stop it, Arabella!" Malum bellowed as he stumbled across the mountain.

"Corvus," I cooed. "Don't run from me, baby girl."

He tripped over a boulder and fell onto his butt. "You said my name?"

I used the advantage to jump on him. Claws extended like a cat, I aimed for his middle.

We slammed together; ice crashed into fire.

He rolled to take the brunt of the impact and I closed my eyes. It was toasty in his embrace. Amazingly warm.

It was even better than a hot shower after lying in a snowbank for hours.

For a long moment, we lay on the rocks, embracing, neither of us moving or speaking.

My short fingernails were curled into the material of his jacket. His fire had put out my ice.

Darn.

I sighed and snuggled closer. His arms and legs were still very much on fire, and they felt nice.

I was fireproof. Slay (in a hot way).

"We need to keep practicing," Malum muttered half-heartedly, and I looked up at him with exasperation. His bronze cheeks turned pink, flames flickering on the top of his head like a crown.

"No. *You* need to keep practicing. I'm perfect."

I snuggled against him and waited for his outburst.

He cleared his throat awkwardly. "You should put your mittens back on."

Before I could process what was happening, he pulled them out of my pockets and tucked them onto my hands.

"Good practice. Team." I yawned.

Eyelids heavy.

Soul warm.

I shook my head to wake myself up.

Malum's arms tightened around me so I couldn't move.

"It's fine, Arabella." I shivered at how he said my name. His voice was like smooth whiskey and high-end tobacco. "I'll carry you back down the mountain."

Nodding, I closed my eyes.

"I'll take care of you, my love," he whispered. "But please stay awake so I know you're okay."

I forced my eyes open.

Handsome bronze features hovered close to mine. His eyes were full of concern.

I leaned forward and kissed the tip of his nose.

He looked thunderstruck. "Why did you do that?"

"Because I wanted to," I said honestly.

Warm lips suddenly slammed against mine as Malum kissed me passionately. He claimed me with his tongue, and I melted. I kissed him back with equal fervor.

When he pulled away, we were both panting heavily.

I fingered my tingling lip and looked at him questioningly.

"Because I wanted to," he said as he started walking back down the mountain. It would be a long trek with me in his arms, but he didn't seem to mind. If anything, he looked pleased to be carrying me.

It made sense.

Men had evolved into stronger bodies so they could carry their superiors (women) around all day.

"Tell me about your childhood," he said out of the blue.

I played with my mittens. "It's not a pleasant story."

"I'm sorry for not asking before. It's *your* story, and I want to know more about you—please, *Aran*."

It was the first time he'd apologized without sounding arrogant. He looked down at me with such a hopeful expression that my heart twisted.

I began to talk.

I told him every gritty detail about what it was like growing up. For some reason, I told him things I'd never dared tell anyone else.

His silver eyes glimmered with understanding. He'd also walked through hell.

For hours, he carried me down a side of a mountain, and for hours, I told him what it was like growing up as the powerless royal heir of the mad queen.

He didn't get angry.

Not once.

Instead, he stayed calm and nodded, tucking me tighter against his chest like he could squeeze the pain out of me.

"It's all behind you," he said as we got back to the war camp.

I was amazed that he'd learned so many terrible things about my past and hadn't threatened to kill anyone. Not once. He was maturing.

I smiled at him as he tucked me gently into bed. "Thanks for not going on a homicidal rampage."

He laughed awkwardly and pressed a soft kiss to my forehead.

Butterflies fluttered in my stomach.

"Move over," Malum said as he pushed his oversized body into my bunk.

"What are you doing?" I shrieked as he fit himself into a space that was designed for a person half his size.

He was pressed flush against me.

"Let's keep talking," he whispered.

I couldn't hide my smile. Even though we'd already been talking for hours, I hadn't wanted our conversation to end.

"You should tell me about yourself this time," I suggested. "What do you miss most about the devil realm?"

"The peace," he said immediately.

He launched into a story about rolling hills and solitude. With his baritone voice, he should have been a storyteller. My toes curled.

He weaved a fairy tale.

I never wanted him to stop speaking.

I fell asleep with his warm body squished against mine, wild tales of ponies with bows and rolling hills dancing through my head.

The leader of the kings was slowly dropping his mask, and I was intrigued by the man it was revealing.

Flames danced in the air around us and cast a golden glow.

With my head tucked beneath his chin, I realized what he reminded me of.

Sunshine.

CHAPTER 41

ARAN

BATTLE

TRAVAIL (NOUN): a state of great suffering of body or mind.

DAY 29, HOUR 4

I woke up to sirens wailing.

Lights flashed.

I was convinced an apocalypse was happening, and we were all going to die.

Finally, my luck was turning around.

"*The angels have returned from their scouting mission!*" The alarm system blared over the room's enchanted speaker system.

Never mind.

I grunted as a heavy, warm weight rolled off me.

Someone kissed my forehead gently. "You're perfect," they whispered in my ear.

I rubbed at my tired eyes.

They were gone.

The speakers continued relentlessly.

"*The third ungodly infestation has been located, and RJE devices have been calibrated for coordinates.*" Lights flashed. "*All soldiers report to the cafeteria in .03 hours. Repeat. All soldiers report to the cafeteria in .03 hours. Reminder to move stealthily, quiet must be observed in open areas. Do not compromise the base.*"

Whatever angel hit the preprogrammed emergency broadcast button was getting punched in the throat.

There was literally no need to rush into battle.

It was still dark out.

Men stumbled around the room, getting ready like there was a fire. The twins and the missing kings had returned sometime in the night.

My fingers froze together as ice crawled up my forearm.

The room was a flurry of activity as everyone in our legion panicked. Malum shouted something.

I blinked groggily as I rolled lazily out of bed.

"Let's go." Malum grabbed my arm as I pulled at the covers. His eyes were chips of steel.

I jolted as I remembered how he'd talked to me for hours.

"Wait, did we sleep together all night?" I flushed as I remembered the warm weight rolling off me.

Did he kiss my forehead this morning and tell me I was perfect? Had I imagined it?

"That's not important right now," he said in a clipped tone. "Get ready." The warrior was back.

"It's important to me," I said as I got ready.

When I was dressed, Malum grasped my arm and pulled me out of the room, straight into a punishing blizzard.

What was with all the grabbing this morning? He held on to me like he was afraid he'd lose me.

Wind burned where it touched my exposed face.

The ground was iced over, and the pine trees were

completely coated in white. Branches were frozen and made no noise.

Dangerous icicles glinted.

The only sound was our crunching footsteps, frosty breath, and screaming wind.

It was eerie.

The twins jogged in my peripheral vision, and my heart hurt as I remembered they'd left me. They were supposed to be different from the kings. They weren't supposed to leave without a word.

Scorpius and Orion sidled protectively in front of me. Malum kept his hold on my arm.

They turned their heads back toward me. Once again, they had streaks of dried blood on their faces.

"Where did you two go?" I asked.

"We can't say," Scorpius said with a strange expression. Orion stared at me over his shoulder.

"Whatever." I pushed my pipe between my lips and inhaled sharply. "I guess we all have our secrets." I exhaled, and smoke curled around my face.

The arm pulling me along the path caught fire. I leaned closer to the warmth and narrowed my eyes up at Malum as I tried to figure out what had pissed him off this time.

His cheeks turned bright pink under my scrutiny, and he purposefully didn't make eye contact.

I stumbled as I realized he was intentionally on fire. He was warming me. Another frozen piece of my heart thawed. I played with the edges of my sleeves.

"Be careful," he ordered. "Keep your mittens on."

I arched my brow at his tone, and his blush intensified.

"Don't tell me what to do with *my* mittens," I said as we moved through the trees.

The corner of his lip curled up. "Don't be a brat."

I stuck my tongue out at him.

The demons sprinted past, kicking up snow in their wake.

Malum's grip on my arm tightened, and I realized he was still dragging me.

"I don't need you to lead me like a dog." I tugged away from him.

"No, you don't." He didn't release me. "But you do need me to warm you."

He had me there.

"Your fire is nice," I admitted sheepishly. "Thank you."

Malum tripped and his gaze shot to my face. He stared at my face with a strange intensity and said, "You're welcome."

Energy strummed between us.

When we entered the cafeteria, and the gathered soldiers fell silent at our arrival. They waited for our directions. The space was much less full compared to the first day we'd gathered.

We were losing soldiers at an alarming rate.

"Did everyone read the new battle plan that we delivered to your barracks the other day?" Malum shouted.

Soldiers nodded.

No one spoke.

"I have a question," Knox said as the group of angels approached him.

I backed away as they started to argue.

Jax asked the room, "Does anyone else besides the angels have any questions?"

Some soldiers turned to each other, but no one else spoke up. Workers hustled around the room, handing out enchanted swords and other various weapons to everyone.

Sadie stood off to the side, whisper arguing with Cobra, and I headed toward her.

I walked into a wall of male.

It was the twins.

"We need to talk," John said, his voice imploring as he wrapped his arm around me.

I shrugged him off and backpedaled. "You two left without a word—what the hell?" My voice cracked.

Luka made a pained noise and grabbed my shoulder. "We left a note on the bureau. Did you read it?"

"I didn't get any note," I said.

"Shit," John swore. "You must have been worried."

My stomach hurt as I thought about everyone leaving me alone yesterday. What if Malum had killed me? Everyone knew what he was like.

Well, what he *seemed* like. It was hard to fear someone after they cuddled you all night.

Jax shouted, "One minute until we RJE to the camp! Stick to the plan!"

John said quickly, "We had to go to our home realm because we needed to figure out what's been happening to us." The three of us strapped enchanted swords onto our hips, and Luka helped me adjust my holster. "We've been ill."

My stomach dropped.

The twins' faces still looked pale, and they had dark circles beneath their eyes. I'd noticed they'd been looking unwell recently, but I hadn't gotten the chance to ask them about it with all the war strategizing.

"Are you okay?" I asked, all anger leaving my body as panic set in. The twins needed to be fine. Sun god, we were about to walk into battle.

Worry made my legs weak.

"We'll be fine," Luka reassured me as he twisted his fingers around one of my curls. "We just need to tell you everything we've learned—it affects all three of us."

"What is it?" I asked, afraid of the answer.

"Fifteen seconds!" Malum shouted, and RJE devices whirled. The rest of our legion surrounded us. Zenith made a quip, but I was so nervous for the twins that I didn't hear him.

Orion and Scorpius grabbed my wrists. Malum stood directly behind me and engulfed me with his larger frame. The twins sidled closer.

Five men surrounded me.

Crack.

I opened my eyes, and we were on the edge of a forest, a wall towered a few feet away.

Jax and Malum pointed, and soldiers nodded as they fanned out under the cover of dark until only a few of us were left to infiltrate the structure.

I breathed deeply, but my lungs didn't work.

The pipe was heavy in my mouth.

"Let's go," Jax mouthed as he put in his earpiece and pulled up the black hood that covered his face.

Everyone followed his lead.

The shifters climbed over the brick wall first, moving stealthily and gracefully with their heightened animal instincts.

"It has to do with our enchanted jewelry," John whispered hurriedly in my ear, and I looked over. He wasn't wearing his earpiece and hadn't pulled up his hood. Neither had Luka.

More people climbed over the wall.

It was almost our turn.

"We confirmed with our aunt, who was the one who gave us the jewels," John spoke quickly. "They form a soul connection between wearers when wedding vows are said aloud."

The assassins climbed over the wall, and the demons followed.

Luka said, "However, enchanted jewels are extremely rare and can take on lives of their own."

The angels unfurled their wings and flew over.

John continued, "Our aunt thinks that's what's happening with us." He frowned. "She thinks the soul connection is already forming between us because it senses something is wrong with one of our souls."

My stomach plummeted.

The kings started climbing.

"What do you mean?" I asked, the words numb on my lips as my vision blurred.

Both twins frowned like they didn't want to say it.

John blurted, "She thinks something is wrong with your soul and it's affecting us. We're having strange pain down our backs and disturbances with our vision. We both feel—empty lately. It's hard to describe."

Oh no.

I knew exactly what pain they felt across their backs; I knew they were seeing in gray tones; I knew exactly the feeling of emptiness they were describing.

I wanted to vomit. Cry. Scream. Faint.

"What are you three waiting for? Climb over." I jumped as Malum's voice crackled through the earpiece hanging around my neck.

"We'll figure it out later—we just wanted you to know what we've found," John said as he pulled the hood over his head. "It's not a big deal, we don't know anything for certain yet."

Luka nodded as he mimicked his motion. "Don't worry."

Too late.

I was having a full-blown panic attack.

What was wrong with my soul? Was I soulless?

It would make sense.

The twins gestured to the wall, and with tingling limbs, I climbed over as they followed close behind.

"What took so long?" Scorpius snarled when I got to the other side.

I barely noticed the courtyard, festive lights, and tinkling bells.

I barely noticed the black corridors.

Ungodly screeched. Animals roared. Blood splattered.

Jinx yelled inside my head.

I was a visitor inside my own body, a soulless husk of bones that fought mindlessly. Perhaps that was all I'd ever been.

An ungodly shrieked in my face.

Malum shoved me aside and ripped its head off with his bare hands.

An infected stabbed an enchanted sword at me, and I dodged, then spun and gutted them. An ungodly ripped from their flesh, and I gutted them too.

Some infected shouted taunts, some fought silently, and others pleaded for mercy that was not mine to give.

The twins fought surrounded by dark shadows.

I grunted as an infected landed a punch to my stomach. Before I could retaliate, Scorpius viciously broke both his arms and legs.

Later, an infected male screamed something derogatory in my face. Luka grabbed his tongue, slicing it clean out of his mouth before gutting him.

I blinked.

A man got too close to me, and John stabbed him, then stomped on his face.

I blinked.

Orion cracked the neck of an infected who almost landed a blow on my arm.

I blinked.

Malum lit three infected on fire as they approached me.

I blinked.

Scorpius and John sliced the limbs off an infected whose sword lightly grazed the side of my leg.

I blinked.

Luka and Orion silently disemboweled an ungodly together.

I blinked.

Malum set a room of infected on fire.

I blinked.

My sword skewered three infected at once, and John yelled "good work" at me while the men handled the ungodly.

I blinked.

Green and red were splattered across corridor walls.

My boots stuck to the floor as I ran after my prey. I left a trail of cobalt ice in my wake. Smoke curled from the pipe permanently lodged between my lips.

The haze stole time.

Purpose.

Meaning.

An ungodly shrieked into my face, and I screamed back.

Sun god save my broken soul.

CHAPTER 42

ARAN

SPIRALS

PHTHISIS (NOUN): a progressively wasting or consumptive condition.

DAY 30, HOUR 13

Knock.

A person stood outside the closet door.

Ice coated the floor beneath me.

Knock. Knock.

Did no one have respect for the champions of war anymore? If I were a man, they never would have interrupted me.

I was obviously holed up in the dark closet of the medical barracks for a *reason.*

The reason was an extremely important meeting between two champions of the gods. Highly classified business.

Supplies were piled high all around, and my knees were tucked against my chest. A box of needles dug into my ribs. Outside the closet, doctors ran about, treating wounded soldiers.

A gurney rattled as a man cried out in pain, and across the room a woman moaned.

Doctors yelled instructions.

Knock-knock-knock-knock. Two shadows obstructed the sliver of light under the door.

"Go away," I ordered.

"You've been in there for hours," John said. "People are starting to worry—I'm worried about you, Aran."

I inhaled enchanted drugs and enjoyed how the smoke burned my lungs.

"You don't need to," I said hoarsely. "I'm doing amazing."

There was a pause.

"For some reason I don't believe that—please come out." John sounded tired and frustrated. "We still need to talk about what we told you earlier. All three of us can face this together."

"Later," I said. "I'm having an important meeting."

An elbow jabbed my stomach.

Sadie repositioned herself.

"Sorry," she whispered, then rammed her elbow into my face. "Sorry again, my foot's numb, and I'm trying to get feeling back into the damned thing."

"Control your limbs, woman."

She huffed as she knocked over a box of supplies. "Cool the attitude. I'm *not* the one who insisted we needed to talk in a closet after a battle. You know I love you, but sometimes—it's hard to be supportive." She paused. "This is one of those times, in case it isn't clear."

"Wow," I said. "Excuse me for trying to have an important *business meeting* with just the two of us."

"Why are we having a business meeting in the closet?" Sadie asked.

"For the privacy—duh."

Sadie flung herself forward and strangled me. Her acrylic nails jabbed my skin. Boxes fell over and needles clattered on the floor.

Never mind. It was a hug.

Sadie held me tight. Even fully clothed in our uniforms, her body heat contrasted with my chilled flesh. I shivered and hugged her back.

It was nice.

My nose wrinkled, and I coughed at her stench. "This is kind of gross," I said as I tried not to inhale through my nose.

She squeezed me harder. "I'm not the one who said we didn't have time to shower. Just don't think about all the gore rubbing between us right now. Dripping and mixing—"

I shoved her off, and she laughed as more boxes fell.

She was insane.

A third shadow appeared outside the door. "Get out of the closet, Sadie," Cobra ordered, "or so help me sun god, there will be consequences."

Sadie clacked her nails together. "Try anything and I'll tell Jax that you've been secretly bullying me."

Cobra hissed like a snake as he kicked against the door. "He'll *never* believe you."

"Please," Sadie said. "We both know that's not true."

"Aran, are you sure you need more time in there?" Luka asked, his voice tight with worry.

"Yes," Sadie and I replied in unison.

Cobra and John whispered something to each other. After what sounded like a long tense debate, the three men walked away from the closet.

I didn't trust them.

"Finally, they're gone," Sadie said. "Now we can—what were we doing again?"

"Talking about *highly* classified secrets," I whispered conspiratorially.

"Well, then get on with it." Sadie clapped. "You said we had an emergency that we needed to solve. Let's do it."

She clapped again in my face.

"Really?" I asked.

She clapped as fast as she could.

I fantasized about a friendless, lonely existence.

"Did you hear that?" a doctor asked, their shadow pausing outside our door.

Sadie whispered in a spooky voice, "Thisss isss a poltergeist, you didn't heaaaaar anything or I will haunt youuu."

I smacked her arm.

She hit me across the face and her nail took a chunk out of my cheek.

We both raised our arms and smacked at each other as fast as we could for five minutes.

"Don't worry." She wheezed between laughs as she put her talons down. "No ghost would want to haunt you. You'd haunt them."

A male soldier screamed, then started sobbing uncontrollably, and the doctor outside our closet ran to assist him.

"Pussy," we both said at the same time.

It wasn't funny, but postbattle delirium had set in.

The closet was exacerbating our instability; however, there weren't many quiet places you could meet these days and not have men watching you like perverts. We were making do.

"That's actually part of the reason I dragged you in here to talk," I said as I tried to calm my racing heart.

Sadie stopped laughing.

Awkward silence expanded.

"You're a pussy?" She asked.

"The other part."

"Oh," she said. "If I'd known you actually had a ghost problem, I never would have mimicked one. What do you need me to do? An exorcism?"

I smacked her. "That's not a real thing."

She punched me. "Do *not* disrespect the time-honored tradition of violently extracting ghosts from people."

"What are you going on about?" I asked.

Sadie shrugged, "That's for me to know and for you to find out—be *gone*, evil spirit."

I huffed. "It's not a ghost issue. I'm in good standing with the poltergeist community. I meant the haunting part."

Needles clattered like Sadie was playing with them. "I'm not going to lie, I have no idea what's going on right now. A part of me thinks I don't want to. Spell it out like I'm stupid."

It was only on account of our friendship, and the fact that I loved her like a sister, that I refrained from a sarcastic reply.

"Stop playing with stuff," I said.

"Oh my sun god," Sadie whined. "If you don't tell me what's going on, I'm going to stab you with a needle. The suspense is killing me. You know I'm not patient, come onnnn. Just blurt it out."

"Some things," I enunciated each word, "just can't be *said*."

"Just give me a hint," Sadie demanded. "Is it about the ungodly? Your dead mother? Is the cannibalism coming back to haunt you? I always worried that would happen. Is it the kings—because I noticed they've all been acting weirder than usual around you lately. Malum made a show of opening the door for you the other day, and I was honestly worried he was going to bludgeon you with it—but he didn't, and then you thanked him and he turned red like a tomato. It was all very strange. Side note—does he have a rosacea skin condition? I might have a cream recommendation.

I pressed my palms against my eyes until I saw stars. "It has nothing to do with any of that. *Please* stop talking."

Sadie ignored me. "Is it the fact that 'whore' is carved on your back? Did you wish she wrote 'slut' or something a little trendier? I've always wanted to ask you that but didn't want to sound insensitive."

"Too late," I said.

She continued, "Is it because it hurts when you're turned on? Or is it because she wrote it super inconsistently and the *w* is so much bigger than the *h*? Honestly, that's also always *really* annoyed me. Like how hard is it to carve a word evenly into someone's skin? The lack of basic decency, and any eye for proportions, is horrible."

"Are you for real right now?" I asked.

Needles clattered. "Yeah," she said brightly, "I honestly feel so much better after telling you. A huge weight off my shoulders. At first I thought this whole postbattle hiding-in-a-medical-closet-thing was a little weird. But I get it now."

"Sadie," I snapped.

"What?"

"We're in here because I don't have a soul. I'm a soulless monster—I'm *missing* my fucking soul."

Stunned silence.

"So you don't want me to give you the skin cream recommendation?"

"No."

She patted my back. "I will admit, sometimes I also feel

soulless because I struggle with making moral choices. I think it's because of extended time with Cobra, but—"

"No." I cut her off. "I'm *actually* missing my soul. I have a *hole* inside my chest." I thumped against my sternum.

"Okay, let's not panic," Sadie said calmly. "Explain."

My voice quivered. "The betrothal jewels the twins gave me are linked to souls, and apparently, enchanted jewels can be sentient."

The jewel of death pulsed against my chest and diamonds vibrated on my wrist as if agreeing with my statement.

I continued, "The twins said that for some unknown reason, the jewelry I'm wearing has gone ahead and completed the bond between us."

I let Sadie process what I was saying and waited for her to make the obvious connections.

"You got married without telling me?" she asked shrilly. "I was going to be your maid of honor and give a funny speech. I've already written it."

She burst into tears, then started wailing at a heinous pitch.

I pushed my pipe deeper into my mouth.

Why I'd thought Sadie would ever react like I expected was beyond me. I rubbed circles on her back as she sobbed and said, "Let it out."

"It's just really hard." She gasped, dug around in the boxes, then blew her nose loudly on what I could only hope was a tissue. "You would have been such a beautiful bride— do you know how this makes me feel?"

"Um."

"Horrible. Dejected. Shattered."

I drawled, "Oh yes, me being married against my will *while* fighting against monsters—by sentient jewelry, that is apparently killing the men I'm tied to because I'm probably missing my soul—is hard for *you*."

I slapped her on the back of the head.

She sniffled. "Are you being sarcastic?"

"Not at all," I said.

She did loud breathing exercises, then said, "I can't have this conversation until you promise you'll still have a ceremony and I get to be your maid of honor."

Three point one, four, one, five, nine, two, six, five, three, five, eight, nine. The numbers of pi helped give me some perspective.

"Fine," I agreed. "I'll have a wedding just for you."

Sadie squealed and chucked herself at me. I fought against her hug, but she must have channeled her shifter strength, because she pinned me to the icy floor.

"You're going to make the most beautiful bride," she whispered into my ear. "Also, I want to wear a white bridesmaid's dress."

"Get off me."

She chuckled and pulled away.

"Can we please now talk about this seriously?" I asked. "I'm kind of panicking."

"I understand." Sadie sniffled. "I was really freaking out about your wedding. It really took a toll on me."

"I'm glad you recovered," I said sarcastically.

"Me too." She patted my head. "And you're very brave for talking about your jewelry issue. I'm proud of you."

"The twins have been sick lately," I whispered.

Guilt twisted in my stomach because I should have told them the extent of my problems. I never should have pretended I was a normal woman who could do something as mundane as have husbands.

Mother's cruel smile flashed in my mind.

"Soul bonds go both ways," I said. "You have connections to your mates' souls, *and* you can feel their emotions. Good and bad. That's what you have with your mates, right?"

"Yeah," she said.

Smoke whistled through my lips. "I don't feel anything from the twins, and all they feel is my pain. Every time I'm aroused, they feel pain in their backs, just like I do. The jewels didn't work properly because they're attuned to souls —and I don't have one."

"That seems like a logical leap."

"It's not." My voice cracked. "I'm empty, so there's no soul to join. It connected them to the only thing I've ever had."

"Which is?" Sadie asked with confusion.

"Suffering."

CHAPTER 43

ARAN
THEY KNOW

TRAGICOMEDY (NOUN): a drama or situation blending tragic and comic elements.

DAY 30, HOUR 14

The closet door was ripped off its hinges.

Light blinded my corneas.

"Get out," Malum said viciously.

I squinted up at the leader of the kings. Scorpius, Orion, and the twins surrounded him.

Malum blocked the doorway. "*Now*, Arabella. Your closet time is fucking over."

"Really? You couldn't just open it?" I asked. He placed the door, which he'd viciously ripped off the wall, on the floor.

Behind him, blood and gore was splashed across the medical barracks like a crime scene. Doctors paused stitching up soldiers to gawk at their mangled door, and soldiers paused their moaning to gape at their leaders.

The men glared down at me.

I sighed.

Malum made a harsh noise as Cobra hurried forward and pushed past him. The snake shifter fell to his knees beside me, and with surprising gentleness, he pulled a needle out of Sadie's arm (apparently, she'd been playing with one in the dark?) and patted her arm like he was making sure she was okay.

I gaped at my best friend and pointedly looked at the discarded needle.

She winked.

"You're a freak," I mouthed at her as Cobra gingerly picked her up and cradled her against his chest.

She smiled over his shoulder and waved her long nails. "Takes one to know one. Let's finish this talk later." Her mates coalesced around her and whispered sweet nothings in her ear as they left the medical barracks.

No one kissed my head and gently offered to pick me up. No one whispered anything nice into my ear.

I got *glared* at.

In fact, both the kings and twins were frowning down at me with all their arms crossed, even John.

I squinted, unsure for a second if the haze had returned and I was hallucinating, because they all looked livid. From their expressions, you would think I'd have done something unforgivable, which was strange because they were literally okay with *murdering* people.

Last time I'd talked to the twins, they'd been concerned but not angry. The kings also hadn't been mad.

In the past day and a half of battling ungodly, something had changed.

Did someone tell the kings that women had rights?

Scorpius muttered something scathing under his breath, and Malum nodded in agreement.

Scarlet flames crackled across Malum's shoulders, and the medical barracks went dead silent. It felt like everyone was holding their breath, waiting for an explosion.

I remained seated and sucked on my enchanted pipe.

There were two steps to being *that* bitch: (1) protect your peace from men, and (2) never pay retail.

Horse settled onto my shoulder. His smoky head nuzzled against my cheek while I gently stroked his feathers.

I didn't need men because I had something *much* smarter, cooler, and better looking: a bird.

For the first time since I'd met them, the twins seemed twisted. Evil. Wrathful. Their dark eyes radiated danger.

The kings looked similar.

Silver flames glowed in Malum's eyes. The eye on Scorpius's neck blinked open and glared at me accusingly. Orion frowned.

Malum lunged forward like he was going to instigate a fight.

He stopped inches away from me.

If he was trying to intimidate me, it wouldn't work. I had a secret weapon. I possessed something they never would —class.

And the ability to put a cute outfit together.

"You can all go take a large, misshapen piece of wood— and shove it up your asses." I made an obscene gesture. "Leave me alone and get control of yourselves. You're frightening me."

Malum bared his teeth. "Good. You should be afraid."

How is this the same man that cuddled me?

Flames sizzled.

A body lunged. Quicker than I could follow, fingers wrapped around my throat.

"Go fuck yourself, Mal—"

Nails dug into my skin.

I froze.

Pale cheekbones, sharper than glass, hovered inches from my face. Unfocused milky eyes stared off into space, and wine-red lips were smashed into a thin line.

Bergamot and musk were spicy with fury.

I was drowned in Scorpius's rage.

"What's your problem?" I asked, unbothered by the pointer finger digging into my jugular.

Scorpius's jaw clenched, and he didn't speak. His tattooed eye was wide open, staring at me.

I blew smoke in his face.

Nails pinched as they dug deeper into the sensitive skin on my neck.

Behind Scorpius, the twins stepped forward. Darkness glistened around them.

I waited.

Neither of them made a move to pull Scorpius off me.

They flanked him.

I ignored Scorpius slowly asphyxiating me and stared at the twins.

"Traitors," I gasped out, my voice raspy from lack of air.

John didn't move, didn't flinch. He did nothing to show that he'd heard me. His familiar dimples had transformed into harsh lines that highlighted the fury on his handsome face.

He was a stranger.

"Is it true, Aran?" he asked cryptically, voice hard and deep.

"What?" I asked. My heart hurt.

John took a step closer. "Tell me right now that it's *not* fucking true." Darkness glinted and twisted around him like living shadows.

I blinked.

John's image changed.

A cape of darkness was draped across his shoulders and blew on a phantom breeze. A jagged crown sat atop his dark curls and his eyes were pools of darkness. His features were hard.

There was nothing boyish about him.

I blinked.

The crown and cape disappeared, but his rage remained.

Scorpius's grip on my neck tightened, and I choked on air.

Betrayal mixed with asphyxiation, and suddenly it hit me —I'd had enough.

Kicking out and flexing with all my might, I ripped my neck out of Scorpius's grip and climbed to my feet.

I stalked toward the man I thought I loved.

Chest to chest with John, I asked him, "What are you talking about?" He'd taken off his combat boots to stitch a foot wound, but I still had mine on.

We were eye to eye.

Up close, John's darkness shimmered. Ice spread across the side of his face where I breathed on him. His expression was severe.

A stranger stood before me.

It wasn't John who answered my question.

Scorpius's voice was cruel behind me. "I heard what you said to Sadie."

The hair on the back of my neck stood up.

"You shouldn't listen to other people's conversations," I replied, still facing John. "I don't owe you any explanation for something you weren't meant to hear."

"Please," Scorpius spat. "Save your excuses."

John's frown deepened.

Malum made a strangled noise.

Ice expanded out from me like an infection. Scarlet flames leaped higher in my peripheral vision.

A soldier whistled, and I jolted as I remembered where we were. Someone's amputated arm was lying on a silver tray a couple feet away. Doctors and soldiers were staring at us with open mouths.

A tension headache throbbed in my left temple.

"I'm not doing this." I stalked out of the medical barracks. The freezing wind slammed the door shut satisfyingly behind me.

I only made it a few steps into the blizzard before I was picked up and thrown over a flaming shoulder like a sack of grain.

My mind flatlined, and I hung limp.

Snow whipped around the realm in a frenzy.

I slammed frozen hands across Malum's flaming back, cobalt blue streaming from my fingertips as trails of ice covered his coat.

The world was viciously cold and angry.

So was I.

Cobalt dissipated as the scarlet flames on Malum's shoulders spread down his back. I hit him repeatedly, kicked my legs, and screamed into the howling wind as I froze him.

He thawed.

I covered him in streaks of cobalt.

Flames turned ice into water; ice chased away flames.

We were locked in battle.

Malum abruptly stopped walking, and he went impossibly still amongst the frozen white trees.

His hand settled on my ass; fingers splayed possessively. It was deliciously warm, and I hated myself for noticing.

"Hurt me as much as you want, my Revered."

Malum's voice was gravelly. "I prefer it." His voice dropped an octave, and the hand against my ass started to burn like it had caught fire. "But you have a lot of explaining to do."

He resumed walking down the path.

"I'm not yours," I said as he hoisted me into our barracks.

I waited, but he didn't put me down on my bunk like I expected—he stalked into the bathroom, turned on the hot water, and tried to throw me into the tub.

I punched and kicked with all my might, but he used his freakish size to overpower me.

He pushed me under the spray.

Why was everyone obsessed with the shower lately?

Men discovered personal hygiene one day and suddenly it was *talk to me in the shower, meet me in the shower, get in the shower, Aran.*

The water sputtered.

Hot drops turned into snowflakes; ice hissed as it trailed across the ancient porcelain tub; the spray slowed as the showerhead turned cobalt blue.

The temperature plummeted below freezing.

Malum sighed, and his breath puffed out in a cloud of condensation. "Calm down." He turned the nozzle up as hot as it would go.

Flames jumped off his arms and crawled along the walls. Once again, ice turned to water. Pipes groaned, then hot water filled the space with steam.

He manhandled me so I stood under the heat, then he caged me against the wall so I couldn't escape.

We were sopping wet.

"Great, now you're *waterboarding me.*" I sputtered. "And you wonder why I don't want to be your mate? Grow up."

I slammed my fist at his throat. He dodged at the last minute, and the blow glanced off harmlessly.

"You don't want to do that." Silver eyes glinted with pure aggression.

I bared my teeth and let him see his death in mine as I lunged forward to strangle him. John and Luka stepped under the spray and restrained my arms.

"All this because I don't have a soul?" I laughed harshly. "I knew you kings would turn on me as soon as anything got difficult."

Flames trailed out of Malum's nose as he breathed.

I tried to wrench my hands free, but the twins were unrelenting.

They held me immobile.

Turning my head, I stared at John. "I *trusted you*." My voice was raw.

He didn't release me.

My heart crumpled.

It hurt.

I looked away, unable to handle the sight of the people I'd thought I'd spend my life with turning on me.

They were ripping out my heart and stomping on the already broken pieces.

There was nothing left inside.

The fight left me.

Insides melting, I slumped forward. The twins' grip kept me from face-planting onto the edge of the tub, smashing my face open, and bleeding out.

Another missed opportunity.

"Why didn't you tell us?" Scorpius snarled like a broken record as he pulled the shower curtain wide so all the men could lean over me. Cage me inside the shower.

Tears welled.

My eyes burned.

I tilted my head forward and let my hair obstruct my face because there was no way I would cry in front of these men. They didn't deserve it.

"WHY would you keep this secret?" John's voice cracked as he asked, his harsh grip softened, and he shifted so he was half hugging, half holding me up. "How could you not tell us?"

He sounded dejected.

I stayed limp.

It wasn't their problem that I didn't have a soul. It was their problem that I hated them and would never talk to any of them ever again.

Callused fingers wrapped around my chin, and Luka tipped my head up, so I was staring at him.

His face contorted with pain as he asked, "Aran, how could you not tell us that you feel pain every time you were aroused?"

My thoughts blanked.

"Oh," I breathed out as my lips parted. *So that was what this all was about?* Exhaustion, confusion, and relief washed over me.

Then, like his words had detonated a bomb, the men exploded.

CHAPTER 44
ARAN
COMPROMISES

Metanoia (noun): a transformative change of heart.

DAY 30: HOUR 15

Malum bellowed like a wounded animal and whirled.

He slammed his fist into the concrete bathroom wall. "You've been in pain *every single fucking time you've been turned on. Do you understand how messed up that is? All three of us touched you in the changing room*!" He screamed as he punched, then his voice dropped and he whispered brokenly, "We never should have touched you. You made a pained noise, and we didn't realize."

He gasped like he was holding back a sob.

Scarlet flames filled the bathroom with suffocating smoke.

Ice formed on my fingertips. Hot water melted it away. My clothes hung off me, soaking wet and dirty from the battle.

Grime pooled at my feet before it washed down the drain.

I didn't regret not telling the men, but I regretted that this was what we'd come to—spiraling in a tiny bathroom.

Six large bodies crammed into a space built for two. Max.

Everyone was squished together.

Slumped over on the edge of the tub, bumping into everyone, Scorpius pulled at his hair dejectedly.

Water sprayed off me and onto him. His pale skin was speckled with pink.

He looked ill.

Orion staggered and collapsed down onto the toilet seat. With his legs intertwined with Scorpius, he hyperventilated. Malum kept driving his fists punishingly through the concrete.

The kings were a mess.

The twins weren't much better.

John and Luka stood on either side of me in the shower. Our sopping-wet bodies were pressed flush against one another, and tremors rocked through all three of us. Scorpius's back leaned against our legs.

I didn't know which one of us was shaking.

Perhaps we all were.

The room spun in a blur of water, fire, and rage.

I turned my head to the side and came face-to-face with angry, dark eyes. Dimples framed a frowning mouth.

John reached out and enveloped me in a punishing hug. His arms trembled as he whispered something I couldn't understand against the side of my neck.

Someone else's hands turned me around, so my back was flush to John's front.

I blinked through the hot water.

Luka grabbed my chin and tipped my face up. He spoke

slowly like the words themselves were painful in his mouth. "Why didn't you tell us?"

He waited for my response.

My brain had liquefied, and my thoughts were static. I tried to move my lips, but they were numb. My tongue was heavy. Dead.

Luka pulled my fingers away from my mouth, and it took me a second to realize I'd been picking at my lip.

The bathroom fell eerily quiet. The only sound was running water and heavy breathing as all the men went still and waited for my response.

Luka's grip on my chin tightened. "Answer me, Arabella. Why didn't you tell us?"

John spoke. "Lately—through our new bond—I've been feeling agony streak down my back at the strangest moments. I had no idea where it was coming from—that was *you* feeling attraction…wasn't it?"

I shrugged.

John's arms tightened around me. Luka's fingers spasmed. A crown of shadows protruded off both their curls.

They looked equal parts terrified and terrifying.

"She shrugged," Orion whispered loudly.

Scorpius let out an unholy sound, and he slammed his fists down onto the bathroom sink.

It cracked.

The silence fractured.

"I didn't want you guys to worry," I said with honesty.

Luka's eyes narrowed into slits.

Malum whipped his head in my direction, and scarlet flames shot from his mouth. "Why wouldn't you tell me? I kissed you. Touched you." His voice cracked. "I *hurt* you."

The temperature increased.

"It wasn't too painful," I said reassuringly. "I promise."

"She's lying," John whispered. "I felt it—it was agonizing."

"No. It wasn't that bad," I repeated desperately.

Malum's expression was distraught. He looked devastated.

Luka's fingers tightened on my chin as he brought his face forward, lips inches from mine. A shadowy cloak hung off his shoulders, and I could taste his minty breath like it was my own.

He whispered, "What chthonic spirit possessed you? Why would you *ever* let us *fuck you* without telling us about this?"

"It wasn't a big deal," I said. "That's why I got so drunk. It never hurt."

I needed them to understand.

His eyes widened, and his hand dropped from my face. He slammed back against the tile, gripping his chest like he'd been shot.

Malum shouted something vulgar. Orion gagged. Scorpius pounded his fist against the broken sink.

Luka spun around, punched the shower wall, and screamed.

Tile shattered.

John held me. "Please, never again," he pleaded. "Please *never* pull this shit again, or so help me sun god, it won't just be the kings committing crimes against the realms." He pressed a soft kiss against the side of my neck, the heat from his skin warm against my chilled flesh.

Pain streaked down my back, and I winced.

John let out a string of colorful expletives. "Sorry." He gritted his teeth. "I shouldn't have done that. Shit."

He hyperventilated and pulled away.

I turned around, shoulders banging against Luka in the

small space, as I hugged John with all my strength. "Don't release me right now," I said. "Please."

John's arms came back around my sopping-wet clothes.

We held each other.

The rest of the men kept screaming and punching, my secrets detonating like bombs, as they destroyed the bathroom.

"Why didn't you tell me?" John whispered brokenly against my hair, and I heard the unspoken question in his voice.

He was the person I told things to. He was my friend when the other men were my enemies.

It was different between us.

I inhaled his familiar sandalwood scent. "Because I didn't want mother to take sex away from me too. I *wanted* to be with you in every way. No matter the circumstances. If you knew, you wouldn't have touched me."

John made a wounded sound.

"I need your touch," I admitted.

His shaking fingers tangled in my wet curls.

Memories of him taking me in the field in the Legionnaire Games played through my head on repeat.

I swayed, but he held me up.

"No more," John begged, lips pressed against my head. "Please—no more secrets. I don't think I can survive it."

I felt nauseous.

I inhaled courage and blurted out, "I-think-you're-in-pain-because-I don't-have-a-soul." Water sprayed off my frozen lips.

He didn't rear back like I expected.

John squeezed me tighter and whispered, "That's bullshit —you're *wrong*. If you were missing a soul, there would be no bond to form."

I pulled back to put some space between us, which put me flush against Luka, who rubbed his hands up and down over my arms like he was trying to warm me.

The Necklace of Death pulsed against my chest.

I reached my hand up under my sweatshirt and held it; the stone was warm and vibrating like it was alive.

John's eyes widened as he stared at where I gripped the necklace under my clothes.

I said quietly, "I need to take the jewelry off so you both can stop hurting."

Luka stopped rubbing my arms comfortingly. His hands stilled, and he gripped my biceps tightly.

John shook his head. "It has already completed the bond. Taking it off will do nothing." He moved closer.

My back was flush against Luka.

I was pinned between the twins.

Luka whispered in my ear, "The jewelry is a symbol of our love for you. Now that we've bonded, it's connected us, body and soul. We're your husbands, and you're our *wife*." His voice strummed with possessiveness, then the inflection changed and he begged, "Please don't take it off."

John trembled like he was freaking out.

"But it's hurting you both?"

"You think we care about a little pain?" Luka asked in disbelief.

"That's exactly how I felt," I countered.

He frowned.

John tangled both his hands in my hair and said, "We'd walk through hell for you. This pain is *nothing* to us. What matters is *your* pain. You're our wife. It's our duty to protect you, and we've failed."

"You don't need to protect me," I said. "I can protect myself."

That was the part the men kept forgetting.

John's eyes filled with sadness as he twirled a wet curl. "We don't *need* to love you, but we *do*. We know you can protect yourself, but you shouldn't have to—please don't keep secrets."

I dropped the necklace. Feeling pathetic, I admitted, "I don't want to take it off."

It vibrated warmly against my chest, a comforting reminder that they cared.

I wasn't alone.

Not anymore.

The twins exhaled loudly with relief.

Malum turned off the shower, and I was startled as I realized the kings had moved. The three of them were crowding around the edge of the tub.

Five sets of eyes stared at me like they were trying to see into my soul and uncover any secrets I might have.

There was a loud crash, and the twins shifted to shield me with their bodies. The kings whirled and crouched in unison, a shield of muscles and aggression.

I stood on my tiptoes to look over John's shoulder.

Malum flung fire through the bathroom.

The door, which was already half hanging off its hinges because of Malum, was thrown open.

The demons dodged the ball of flames.

The men relaxed.

Vegar's eyes widened as he took in the ruined bathroom, and Zenith blinked in shock behind him.

The demon's mouths opened and closed as they took in the scene.

Zenith pointed at me. "You're an idiot." He shook his head like he was disappointed.

"Wow," I said, "Blame the only *woman* for the men's destruction."

Zenith flung his hands in the air, inky lines trailing down his face. "They're fucking idiots—their bullshit is expected." He waved dismissively at the men, then pointed again at me. "But I thought *you* were better than them. You're supposed to be beyond this display of stupidness."

I glared back at him. I totally respected holding women to a higher standard (because we were better than men in every way), but this was taking it *too* far.

"But I did nothing," I deadpanned.

Zenith rolled his eyes. "Control them." Vegar winked at me.

I choked. "They're not my *dogs*?"

"Are you sure about that?" Zenith asked in a disbelieving tone, like he thought I was an idiot.

"We did pledge to serve as your hounds," Orion whispered. Scorpius and Malum nodded in agreement.

John covered his laughter with a cough, and Luka slung his arm around my shoulder.

I had no words.

The demons shook their heads and walked away. Zenith called over his shoulder, "We're going to have to give a battle report tomorrow and deal with soldier losses. Stop with the bullshit."

"We're done," Malum said with exasperation, like it was obvious his meltdown had concluded.

Personally, that was not *obvious* to me, but what did I know?

I slumped against the twins and asked, "Can we sleep together tonight?"

John went still against me. "I thought we covered this?" his voice brimmed with concern.

It took me a moment to realize what he was insinuating. "Not like that," I groaned. "I can barely keep my eyes open."

He brushed wet hair behind my ears. "Sure, you can sleep on me tonight. Luka gets the floor."

Luka stiffened but didn't argue.

John lifted me over the mangled side of the tub— concrete had fallen from the ceiling and crushed part of it— and he escorted me out of the ruined bathroom.

Malum blocked the door. He cleared his throat, and his cheeks turned bright pink. "Actually, could all of us sleep —together?"

I blinked, unsure if I'd entered an alternative dimension.

"You three want to sleep with me *and* the twins?" I asked. "Tonight?"

"Personally, I want to fuck you and John," Scorpius said boldly. "At the same time. Preferably, while I choke the living daylights out of you both."

Everyone gaped at him.

"Ignore him," Orion mouthed. "We just want to sleep." He peeked at Luka shyly.

Malum rubbed the back of his neck and said, "We need the physical contact, especially after the battle, and—everything we've learned."

He continued, "Since we know the twins are now your husbands"—he gasped like he was choking—"we want to show you we are…willing to compromise."

"How would we fit?" I asked.

Malum looked chagrined. "I have an idea."

An hour later, I stared at the ceiling. John clung to my left side, and Luka was reaching across him to play with my hair. Orion's arm was flung over me from the right side. He was lying next to Scorpius, and both of them were lying on top of Malum.

We were a pile of bodies.

The kings had pulled all our mattresses off the bunks and pushed them together in the middle of the room to make a superbed.

The five of us were buried under a mountain of blankets.

I shivered, and the men shifted around me.

Someone mumbled something, then an arm pressed against my right side. It radiated warmth. I sighed with relief as my toes curled with delight.

"Go to sleep," Malum whispered underneath his mates.

I yawned, "G'night."

John whispered something I couldn't hear and pressed a soft kiss against my cheek. I smiled.

As sleep claimed me, my smile dropped away.

The nightmares came quickly.

Mother sliced an enchanted knife through my back while I screamed. This time, guards had to hold me down because I was fighting for my life. Begging. Pleading. Another guard joined the four restraining me.

But for the first time, I recognized it wasn't real.

That time in my life was over.

My present was filled with something I'd never had growing up: love.

CHAPTER 45
SCORPIUS
TORTURER'S BREATH

FIKE (VERB): to move restlessly.

DAY 30, HOUR 23

When I'd overheard Sadie say that the wound on Arabella's back caused pain when she was aroused, I'd blacked out with unadulterated rage.

The world had gone silent.

The emotions that had ripped through my sternum had made me want to tear ungodly apart with my bare hands. All I'd been able to hear was Arabella's voice on repeat in my brain—the resignation in her tone as she'd whispered about how her mother had mutilated her.

I'd wanted vengeance.

Craved violence.

The urge to hurt someone, myself, *anyone*, had hit me like a tsunami. Voicing what I'd heard aloud to my mates and twins was one of the hardest things I'd ever had to do, second only to watching Arabella suffer in the Legionnaire Games.

It was a dagger through the heart.

How much more could one woman go through? How was she surviving?

Her male disguise had been a shock, her secret heritage had been a surprise, the slur carved into her back had been unacceptable, but *this* was too far.

When I'd told the other men, their breathing patterns had changed. Their feet stumbled, joints popping as they'd struggled to stay upright.

Corvus had carried Arabella through the blizzard, back to the room, and deposited her in the shower. When asked why she'd kept such a horrible secret, Orion had said she'd *shrugged*.

Shrug: a gesture that conveyed indifference.

We'd spiraled.

We'd failed our Revered worse than any Protectors in history. We were abominations to devil kind, and we didn't deserve her as our mate. We'd touched her, kissed her—tortured her.

Now I was locked in a new type of hell.

I was in her memories.

Her nightmare.

I drowned in her pain, and I didn't know how much more I could take. I didn't know how she was still functioning.

She was the strongest person I'd ever met.

Arabella screamed as five guards held her down and her mother carved "WHORE" into her flesh. I knew it was five because there were five different male breathing patterns surrounding my Revered.

She was being tortured, whimpering and screaming in pain.

I could do nothing but experience it.

The blade sliced deeply through her skin. It scraped against bone, and Arabella screamed.

Her mother chuckled.

I wanted to die.

Locked in sleep paralysis, I could do nothing but experience the atrocity that was committed against my Revered.

At first, I screamed and fought to wake up, unable to stomach what I was experiencing. Then I went quiet. The five breathing patterns were unfamiliar from any of the others I'd heard in her nightmares.

I focused on memorizing every doomed breath they took.

For hours, Arabella begged, and I listened so if I encountered the men in real life, I would immediately recognize them.

They would pay.

CHAPTER 46
ORION
TORTURER'S DEMISE

PARAMNESIA (NOUN): a disorder of memory.

DAY 30, HOUR 23

Five men held down my sweet Arabella while her mother carved into her flesh. I experienced everything that she had.

My Revered screamed in pain, and I suffocated.

The pain was heinous, but it was her suffering that broke my heart.

I was helpless to do anything but experience it.

I couldn't help her.

Four of the five letters were carved into her back before I found the willpower to examine the men holding her down.

With one glance, I memorized their faces.

Then I focused on Arabella. As she begged. As she cried. As she screamed. As tears dripped down her face.

I planned out all the things I would do to the men who held her down while her mother sliced into her.

Their eyes would be removed because they'd looked at her.

Their lips would be carved off their faces because they'd smiled while she screamed.

Their fingers would be removed because they'd touched her bare skin.

Their muscles would be extracted from their bodies because they'd used them to restrain her.

Unlike Scorpius, I would get no pleasure from hurting them, but I would do it because it had to be done. They'd brought it upon themselves when they'd held down my Revered. They'd brought it upon themselves when they'd smirked while she'd begged for help, and they did nothing.

They would die because they were already dead men walking.

I would do it for her.

Because that was what you did for those you loved: you hurt those who hurt them. You protected them. You removed the monsters from their lives and became *their* monster.

For Arabella, I would do anything.

I was her monster.

CHAPTER 47

JOHN

SHARED PAIN

NYCTOPHOBIA (NOUN): abnormal fear of darkness.

DAY 30, HOUR 23

All the kings were whimpering in their sleep, and Arabella was convulsing.

I was wide awake in the bedroom.

Blazing pain coursed down my spine, and as I concentrated on the agony, I realized it was in a pattern.

I felt every slow slice of the enchanted blade through flesh.

I felt what Arabella felt when the slur was permanently etched into her skin.

The knife nicked her bone, and I gasped.

I'd bitten through my tongue hours ago to hold back my screams as I convulsed. Luka twitched against me, his breathing labored, and I knew he was experiencing the same thing.

The completed soul bond was making us live through Aran's nightmare.

I shook and ground my teeth together.

I was glad the jewelry had completed the bond, because now I understood exactly what Aran had been through. I *knew* firsthand how badly she'd been tortured. I focused on the pain of her past as I held her in the present.

The worst part was Aran was also experiencing it.

I'd tried to wake her up, but she was in the grips of something that was much more than an ordinary dream. The kings yelled out. For some reason, their bond sickness was also making them suffer.

I endured in silence and did the only thing I could do. I tried to comfort Aran. I squeezed her tight against me and prayed that even in the depths of hell, she'd realize she was no longer alone.

I would stand by her side.

No matter the circumstances.

A single thought repeated in my brain and brought me peace as I convulsed—never again would she suffer alone. Our souls were bound together.

Her pain was my pain.

I drifted off to sleep with her in my arms.

CHAPTER 48

CORVUS MALUM
TORTURER'S APPEARANCE

IGNICOLIS (NOUN): A worshiper of fire.

DAY 30, HOUR 23

I was trapped in another one of Arabella's memories.

I'd thought they couldn't get any worse.

I'd been wrong.

My Revered was held down by five guards as her mother dragged a blade through her bare skin. Her dress had been pulled off, and she was topless.

The guards holding her were leering at her naked skin, their eyes wide with lust and excitement as she was mutilated.

Her pain was unimaginable.

I ignored it.

I stared at their sick expressions and memorized their faces, and I planned their demise.

It would be slow.

Guards stood along the perimeter of the room. None of them moved to help. A few looked away like they were horrified, but they didn't move a muscle to assist her.

They were all complicit.

The few faces I recognized, I ignored, but the new faces I studied and added to my list.

There were twenty-five guards in the room that night while my Revered was tortured.

Arabella's cunt of a mother ranted about how she was a whore for daring to try to lose her virginity. She told her she was filthy and pathetic. She told her no man would ever love an impure whore like herself.

Midscream, Arabella winced, and it wasn't from the blade carving her flesh.

I felt her emotions.

Her self-doubt.

My fury morphed into unadulterated pain. It radiated from my sternum and destroyed my organs.

The gray tones of the memory disappeared, and I woke up to my mates sleeping around me on a mattress in the middle of a dark room.

Wetness streaked down my cheeks.

I was crying.

Pinned beneath bodies, I reached desperately through the fray until my hand found ice-cold skin. Arabella was trembling and whimpering.

Panic filled my throat, and I shifted until I was pressed flush against her.

I gathered her into my arms. John was wrapped around her on the other side. He reached out and grabbed my forearm.

I paused.

No jealousy or anger filled my chest.

The cunt's words, that no man could ever love someone like her, stabbed through my brain on repeat.

I'd felt my Revered fill with doubt. I'd heard her whimper. A part of her had believed her mother.

Arabella shivered uncontrollably.

I conjured a flame in my hands and brought it against her chest to warm her.

John mumbled something in his sleep. His hand squeezed my forearm tight, like he was afraid I'd push him away.

Luka's fingers were tangled in her curls.

Orion and Scorpius shifted in their sleep, so they were draped across me as they reached for Arabella.

My flame burned hot in the center of all of us.

Sadness for what my Revered had been through transformed into determination.

Arabella would be protected and loved by *all* of us. I'd spend every second of the rest of my immortal life proving her mother wrong.

It was the very least she deserved.

CHAPTER 49
LUKA
DIFFERENT PERSPECTIVES

Pauciloquy (noun): brevity in speech.

DAY 30, HOUR 23

John and Aran twitched beside me.

Distantly, I felt the pain of a knife carving a word into my spine. The agony was muted because my mind was elsewhere.

The only thing I could focus on was the feeling of damp curls wrapped around my fingers and John's back pressed against my front.

I was touching the two people in the world who meant everything to me.

The pain across my spine should have been overwhelming, but I kept forgetting to feel it. My mind was too overwhelmed with obsession.

My skin buzzed with contentment because the two people I was dependent on were in my arms.

All of us were together, so everything would be okay.

They were my everything.

Physical pain didn't matter because I was touching them.

I was so grateful to be holding them that a tear trailed across my cheek. Love filled my chest.

Every night that I got to sleep beside them was perfect.

I only wished they weren't also experiencing the agony. I wished I could take the pain away from them. I'd bear anything for them. They owned my heart and soul.

CHAPTER 50
ARAN
DISAPPEARING MEN

PANTAPHOBIA (NOUN): total absence of fear.

DAY 31, HOUR 10

I woke up alone on a mattress pad in the middle of the floor, with a pile of ice-covered blankets covering me. The pillows were coated in frost.

Snow slammed violently against the dark window. If it weren't for the clock, I would have thought it was night.

For the first time in years, I felt well rested.

Mentally, I was doing better. Physically, I was struggling.

My shoulder muscles ached from fighting for hours, and my fingers were sore from gripping a sword hilt.

I hobbled off the mattress with my pipe between my lips.

The arches of my feet cramped as I walked, since I'd sprinted in heavy combat boots for hours.

I cracked my neck loudly and looked down. I was wearing male sweatpants that I didn't remember putting on.

Horse cawed as he settled onto my shoulder, and his long

feathers hung almost to the floor. I stroked his elegant neck. He preened and smoke wisped off him.

Sightlessly, I stared at the wall and smoked, enjoying the stillness of the quiet morning.

Horse tucked his long neck into his chest and slept.

Smoke warmed my frozen lungs.

A drawer shut, and I jumped at the loud noise.

Turning around, I took in the room and frowned. Orion and the demons were getting dressed.

My stomach churned.

It was eerily quiet because there were only four of us in the room.

John, Luka, Malum, and Scorpius were all missing.

Again.

My gut told me they weren't at breakfast.

Whatever, I wasn't going to let their absence ruin my newfound feeling of peace. I felt like I could take on the world.

I could do anything.

Bundled in my clothes, I walked out of the barracks into the blizzard. Head down, I pushed forward through the storm to get to breakfast. During our first week at the camp, the snowfall had been mild, and the days had been mostly full of sunshine. We hadn't had a pleasant day since.

I traveled further down the path.

Enchanted jewelry warmed and pulsed faster against my skin.

Then it hit me.

I went still as I looked around.

Nothing.

No pain.

The bond sickness with the kings was gone.

"Holy sun god," I whispered with awe at the richly colored forest.

All the pieces clicked together.

The strange dream I'd had about the Necklace of Death; the new vibrant colors; the lack of emptiness in my chest; the enchanted pulsing jewelry.

I stared down at my diamond covered wrist in astonishment.

My new soul bond with the twins must have broken my toxic connection with the kings.

I was *free*.

I tipped my head back and laughed with abandon.

It was a miracle.

Immediately, my euphoria abated as I remembered how the bond was hurting the twins. There was still something wrong with my soul.

I rubbed at my aching sternum and breathed deeply. I tried to calm my racing thoughts.

You'll figure it all out.

"What are you doing?" Orion yelled over the wind as he sprinted toward me. "Why didn't you wait for me?"

I composed myself.

"Breakfast," I answered casually.

A hand on my arm stopped my forward progress through the snow.

"I can't tell you where they went," Orion said like he could read my mind. Snowflakes gathered on his dark eyelashes, the white contrasting with his golden skin. "But don't worry, everything is going to work out. I promise."

I sighed.

Staring into his eager eyes, I realized I couldn't tell him about the fixed bond sickness.

He'd be devastated and convinced that I'd chosen the twins over him and the kings.

I didn't want him to suffer.

I didn't want any of them to suffer.

Not anymore.

"Let's go eat." I held out my hand.

Instead of taking my hand, Orion draped his arm over my shoulder and pulled me flush against him. I melted into his embrace.

The silence between us was peaceful.

He led me into the cafeteria, pulled my chair out at the table where Jinx was sitting, then went and got food for both of us.

At the beginning of the war, each of the tables had been full of soldiers eating and talking boisterously.

Less than half the tables had people seated at them.

Everyone spoke in hushed murmurs.

I started to count the number of people present but stopped because it was nauseating.

We'd walked into the last battle with fifty-nine soldiers.

There were *not* that many left.

Later, I'd go find the sheet that all the soldiers had signed after the battle so we could have an accurate casualty count. I'd call the High Court and give them an update. I'd probably have to stand through another funeral. Then I needed to research bonds to understand exactly why the twins were hurting. I'd—

"Stop thinking so strenuously," Jinx said across the table.

I arched my eyebrow at her. "I'm not."

"Sure, and I'm not missing my leg and assigned as your guardian." She made a face.

"You're stupid," I thought loudly in my head, just to be spiteful.

Jinx petted her ferret scarf and didn't react. She must not have heard me.

What was the point of having a mental connection if it didn't work half the time?

"It works," Jinx said. "I just was ignoring you."

I clicked my tongue. "Awkward."

She didn't reply.

I smoked and stared at the table while she ate.

It was pleasant.

"How's my favorite soulless bestie doing?" Sadie asked as she slapped me across the back. I spit out my pipe.

Jinx startled and knocked over her cup of water.

The tranquil vibes were broken.

I picked up my pipe and dusted it off.

Sadie had a manic energy about her that always ruined a peaceful environment. It was one thing I liked most about her. She kept life interesting.

She slumped into the seat next to me and propped her boots on my lap like I was a footstool.

"Really?" I pushed her feet off my thighs. I lowered my voice and whispered, "Also, I don't need everyone knowing about my soul issues."

"Don't worry." Sadie grinned around a bread roll and elbowed me. "Your secret is safe with me." She mimed locking her lips and throwing away the key.

"Clearly," I said as I watched her shove a chunk of butter into her mouth alongside the half-eaten roll.

How she'd seduced not one, but *four* men, would forever be a mystery to me. Not that they deserved her (they didn't), but it was still a mystery.

"What are you two blathering on about?" Jinx asked as she cleaned up her spilled water.

Sadie blurted, "Aran doesn't have a—" I kicked her under the table "—nothing," she finished lamely.

Jinx frowned and stared at us, which was disconcerting because she was wearing dark sunglasses. She shook her head and mumbled something about how we sometimes used our brains. That, or she was talking about a satisfying rain—I couldn't tell.

Jinx stroked her ferret and demanded, "Explain right now what you were talking about." Her pursed lips gave her a matronly appearance.

I narrowed my eyes. "I think we should talk about *you.* How old are you again?"

Sadie's butter knife clattered loudly against her plate as she stared at the child, who did not resemble a child anymore.

She gasped. "Wait a second. Aren't you supposed to be fourteen?"

"I'm going through my species's version of puberty," Jinx said coldly as she cut her meat into tiny pieces.

"So your species skips the teenage years?" Sadie gaped at her. "I think you're taller than me now. Stand up, let's measure."

Sadie stood up.

Jinx's knuckles turned white around her knife. "Sit down. I know I'm taller than your malnourished corpus," she said scathingly.

Sadie dropped back into her seat with a huff and opened her mouth—

"Corpus means body," I said before she could ask.

Sadie shoved another roll into her mouth and said to Jinx, "Well, that's rude." She added a second roll before she'd swallowed. "I can't believe you're already taller than me—wait, did you grow boobs? You're always wearing that oversize sweatshirt. Take it off so we can see."

Jinx pointed her steak knife at Sadie. "Shut up."

Sadie's face turned red as she tried to hold back her questions.

"I got your favorite foods," Orion whispered as he took the free seat next to me. I leaned close, discreetly inhaling his raspberry-and-chocolate scent.

"Thanks," I said as my stomach growled and I started eating.

Cobra joined the table and set his tray down with a loud clatter. "Did all your men abandon you, Aran?"

Sadie choked, and both of us slapped her back at the same time.

"Don't talk to her like that," Orion said loudly, and everyone in the room froze.

All noises stopped.

"You don't need to defend me," I said, momentarily rendered speechless by the handsome prettiness of his features.

Orion frowned and said at full volume, "He knows nothing about our mates. No one should be allowed to speak to you like that." Wide, unblinking eyes stared straight into my soul. "Do you want me to hurt him?"

"I thought that was Scorpius's thing?"

Orion leaned close so our faces were inches apart. "No. Scorpius enjoys pain. That's all. I'm also your Protector, sweetheart."

His hand gently cradled the back of my head. His lips pressed softly against my forehead like I was something precious that needed to be handled with care.

I forgot how to breathe.

I ignored the pain in my back.

Orion pulled quickly away from me. "How could I forget about your back?" he gasped. "I'm so sorry. Please forg—"

I slammed my lips against his.

He groaned into my mouth and kissed me back passionately.

"When did you guys start making out?" Sadie asked, and we pulled apart.

"Pervertsssss," Cobra hissed as he dug into what appeared to be a rare piece of steak. He shared a piece with Sadie.

Shifters are weird.

The rest of the meal passed in relative peace. It was relative because the entire time Jinx argued with Sadie, and Cobra argued with me. Orion watched us all with mild confusion.

Afterward, we stomped through the blizzard to the strategy room.

I studied the books.

Fifteen dead in total: fourteen foot soldiers and the last devil from the devil legion. I had a terrible feeling about the last death.

I wrote out the numbers numbly.

Forty-four soldiers were left, less than half the hundred men and women we'd started with.

So many dead.

The angels didn't bother to show up to give the report. A sign of their defiant cowardice.

I spoke in a monotone voice to Dick. He was optimistic and thought the war was going well.

Behind him, Lothaire stared at me with an intense expression. "You can do this. Keep going." He mouthed. "It's almost over."

I gave him a small smile.

It was strange to have a parental figure that cared. It was even stranger that a violent one-eyed vampyre was my father.

I never saw it coming.

He beamed at me like he was proud.

Warmth filled my chest.

When the screen clicked off, hives broke out across my chest. There was only one infected settlement left on the map, but unlike Dick, I had a bad feeling in my gut.

The next day, the men returned.

Two days later, the angels told us the new coordinates in a monotone voice. They'd worked fast.

There was no time to recover.

No dallying.

Once again, we went to war.

CHAPTER 51
ARAN
THE RECKONING

SCHLIMAZEL (NOUN): a consistently unlucky person.

DAY 34, HOUR 22

We RJE'd into a blizzard.

This was it.

The forest outside the last infected settlement.

The battle that would end the war.

Even with layers of protection, the freezing temperatures hurt as the snow pummeled us. My eyes stung as my lashes crusted with ice.

Forty-four of us trudged forward through the storm.

Hunched low.

I shivered and blinked rapidly as I tried to see. An arm wrapped around my shoulder, and a glowing scarlet ball of warmth flickered over a bronze hand in front of my chest.

"We're supposed to be concealed," I said, and my voice was swallowed by the wind.

A gruff male voice spoke close to my ear. "Your Protectors are blocking us from sight. Don't worry, my Revered."

Scorpius and Orion shielded us with their bodies.

Malum's ball of fire glowed maroon. I raised my mittens up to it.

The sting of the chill abated.

Malum pulled me tight against his side and shielded me from the worst of the snow.

He held me like we were on good terms.

We weren't.

I shivered again, and the intensity of the flame increased.

"Why won't you tell me where you went?" I asked.

Malum went rigid and Scorpius glanced back over his shoulder.

The two kings had returned yesterday covered in blood and once again they'd refused to talk about where they'd gone.

"Not now." Malum shook his head. "Later, Arabella. I promise. It will all become clear."

"Fine, we'll talk later." I pulled away from his embrace.

He made a harsh noise, but he let me go. Moving more stealthily than a man of his size should have been capable of, he positioned himself beside his mates.

Without his flames, the cold intensified.

My bones hurt.

Teeth-chattered.

I trembled with shivers.

Out of nowhere, a glowing ball of fire floated in front of me, and the heat cut through the cold.

Malum was walking ahead, and seemed to be ignoring me, but his fire trailed beside me.

"Thank you," I called out so he could hear me.

"Shush," Rina snapped.

Malum looked back over his shoulder and winked.

Heat warmed inside my chest that had nothing to do with the ball of fire.

We marched through the wintry forest. The kings were in front of me, and the twins were behind.

I was surrounded by a wall of flesh.

A personal army of monsters.

As we stomped through the ankle-deep snow towards the infected settlement, my sense of foreboding grew.

I wanted to turn and run. I forced myself to keep moving forward with everyone else.

We only had forty-four soldiers left.

With the current casualty rate, the twenty-two men left to secure the perimeter had a ninety percent chance of death.

Fumbling with my mittens, I pulled out my pipe, shoved it between chattering teeth, and inhaled greedily.

Immediate calm descended as warm smoke filled my lungs.

The ball of fire burned hotter.

A hand patted my back gently. "Keep moving," John said as he hunched behind me. His voice was unmistakably hoarse, even in the howling wind.

I hadn't realized I'd stopped moving.

I was bent over, smoking.

Instead of walking forward, I turned to John. "Are you okay?" I asked as I looked back and forth between him and Luka pointedly.

The twins were shrouded in glittering darkness, a tangible force that wrapped around them.

"We're fine, stop worrying about us." Luka's voice was unfamiliar and rougher than John's. "Please." He huddled closer so he could be heard over the wind.

It was obvious the twins were in physical pain.

They held themselves differently. They hunched forward slightly, like they were protecting an injury.

They'd left the camp, and something bad had happened to them.

When they'd returned from whatever secretive place they'd gone, their lips were pinched tight and eyes glossy from pain. They'd walked differently.

A small part of me was still angry at them for disappearing again. A larger part of me was just plain worried.

They were putting on a brave face, but something was horribly wrong. I was terrified it was my fault.

"Focus on the battle, Aran." John punched me gently in the arm. "Nothing's going on."

I exhaled a cloud of smoke. "I don't believe you." My words were swallowed by the blizzard.

"We don't have time for this, we have a war to win," Scorpius snapped, and his tone left no room for argument. "We need to move."

I inhaled smoke and trudged forward as the kings and twins resumed their protective positions.

Horse cawed as he settled onto my shoulder.

He nuzzled my face, his wispy form barely holding shape under the storm's onslaught.

We moved as a unit in silence.

Soldiers off to war.

Time folded in on itself.

I blinked.

We entered the courtyard and Malum's flame dissipated.

Rina told me to put my pipe away and put my black hood on.

I ignored her.

Smoke filled my lungs.

I blinked.

Twenty of us crept through familiar flame-lit corridors. Ice melted off uniforms and dripping sounds echoed down the quiet corridor.

I looked down.

Unlike everyone else, I was still covered in a sheen of cobalt.

The ice wasn't melting off me, it spread beneath my feet with every step I took.

Someone shouted.

Glowing blue swords were drawn.

I blinked.

Wings clattered above, and swords stabbed down from the ceiling, expertly hitting targets. Down the corridor, a gruesome roar echoed—the warning sound of a bear shifter—and the hairs on the back of my neck stood up.

Infected screamed as we eliminated them.

Ungodly chittered as they ripped from their corpses. I sliced off their heads before they could react.

"Good work," Malum shouted. He was nothing but a blur of darkness. I squinted as I tried to discern where the rest of the soldiers were in the smoky corridor.

A hand grabbed my shoulder and yanked me back.

An ax flew out of nowhere and missed my pipe by inches.

"Pay attention," Luka shouted.

Two figures closed ranks on either side of me, and I sucked on my pipe greedily, grateful it hadn't been hit.

"I am," I said as I swung my enchanted swords forward and sliced the neck off an infected.

"We've got your back," John shouted. There was a grunt and a thump as a body hit the ground behind me. The twins fought behind me.

"I've got your front." I dodged ungodly pincers and protected them.

That was the last thing I said for hours.

The battle raged in the halls.

I blinked.

We'd been fighting for what felt like an eternity.

Sweat froze as it dripped down the sides of my face, making my skin feel uncomfortable.

We sprinted down the hall as a group. The twins and kings ran in front of me with their swords drawn.

There was a fork ahead in the corridor, and everyone turned left.

A hidden door opened at the exact moment I passed, and an infected flung herself at me. As our swords clashed, I skidded backward down the right path, away from the group.

There was a loud crack as the side of my head slammed against the stone.

Disoriented, I stumbled and touched my ear gingerly. Instead of bone and blood, a broken earpiece fell out.

I had no time to feel relief.

A blur of blue arched toward me. I barely spun and got my weapon up in time. The infected was a bulky male who towered over me in strength and height.

He was strong, but I was faster. My blade sliced clean through his neck, and his head rolled.

An ungodly ripped into existence.

I stumbled backward because it was larger than any ungodly I'd ever seen. Its head scraped across the towering ceiling.

Twirling my sword, I sliced off one of its arms.

A pincer slammed into my chest and flung me backward.

It lunged again, and I barely dodged the blow.

I needed a plan of attack. It was too tall for me to swing

my sword and slice its head off. I would have to jump if I was going to pierce through its chest.

"Run!" Jinx's voice shrieked in my head.

I turned and sprinted down the dark corridor as fast as I could. A horrible chittering clack echoed loudly behind as the ungodly sprinted after.

In a split second, I processed everything that had happened and all my options.

"HELP!" I shouted as I ran, my heart sinking in my chest. I couldn't hear anything but the ungodly chasing me, which meant no one could hear me. I needed that earpiece. Of all the times for the bond sickness to be gone.

"HELP!" I screamed again with all my might, because while it was a long shot, it was my only option.

I just needed one person to hear me.

Just one.

I squinted as I tried to discern what glowed up ahead. Maybe the corridors looped together in a circle? Maybe the other soldiers were up ahead?

Jinx screamed in my head, *"Wait, don't ru—"*

A sword swung forward, and instinctive reflexes were the only thing that stopped me from getting my head removed. Sparks flew as our swords slammed together. Multiple swords glowed, and I backed up, blocking blow after blow with everything I had.

"Behind you!" Jinx screamed, and I threw myself to the side as I remembered what was chasing me.

The ungodly was unable to change its trajectory and slammed into the infected, pincers slashing.

Not good.

My stomach tightened with horror.

Ungodly exploded out of the downed bodies, and I was surrounded by slashing pincers and screeches.

For a second, the world slowed.

The analytical side of my brain took over.

I could hear my heart pounding through my veins; I could feel every ridge of the metal hilt in my fingers.

There were two possibilities: (1) I could let them tear me apart (chances were high that they wouldn't know to eat my heart and I would wake up after the battle was over), or (2) I could fight with the goal of creating an opening and running away from the group.

Enchanted smoke filled my lungs, and I rolled my pipe with my tongue.

Even if I survived, the oversized ungodly would still pose a threat to the men.

A pincer swung toward me. I sliced it off.

I made my choice.

My thoughts went blank, and I fought desperately, blue swinging in an unfollowable blur as pieces of ungodly rained down. I tried to create a path for myself.

For each one I downed, another seemed to appear.

The shadow of the oversized ungodly loomed behind the fray like he was waiting for me to tire.

He was smarter than the rest.

But I also wasn't stupid.

Mind blank with concentration, I barely processed the vibration that shook the stone beneath my feet.

There was a bone-chilling roar.

Something immense slammed against me. My head cracked against the wall, and I fell, slumping against the stone.

I braced myself for the attack.

A furry body moved, and I squinted in the dark.

Ungodly shrieked as they were slaughtered, and razor-sharp claws glinted as they sliced mercilessly.

Groggily, I rubbed at my eyes as I tried to push the confusion from my brain.

"Stand up!" Jinx's voice was fuzzy and barely audible. *"S —protect—you. Find—sword. Do—now!"*

Head aching, vision spinning, I crawled through the debris toward the blue glow.

I reached toward a sword.

My fingers…just…barely…wrapped around metal. A wall of muscle and fur slammed against me.

Everything went silent.

In slow motion, as if I was merely spectating, I sailed through a brick wall, and my teeth chattered against my pipe.

A white-and-black, striped creature flew through the air with me. Razor-sharp claws were bright pink and decorated with rhinestones. It had twin fangs longer than my arm.

Moisture blurred my vision.

Sadie had heard me.

Against all odds, she'd heard my call for help.

The ceiling where we'd stood fell down on the ungodly, and the corridor disappeared in a pile of rubble.

My body turning midair like a rag doll, my eyes widened as I saw what we were flying toward:

A vacuum of swirling energy.

A portal.

This can't be good.

We slipped through time and space and kept falling.

Sadie turned midair and cushioned me.

We slammed into concrete.

Time lost all meaning as we lay in a pile of bruises and broken bones. Everything was silent. It was almost peaceful —until it wasn't. The saber-toothed tiger cushioning me shifted back into a scrawny woman.

The world snapped, and sounds rushed back into my ears.

Fear mixed with adrenaline, and I stumbled to my feet. I stood in front of Sadie's naked body.

The room spun, my vision blurred, and my hips ached with throbbing pain as I pointed my sword forward protectively.

Blue glowed all around.

I blinked furiously to clear my vision.

A rock pinched the side of my mouth, so I pulled out my pipe and spit it into my palm. It was my tooth.

I shoved my pipe back between my lips and inhaled smoke desperately as my eyes slowly focused.

We were in a sprawling brick room.

The temperature was unbearably warm, and my clothes were suffocatingly heavy. I broke out in a sweat.

The walls were covered in pictures. Flame sconces provided the only source of light. The ceiling towered high above and was at least thirty feet tall. There were no windows or doors.

On the far wall, an expansive tartan hung off the ceiling and showed the locations of the mountains, valleys, and infested settlements within the realm.

It was a map.

In the far north, next to the third battle location, large red Xs were once again laid out across the mountain range near the valley. I squinted. At the bottom corner of the map, there was a key that said "X - villages."

My stomach pitted with unease, because even if we were successful in clearing the last compound, there was likely still more infected.

The war wasn't done.

I exhaled with shock, a puff of smoke curling from my lips as I took in the rest of the room.

I stared forward numbly.

A hundred or so people stood before me, most of whom had enchanted swords hanging off their hips.

My brain processed anomalies: there didn't seem to be any bathrooms, and there weren't signs of food, but the room didn't stink of waste, and the people weren't starving.

The portal swirled in the center of the towering ceiling.

A rushing sound filled my ears.

I backed up slowly. We were lucky we'd fallen near the corner of the room so we had protection at our backs.

That was where our luck ended.

In the dim lighting, the crowd of people's eyes glowed with a familiar, vibrant green sheen.

The nearest infected were about ten feet away.

They stared at us.

I crouched low, stance wide and protective. No one was going to hurt Sadie. Not on my watch.

CHAPTER 52
JINX
SURVIVAL

Thanatophobia (noun): fear of death.

DAY 36, HOUR 3

Through our guardian-angel connection, I saw through Aran's eyes.

She was surrounded by dozens of infected, pain radiated through her body from multiple contusions, and Sadie was naked on the ground behind her.

She crouched low and inhaled enchanted smoke.

She swept over the infected with a disturbing nonchalance as she analyzed the situation. Her thoughts were freakishly calm.

"Where are you?" I screamed through our connection, but the sound was jumbled and fuzzy.

Helplessness filled me.

Please not now.

I choked on guilt. It was my fault that our connection was inconsistent.

Desperate to do something, I grabbed my crutches and pulled myself upright out of the leather chair.

I spent the battles alone in the strategy room, meditating, and Warren knew not to disturb me. HE spent the time exploring the forest as a ferret.

Now I wished I weren't alone.

I needed help.

Someone.

Anyone.

I clutched at my temples with trembling fists because I couldn't think. I was panicking. My heart pounded in my chest as I struggled to breathe.

I was Aran's guardian; I was supposed to guide her in times of distress.

This situation went beyond mere peril.

Her odds were impossible.

My crutches slammed into a chair, and I tipped over. I barely noticed.

"Can you hear me? Aran, can you hear me?" I screamed repeatedly through our link.

Nothing.

Sadie groaned with pain as she became conscious, and Aran whispered down at her through the corner of her mouth, "Don't make any sudden movements or noises."

Dragging my crutches in one hand, I crawled across the floor toward the enchanted pad built into the desk. I needed to alert the High Court.

Sadie's eyes shot open.

They glowed bloodred.

She tilted her head slowly to the side, face blanching as she took in the portal on the unreachable high ceiling, and the crowd of infected with enchanted swords.

"Can you shift?" Aran whispered. "Can you shift and leap against the wall and throw us through the portal?"

Sadie scrunched her face like she was concentrating, then her expression shuttered as she looked at Aran dejectedly.

"No," she whispered. "My cat form sustained too many injuries. It's happened before. I won't be able to shift until I've rested and healed."

Aran swore under her breath.

Using the table legs to hoist myself up, I slammed my palm against the enchanted pad. It warmed under my fingertips and projected the High Court's logo onto the chalkboard.

I hit the symbol.

The projection shimmered as it called.

My heavy breathing was too loud in the quiet room as I waited.

There was a loud click, then the symbol turned into letters that read "Members of the High Court military council are currently occupied. Please call back later."

I screamed with frustration and punched the tablet.

The projection turned off.

How in the realms could the military council be busy during a military battle?

I watched through the connection.

"I can stand." Sadie pulled herself upright.

Aran hissed under her breath, "Move slower. We don't want to agitate them."

"Don't we want to kill them?" Sadie whispered as she moved with painstaking care.

I gritted my teeth and spat aloud, "No, you imbecile." How she'd managed to remain so dumb, even after what had been done to her, was beyond my understanding.

"Not if we don't have to," Aran whispered softly. "We

want to survive. Best-case scenario, we climb back up and out the portal without disturbing them." She paused as an infected shouted something and made an unfamiliar hand gesture. "Worst-case scenario, we kill them and they shift into ungodly. We can't fight off this many and live."

Sadie grimaced as she realized their predicament. "You'll survive," she mouthed.

Aran shook her head and said under her breath, "They could still eat my heart."

Sadie's eyes filled with moisture. "They probably wouldn't."

"It doesn't matter," Aran whispered coldly. "Either we both walk out of here alive or we both die. There is no third option."

Sadie gulped, her bloodred eyes widening at whatever she saw on Aran's face. She rasped, "I love you." It sounded like she was saying goodbye.

"I love you more." Aran's voice was hard as steel.

Sadie's eyes shone with moisture. "I love you most."

"Impossible," Aran replied.

There was a loud scraping noise as an infected took a step toward them, its boot scuffing across the floor. Its gaze was mindless.

Aran took a step back protectively.

"What do we do if they attack?" Sadie asked, voice quivering.

Determination flooded through Aran. "Then we fight, and we try our best to maim but not kill." Her voice was barely audible, and her words were clipped like it hurt to speak them aloud. "We keep them all alive."

"That will be difficult with your sword." Sadie nodded to the weapon in Aran's hand.

Aran nodded, unease chipping away at her determination. "We'll try our best. If we have to fight the ungodly, then we will. You will not die here."

Sadie smiled sadly.

Aran's unease became outright horror.

They both jolted as an infected woman standing a few feet away screamed something at them. It sounded like a swear word, but her accent made it impossible to decipher.

Aran slowly raised her sword higher.

"Where do you think we are?" Sadie asked as she grabbed Aran's hand and squeezed. "It feels familiar somehow."

Aran looked up at the high ceilings, then her eyes lingered on the portrait-covered walls.

In the strategy room, I held my breath as I waited. *"Please say the location aloud. Please say it aloud. Please say it aloud,"* I sent down our connection fervently.

Sun god bless Sadie and her ridiculous need to ask questions.

This was it.

My only hope.

I could feel Aran's brain processing patterns and connections at a familiar lightning speed. For all her faults, Aran wasn't an idiot. She had more brains than the rest of the other champions combined.

Now it was their only hope.

Sweat dripped down the side of my face, and my chest pounded so hard against my sternum that I felt lightheaded.

Aran whispered, "The floor sounded hollow. The heat. The portraits."

"What?" Sadie asked with confusion.

"We're in the basement of where we first battled," Aran said with horror as she wiped at her brow.

Feet shuffled, and there was an ominous rustle as infected

brandished their enchanted swords. The dimly lit room glowed blue.

"They're moving closer." Sadie's hand trembled in Aran's grip.

Aran squeezed her hand. "I'll try to fly." She went to pull her hand away, but Sadie wouldn't release her.

"No." Sadie's voice was uncharacteristically serious. "We both know you can't fly. Don't waste your energy."

Frustration welled up inside Aran, and she bit down on her pipe, jaw grinding with frustration.

"I might not be able to shift"—Sadie's voice darkened—"but I'm not useless." Her eyes glowed bright as she grabbed the shaft of Aran's enchanted sword with her bare hand.

An infected screamed and threw itself at them, the crowd charging as one.

Sadie pushed Aran behind her with surprising strength as she flung her blood at the faces of the charging infected. Blood dripped into their open mouths and eyes.

"Defend us!" Sadie roared.

The three closest infected turned with their swords drawn, and they clashed with the charging crowd.

I pulled out of the connection.

The strategy room was too bright, and it was eerily quiet compared to the screams of the infected and clangs of enchanted swords.

I was slumped over the table.

Ears ringing with faraway battle sounds.

Eyes wide and unseeing.

I was paralyzed, unable to function.

I slammed my palm against the table, then pinched my hand with all my strength—the pain helped me focus.

As I looked around, my thoughts went a million miles a minute as I went through possibilities and plans.

I knew their location, which meant I could get help for them.

The problem was all the soldiers were in battle halfway across the realm.

I frantically grabbed my crutches and moved across the room, almost falling on my face a few times in my haste. Yanking open the RJE drawer, I desperately checked the remaining devices.

There were about a dozen, all with different coordinates. They were programmed for Elite Academy, the third battle location, the second battle location, and the first battle location.

I searched desperately, but those were the only locations.

Through gritted teeth, I screamed.

The one I needed was missing—there was no RJE device for the current battle, they'd taken them all. I had no way to alert any soldiers.

Not bothering with crutches, I hopped the few feet over to the shelves of binders and started tearing them off the shelves.

I couldn't find where they'd put the coordinates.

Curse the sun god. Curse the constant incompetence in the realms. Could nothing go right today?

I threw a binder across the room with frustration, then followed its trajectory with my body back toward the open drawer.

I grabbed one of the RJE devices labeled "Elite Academy" and activated it.

Crack.

Reality shifted.

I fell forward as the shelf I was leaning against disappeared beneath me. My hands slapped against black marble.

Lightning streaked down the walls, and my hair levitated from the electricity.

"*Lothaire?*" I screamed down the empty marble hall. Crystal chandeliers hung unlit, and maroon light streamed through stained-glass windows.

Crawling forward on my hands and knees, I screamed, "*Is anyone here?*"

Lighting slammed against the floor.

Marble burned hotter beneath my hands.

I rolled onto my back and bellowed with everything I had, "*Lothaire?*" Chest heaving, I lay still and waited.

Please, sun god. Please let him be here. Let him hear me.

Precious seconds turned into minutes.

Nothing.

Of all people, I should have known that prayer wouldn't work—not to him. *Never* to him.

I slapped my palm against the now cold marble as I thought about the dates. It was around the time when the academy had a break. Lothaire would be elsewhere.

Screaming through gritted teeth, I stared up at the intricate crystal chandelier and accepted—unless a miracle happened in the next few seconds—there was no way I could retrieve timely help for Aran and Sadie.

The High Court hadn't answered, which wasn't a good sign. The military council tended to disappear for days while they handled "top-secret" business.

There was no one to alert.

No one to rescue Sadie and Aran.

I was the only one who knew where they were.

I activated the RJE device.

Crack.

I was lying on my back next to the table in the strategy room.

Grabbing the furniture, I hoisted myself to my feet using the table legs. I pulled open drawers and grabbed a different RJE device. I desperately searched for the weapons prohibited by the Official Peace Accords that the High Court "supposedly" kept for demonstration purposes.

Thank the sun god that weeks ago I'd paid attention to Dick's presentation.

I'd bet he knew exactly what he was doing when he'd left them.

Finally, I opened the correct drawer. Rifling through the various canisters of chemical weapons, I sobbed with relief when I found the circular enchantment.

I pocketed the high-caliber explosive.

In a fog, I threw myself forward toward the blackboard. Slamming into furniture on one leg, I half hopped, half crawled toward my destination.

At the board, I did the only thing I could do.

Once I was satisfied with my work, I reopened the connection to Aran.

My heart rate skyrocketed.

Sadie was on her knees—hands extended forward toward the now five infected she'd enslaved with her blood—like she was physically pushing them forward.

Infected screamed as they died, and ungodly chittered as they erupted.

Sadie's army of five wielded enchanted swords with much more dexterity than the average infected.

They cut through the crowd.

Slain bodies were strewn across the floor: pincers, hands, scarlet splatter, and vibrant green gore.

From the number of ungodly and infected corpses, they'd given up trying to wound and had resorted to killing.

Sadie had been extremely efficient.

About half the infected were slain, there were a few dozen left.

It was still too many.

Aran stood beside Sadie and killed the infected and Ungodly that got past their enslaved army.

"You've done enough!" Aran shouted at Sadie. "You're going to hurt yourself. Release them."

"No," Sadie snarled.

Her golden skin had a green tint, and blood dripped from her eyes, nose, and mouth. White hair clung to her naked body and was slick with sweat. She shook forcefully with exhaustion.

"Release them now," Aran ordered as she stepped in front of her protectively.

"No!" Sadie shouted as she bowed her back and bellowed like controlling the infected was ripping her apart from the inside. Blood gushed out of her mouth.

Aran screamed an expletive and whirled around. She slammed the hilt of her sword against Sadie's temple, and she dropped unconscious.

In a blur of movement, Aran grabbed her body and dragged her back into the corner. She propped her against the wall and stood over her body.

The five enslaved infected dropped dead.

The room went uncannily still.

There was a loud ripping as ungodly tore from their corpses. Every creature in the room turned toward Aran. Pincers snapped. Swords glowed.

I pulled out of her mind, gasping, stomach churning as I processed what I'd seen.

The urge to go get Warren and get his help was overwhelming, and I almost acted on the impulse, but I stopped myself. He was skilled, but he was still just a teenage boy. He didn't possess nearly as much power as the soldiers who fought against the ungodly.

Stronger people than him had been killed in this war, and this was not a battle—it was a slaughter.

I couldn't live with myself if I hurt another person.

Plus, I didn't have the time to search for him in the forest. Every second was precious.

Before I could think, before I could panic, before I could remember I wasn't a soldier, before I could change my mind, I grabbed my crutches and slammed my hand down on the second RJE device I'd grabbed.

Yet again, time and space warped.

Crack.

I was in a musty brick corridor that reeked of death. Rotting gore was splattered everywhere.

Gagging, I slammed my crutch against the brick floor. It sounded solid.

Ignoring the leftover substances from an old battle, I lowered myself down awkwardly and pressed my ear to the floor.

I distantly heard the muffled sounds of war.

Patting my pocket to make sure I had what I needed, once again, I didn't give myself time to think about what I was doing.

I started to use my crutches to move forward, then stopped.

Looking down at the rubble, I awkwardly bent down and picked up a jagged piece of broken brick. I pulled my pants up and sliced it deep across my leg.

Then, as fast as I could, I crutched into the darkness.

Toward the screams.

CHAPTER 53
ARAN
THE TRUTH IS SPILLED

MAKEBATE (NOUN): one that excites contentions or quarrels.

DAY 36, HOUR 4

It was the underside of the *e* as it was carved into my back.

It was the fiftieth mile of what was supposed to be a forty-mile run—legs pumping furiously, lungs rattling for relief—as Lothaire screamed at us to run faster or we'd do another lap.

It was hour three of being set aflame by Mother.

I suffocated.

Persisted.

Drowned in a melee of screams.

I hallucinated that Lothaire stood off to the side, watching the battle. "You're *my* daughter," he said proudly. "You're powerful, I know it."

"I'm your daughter. I'm strong," I whispered as I swung, hoping if I said it aloud, I'd believe it.

Blood splattered across my face, and I barely noticed the warm fluid. Green gore sprayed from carapace shells as I mercilessly sliced them to pieces. A woman screamed in my face as she died.

Despite it all, the haze hadn't swallowed me.

The world flashed in vibrant colors, and time moved at its usual speed. Terror for my best friend replaced any emptiness I might have once felt. My necklace and bracelet pulsed.

I dodged a pincer, then sliced off the ungodly's head.

Sweat poured down my face, and the oppressive warmth kept my fingers clammy. There was no ice.

I kept my back pressed against Sadie's unconscious form.

The corner provided cover.

It was the only upper hand I had.

I stabbed an infected through the heart, turned and disemboweled another, then sliced through the heads of both ungodly as they ripped free.

They fell in pieces before they could rise to their full height.

Death himself hadn't wrapped his cloak around my shoulders. Not yet. I existed in the in-between: a land of fortitude and intrusive thoughts.

It was just me, the battle, and the familiar out-of-breath, winded, barely alive feeling.

My arms prickled with numbness.

Hours of blocking heaving blows and swinging my sword were taking their toll. My fingers were cramped around the hilt. I couldn't remove them even if I wanted to.

Terror for Sadie, who was slumped helplessly against the wall behind me, had me repeating a stream of expletives to myself.

She should have woken up by now.

But I'd had to do it.

She'd been losing a significant amount of blood and had

been in danger of permanently harming herself from exhaustion.

The mental war raged as I refused to give in to the exhaustion.

The physical war persisted.

Life was intolerable torment, and anyone who thought otherwise had never stood over their closest friend and swung a sword as they held back a room full of mindless monsters.

Time marched forward as I sliced and blocked.

A large middle-aged male infected slammed his enchanted sword down with so much force that my right arm went completely numb.

I felt nothing.

I couldn't move my shoulder or forearm.

Slamming my foot into the man's knee, I used my left hand to rip the hilt out of my unmoving fingers and rammed the blade through his stomach.

Right arm useless at my side, I resumed fighting with my left. I wasn't fully ambidextrous, but my nondominant hand was sufficient.

Sufficient was enough.

It had to be.

For Sadie.

Sweat blurred my vision, and I couldn't see beyond my attackers and the pile of carcasses at my feet. They kept coming, and I kept getting more tired.

I barely blocked a swing. The edge of an enchanted sword sliced down the outside of my thigh, and I screamed.

Lunging, I decapitated the infected and killed the ungodly as it emerged.

But another infected appeared in its place.

Again.

Another infected appeared.

"*Wake up, Sadie!*" I screamed desperately, but there wasn't so much as a twitch from the legs I bumped against as I fought.

Tears of frustration poured down my face because if she'd died, it was my fault. I'd killed her by knocking her out.

I sobbed as I fought.

Gasped for air around body-shaking sobs.

A sword swung low and cut shallowly across my shins—I didn't react quick enough. As I collapsed to my knees, I focused on my shoulder muscles.

Wings exploded.

My shirt was covered in cuts and provided no resistance. It fluttered off me in shreds. Left hand swinging the sword to block blows that rained down from above, I clumsily grabbed a feather with my numb right hand. With every ounce of will I possessed, I ripped it off.

It burned like a motherfucker.

With no precision or accuracy, I flung the feather into the crowd. An infected screamed, and I took it as a good sign. I ripped another feather and did it again.

Again.

And again.

Bodies screamed as everything blurred.

Sweat mixed with tears, and I grabbed the brick wall to hoist my body up. A last-ditch effort. The final stalwart defense that my friend deserved.

I didn't move.

My wings were too heavy.

Lying back against Sadie's body, wings spread wide—a fallen angel who'd never gotten to fly—I dropped the sword and ripped at my feathers with both hands.

Flung them at the faceless bodies.

I knew in my gut that it was the end; there was nothing to

analyze. No strategy left. I prayed they'd eat my heart, because I couldn't live in a world without Sadie.

I hiccuped between gasps.

Tears streamed down my face as I flung feathers blindly.

In the end, I wasn't strong enough; in the end, all the power in the world wasn't enough to save us.

Please sun god, save Sadie. Take me instead, the world needs her lightness. I sobbed. *The world doesn't need any more darkness, and that's all I can give. It needs her. So badly. She has so much goodness to offer. She's too pure to end like this. I need her.* Tears blinded me. *I need her so fucking badly. I can't live without her. I can't. Please.*

I wrenched a feather off my wing and flung it.

It clattered across the floor.

Shadows descended.

All around.

Hallucinating, I imagined the ground quaking beneath me. Portraits rattled as they fell off the walls, bricks rained down as the ceiling opened up, and a divine figure dropped from above.

The shadows turned toward the figure.

They stopped ascending.

I blinked.

I wasn't imagining it.

The monsters had really turned around.

Before I could be grateful, a heinous sound, too unimaginable for words, made every muscle in my body seize in agony. I was paralyzed by it.

Then it stopped.

Blessed relief flooded through me, and I gasped for air. Sadie was limp and warm beneath me.

I blinked, blurry vision clearing.

A handful of infected and ungodly stood in the center of the room, and all of them were frozen still with their mouths open wide as their eyes danced with a strange kaleidoscope of colors.

I'd never seen anything like it.

A soft voice chanted.

I pressed shaking fingers to my eyes and dragged them away, but the scene remained.

I rolled off Sadie and crawled forward on my hands and knees through piles of substances I refused to think about. My heavy wings trailed behind me like a downed butterfly's.

Head lifted high, I squinted as I peered between the legs of the infected.

I stopped.

Immediately I wished I hadn't crawled forward, because now the image was burned into my memory.

Jinx was crumpled on the floor in a pile of bricks, and her one arm was dislocated at a horrible angle—but that wasn't the scary part.

Her sunglasses were off, and her eyes glazed pure black.

Her one hand was outstretched, fingers bent in different broken directions as she pointed at the frozen figures and chanted, "*Anima tua est mori.*"

A gold cuff glowed brightly on her other wrist like it was leaking sunshine.

Light illuminated the mangled bodies that covered the floor, and the temperature in the already warm room skyrocketed.

Long tendrils of a white flame floated in the air between the frozen creatures and Jinx's outstretched hand, creating the illusion that she was connected to our remaining foes by ropes.

The hairs on the back of my neck stood up.

It wasn't Jinx's midnight-black eyes, the white flame, or

her words alone that made my stomach drop; it was the sheer power that radiated off her.

Silky black hair curled up around her head defying gravity as she repeated the chant.

Looking at Jinx was like looking at Lyla.

No.

It was worse.

The adage "you don't look fate in the eyes" seemed more like genuine advice and less like a whimsical saying. She was power incarnate, a type of power that didn't seem native to the realms of the High Court.

She dropped her outstretched hand, and the white ropes dissipated.

The bodies of the infected and ungodly dropped—Jinx was the only one still alive.

They were all dead.

Black receded, and Jinx's eyes went back to normal. Her breathing was labored and loud in the aftermath of whatever she'd done.

The sunshine exploding from her cuffed wrist extinguished like it had never existed. The room plunged into shadows.

"What are you?" I croaked.

She lifted her head in my direction and whispered, "You already know." Her words trailed off into an agonized moan as she convulsed on the floor.

My heart clenched with worry as my mind rebelled.

I tried to crawl forward to help her, but exhaustion punched through me, and I collapsed face first onto blood-covered stone.

The threat was eliminated.

But was it?

As I drifted into consciousness, the Latin saying, "*Anima*

tua est mori," repeated inside my head. Its literal translation was, "Your soul must die."

The white ropes made of flames had been their souls stretching as she pulled them out of their bodies.

She'd consumed them.

The kings were the chosen soldiers of the sun god, and even they could only see souls and judge them; they couldn't *take* them.

The power to consume a soul was the ability of a dark god.

Jinx had destroyed them all—she was a terrible creature of lore.

She was a soulmancer.

CHAPTER 54

CORVUS MALUM
MISSING MATES

Nyctophobia (noun): abnormal fear of darkness.

DAY 36, HOUR 3

My thoughts blanked.

Arabella and Sadie were missing.

Once again, I'd lost my fucking Revered in the middle of a battle. Once again, we failed her.

This time, she wasn't nearby.

We'd checked.

For some heinous reason, the bond sickness wasn't working when we actually needed it.

I opened my mouth and bellowed, scarlet flames pouring out as I burned the infected and ungodly to ash.

Since we'd come to this realm, since I'd realized what Arabella was to me, my powers had been intensifying. My flames burned hotter and brighter, and I had no urge to hold them back.

The fire wanted to destroy the world, and I wanted to destroy the world for her.

Our interests were aligned.

"We can't find them anywhere. We've done an entire sweep of the castle," Jax's panicked voice crackled over the earpiece.

"Where the fuck IS MY REVERED?" I bellowed like a mad man.

When we'd realized that both Arabella and Sadie were missing, I'd ordered everyone to fan out and search for them.

Finding Arabella was the priority.

Fuck the war.

Fuck the High Court. They'd cautioned me against unleashing too much of my power because they didn't want me to go mindless with rage and accidentally kill the soldiers on our side.

Too late.

I was mindless.

Flames of pure destruction poured off me as I scorched the last dozen ungodly that remained. Before their ashes had touched the ground, I'd already turned and was running down the hall toward the group.

We had to find Arabella.

I couldn't lose her.

I wouldn't survive.

CHAPTER 55
ARAN
CONFESSIONS OF A MONSTER

LACUNA (NOUN): a blank space or a missing part.

DAY 36, HOUR 8

"Wake up." I slapped Sadie on the cheek, then leaned over and repeated the action on Jinx.

I'd opened my eyes about an hour ago and found myself in a room filled with dead bodies.

Sadie and Jinx were passed out among the carnage.

After retracting my wings, I'd stumbled over to Jinx and picked her up gingerly. Then, I'd carried her over to where Sadie was slumped over.

The first issue was Jinx's dislocated shoulders and fingers; one by one, I'd set them back into place. I couldn't do anything about her bruises or potentially broken bones, so I'd braided her messy hair to get it off her face. I'd wiped the dirt from her eyes.

I'd turned to Sadie.

Spitting on a scrap I'd torn from my ruined shirt, I'd wiped the crusted blood away from her nose, eyes, and mouth as best I could. After she looked better, I'd torn off more strips and wrapped them around a couple of the deepest cuts on her arms and legs.

Then, I'd worked on my leg.

Half my thigh had been cleaved off.

I'd started to wrap my shirt around it, then I'd realized the missing skin would regrow in the material. I'd quickly ripped the fabric away.

Head spinning and vision tunneling, I'd started to pass out, so I'd lain flat on the floor and tried not to think about the wound. It burned horribly and sent stabbing streaks of pain down my leg. Ignoring it was easier said than done.

That was the last of my healing efforts.

Now I lay on the floor between Sadie and Jinx, my leg propped up against the wall with the half-missing part of my thigh out of harm's way.

"Wake uuuuuup," I said morosely as I reached my tired arms out and slapped at their sleeping faces.

I knew they needed rest to recover. However, I also knew that we were trapped in a room full of dead bodies, and I was scared.

I had not gone through hell for them to just sleep it off while I suffered.

"Wake up!" I shouted and clapped my hands, going for the surprise effect. Sadie startled, and I turned my head with excitement.

She snored.

A stray eyeball rolled across the floor.

I gagged.

"You're losing friendship points right now," I groaned as I closed my eyes and tried to pretend I was on a breezy beach somewhere, drinking and smoking.

The problem was my leg throbbed and I was in agony.

Also, the room *reeked*.

Sharp rocks bit into my back uncomfortably, and it was oppressively warm.

This beach sucks.

My heart skipped a beat as I realized the worst thing yet —I was missing my pipe.

Patting around the gushy floor with my eyes closed, I desperately searched. *Please sun god,* I prayed. *Since you literally didn't save me at all, at least save my pipe. It's the least you can do.*

My fingers trailed through something fleshy, and I pretended it was a rock covered in wet sand (I was 100 percent aware that it was someone's detached spine).

I couldn't find my pipe.

Despair settled in my bones that all was lost.

"No," I whispered dejectedly into the darkness.

There was only so much a woman could take before she broke.

I touched my face—my pipe was still in my mouth.

I breathed in enchanted smoke greedily.

I held both Sadie's and Jinx's limp hands in mine, and my chuckle turned into a broken plea. "Please wake up."

I waited in silence.

It felt like an eternity passed.

Hope was fading.

Sadie suddenly woke up with a scream. She lunged forward and wrapped her hands around my neck. "Who took my bread roll?" she bellowed groggily.

It was too much.

I burst into tears and wrapped my arms around her in an awkward hug as she choked me.

"Aran?" she asked with confusion as she stopped choking me. "What happened?"

I opened my mouth, then closed it as I thought about *what* exactly had happened.

In all my melancholic despair, I'd forgotten to plan an explanation for how the handle of my sword had slammed into her forehead and knocked her unconscious.

"Wait a second," she growled, and her fists pummeled against me. "*Arabella Alis Egan, how dare you!*"

I squealed and protected my fleshy bits.

"It isn't what you're thinking," I yelled in defense.

She stopped punching me. "So you didn't knock me out because I wasn't listening to you?"

I pursed my lips. "It's exactly what you're thinking."

She whacked me across the top of the head, but the blow was glancing and filled with love.

"What's going on?" Jinx asked groggily, and I froze midwrestle.

Sadie gasped, "What's Jinx doing here?"

Why had I wanted them to wake up?

"You have some explaining to do." My voice cracked and it felt like I was falling.

The pieces were already clicking together in my mind, but I needed to hear her say it aloud.

Jinx grimaced as she stared at her mangled fingers and nodded curtly. Sadie's eyes cast a red glow and illuminated the three of us.

We sat in uncomfortable silence.

Jinx coughed, a harsh rattle. Still staring down she said softly, "Twenty-five."

The room was stuffy with heat and too quiet, as if the dead were holding their breath and listening.

She didn't elaborate further.

Sadie asked, "What?"

A bead of sweat streaked down the side of Jinx's face. "I

recently turned twenty-five years old. My species goes through puberty differently because I'm not from these realms—I'm a soulmancer."

Sadie stiffened.

Jinx continued, "On the Creature Classification Scale, the High Court labeled me a six when I was just a toddler. The scale only goes to five. They shackled me to repress my abilities." She held up her bare wrist where I'd seen the gold cuff had glowed.

Neither of us breathed.

Jinx didn't look up as she spoke. "When I was a baby, the High Court confiscated me from traffickers. However, my *saviors*," she spat, "didn't integrate me into society because I was deemed too dangerous. I was caged and held until my purpose could be discovered."

She laughed without humor, and it came out as a wheeze. Something rattled in her chest.

Jinx continued speaking like she was far away, lost in some horrific distant memory. "At least the former occupant of my cage was a human monster who had the decency to not be a *complete* moron—they'd given him a bookshelf filled with treatises on philosophical discourse. As you can imagine, it was the only thing that kept me sane."

"No," Sadie rasped.

Jinx jumped and looked up like she'd forgotten we were present.

Sadie shook her head. "I can't imagine how that kept you sane. When I was being tortured as a child, I just wanted to read fantastical romances filled with smut and depraved acts. It calmed me down."

Jinx sniffed. "Shocking that a woman of your intellect would turn to such drivel."

Her haughty demeanor was ruined by another coughing fit.

Sadie either missed the point, was in denial, or was purposefully trying to break the somber mood. She beamed at Jinx and offered, "When we get out of here, I'll give you a list of book recommendations." She winked (or twitched; it was hard to tell because she had two swollen black eyes). "Now that you're twenty-five, I can give you the *real* dirty recommendations. Let me tell you, you're going to be *sweating*."

"Are you serious right now?" Jinx stared at her incredulously.

Sadie smirked. "It depends on how queasy you get at the word *moist*. We'll start there."

Jinx tried to turn her back to Sadie, but she winced in pain as and gave up by flopping back onto the rubble.

The three of us sat in silence.

It was nice.

"So?" Sadie asked. "What's the rest of the story? I'm invested."

"I'm not talking to you." Jinx purposefully looked away from her.

Sadie asked in an innocuous tone, "Hm. Are you sure you're not fourteen? You did tell everyone I was your mother."

Jinx's head whipped back around. "No, I did not. *You* did that."

A headache throbbed behind my left eye.

My half-mutilated leg burned.

I inhaled smoke desperately. "Sadie, stop it!"

She pouted. "What did I do?"

"Jinx, tell the story." I pointed my pipe at her. "You owe me that much."

The youngest-looking twenty-five-year-old in history narrowed her eyes at me, but agreed with a curt nod.

Chest rattling with each shallow breath, she said, "Ten years ago, the High Court found a purpose for me."

She stared down at her mangled hand and avoided eye contact.

My stomach twisted with knots.

Back at Elite Academy, when the Kings had unleashed their powers, Orion told Jinx her soul was irredeemable because she'd committed a heinous crime against people she loved.

I shivered.

It was all so obvious.

"I don't know the entire story." Jinx's voice was barely a whisper. "I only have small tidbits from what I've overheard and the things I've pieced together. What I know for sure is there are two key leaders, and their plans involve manipulating certain individuals, whom they call players. They've been doing it for decades—maybe even generations."

"Manipulate what people? Who are these players?" Sadie asked.

I dug my nail into my lower lip.

Jinx didn't look up.

I ripped off a chunk of skin and inhaled smoke until my lungs ached. Copper flooded my mouth.

Jinx continued like Sadie hadn't spoken, "Over the years, I overheard them worrying that one of the most important players that they'd planted, wasn't cunning enough to wield the power they'd given them. Their methods of fixing the problem didn't seem to be yielding results. They were getting frustrated and desperate."

The knots in my stomach turned to razors.

Sadie's eyes widened.

"Then, ten years ago, they said they'd found a perfect solution. I was fifteen at the time," Jinx said slowly, then fell silent.

I did the math.

The numbers added up horribly.

I looked around the room, barely seeing the dismembered corpses as my thoughts blanked.

Dread stretched among the three of us.

"Just say it," Sadie broke the silence with a whispery rasp.

I shivered as I wiped sweat off my forehead with a trembling hand. I wanted to tell Jinx not to speak, but I couldn't find the strength to say the words aloud.

Jinx looked up, and her too wide dark eyes held mine. "There was a side player, a fourteen-year-old, who'd just received record high scores on an analytics test. She was rumored to be brilliant. But that wasn't the best part." She kept eye contact. "She was the daughter of a woman who was infamous for her cruelty. As a result, they theorized that the player's brilliance was likely dangerous—it was exactly what the leaders needed."

I didn't breathe.

In my periphery, Sadie looked back and forth between our locked gazes with horror.

Jinx's lips moved.

I heard her speak as if she was talking from far away, down a long tunnel.

"The High Court took me to the fae palace in chains."

Her voice warped.

"They removed my shackle and ordered me to take a piece of the brilliant player's soul while she slept."

My vision narrowed.

"They RJE'd me immediately to the shifter realm and

ordered me to give the piece to the idiot player while she slept."

Her words echoed from every direction.

"The two leaders were so impressed with the results that they elevated the brilliant player's position in their plans. One leader vouched for her, and the other vouched for the improved idiot player."

I gasped for air.

I just wanted her to stop talking.

Jinx continued, "A new plan was created to bring the two players together and use them to achieve the objective, which is still not clear to me. Secret, highly illegal enchantments were done on the idiot player to identify her fated mates. I was ordered to ingratiate myself into the family of one of those mates, and four discarded players were used to make my adoption seem legitimate."

Sadie heaved beside me.

"I was ordered to build a relationship with the brilliant player. There were—" Jinx paused like she was searching for the correct word. "—checkpoints over the years to update me on my role."

A bead of sweat dripped down my spine.

My hair stuck uncomfortably to my clammy skin, but I didn't brush it off. I was too numb to move.

"From what I gathered, both leaders had some type of ability to communicate mentally with the players. However, the brilliant player was damaged by the soulmancy, and a connection could not be established. Even the Angel Consciousness could not forge a link."

A wave of nausea rose up my sternum.

I swayed as a tunnel narrowed around me.

"I was the only one who could form a connection. I was ordered to be her guardian and help her eventually establish a link to the Angel Consciousness so she could earn her wings. Soulmancy is not an exact science, and there is much that I still don't know."

My hearing cut out, and the world went stuffy with static.

Jinx continued mercilessly, "I spent years trying to connect with the soul I'd mutilated. I was inside the player's brain so often she was convinced she had a monster in her head. There were even some shared physical manifestations —when she was enraged, her eyes turned black like mine."

I collapsed onto my side, pressed my cheek to the sticky floor, and gasped.

"Aran—Aran—Aran!" Sadie shouted as she shook me, sounds resuming as she jostled my shoulder.

I groaned.

"I took a piece of your soul and gave it to Sadie." Jinx moaned like she was in pain. "I mutilated you both—and the worst part is you think of me as family."

Sadie trembled as she gripped my shoulder. "You're the numb," she whispered, "but I heard the moon goddess say she was the—"

Jinx cut her off, "The leaders have mental connections with their players. You were dying, and they told you what you needed to hear so they wouldn't lose their investment."

"Why does it need time to recharge?" Sadie asked with confusion.

Jinx shrugged. "From what I can gather, it is extremely rare for a split soul to take in someone else's body. My theory is that your body still recognizes it as foreign matter and tries to expel it after you use it, but it has nowhere to go. So it recharges and comes back."

I covered my mouth with horror.

"But it doesn't sound like Aran's voice," Sadie argued.

Jinx shook her head and looked morose. "Of course it's

not her speaking voice—it's a piece of her *soul*. Although, I've always found it surprising that you hear it as a voice, it must be your body recognizing that it's a pattern of thinking separate from your own. However, there must be a fundamental compatibility between you two that defies physics for it to guide you like it does. A specialized analytical piece of Aran tries to save you from the inside—it's mind-blowing if you think about it."

I reached over and grabbed Sadie's hand.

We looked at each other.

We were bonded in friendship down to our very souls.

It was almost heartwarming, if horrendous soul mutilation could ever be called such a thing.

Our hands were shaking as we held each other.

"But Dick was the one who whipped me—" Sadie's voice filled with horror. "Is he the leader?"

Jinx's voice was monotone. "I've been enchanted not to disclose the names of the leaders."

"He looked me in the eye and lied to me," Sadie snarled. "No wonder that halo thing they gave me never did anything. It was all a ruse to make me compliant in their games."

I shivered even though it was feverishly warm.

"What's the point of it all?" Sadie asked.

Jinx shrugged. "Control of the realms. Politics. Power. War." Her eyes were deadened. "The usual things."

"My depression?" I asked, my voice exploding louder than I'd meant to speak.

"You're missing a piece of your soul," Jinx stated softly.

"That's why our guardian connection is so unreliable," I said numbly. "That's why the soul bond with the twins only shows pain."

"Correct," Jinx said tiredly.

Muted colors. Empty feelings. My mind palace had gaps when I was fourteen years old. I thought I was abducted by aliens. Dick and the hooded man were always around.

So many things made sense.

I asked, "What was the voice that overtook the people and spoke in rhymes to Sadie and me?"

Jinx sighed heavily. "Members of the Angel Consciousness that worked with the High Court to guide you."

I fired off another question. "I've heard a male voice speak to me when I've done…things."

"The leader." Jinx scoffed. "They couldn't forge a mental connection, so they tried to actually speak aloud to you."

Dick was nearby when I'd ate my mother's heart. He was also nearby when I killed in the beast realm. Both times that I'd heard a voice.

"Did it cause the bond sickness?" I asked warily.

Jinx picked at the rubble. "I don't think so. It seems to be a genuine effect of how the kings treated you. It was probably fixed when you bonded to the twins because your soul changed."

That was also my deduction.

"The reason I can't fly?" I asked. "The ice I can't control?"

Jinx shrugged. "I don't know. I'm not omniscient."

My head spun.

I couldn't think of anything else to ask.

Sadie spoke up. "You said there were four discarded players used to make your adoption to Jax's family legitimate." Her raspy voice had an edge to it I'd never heard. "There is only Jess and Jala…who are the other two?"

Jinx didn't answer.

The energy shifted, and suddenly the sweltering room felt freezing.

"Jen and Jan," Jinx whispered, her voice barely audible. "They were twins."

"What happened to them?" Sadie asked.

"Randomly, some people are immune to my—abilities. Like Warren. I don't know why or how it happens."

Sadie stated harshly, "They were immune. What did you do?"

Jinx's eyes were wide like she'd seen a ghost. Her broken fingers tangled in the fabric of her ripped shirt. She said nothing.

"What happened to them?" Sadie asked, her voice hard as steel.

"The leader killed them because I couldn't wipe their memories." Her voice cracked. "I tried to save them." She shuddered. "But he killed them."

"You wiped our memories," I whispered. "We don't even know their names."

Sadie covered her mouth as she made a wounded noise.

Jinx curled up like she was trying to make herself smaller and whispered, "They made me do it. And now you'll never be able to remember."

No one spoke another word.

This time, the silence hurt worse than the physical pain.

CHAPTER 56
JOHN
BLOOD TRAILS

ERYTHROPHOBIA (NOUN): morbid avoidance of the color red.

DAY 36, HOUR 12

"We've checked everywhere. They aren't here!" I yelled with frustration and kicked debris down the corridor. I pressed my hand against my chest and focused on the empty feeling inside. It was the only thing that kept me from losing it completely.

"Where are you Aran?" I whispered dejectedly as I stepped over the burned remains of ungodly.

The world was colored in shades of gray. Every breath I took pulled at the freshly healing wound that covered my back, which hurt far worse than any ordinary injury.

I welcomed the emptiness.

The coldness.

The pain.

It all meant one thing—Aran was still alive.

Luka gripped my bicep; his eyes were unfocused as he stared down the empty corridor. He hadn't spoken since we'd realized Aran had gone missing, and darkness shimmered, stretching around him in an amorphous mass.

He looked how I felt.

Haunted.

"They aren't here," Cobra hissed, slit pupils glowing bright green as shadows writhed across every inch of his pale skin. "My snakessss have combed the structure. They're gone."

Xerxes rubbed at his chest. "Our bond is growing fainter, which means she's injured. We need to find her soon."

"Where the fuck would they have gone?" Ascher asked, his tattooed knuckles cracking as he slammed his fist into the brick wall.

"We need resources," Scorpius said harshly. "We need to leave and get help. The angels and assassins are handling the soldiers and perimeter, so we're wasting time waiting. We need Lothaire. The High Court. Fucking anyone. Now."

Orion nodded.

Footsteps echoed, and excitement burned my throat. Luka's grip tightened on my arm, and we both held our breath.

Corvus appeared around the corner and barked, "Did you find them yet?"

It wasn't Aran. Hope plummeted so swiftly that I felt lightheaded with disappointment.

"No," Jax snapped as he glared down at the corpse of an infected.

Corvus growled like a wild animal and staggered back. Flames shot off his tongue as he said, "All the ungodly are dead. They aren't here."

"We need to get help," I said, and all the men nodded as we moved together.

Corvus slammed his hand down on the RJE device.

CRACK.

We knelt in the strategy room.

"The board!" Jax shouted, and all of us turned to see what he was gesturing at. The room exploded in expletives and noise.

Scrawled across the blackboard in large letters was, "Sadie and Aran, portal back 1st battle, trapped in basement w/ ~100 ungodly. BRING REINFORCEMENTS. SPEED. FOLLOW MY TRAIL -Jinx."

Before I'd finished reading the message, Orion grabbed an RJE device from the drawer.

We all flung ourselves at him as he activated it.

CRACK.

"Aran, where are you?" Scorpius yelled, his voice projecting down the long, ruined corridor.

The stench of decomposing bodies was overpowering as I got to my feet. I looked around the dark structure, and dread filled my gut because there was no response.

No sounds.

The compound appeared abandoned.

"I smell Jinx's blood trail," Jax roared roughly as his head morphed into the maw of a bear. He sprinted down the corridor, and the rest of us followed without question.

I squinted down at my feet as we ran.

Red drops were splattered in a line between round imprints from crutches. I ran faster, heart pounding in my chest as I tried not to think about finding Aran in pieces.

Luka kept hold of my arm as he ran beside me.

Jax skidded to a stop in front of a gaping hole in the floor that appeared to be caused by some sort of blast. All the shifters leaped down the opening. The rest of us followed them into the dark.

I was terrified of what we might find.

The stench of rotting flesh increased exponentially.

There were bodies everywhere—piles and piles of mangled corpses. So many bodies that it looked like the ungodly had fought an entire army.

Nothing moved in the room.

"Arabella?" Corvus bellowed desperately as Jax roared, "Sadie? Jinx?" Everyone held their breath as they waited for a response.

It was dead silent.

Nothing.

I wanted to sob. I wanted to scream. I wanted to fall to my knees and plead with the sun god for Aran's safety. I wanted to curl up into a ball and protect myself from the sheer agony coursing through my soul.

Standing up straighter, I scanned the room.

I would find her, and she would be okay because there was no other option. Somewhere along the way, she'd become the reason I got up in the morning.

Aran was an intoxicating combination of dark humor and sweetness.

Other people were intimidated by her harsh disposition, but I'd always preferred the darkness—I was its prince, after all.

The shimmering void expanded around Luka. With each body I scanned that wasn't Aran's, I considered how far I'd go to save her.

There were spine-chilling creatures kept in the under-world, some of which had advanced tracking abilities. Sure, they were class five creatures who would likely commit unspeakable atrocities if they were released. Still, they could help us find her.

I staggered over a man's mutilated sternum.

His rib cage was intact, but his heart had been ripped out in the battle.

I empathized.

Across the room, Corvus bent down and threw body parts aside as he searched for her like a madman. Scorpius stood perfectly still and listened. Orion carefully climbed through the gore, eyes wide and unblinking as he searched beside us.

Luka and I combed through the faces, his grip painfully tight on my arms.

The shifters fanned out, looking. "Ssssadie?" Cobra hissed brokenly, shadow snakes streaming off his skin like a black tide.

No one responded.

They weren't here.

I needed to do something. Every second that passed was a second Aran could be dying. I refused to accept a world without her.

It didn't matter that our soul bond was corrupted.

It didn't matter that the world was gray.

It didn't matter that I was empty behind my sternum.

I'd endure all of it a thousand times over if it meant I got to spend my life with Aran under my arm. My back burned with pain as I moved, a reminder of what I was willing to do for her.

Anything.

I would give up everything.

Without her by our sides, Luka and I were nothing. There was no point to any of it. As soon as we'd realized Aran was missing, the disconnect from other people that we'd always felt had returned tenfold.

We didn't care about others.

We pretended.

But there was no point in pretending anymore if we didn't have Aran.

There was no point in living.

We weren't built for this world.

I unleashed my power and darkness expanded into a floating doorway. Luka's eyes widened as he realized what I was doing. It was highly illegal to release creatures from the underworld; it was a maximum-security prison for a reason.

The High Court would label me with treason and hunt me until I was eliminated.

"To help find her?" he asked.

I nodded.

My twin's face contorted with determination. "Good. Let's go."

The ruination of the world be damned. She was ours and we would get her back. We stepped forward together into the—

"*She's here! I hear three people breathing!*" Scorpius shouted, and we both halted. As soon as the meaning of what he'd said processed, Luka and I withdrew from the void.

It winked out of existence.

Jax pushed aside a large slab of the ceiling and revealed Sadie and Aran, who were holding each other. Jinx was leaning against them.

All three were unconscious.

Dirty.

Covered in blood.

Their chests rose and fell as they breathed.

Shadow snakes swarmed over all three of them, and Cobra hissed, "They're all alive." He staggered and whispered, "They're okay. She'sssss okay." He looked around at the carnage, face shining with pride. "They did this."

Everyone looked around.

"Holy sun god," Scorpius whispered as Orion whispered in his ear and described the room's devastation.

The massacre took on a new light.

"No," Corvus said with disbelief, eyes widening and jaw dropping as he looked back and forth between Aran—blood-coated enchanted sword lying beside her—and the dozens of mutilated corpses.

He stared at her like he'd never seen her before.

That's my girl.

Satisfaction welled.

I'd never doubted her abilities. She was immensely capable. Sun god, power perpetually dripped from her fingers.

From Luka's unsurprised expression, we were on the same page.

We'd always seen Aran for what she was; it was the kings who kept misjudging and trying to pigeonhole her.

Moment of shock over, everyone exploded into motion.

As I took in the gruesome wound on Aran's thigh, the world became a blur, and it felt like I was moving underwater. Horror filled me at the fear and pain she must have experienced. She'd been all alone, trapped down here with monsters, bleeding out with no way of escaping.

My girl must have been terrified. Luka trembled beside me as he came to the same conclusions.

Time lost all meaning.

I wanted to cry, but my eyes were bone dry.

Corvus hoisted Aran into his arms, and all of us surrounded her. Touched her reverently. Reassured ourselves she was okay.

Cobra picked up Sadie, and Jax scooped up Jinx.

The RJE device was activated.

Crack.

The snow fell softly.

Sunlight shone in muted shades.

We sprinted into the medical barracks. We screamed at doctors as they ran around frantically. They attached the girls to tubes and gave them enchanted medicine.

There was barely anyone else being treated—the usual injured foot soldiers were missing.

I didn't care.

Luka tangled his fingers in Aran's curls, and I held her hand.

The kings also sat around her still form and kept their hands on her like they were afraid she would disappear.

The shifters were similarly gathered around Jinx and Sadie. The boy named Warren staggered into the room and shouted.

A doctor announced that it was good that they were all in a healing sleep, and Corvus screamed flames into his face.

I agreed with his sentiment.

Sixteen hours, twelve minutes, and fours second after we'd found her, Aran woke up. One eye was a darker blue than usual and highlighted the gray tone in the other.

She didn't smile when she saw us.

She didn't frown.

She stared blankly forward with a shell-shocked expression.

Her head whipped to the side where Sadie and Jinx were hooked up to fluids, still asleep. Ripping a needle out of her hand, she staggered over to them while we tried to stop her.

She ignored us.

Pushing the shifters out of the way, she stood between their sleeping forms and grabbed their hands.

She fell to her knees.

Bowed her head like she was praying.

And laughed.

CHAPTER 57
ARAN
BONDS THAT CAN'T BREAK

ACATALEPSY (NOUN): an ancient Skeptic doctrine that human knowledge amounts only to probability and never to certainty.

DAY 38, HOUR 12

I was covered in ice and it felt like a hug.

The bottom of the bunk above my head was also iced over.

After everything that had happened, weirdly, I didn't feel any sadness.

I was overwhelmed with gratitude that all three of us had survived against unmistakable odds.

When we'd gotten back to the camp, immense relief had bowled me over.

It was over.

All three of us had beaten horrible odds and lived.

It felt like a miracle.

On top of surviving, for the first time in my life, I had

closure over why I'd started suffering when I was fourteen years old.

Most of all, I was grateful that my entire soul wasn't missing like I'd initially thought. A small piece I could handle. It made it a fixable problem.

I'd successfully processed my grief (I was delusional).

The body draped across me like a blanket shifted, and I grunted as they kneed me in the crotch.

"Are you still crying?" Sadie asked as she sniffled and buried her face in the blankets near my head.

"Uh—yes," I lied, just so she wouldn't feel alone.

Sadie sobbed, "Me too."

"I didn't notice," I replied. She'd been wailing for hours straight, and I was concerned about how she was still going.

Her labored breathing was loud in the mostly empty bedroom.

She was safe and alive.

In my arms.

Sadie's mates and the rest of my legion were waiting for us outside in the blizzard. They stayed away outside out of respect for us—Sadie had also threatened to enslave everyone with her blood if they didn't leave us alone.

The latter had played a big part in them giving us the room.

"Can I leave now?" Jinx asked from the floor beside the bed. She was wrapped in blankets and had bandages around her head. Sadie was holding her hand, and I had my free hand on her shoulder.

Jinx complained but didn't pull away from our touch.

When I'd woken up after a restful sleep, I'd had startling clarity that Jinx was as much a victim as the rest of us. She'd been beaten and abused by the leaders for years. She'd lost a leg in the Legionnaire Games, just so I could earn my wings.

Jinx was a pawn as much as any of us.

If I could try to forgive Lothaire for abandoning me as a child, then I could do the same for the woman who'd been tortured worse than any of us.

When we needed her, she'd saved us.

A few weeks ago, I would have spiraled at her revelations and moped. I would have refused to forgive her and would have punished us both.

But I wasn't an empty shell anymore.

A necklace and bracelet pulsed warm against my skin, reminding me that my soul wasn't as empty. I was connected to the twins.

There was a bit of color in my life, and the cold didn't feel as pervasive with my best friend lying in my arms.

I'd slaughtered too many infected. I'd spent too many hours slicing people to pieces because they were unlucky enough to be taken over by monsters. I wasn't going to cut Jinx out of my life.

It was messed up, but war had given me perspective.

I just wanted the killing, the hate, the violence to *stop*.

I wanted peace for all of us.

And sun god, for the first time in my life, I *understood* why I was the way I was. I no longer felt like I was going insane.

Sadie let out a long dramatic wail, and I grimaced as I patted her head. She was taking the death of the twin girls and mutilation of my soul extra hard. I wanted to join her in grieving, but since I had no memories of the girls, I couldn't find the emotions.

All I could focus on was the three of us were alive.

It was a miracle.

For a period back in that room, I'd been certain that Sadie was going to die.

I'd been a few seconds away from losing her.

Jinx shifted and I patted her head. She gave me a death glare, but didn't pull away or say anything mean.

For her, that was a declaration of love.

Back in the settlement, after Jinx had finished confessing everything, she'd started to crawl away from us. She'd thought we'd blame her. She'd thought we wouldn't want her to be a part of our family anymore.

She didn't understand how this family worked.

We'd all been used. We'd all been mutilated, each of us in different ways. We'd all been treated as pawns.

"So," I said conversationally. "How do we stop the leaders?"

"I'm going to tear them to shreds," Sadie said as she punched my pillow.

Jinx sighed loudly and shook her head. "I've told you both, we don't. They have an entire institution behind them, and the leaders are insanely powerful. They are *more*."

"What does that mean?" Sadie asked with confusion.

Jinx looked back at us, midnight-black eyes wide and haunted. "Some things in life are beatable. Some are only survivable. This is the latter."

"I don't accept that," Sadie said.

Jinx stared blankly.

Her pale features were stark and slightly uncanny. It finally made sense; they were too sharp to be from these realms because she *wasn't*.

She was a class six creature.

A trafficked child.

She was a monster soulmancer.

She was my sister, and I wanted to gut the people who'd hurt her.

"Here I opened wide the door—" Jinx closed her eyes. "—darkness there, and nothing more."

Ice spread across the sheets, and Sadie shivered but didn't complain.

Sadie trembled against me. "Is that also from Nietzsche?"

"No, a genius named Edgar Allan Poe." Jinx leaned into our touch and rested her head against the side of the bed. She whispered, "I thought for sure you'd both hate me. I thought"—her voice cracked—"that I'd be completely alone."

I whispered, "You're stuck with us."

Sadie laughed weakly. "We all have our problems."

Jinx's face twisted with confusion. "How can you say that? I mutilated your souls?"

Acceptance was a foreign emotion in my chest as I replied, "It happened a long time ago. Crying about it now won't change anything."

Sadie sobbed harder and whispered, "I have a confession—once in the beast realm, I enslaved Aran with my blood when she was asleep, and I made her get me food from the kitchen because I was so sore from training, and she doesn't remember it."

I rolled my eyes and replied, "Once I found a kitten and gave it to Sadie as a gift, and it kidnapped her."

Sadie barked with laughter and hiccuped as she remembered how Xerxes had spied on us. The sound was so ridiculous that I chuckled.

"What even is our lives?" she asked between gasps.

"I think we're lucky," I whispered, and Sadie looked at me with confusion.

I explained, "At this rate, we probably shouldn't be alive. But here the three of us are—it's a miracle."

Sadie's lower lip trembled as she thought about it, then she let out a half scream, half sob. "You both are so special," she wailed loudly.

"You're ridiculous," Jinx grumbled, but she reached up and grabbed my frozen hand. Her fingers were heavily bandaged.

"What do we do now?" Sadie asked as she wiped tears from her eyes.

Jinx said, "What we've always done."

"We survive," I said with conviction.

I pushed Sadie off me so I could sit up. She clung to me dramatically, and I swallowed more laughter because I didn't want to hurt her feelings. Something about watching her sob was so funny to me.

Yes. I was a bad person.

Sadie moaned dramatically, "It's so much work. I'm tired."

Jinx glared at her.

I looked back and forth between the sister who'd stolen my soul and the sister she'd given it to.

I felt so sun-god-damned lucky.

My soul had been gifted to the one person I was closest to in all the realms. It had made her stronger and helped her survive.

I shuddered to think what Sadie would be without me. I was literally her best friend and the analytical voice inside her head that allowed her to fight well.

Ever had an *impact* on someone's life? *Same.*

"You would be so lost without me." I grinned at Sadie.

She punched me in the tit, and I yelped.

"Don't be insensitive." She sniffed. "This is a very emotional time."

"Is it really?" I dodged another punch.

The door slammed open, and a towering shadow entered. My adrenaline went through the roof. Without thinking, I flung myself out of the bed and stood protectively in front of Jinx and Sadie.

"Um, sorry to interrupt," Malum said awkwardly as he rubbed the back of his neck, pink staining his cheeks. "A worker just told us that the High Court is looking for us. They want us all present to debrief in the strategy room."

My chest deflated, and I looked back at the girls. Jinx's panicked expressions reminded me of what was at stake.

It didn't matter how much I hated the High Court; we had to wait and plan.

We had to pretend we didn't know.

We had to survive.

Jax pushed into the room behind the blushing king, he looked over Jinx like he was making sure she hadn't gotten injured while in the bedroom with us (a very real possibility).

"Are you okay?" the towering shifter asked with concern as he reached down and hugged her like she might break. The golden chains in his long braids tinkled as he held his sister.

Jinx hugged him back. "I'm fine. Sadie and Aran are being weird." She inhaled and rested her head on Jax's shoulders like she was taking strength from him.

Sadie made a face at her.

I blew her a kiss.

"I don't care what's happened in the past." Jax's expression was serious as he stared down at Jinx. "You'll always be my baby sister," he said fiercely. "I will always stand beside you protectively."

Jinx sucked in air shakily.

"I need to hear you say it—please." His voice cracked.

"You'll always be my brother," Jinx whispered. "You'll always be there for me." She gently kissed his cheek.

They continued to embrace for a long moment, then

they pulled apart. Jax draped one arm over Jinx's shoulder and the other over Sadie's. He nodded at me as they left.

I tipped an imaginary hat.

Warmth dethawed another portion of my heart.

Dick was projected onto the screen. The cloaked man and Lothaire flanked him on either side.

Lothaire stared at me and mouthed discreetly, "I heard what you did." The corner of his mouth lifted. "Good work, daughter."

Pride swelled.

"There were no foot soldiers left," Knox said grimly as he stood at the front of the room and gave the battle report. "None survived."

Holy sun god.

My smile slipped.

With everything happening, I'd forgotten about the rest of the battle.

I lifted my head and locked eyes with Sadie, who also looked stunned. The rest of the men looked resigned. They'd already known.

"You're telling me," Dick said harshly, "that all the soldiers stationed on the perimeter are dead. *All* of them?"

Knox nodded. "The twenty of us who went inside are all that remain. The academy, shifter, angel, and assassin legions are all that are left."

"How?" Dick spat.

Knox swallowed thickly and said, "There seems to be a large group of infected that rushed outside as soon as the battle began. It was not a handful like usual, it was dozens."

"Why the change in behavior?" Dick's eyes narrowed, and his tone was poisonous. "Where did they go, soldier?"

"I'm not sure, sir. It's our belief, however, that it wasn't that many and the war is over. We've wiped out most of the ungodly. The last ones can be eliminated as they're found." Knox bowed his head deeply and stepped back from the screen.

Dick stared down at where he'd stood with disgust on his features.

I inhaled fortitude and lifted my head high. "I know where they went," I said.

Dick's head snapped up.

It took every ounce of control I possessed not to flinch as he looked at me.

The angels turned around and glared.

Lothaire nodded at me, like he was encouraging me to continue. He believed in me.

His approval gave me strength.

I took a deep breath.

"In the battle, we found another map of the realms," I said calmly. "However, this one contained a key—the red *X*s on the mountains by the third valley are villages. It's likely that the last stronghold of infected is located there."

Silence.

The room exploded in murmurs. In my peripheral vision, the angels gave me death glares. They wanted the war to be over, and so did I. But I wasn't going to pretend the threat was eliminated when it wasn't.

This war would haunt me for the rest of my life.

I needed it over.

For good.

Once I left this sun-god-cursed realm, I was never

coming back. The corrupt High Court would have to drag me kicking and screaming.

"How many infected are suspected?" Dick asked.

My heart thumped erratically in my chest as I thought about what he'd done to Jinx. What he'd done to all of us.

He was a leader, and we were his pawns.

I wanted to snap his neck.

Ice spread across my fingers, and I tucked them behind my back as I stood at attention.

"Unclear, sir." I kept my eyes dead and expression blank. "Most likely a large number. There were multiple *X*s on the map."

The angels murmured to one another with discontent.

"There are only twenty of you left." Dick enunciated each word like he was thinking. "And because of the peace accords, we can't recruit additional soldiers."

Lothaire looked worried.

"All of you will RJE to the valley and hike to the mountains. You'll eliminate the last ungodly, and this war will be *over*. We can't give them time to escape. You'll go tomorrow."

Rina gasped.

The corner of Dick's lips pulled up in a sneer, and he turned to Malum. "Since you've found all your mates, you'll activate your powers to ensure this battle is won. You're the kings of the sun god for a reason—prove it."

Malum made a noise of disbelief. "But, sir—"

"We've paid for your therapy," Dick said harshly, "and we've been informed that you've been practicing—is that not true?"

"It's true," Corvus said. "Howev—"

Dick interrupted, "Then it's decided. Good luck, soldiers."

The screen went dark.

"See you tomorrow on the battlefield," the angels sneered at me as they left the room.

From their tone, they thought this was my fault.

Sadie and Jinx both turned to me with worry.

"You guys go ahead. I need to speak to my legion." I tried to sound reassuring, but I shivered with nerves and ice spread across the floor beneath me.

They reluctantly left the room.

Seven men stared at me expectantly.

"Um, you two can also go," I said to the demons.

Zenith rolled his eyes and sat down in a leather chair. "No, thank you," he said. "We'll stay here where it's safe." Vegar nodded as he sat down next to him.

"It was an accident," Malum mumbled petulantly, referring to the bathroom he'd destroyed in a fit of rage. "No one got hurt."

Zenith scoffed. "We're staying." He turned in his chair to face Vegar and gave us his back, a clear dismissal.

"Whatever." I stomped out into the raging blizzard, and five men ran to surround me.

John threw his arm over my shoulder and tucked me against his side as he turned to protect me from the harsh snow.

Luka wrapped his hand around my curls and leaned close. "Are you okay?" he whispered, dark circles stark under his worried eyes as snow gathered on his lashes.

"I think so," I said honestly.

He pressed a soft kiss onto my forehead.

Like personal guards, Scorpius and Orion fell into protective positions in front of me. Malum walked behind me, his flames shedding warmth that fought against the icy wind.

They formed a wall of protection.

When we got back to the sleeping barracks, Scorpius dusted snow off my hair while Orion helped me out of my coat.

Malum knelt at my feet and pulled off my combat boots, and I opened my mouth to complain that I could do it myself, but he gave me a death glare. "Let me serve you. Your leg is still healing."

"It's healed." I smacked my leg to demonstrate and nearly threw up. It burned with agony.

Malum grabbed my wrist. "What the fuck? Don't hurt yourself." His eyes widened like he was panicking.

"Let me clarify," I said calmly. "It's *almost* healed."

"No. It's not." He dragged his hand over his shaved head and breathed shallowly.

I accidentally (on purpose) kicked off my combat boot straight into his gut to show him how well it worked.

"Don't hurt yourself!" Malum barked with concern as he caught my boot.

Yet again, he missed the point.

The twins grabbed the blanket off my bed and wrapped it around my shoulders.

When they were content that I was warm, the men stepped back.

Malum raked his hands down his face and paced. "Fuck, what are we going to do? Arabella fell *asleep* every time we tried to have her stop us. The ungodly seem mostly immune to fire, and there's still a chance we could kill the angels and assassins."

He was spiraling.

"Or they might be fine and we're worrying for nothing," Orion whispered. "At least the infected would die."

Luka played with one of my curls. His attention was fully on me, and he acted like the other men didn't exist.

Unfortunately, I couldn't do the same.

"We could always just kill them all," Scorpius said dispassionately. "Who cares if the angels or assassins die?" He smirked like the idea excited him.

I grimaced. Sometimes I forgot how cavalier he was about other people's deaths.

It was creepy that I *didn't* find it disturbing.

The men looked around like they were waiting for someone to come up with a solution, and my stomach plummeted as I thought about everything I'd learned.

"I'm missing a piece of my soul," I blurted because apparently, I was in the mood to trauma dump.

"What?" Luka asked as he stared at me. "We told you we don't thin—"

"I confirmed it. I have sources," I said quickly before I lost my courage. "I'm missing a piece of my soul. The High Court took it from me when I was fourteen."

I left out the part about Jinx taking it and giving it to Sadie, because some things in life were personal.

Knowing the men, they'd probably get jealous.

There was a long pause, then Malum went up in flames. "Who did this to you? I want names. Now." Scarlet exploded from his mouth.

I pushed my pipe between my lips and closed my eyes as the first drag of enchanted drugs calmed me. "I'm not sure," I lied. "We can worry about that later." It was partially the truth because I didn't know who the other leader was.

Luka moved closer, his features contorted in pain.

All the men stared at me like they were grieving for me.

I shrugged because I honestly wasn't that upset about it. A part of me had always known something wasn't right.

I no longer felt crazy.

Chuckling awkwardly, I said, "I always had a feeling I was a soulless bitch."

No one laughed.

Tough crowd.

"We're the lost princes from the Olympus realm," John blurted, and darkness glittered around him and expanded. "We kept our identities a secret from the realms because we struggle with our—people skills." He glanced over at Luka. "Our powers form a portal to the underworld, the maximum-security prison run by our father, King Hades. We're not supposed to tell anyone. Ever. It's a family secret."

I blew out a puff of smoke. "I know. You already told me you were the Princes of Darkness?"

John frowned. "But we didn't tell you we were from the Olympus realm. We didn't *explain* who we were—or what we could do."

It hit me. "Oh my sun god!" I exclaimed. "Is that where our truth journals are from?"

"What?" Luka asked.

Orion nodded and whispered, "I think so."

John flashed his dimples and punched my arm. "Really. That's all you have to say?" My bicep went numb, and I lost feeling in my fingers.

I punched him back with my good arm as hard as I could, and he laughed.

"And I'm the Queen of the Fae Realm. What do you want—a medal?"

John grinned at me and ruffled my hair. His smile slowly dropped as he stared at me.

"Are you really missing a piece of your soul?" he whispered.

I nodded.

He looked horrified.

I took a deep breath. "That's why our soul bond is corrupted. The betrothal jewelry probably sensed I was broken and tried to forge the connection to help me. It's probably what overrode the bond sickness. I'd assume it's corrupting your souls or something, but I don't know."

I expected the twins to recoil with disgust.

Both took a step closer.

"So we're helping you," John said with awe in his voice.

They both looked at me like they were enraptured and not at all disturbed by what they were learning.

"We're never letting you go," Luka said with steel in his voice like he could read my thoughts.

Malum breathed harshly, "So you've been mutilated?" Both Scorpius and Orion looked at him with concern.

I stopped breathing.

My heart beat erratically.

This was what I'd been waiting for; these were the consequences that had my thoughts racing and fear filling me ever since Jinx had revealed the truth.

I'd known it was coming.

"Yes." as I pushed my shoulders back and sized up Malum. "Which means I'll *never* be your perfect Revered. I probably won't be able to help you control your fire in any way. I'll corrupt you—just like I corrupted the twins."

I paused. "I'm useless to you."

Molten silver flashed.

Scorpius made a harsh noise under his breath, and Orion's eyes widened. A muscle in Malum's jaw jumped.

"Is that so?" he exhaled, and fire came out of his nose.

"I'll never be your perfect Revered," I said softly. "You don't have to pretend anymore. I know I drive you crazy."

Malum transformed into a creature of bronze and malice. "You're right," he said.

White teeth flashed.

My heart stopped beating.

It was a cold, dead, useless thing in my chest.

Malum smiled cruelly. "We don't have to pretend anymore."

CHAPTER 58
ARAN
POISONED BONDS

POLYAMORY (NOUN): the practice of engaging in multiple romantic relationships.

DAY 38, HOUR 22

I took a step back and bumped into Luka as Malum stalked toward me swiftly. A vicious predator locked on its prey.

He stopped inches away, towering over me and exuding waves of vitriol and hate. "You think that after all this time —" He breathed harshly. "—I've been fucking *pretending* to be into you?"

"Maybe," I whispered.

Silver eyes flashed with unholy rage.

Bronze features rippled with unspeakable emotions as he tipped his head back, opened his mouth, and fell to his knees.

He bellowed.

Fire burst from his lips as he said, "I care so much about you that it drives me *crazy*—morning, day, and night. I wake up, and my first thought every—single—day is that I hope *you*'re feeling okay. I go to sleep thinking about your sorrowful blue eyes. I fist my cock in the shower thinking about your pink tongue and pouty lips." His voice rose, and he shouted, "*How the fuck could all this be an act?*"

"I don't know," I yelled back, overwhelmed by his impassioned display.

Ice spread across my hands and traveled up my forearms.

He pointed a flaming finger at me.

"I am so obsessed with you, woman, that it's *killing me*!" he roared.

"Uh." I rubbed the back of my neck awkwardly and mumbled, "I didn't realize you cared about me that much."

"*Care doesn't encapsulate a tenth of what I feel for you!*" He gripped his shaved head. "*Aran, I'm so fucking infatuated with you that I'm foaming at the mouth for a smidge of your affection!*" He gasped shakily. "And you have the audacity to tell me I don't really care."

Handsome bronze features contorted like he was tortured.

My heart pounded painfully against my sternum.

"What more can I do?" he asked, still on his knees. "I've shown you time and time again that you're my everything —*you are my soul*. You're the reason for my existence. Without you, I'm nothing." He thumped a flaming hand against his chest. "You're my Revered."

I shivered.

"That's the problem," I said. "I'm not an *ideal*. I'm an imperfect person."

Steele eyes narrowed with confusion. "What the fuck are you talking about?" Scorpius and Orion walked up and stood on either side of him.

I waved my hand at them. "You three want me to be your Revered—this perfect mate that will save you. You don't want *me*." My voice trailed off. "You don't want Aran."

The twins shifted closer, their jewelry vibrating against my skin. John rubbed my back as Luka twirled one of my curls. They were pillars of support.

Scorpius frowned, his features sharp enough to cut glass; Orion's eyes widened, dark lashes fluttering; Malum scowled.

"You've got to be joking?" Scorpius asked in disbelief. "Arabella, *you're* our Revered. Of course we want *you*. Do you think I sit in the shower talking to anyone else for hours? Sun god—I don't even want to do that with them." He gestured to Malum and Orion. "I've told you things that I've never told anyone." His voice quieted. He whispered like he was embarrassed, "I've opened up to you."

Orion nodded as he stared at me, unblinking. "You're the only person I can talk to without having to hide who I am. From the moment I first met you, a piece of me knew what you were to me. My everything."

Malum stood up swiftly, determination on his face. "We can prove it to you right now."

"What?" I asked, looking between the kings.

"You think we don't want you because your soul has been mutilated—which we *will* be getting answers about later." He raked his hand over his shaved head and nodded. "There's a simple solution, one that also helps with the problem of unleashing our powers in battle."

I rolled my pipe between my lips.

Malum's tone was serious. "We can bond, and all of us can finally be together."

I choked on smoke.

"It's all up to you," he continued intensely. "Will you accept the three of us as your mates? Will you let me be your Ignis and Scorpius and Orion be your Protectors?"

"Please," Orion whispered, and Scorpius took a step back like he was afraid of my answer.

The three of them vibrated with fierce energy.

"Even if our mating bond is corrupted because of your missing soul," Malum said forcefully, "we still want it."

They nodded in agreement, like what Malum was saying wasn't the opposite of everything they'd ever wanted from their mate.

I struggled to breathe.

"We want *you*, Aran." Bronze features gleamed with emotions. "Flaws and all."

My tongue was heavy in my mouth, and I struggled to speak.

After a long moment of gasping, I finally said, "How does forming the bond prove anything?"

"It proves we don't care if you're not perfect." Scorpius stepped forward and caressed his graceful fingers down the side of my face. "We don't care if the mate bond is messed up—we don't care if you're not a *perfect Revered*, like you put it. Corvus is right, we just want *you*."

"Please," Orion mouthed.

I was shell-shocked.

How could they want the bond when they knew it could hurt them like it was hurting the twins?

They were supposed to want me to help fix their powers and make them stronger. They weren't supposed to want me when I could break them further.

"But what about my back?" I said weakly.

"I refuse to hurt you," Malum said immediately. "The bond is formed through intimacy and acceptance—but it's not an exact science."

Scorpius explained like he'd put a lot of thought into it, "The crucial part is that we all mentally accept the mating bond. The intimacy is more symbolic of what's occurred, but the key is your acceptance. We can make your participation as painless as possible." His lips turned up wickedly. "For now."

Malum looked at where the twins were touching me. "We think it will also help your bond with the twins. If more souls are involved, it will counteract the damage." He exhaled. "I know how much they mean to you."

I glanced at the twins and was momentarily shocked by how horrible they looked. The pallor to their skin and dark circles were worse than the days prior. They were suffering because of me.

"Don't worry about us," John said as he flashed a dimple, but he ruined it by wincing as he shifted like he was in physical pain.

Orion whispered, "If all of us are connected to your soul, we can alleviate what's been done to you."

"Let us help you," Malum pleaded.

Scorpius shook with barely constrained anticipation. "Let us own you. Body and soul. No matter the consequences —please."

I rubbed the back of my neck, possibilities and probabilities unfolding in my mind's eye. Mentally I made a checklist.

Pros to bonding with the kings:

1. It might help ease the twins' pain.
2. It might give me the ability to stop the kings once they began using their powers and potentially save the angels and assassins tomorrow.
3. The lack of bond might be why I was struggling to fly.
4. I'd finally have a big family to call my own.

Cons to bonding with the kings:

1. Their overbearing possessive slightly stalkerish personalities.
2. Mitch.

I sighed because it was a *super* close one; Mitch alone was making it hard to agree to their proposal.

Luka whispered in my ear, "Whatever you decide to do, we'll stand by you. No matter what."

I leaned against him and closed my eyes as I soaked up the support of the twins. When I opened my eyes, the kings were still staring at me with pleading, desperate expressions.

You didn't know who someone was until you saw them suffer. Times of torment revealed more truths than any times of peace ever could.

They were serious.

They didn't care that I was broken.

They didn't care that I also needed the twins.

Something in my expression made Malum look away with devastation.

I had feelings for the kings, and I didn't want to see them hurt.

You could let the dark times rip everything away from you, or you could survive them and build something brighter.

It wasn't really a choice.

"Okay." I cleared my throat. "Yes. I'll be your mate."

Orion's jaw dropped, and Scorpius covered his mouth with his hand.

John chuckled and ruffled my hair, and Luka gave me a soft kiss on my cheek.

Malum stumbled back like he'd been punched. "You mean it?" he whispered with shock as his cheeks turned bright pink. "You really mean you're going to accept the bond—Aran?"

I shrugged and tried to act like him saying my proper name didn't make my stomach flutter. "It makes sense," I said with feigned casualness. "The logic is sound."

My heart beat irregularly in my chest.

Turned out I liked to make major life decisions spontaneously. I'd agreed to marry the twins on a whim, and now this.

This was either going to be a special moment or an impulsive choice that I would regret for the rest of my immortal life.

Only time would tell.

Malum leaned forward and reached for me like he was going to tackle me to the floor, but he pulled his hands back at the last moment and grimaced. "We have to mate now because we fight tomorrow. We also have to do it without hurting you."

Scorpius pushed past him, grabbed my face with both hands, and kissed me passionately. He tasted like bergamot and sin. I moaned into his mouth as his tongue speared against mine.

Little streaks of pain exploded down my spine.

He yanked his lips away from mine. "How was that?" he rasped.

"Mmmm," I answered intelligently.

Milky white eyes looked off into the distance. "Your back, Arabella. How is your pain level?"

"Bearable," I said honestly.

Scorpius dragged his nails across my cheeks. "It better be." He smirked. "Here's what we're going to do."

❄

"Are you sure about this?" I asked for the millionth time as I rolled my pipe between my lips.

This was different from how we usually kissed. All those moments had been explosive bouts of uncontrolled passion.

This was deliberate.

Planned.

A conscious choice to be intimate.

The bedroom was shrouded in shadows. Night had fallen and a blizzard raged.

The kings stood on the superbed in the middle of the floor. We'd once again pushed our mattresses together.

I sat on the corner on Luka's lap with John's head in my lap.

Every time I fidgeted with my pipe, John grabbed my fingers and brought them back to his hair. If he was a cat, he would have been purring as I played with his messy locks.

Luka's thumbs traced soft circles underneath my sweatshirt.

I was cozy and warm.

I was also freaking out.

"I don't think this is going to work," I said anxiously as I tugged at John's hair.

John snuggled deeper into my lap and mumbled, "It's fine. Stop panicking."

"I'm not," I lied. Ice spread from my fingers onto his hair, but he didn't seem to mind.

Orion held his hands out cautiously like he was talking to a skittish animal. He whispered, "It's okay, sweetheart. The important part is that you mentally accept all of us as your mates. The physical part is simple—just tell us what you want us to do." He glanced back and forth between Luka and me.

"We can give you suggestions," Malum offered, his voice rougher than usual. "If that helps."

I nodded, unable to do much else.

Malum frowned. "Just make sure you tell us if your back hurts—*please*. We'll stop immediately. You have to tell us. No more enduring in secret."

"I will. I promise."

Scorpius cocked his brow, looking every bit the arrogant king. "Do you want us to take off our clothes?"

My breath caught.

Scorpius smirked like he knew what he was doing to me. "From your inhale, I'll take that as a yes."

Luka nuzzled his face against the back of my neck as the three kings stripped, revealing layers and layers of cut muscles.

Cherry blossoms drifted across Orion's golden shoulders as he stared at me, steel glinted across Malum's bronze neck, and a tattooed eye lazily opened across Scorpius's pale skin.

The three of them were works of art.

When they pulled down their sweatpants, I forgot how to swallow. *Holy mother of the sun god.*

Abdominal muscles tapered into deep *V*s across their torsos. I'd caught glimpses of them naked getting with other girls and while we changed dozens of times, but this felt different.

There was a gentleness about them that was new.

In tandem, they fell to their knees. Their muscles flexed, powerful bodies radiating strength.

John shook his head on my lap, and I realized I'd stopped playing with his hair. His eyes were open, and he watched Scorpius with hooded eyes.

I felt exactly the same way.

Luka's fingers tangled around my wild curls, and I turned

around to see if he was watching. His eyes flickered between me and Orion.

I wasn't the only one enjoying the show.

I turned back to the kings.

Malum had moved. His face hovered mere inches away from mine. "Do you, Aran, accept us as your mates? Will you let me be your Ignis? Will you let them be your Protectors?"

My tongue was heavy in my mouth as I whispered, "I accept you as my mates."

Malum's smile was wicked. He finished crawling to me and leaned forward.

He gently kissed me. Whiskey, tobacco, and heat exploded across my senses. I'd never tasted anything so delicious. He pulled away, and the pain on my spine dissipated. He licked his lips, silver eyes gleaming with desire.

Orion whispered, "We accept you, Aran, as our precious Revered."

I leaned in for more kisses.

"No, precious," Malum whispered, cheeks flushing maroon as he backed away. "No pain. You tell us what you want us to do. You're in control."

"Um." I was too chicken to say the words aloud.

Scorpius smirked like he could read my mind. "I know you've imagined us, Arabella." He licked his lips. "I could hear your breathing change every time we fucked people at Elite Academy. We were fantasizing about you—and you were fantasizing about us."

Orion mouthed, "Whatever you want, sweetheart. Just say it."

I took a deep breath. "I want Malum and Scorpius to fuck Orion," I said before I could lose my confidence.

Malum smiled. "That can be arranged."

I moved to cover my flushed face, but Luka caught my wrist and held my hands down.

"Don't be afraid," he whispered into my ear, and I shivered.

"Keep your eyes on us, Arabella," Malum commanded, his voice rough and heated.

He turned and kissed Orion roughly. Scorpius licked his fingers wantonly, then slowly dragged them down Orion's body.

There was a loud slapping noise as Scorpius left handprints across Orion's ass. Then he parted his cheeks and spit obscenely.

Luka groaned in my ear.

I agreed.

John shifted on my lap, his hands wandering beneath his pants.

Orion stared at me as he writhed in pleasure—he was shockingly pretty compared to the rough handsomeness of his mates.

The three of them were divine.

Luka massaged my scalp as I played with John's hair. Gentle zips of pain streaked down my spine, but I barely noticed it. I was too entranced with what was unfolding around me.

Malum and Scorpius fucked Orion like they were savages. They pounded into him with their heads thrown back in pure ecstasy. Powerful muscles drenched in sweat.

Their grunts and moans filled the room. After what felt like hours, they pulled their hard cocks out of Orion's holes and crawled over to me. Each one of them gave me tender kisses, then Luka picked me up and gently handed me over to Malum.

John grumbled but let me go.

Malum sat so I was sprawled across his naked thighs. He repositioned us so his thick penis jutted out between my legs. "You're doing so well," he whispered huskily. Orion and Scorpius took turns sucking him off while I sat on his lap.

Desire pooled between my legs, but my pain level stayed manageable because no one was touching me. After Malum came down Orion's throat, he laid me down beside them and tucked me under the covers so I was cozy.

I gasped as they resumed making love beside me.

Everything was a blur of masculine moans, grunts of ecstasy, and heavy panting as they leaned over—each one giving me featherlight kisses as they found their release.

An hour later, I drifted asleep with the kings piled naked around me.

"So glad you're back with us, safe," Malum whispered.

"Me too," I agree.

"Love ya," he said.

Orion whispered. "I love her most."

Bodies shifted and nails dug into the sensitive skin on my neck. "False," Scorpius said fiercely. "My love is superior."

"No, it isn't," John and Luka said simultaneously.

"I love you all," I whispered softly as I fell asleep.

I dreamed, and it felt like peace.

CHAPTER 59
ARAN
THE FINAL BATTLE

AGATHOKAKOLOGICAL (ADJECTIVE): composed of both good and evil.

DAY 39, HOUR 5

It felt like I was floating on a bed of roses.

I was ethereal.

Light.

Warmth seeped into my bones, and peace radiated through me. I curled up around the source of heat. It felt divine. Pleasure and happiness bubbled.

"*Report for the final battle. Repeat, all soldiers report now for the final battle.*" Enchanted speakers blared, and sirens wailed.

I was wrenched awake.

The heat disappeared, and the room became a blur of movement as men scrambled to get dressed. At some point, the demons must have returned.

I sat up. Outside the window, the blizzard gusted in the darkness of early morning.

John pulled me to my feet. Luka handed me a pile of my folded battle clothes.

I sighed. I was getting awfully tired of going into battle.

Sirens flashed brightly.

Speakers repeated the directive with increasing urgency.

"How are you feeling?" Malum asked as he knelt at my feet and laced up my combat boots while I zipped up my coat.

"I feel good. How about you?" I stretched, leaning side to side. "Do you think the mating worked?"

Standing up, he said, "Maybe. I'm not sur—"

His lips parted with surprise as he stared down at me.

"What?" I asked as I rubbed at my face, wondering if I had something on it.

He hollered, "*Everyone look at Arabella!*"

The men paused getting ready, and one by one, their eyes widened with shock.

"What?" I repeated impatiently, but none of them said anything. Rolling my eyes, I stomped over to the destroyed bathroom.

I stared at my distorted reflection in the cracked mirror.

Sirens flashed.

Speakers wailed.

My fingers shook as I brought them up to my neck. The skin was uncomfortably cold to the touch, and I pulled my fingers away because they burned.

Shine refracted across the mirror.

A three-dimensional ice skull was tattooed across my throat. That wasn't all. Just like Orion's cherry blossoms, flakes of blue-white sparkling snow drifted across my skin.

Gold gleamed on the top of my ears and formed pointy caps that resembled fae ears.

Pinpricks of chill drifted down my throat and the snow

danced along my collarbone as if it was carried on a wintery breeze.

"What in the holy sun god," I whispered, and my breath was a frosty puff.

I'd actually done it.

I'd accepted the kings as my mates.

"We're mated." Malum's baritone voice vibrated behind me, and I whirled around. Scorpius and Orion stood beside him.

All three of them were beaming.

For the first time since I'd met them, they appeared young and happy. Carefree.

"Do you feel any pain?" I asked as I looked over their healthy complexions, searching for a sign they were concealing discomfort.

White teeth flashed, and Malum said, "I feel amazing." His mates—no, *our* mates—nodded in agreement.

John pushed past the kings and entered the bathroom. "If anyone cares, I also feel great." His dimples flashed. "I need to test something."

I opened my mouth to ask what he meant, but my question never got out. He gripped my face with both his hands and slammed his lips against mine.

Pinpricks of pain exploded across my spine, and I winced.

"Sorry," he panted as he wrenched himself away from me. "Shit." He looked over at his twin. Luka shook his head like he was telling John not to say anything.

Weird.

"Did you feel my pain?" I asked John, worry gnawing at my stomach because of the concerned expression on his face.

He waved his hand dismissively. "No. I didn't feel anything. The kings were right, our bond doesn't hurt anymore." His smile dropped. "But it's you I'm worried about."

Relief filled me. "That's amazing!"

John narrowed his eyes. "No, it's not. You're still in pain. That's what matters."

The dark circles had receded from his eyes and his olive skin looked healthy. Luka also looked much better.

I felt faint with relief.

The six of our souls were really connected. There was enough power flowing between all of us that my broken soul no longer corrupted the twins.

I wanted to cry.

John winked at me, then slammed his shoulder into Scorpius as he left the bathroom.

Scorpius licked his lips sensually. "I heard you got a skull."

Those same lips had wrapped around Malum's cock. They'd kissed Orion as he thrust into him from behind.

"Interesting, my little Revered," he said. "We'll see what you can do."

I drew up to my almost six-foot height. "I'm not little. And we'll see what you can do, *Protector*."

He crossed his arms over his chest, the picture of male satisfaction.

Orion whispered, "You look beautiful, sweetheart."

"You're our ice queen," Malum said reverently, like he couldn't believe the turn of events.

They stared at me with adoration.

"*We need to go!*" John yelled with urgency, and the demons shouted in agreement.

Minutes later, I RJE'd with the remaining twenty soldiers back to the last settlement location.

Lavender light shimmered as the sun rose over the valley.

The snow fall was mild.

We climbed up the mountain where the X's had been drawn. A few hours later, we crested the top.

A flat plateau sprawled between the mountain peaks.

Someone gasped.

Dozens of freestanding structures were sprawled across the flat plain. They were wide and low-roofed. Each one could easily house dozens of infected.

The size of the village was shocking.

No one spoke as we all processed the sheer impossibility of our task.

There were only twenty of us.

Angels spread their wings wide and crouched as they prepared to take to the sky. The assassins were shadowy blurs as they darted back and forth like they were preparing to race forward into battle.

Sadie sliced open her palm and her blood levitated into the air. The shifters formed a protective circle around her.

Everyone was ready to die.

"No," I said.

Sadie looked over at me with confusion.

"No," I repeated louder.

Not again.

I'd almost lost her once, I would not make the same mistake.

Pushing my pipe between my lips, I turned to the twins and said, "If we lose control, stop us. Use force if you must." The Necklace of Death pulsed under my clothes. "We're all connected, and I have a gut feeling you're the only ones who won't be entranced."

"What?" Luka furrowed his brow with concern. "No, we will not—"

I hugged him, and he went quiet.

I mumbled into his neck, "As long as my heart is not eaten, I'll be fine. Don't worry. Just don't let us hurt anyone we shouldn't. Please."

Luka hugged me back tightly, and John wrapped around me.

"What's going on?" Knox asked.

The twins let me go, and I turned to the leader of the angels. "Everyone needs to stay back and stay out of our way. I advise that you climb back down the side of the mountain and wait it out."

"Why would we do that?" Rina scoffed.

I rolled my pipe between my lips and exhaled Horse. He settled onto my shoulder in a plume of smoky feathers, his long regal neck turned away from the angels dismissively.

"The High Court ordered us to use our mate powers." I gestured to the kings.

"And what's that supposed to do?" Rina asked haughtily, but her eyes gave her away. They flashed with fear.

She'd seen what the kings had done in the Legionnaire Games. She knew exactly what I was referring to.

The kings looked at me grimly.

"Are you sure you want to do this?" Sadie's ruby eyes glowed with concern.

I nodded. "Climb down to safety and hide. We'll handle the last of the ungodly." The unspoken, *otherwise we're outnumbered and could lose the battle*, hung in the air between us.

She stared at me for a long moment, then nodded and gestured to her mates. "Let's go down and wait it out. Aran can handle this."

My stomach knotted. I rubbed at the black fabric which covered my neck and concealed my new tattoo.

I hope she's right.

Cobra narrowed his eyes at me like he wasn't going to

obey, but at the last moment he shook his head and followed Sadie. "Don't get yoursssself killed," he hissed as he stomped past.

"Don't question our ability to protect our mate," Malum snapped. Scarlet flames danced across his head.

Cobra bared razor-sharp fangs at him, then disappeared over the edge of the mountain. The assassins were a blur of shadows behind the shifters.

The angels remained.

"You should go," I repeated.

"Angels don't run and hide," Rina spat. "We're staying."

Whatever. I tried.

Cracking my neck back and forth, I focused on the village full of infected.

I pushed my pipe between my lips and inhaled enchanted smoke.

"Are you ready?" Scorpius asked with a grim expression.

"Yes," I said, before I could change my mind.

Cherry blossoms swirled off Orion's neck, a pink pretty in the lavender sunlight. They traveled through the air and circled around the structures.

I tensed my muscles.

Click. Click. Click. Click.

The gold hardware on our ears floated upward and separated into shards of a crown.

Unlike last time, the kings' eyes didn't darken.

Ice talons exploded from my fingers. Scorpius's and Orion's talons looked the same, but Malum's had changed.

They were made of fire.

Malum tipped his head back and said, "As the Ignis from the illustrious House of Malum, I invoke the power of my mates." He pulled the wickedly sharp dagger from his neck.

He stared at me as he said, "As the crowned King of the Sun God, I invoke the power of my mates."

My skin prickled with power.

It was intoxicating.

"Venimus!" Orion sang. "We came."

I braced myself for the trancelike state—it never came.

Scorpius grinned as he realized and bellowed, "Vidimus! We saw." The eye tattoo on his neck looked around and his milky blind eyes glowed brightly.

It was Malum's turn to speak, but I tipped my head back, and sheer power ripped through my chest.

On instinct, I yelled, "Interfecimus! We slaughtered."

Ice shot from my fingers and formed into a staff. It touched the ground and towered high above my head. A skull sat on the end, and Horse settled onto it. His feathers gleamed with shades of red and gold.

He was corporeal.

I gasped with delight.

Horse opened his long beak and cawed, the sound toe-curling and vicious.

Malum shouted, "Vicimus! We conquered." He held the dagger above his head, and flames poured off him, filling the air.

Ice burst from my fingers and rose to greet his heat.

The lavender sunlight disappeared. Gray clouds rolled in and snow whipped furiously.

The blizzard had arrived.

"*The day of wrath is here*," Orion sang loudly in his sweet, poisoned voice. White-blond hair floated alongside cherry blossoms. He winked over at me. "*The day of wrath is upon us.*"

Doors slammed open, and hundreds of infected poured out of the structures into the unforgiving snow.

Scorpius tipped his head back to the sky and bright light shot out from all three of his eyes.

The white flames above the infecteds' heads flickered green, then midnight black.

Orion sang, "*Your souls have been found lacking. You have committed a heinous crime against bodily autonomy. Redemption is not possible. You will be exterminated.*"

I raised my ice staff.

Slammed it down onto the rocks.

CRACK.

Horse raised his wings wide and screamed into the storm.

Temperatures plummeted. *Lower. Lower. Lower. Lower.* Winds intensified.

Visibility was nonexistent, but I didn't need my eyes to see.

I could *feel* the location of every infected person. Their souls were corrupted by the foul ungodly.

Scarlet flames leaped and rose higher off Malum, and his warmth cut through the ice storm. The twins stepped forward and stood beside the flaming king.

Malum spread his arms wide, and his heat sheltered all of us from my cold.

The ungodly weren't so lucky.

The blizzard was merciless.

My limbs tingled with awareness—I could feel every flake of snow that covered the mountain plateau. It was rapturous. I was free.

I tipped my head back and laughed as the weather raged.

I *was* the storm.

The power was intoxicating.

I felt like a god.

The temperatures kept plummeting. The infected died from the un-survivable cold, then ungodly ripped from their carcasses. The monsters flailed helplessly as snow piled around them.

Colder. Colder. Colder.

Crack. I slammed my staff down on the rocks.

Just like the claws adorning my hands, the snowbanks covering the plateau turned razor-sharp.

Every snowflake transformed into a serrated blade.

Crack.

Hundreds of ungodly were sawed into pieces.

Instant death.

Horse shrieked into the wind as he flapped his majestic golden-red wings. I tipped my head back and yelled with him.

The blizzard raged.

I needed to test every living person's soul; I needed to cleanse all the realms of darkness; I was reckoning incarnate; I was here.

Someone yelled something at me, but I couldn't hear them above the wind.

Turning, I faced the angels who were frozen in place.

I'd start with them.

Almost black flames flickered weakly above the angels' heads. They weren't fully corrupt, but they were close. Far away, down the side of the mountain, eight warm bodies were frozen still, and three of the souls were also nearly irredeemable.

A smirk twisted my frozen lips.

I didn't believe in redeeming the impure. I would execute them to save the pure.

"Stop! You don't want to hurt them," Jinx's voice screamed inside my brain. I smiled because she was wrong.

I did.

Horse flew off my staff and settled onto my shoulder.

Someone bellowed something in my face and shook me, but I barely noticed.

I lifted my staff and—flames slammed against me.

The world burned.

Scarlet fire.

Everywhere.

I staggered back as the numbing cold retreated from my limbs. I slowly came back to awareness. Tiredness hit me like a hammer, and my knees gave out.

Two people caught me.

"You're okay, sweetheart." Orion knelt in front of me, and his lyrical voice washed over me like honey. "You did amazing."

Scorpius knelt beside him. A tattooed eye was wide with worry as it stared at me.

"Good girl," Luka whispered in my ear, and I realized the twins were holding me upright.

Flames danced around all of us.

The warmth intensified as Malum stepped closer. Fire poured off his hands onto me.

"I conquered," he said. "I conquered *you*, my Arabella."

Malum's eyes widened. "That's why you fell asleep each time we practiced. You were never meant to stop me. I was born to stop *you*. You're the powerful one. It has always been you.

Scorpius tipped his head back and laughed. "This entire time, she's been the blizzard—that's my killer."

I tried to smile back, but my lips were numb with cold.

Sheer power strummed through my veins.

I was frozen.

"Go to sleep," Malum whispered, his flames surrounding me in a cocoon of peace. "We'll take care of you. You did so well."

Sleepiness dragged my eyes lower and made my limbs heavy.

Horse shifted on my shoulders.

He was also on fire.

He nuzzled his cheek feathers against the side of my face, then pecked like he was giving me kisses. He chirped three times, and it felt like he was saying "I love you."

I kissed his feathered head gently.

He looked at me with adoration.

Scarlet flames trailed across his feathers, and he disintegrated into ash. The storm carried him away.

I blinked frozen lashes in horror.

A tear froze as it streaked down my cheek.

"A phoenix," John whispered with wonder.

It hit me.

I *understood*.

Mother had set me on fire until I was incoherent. The High Court had mutilated my soul and I'd lived a colorless life—but suffering didn't define my existence.

I didn't *struggle* to control my power.

I *was* power.

Horse and I would rise from the ashes.

We would survive.

I yawned, and in the space between consciousness and sleep, the meaning behind Lyla's warning, "You must embrace the dragon," became clear.

It had been me all along.

I was the dragon of the House of Malum.

PART FOUR
CONVALESCENCE

"All that we see or seem is but a dream within a dream."

—Poe

CHAPTER 60
ARAN
THE AFTERMATH

CONVALESCENCE (NOUN): time spent recovering from an illness.

"Meet the Heroes of the Realms" flashed across the top of the enchanted news tablet that John was reading. Headshots of twenty soldiers were displayed in bright neon underneath. My picture was the largest.

I didn't feel like a hero.

I felt tired.

Drained.

Numb.

The warmth of a mate bond strummed in my chest, but it didn't take away the bone-deep exhaustion. When I closed my eyes, I could see the infected shivering as they froze to death.

The heaviness in my chest reminded me that I could tear the world apart if I needed to. However, the connection was not at all how Sadie explained her mate bonds.

I couldn't identify any of our individual emotions inside my chest.

Malum had meant it when he said his mates *were* his soul in a way that other species couldn't understand.

We were one.

As individuals, we were breakable. Together, we were a terrifying source of endless power.

We were weapons of mass destruction.

It was hard to comprehend.

I wouldn't have believed it if I hadn't felt the power as I murdered hundreds.

But I had.

I'd killed. Again and again and again and again and again and again, until I'd lost count of how many infected and ungodly I'd sliced to pieces with serrated ice.

I should have been catatonic over what I'd done, but I was a little proud.

The last bit was the part that scared me the most.

It didn't help that my soul had been mutilated. The memory of Mother still haunted me. Jinx was under the thumb of leaders who had us all on strings like sick marionette dolls.

Everything I'd gone through these last few months was real.

Having mates didn't make that go away.

Time was warped. We'd fought the ungodly just yesterday, but it felt like the battle had happened weeks, maybe even months, ago.

It didn't help that the High Court had already launched victory parades across the realms and published dozens of news articles. They'd even canceled the funeral for the fallen soldiers. Dick had announced, "It's a time for celebration."

It was all too much.

The world had color and I wasn't empty anymore, but I still spiraled.

It didn't help that we didn't have answers. No one knew why the ungodly had chosen this realm in particular.

Why were they hiding in that basement? Why did they have a village in the mountains? How did they infect people?

So many questions.

But there was no one to ask.

We'd wiped them out.

Maybe that was the worst part about war: you thought it would give you answers, but it only created questions.

Wars started messy and depraved.

They ended the same way.

My thoughts spiraled.

I was in a free fall.

I was drained and reeling. Muscles weak and joints stiff, I struggled to move.

The doctors had diagnosed me with "severe energy backlash."

I'd diagnosed myself with insanity.

Unfortunately, no one bothered to ask for my professional opinion.

According to the doctors, I'd depleted my powers down to a dangerous level, and I wouldn't be able to conjure ice for at least a week as my body recharged. At the most, they said it could take months, maybe even years.

The hairs on the back of my neck stood up as I thought about every time I'd bemoaned the blizzard conditions.

I *was* the storm.

It was hard to comprehend.

I stared down at my bare fingers. They felt naked without ice.

Mother's flames had been impressive because she could

torture multiple people at once. What did that mean about me?

The sheer scale of ice I'd controlled was mind-numbing.

I shivered as I remembered that the Angel Consciousness had never removed the block from Mother's genes. She'd never earned her wings. *Would she have been able to level armies if they had?*

There were too many factors to know for sure. After all, as far as I knew, mother never had mates.

Was I fated to the devils because I was born powerful, or was I so powerful because I was mated to the devils?

I'd never know.

"Are you ready to go?" John asked as he turned off the news tablet and hoisted our bags of packed clothes over his shoulders.

I blinked.

Rubbing at my eyes, I forced my aching joints to stand up straight. I nodded like I was a functioning adult.

Even though his arms were full, he still pulled me against his side. I leaned into his sandalwood scent and inhaled greedily.

Luka came out of the bathroom and smiled down at me tenderly. He looked healthy and hale; his face had regained all its color, and he held himself straight like he was no longer buckling under invisible pain.

I might be half-dead on my feet, but it was a relief that the twins were doing better.

Two more people weren't suffering because of me.

"Ready to get out of here, Your Highness?" Luka asked, his lips turning down as he took in my disheveled appearance. "We need to get you home so you can sleep."

I squinted because I wasn't sure where *home* was.

"Thank fuck for that," Zenith snarled as he walked across

the room, packing his bag. "One more day in this blasted realm and I would have offed myself. Also—" He pointed to the still-destroyed bathroom. "If we get charged for that, I'm blaming all of you."

I shrugged. "Blame it on Malum."

"Oh, I will," he said with a huff.

Vegar came up and gave the frowning Zenith a kiss on the cheek, then the demon turned to us and said, "It was a pleasure working with you." He spoke with grave sincerity.

I saluted him weakly. "I hope we never have to go to war together, ever again."

"Same, soldier." Vegar smiled and saluted back.

Zenith shook his head in disgust. "The sun god better ensure we never have to do this shit again. Eighty soldiers dead. It's sun-god-damned ridiculous we all survived."

Eighty soldiers dead.

Ten sets of eight. Five sets of sixteen. Four sets of twenty.

The number was staggering.

I felt sick.

The door slammed open, and sun rays streamed into the barracks. The layer of snow was gone, and steam rose from the dirt as three towering men entered.

I squinted because the bright light burned.

I missed the storm.

Malum stomped inside and announced, "We've finished filling out the debriefing paperwork, so we're all free to leave." His smile fell, silver eyes narrowing with concern as he stared at me. "Should you be standing? You're supposed to be recovering."

Smoke curled off his tongue, and flames leaped along his fingers.

I sighed.

I can't believe I'd voluntarily mated with a man who breathed fire.

What type of person did that?

I'd accepted the dragon all right, and what had that gotten me? Unimaginable power. Actually, Lyla had been onto something.

"I can stand," I said in a duh tone. My knees trembled, and I clenched my ass to stay upright.

Malum frowned and opened his mouth (most likely to say something stupid), but Orion put a hand on his chest, and Scorpius stepped between us.

"Let's get you home, killer," Scorpius said with a smirk.

Since I'd woken up—after accidentally on purpose slaughtering hundreds of people—he kept calling me "killer" in a proud tone.

It was 10 percent sweet and 90 percent terrifying.

I wasn't sure if I should spiral or beam at his praise, which once again said a lot about my morals.

Self-discovery was disturbing.

Malum mumbled something under his breath and lifted the bag off John's shoulders. "We ready to go?" he asked the twins.

Luka nodded. "Everyone's stuff is packed. It wasn't much."

"I could have carried that," John argued, and Malum looked down at him like he was stupid.

Scorpius laughed. "Okay, *human*."

John crossed his arms over his chest. "We've already been over this. I'm the *Prince of Darkness* from the Olympus realm —I'm only half-human."

Malum smirked. "Okay, *prince*, let a *king* handle the luggage."

"Are you guys serious right now?" I asked. Orion and

Luka rubbed at their temples like they were staving off headaches.

"What?" Malum asked innocently.

John frowned at me. "You know I'm strong enough to carry our bags, right?" He flexed. "Tell him I'm strong enough."

"I refuse to answer that." I yawned and swayed on my feet.

Scorpius lunged and caught me. Long fingers gripped me harshly like he was terrified of letting me go. "Let's get her home," he said.

I tried to push him off me. "I should say goodbye to Sadie and Jinx."

He didn't budge.

Malum looked at me with exasperation. "You already spent three hours with them this morning. If I remember correctly, there was hugging, wailing, and crying." He shook his head. "You can visit each other whenever you want. You both have RJE devices."

I frowned. "Well, maybe I want to say goodbye a second time. Did you think of that?"

Scarlet flames danced across his shaved head.

"That's our cue," Zenith said. "See you never, assholes!"

I waved as the demons activated an RJE device and disappeared. I was going to miss their energy. They were special.

"We're taking you home, where it's safe," Scorpius said fiercely. "Thank the sun god it's summer there. I can't wait to be in the warmth far away from the High Court's bullshit and their news media circus."

Scorpius wrapped his arms around me tighter. He seemed to have forgotten that he was supposed to be holding me upright. Instead, he was half strangling, half hugging me.

I patted his back.

Apparently everyone needed hugs, even sadomasochists.

"Where is home?" I asked.

Everyone kept talking about it like we had one. Last I'd checked, I was from the fae realm, where the general populace wanted to battle me to the death for my throne.

There were a lot of factors at play.

None of them were good.

"It's a place where we can protect you," Orion whispered as he traced his fingers down the side of my face.

"A place where we can protect the world *from* you," John said cheekily.

I kicked him, but missed because Scorpius was still wrapped around me like a pretzel.

"How would you stop me? You can't even carry the luggage," I said.

John gasped like I'd betrayed him. "Big talk coming from the woman who claims she hates killing, but just murdered a bunch of people in an avalanche of ice."

It was my turn to gasp. "How dare you—it was clearly an accident."

The men gave me incredulous looks.

"It was one of those accidental, on purpose situations," I explained awkwardly.

"Whatever you say, killer," Scorpius whispered against the side of my neck.

I groaned.

It was hard to argue your innocence when you had the Latin word for "we slaughtered" magically tattooed across your shoulders. The good news was the new tattoo was hard to read because Mother had carved "WHORE" into my back.

A win was a win.

"You're going to love it." Malum smiled.

I frowned because anything that made him happy was automatically a red flag.

Before I could ask more questions, an RJE device swirled, and the men all reached for it.

CRACK.

We changed realms.

CHAPTER 61
ARAN
THE ESTATE

SNUGGERY (NOUN): a snug cozy place.

I was kneeling on white pebbles.

Birds chirped, and water gurgled in babbling brooks.

Was I hallucinating?

A comfortable breeze blew through my hair. Golden sunshine covered everything in a dreamy haze. Fluffy white clouds drifted lazily through the sky and strange birds flew overhead.

Horse was still missing.

A crushing sense of loss speared me. My heart twisted. With shaky fingers, I pulled out my pipe and exhaled. *He'll come back. He's a phoenix*, I reminded myself.

I focused on the picturesque landscape.

It calmed me.

Rolling verdant hills were intersected by glittering peaceful lakes. Meandering streams snaked between them. Tall flowering trees dotted the hills and offered patches of shade.

We were standing on a pebble path that led to the front gates of a stunning white brick estate.

A miniature pony trotted across the field, and a goat followed close behind.

I spun around—pushing Scorpius off me because he was still clinging—and took it all in.

Swans bowed their heads together in the ponds, and strange-colored ducks quacked as they waddled in a line.

I thought I was a rainy-day-type girl.

I wasn't.

This was what I craved.

The fae realm was pretty, but it was crowded with people, buildings, and a general sense of doom. Mother had carefully cultivated the last bit through years of terror.

This place was different; it was *quiet*.

Bucolic.

Another miniature pony trotted by with a pink bow in its mane. I covered my mouth and fought the urge to cry and chase after it because it was so cute.

"Is this Olympus?" I turned to the twins in awe.

Malum choked. "As if." He pushed me toward the golden front gate of the estate. "Welcome to the Ancient Illustrious House of Malum. This is all *yours*, my Revered."

I stumbled and would have fallen if he hadn't caught my arm.

"You're joking," I said.

Turned out they didn't live in a hut.

Who would have guessed it?

Scorpius smirked and sauntered past. "We don't joke, *killer*." Orion gave me a gentle kiss on the forehead.

"This is the devil realm? Isn't it supposed to be a land of fire?"

Malum pointed up at the golden sun. "It is."

I blinked. "Aren't you supposed to share half a planet with the angel realm? Isn't their side cold? Also—do you see the miniature ponies?"

I'd thought Malum had been spinning a fairytale when he'd described what peace felt like to him.

Now I understood.

He'd been telling the truth.

Malum rolled his eyes. "The sun melted the glaciers that cover most of the other side of the planet, and it plunged the angels into a perpetual ice age."

Team devils, I'd always admired their psychotic attitudes and unwell demeanors.

"Wait." I narrowed my eyes as I thought about geography and climates. "That doesn't make any sen—"

He interrupted, "We don't have any oceans or glaciers on this side of the planet, so our biomes are split. It makes perfect sense."

I stumbled as I remembered the passage about how the OPA had come to be. The sun god had increased the temperature of the realms to kill the invaders.

He was so real for that.

"But this place is actually *nice*," I said as I changed the subject, "and you're a *devil*."

Malum frowned, and flames leaped off the tops of his ears. "Now you're starting to piss me off."

I would have argued further, but I was too distracted because a baby goat with a purple bow jumped past. It chased after the miniature pony.

"What's with all the cute animals?" I debated the merits of sprinting after the goat and forcing it to love me forever. "And the bows?"

Orion and Scorpius looked over their shoulders at Malum pointedly.

The leader of the kings, slayer of monsters, assassin with a knife tattooed across his throat, turned bright red.

Orion had said something about seeing a softer side of Malum at his home, but never in a million years would I have believed *this*.

There was soft, and then there was marshmallow squishy.

Malum cleared his throat. "They were going to be butchered, and I had the land." His face turned maroon. "It was the right thing to do."

I gawked at the man who'd tormented me at Elite Academy.

He refused to make eye contact.

Every time I thought I was beginning to understand him, he showed me another side.

The man had *layers*, or a severe personality disorder that needed heavy medicating.

The twins weren't the Jekyll and Hyde, Malum was.

"Just to be crystal clear," I said slowly, "you hate women and think they're pathetic, but have miniature creatures with pink bows as pets?"

"I don't hate women, I've told you that," he said as he walked quicker toward the front entrance of the stunning estate. "Not anymore."

I walked faster to keep up with him.

I giggled. "If only everyone at Elite Academy could see you with your ponies and goats."

Flames trailed after him. "They're not *my* animals, they're the *estate's* animals."

"And *you* own the estate," I said. "Just admit you like bows and secretly wish you were a woman."

It all made sense.

I gasped. "That must be where all your repressed rage

comes from. There's no shame in owning it, I won't judge. Gender is just a construct—"

Malum stopped walking, and I bumped into him.

He glared down at me. "I don't want to be a woman, Arabella."

"Denial is the first step to accepting yourself." I shot him with a finger gun. "I honestly don't mind." I chewed my lips and really thought about it. "Actually—I think I might *prefer* it."

Bronze fingers grabbed my chin and tipped my head gently back.

Malum leaned close—whiskey and tobacco assaulted my senses—as he whispered inches from my lips, "I don't want to be a woman, I want to *own* one."

My lips parted. I tasted his breath on my tongue, and it was like smoking the world's most dangerous drug.

"Um, what?" I asked, unable to think.

Malum licked his lips slowly. "I want to own *you*, Arabella, body and soul. I want to earn your forgiveness. I want to spoil you. I want to show you what it means to be *the* Revered in the ancient illustrious House of Malum."

"That's a lot," I whispered.

He pressed a gentle kiss against my lips like I was made of glass.

My head spun with lightheadedness.

"The House of Malum is renowned for cherishing its Revereds," Malum whispered as he pulled back. "We will show you exactly what that means." He looked over his shoulder at where the kings and twins were staring at us.

"Um, okay," I said intelligently. "Good luck with that, buddy." I patted him on the shoulder and walked past.

Why did you just call him buddy and pat him like he's a dog? Get a grip, woman.

Unfortunately, I did not get a grip, because I saluted the rest of the men and said, "Aye, aye, soldiers."

They looked at me like I was deranged.

They weren't wrong.

No one spoke the rest of the walk because I'd made the energy weird and off-putting. Clearly, I didn't know how to handle myself in a peaceful setting.

Ornate dragon sculptures framed the front steps of the estate. Towering heavy oak doors swung open as we approached.

As I stepped across the threshold, my skin buzzed.

Memories that weren't mine played through my head. *Men fought in ancient wars. Insane power strummed through their veins. They loved fiercely and fought even fiercer.*

For the first time in my life, I didn't feel trapped.

Everything felt *right*, like I was where I was always supposed to be.

I belonged.

Unlike in the fae palace or Xerxes's manor, there wasn't an army of servants waiting to greet us. The quiet, high-ceilinged foyer was pristine and empty.

The twins looked impressed as they also took it all in.

"Let's show you to our wing," Orion whispered. He grabbed my hand and tugged me down the hall. The floors and walls were covered in dark wood.

Scenes of rolling hills and dragons were carved into the wood—it was stunning.

"Do other people live here?" I asked as I looked down yet another empty hall.

Malum shook his head. "There are groundskeepers from the local village who stop by daily to take care of the animals, but that's it."

Scorpius trailed his hand across the wall reverently.

Malum explained, "It's a tradition in devil culture for mates to live alone. The house is covered in rare wood that's layered with protective enchantments. Devils prefer privacy."

Scorpius bared his teeth and said, "Only those of the ancient House of Malum can enter. Everyone else needs permission. No exceptions."

I looked at the twins with confusion.

Orion saw my face and whispered, "Your soul was already tied with theirs when we mated to you. Now all our souls are connected." He stared at the twins intensely. "The house recognized them."

Scorpius smirked evilly. "I've never heard of a devil mating with more than four people. We'll have to see what happens. I suspect with time, the twins will manifest soul abilities—I can't wait to see what you do, John."

Luka put his arm protectively around John's shoulder. "We're here for Aran." His words were ruined by the way he glanced at Orion with longing.

Scorpius smiled wickedly at John. "No." He ran his tongue over his lips. "You're definitely also our mates."

Orion nodded in agreement, and Malum sized the twins up like he was just seeing them for the first time. He shrugged like he couldn't care less and turned back to me with a hungry expression.

John tried to hide behind me as Scorpius mimed stabbing him. I patted him on the back. "I can't wait to see how this plays out for you, *bestie*."

He glared.

"I heard Scorpius likes pain," I stage-whispered, and he lunged for me, but I ducked and blew him a kiss.

Before he could retaliate, Orion led us into a great room with high ceilings and a brick hearth that roared with fire and stood taller than me.

Scarlet leaped alongside blue-and-black flames.

It was no ordinary hearth.

My breath caught.

Deep leather couches were spread around the room.

I grabbed a fluffy white blanket and collapsed onto the leather. My face flushed from the heat, and I curled my toes with delight.

It was dark and cozy.

Toasty.

The room was perfect.

"Wait, you can't fall asleep yet." Malum yanked the fuzzy blanket out of my grip.

I inhaled enchanted smoke.

One. Two. Three. Four—nope, counting didn't work.

I tried to yank the blanket out of his grip. Unfortunately, Malum was built like the side of a barn. Orion grabbed me around the waist and pulled me away just before I could scissor kick his mate—correction, *our* mate—in the balls.

"If you don't give me that blanket right now, the miniature horses are going to be living with us inside," I threatened, as Orion carried me away from the couch.

Malum pursed his lips as if he liked the idea.

I gawked at the man I thought I knew.

Holy sun god, my mind clicked as I realized why he was so weird.

Malum was a *horse girl*.

Everything made sense.

"We need to show you your surprise." The horse girl raised his hands in the universal gesture of surrender.

I stopped struggling because receiving gifts was one of my love languages. So were words of affirmation, acts of service, quality time, physical touch, and begging for my forgiveness.

It was called having standards.

Orion gingerly put me down.

"I'm waiting." I held my hand out for my present. "Also, I'm suffering from medically confirmed energy backlash. Are you sure this can't wait until after I sleep?"

All the men looked at one another with sheepish expressions.

"You'll want to see this," Orion whispered.

The twins looked at each other and John said, "We also have something to show you."

Everyone was just full of surprises these days.

I gnawed on my lip. "I didn't get you guys anything. Was I supposed to?"

"No," Malum snapped. "Don't be ridiculous."

John narrowed his eyes like he was thinking about it. "I'd like a gift."

All the men glared at him.

The flames in the hearth jumped higher, and the temperature of the room increased.

"We need to show you this right now," Malum said.

Something told me this was not going to be a new purse —which was depressing because I desperately needed one.

"Lead the way," I said with a sigh.

Malum led us out back to stables, where we all got on horses—I made a small scene about being too tired to ride (the day I stopped being dramatic, I'd be dead)—then we traversed across the hills until we arrived at the edge of a dark forest.

Scorpius led us forward, deeper into the dark.

When we got to our destination, my stomach plummeted.

Heart stopped.

"What the sun god?" I asked with horror as I backed away.

CHAPTER 62
ARAN
DARK SURPRISES

IMPEDIMENT (NOUN): a bar or hinderance.

A cloud of smoke released from my lips.

There were bodies in the woods.

Dozens.

Of.

Corpses.

Heart pounding, breath shallow, I blinked furiously and tried to process what I was seeing.

My mind played tricks on me. *Infected screaming for mercy, ungodly chasing me down dark corridors, cold everywhere, slaughtering hundreds, blue flames, Mother laughing, fae guards smirking, pleading desperately.*

I blinked.

"Aran, the war is over." John's face hovered in front of mine. "Breathe with me. In and out."

The memories drifted away.

The kings argued among one another, and even Luka joined their debate.

"What is wrong with them?" I whispered, as I looked around with horror.

John sighed. "You mated us to the kings. Hate to break it to you, but you brought this on yourself."

I rolled my eyes and pushed him away.

Breathing deeply, I hardened my resolve and faced the kings. My vision blurred around the edges as I tried not to focus on what was behind them.

"This is your surprise?" I asked them hoarsely.

Malum rubbed the back of his neck and looked chagrined. Orion stared at me with worry. Scorpius had a satisfied expression.

"We thought you would be excited," Malum said.

I stared at him incredulously.

His cheeks turned pink.

"Recognize anyone?" Scorpius asked proudly.

I grimaced and quickly scanned the dozens of bloody pikes that had emaciated corpses nailed to them. Death by starvation and blood loss.

It was heinous.

"No," I said.

The kings were beyond unwell.

Oh my sun god, was I mated to serial killers? I was going to be sick.

How had I missed the signs?

"I think she's had enough," Luka said. "Let's go back to the estate." I took his arm, grateful for the support.

The twins led me out of the horrible forest.

"*Come back!*" Scorpius shouted as the kings hurried after us. "It ruins the surprise. She just needs to stand a little closer so she can identify them."

My stomach revolted.

"Just tell her later," John said with exasperation.

When we made it back to the bucolic rolling hills, I fell to my knees with relief and pressed my face into the fluffy grass. "Sweet paradise," I moaned.

I stared at a miniature pony and tried to forget the last ten-minutes of my life.

I ignored the kings' attempts to talk to me. They'd lost that privilege.

What happened to normal gifts? Designer purses, limited-edition perfumes, diamonds, silk sheets, and enchanted super-yachts.

How had we gotten to this place where men brought their lovers into dark woods and showed them crucifixion victims?

What did this say about our society?

It wasn't good.

When we got back to the estate, I sprinted to the great room and collapsed in front of the hearth.

My nerves were shot, and I was suffering from a dizzy spell.

I felt like one of the fair maidens Sadie was always talking about from her romance books.

The fuzzy blanket was a warm cocoon around my shoulders.

I shivered beneath it.

My fingers stiffened as ice spread across them. I stared down at them in disbelief. The doctors had said it would take me weeks before the ice came back.

How is this possible?

"Arabella, please listen," Malum begged as he ran into the room with the rest of the men. They relaxed when they saw me.

The fire in the hearth burned brighter. Ice spread off my fingers onto the ornate rug.

A part of me wasn't surprised that my powers were already back.

I tipped my head back and smoked.

"Why did you bring me to a forest of bodies?" I asked calmly as I lay down on the icy rug and smoked.

Snow fell from the ceiling and kissed my cheeks.

I would have laughed, but I was still traumatized by the kings' surprise.

"It was you—even inside," Luka said with awe as he stared up at the snow. "I thought a window was open."

John flashed his dimples as he joined me on the floor. He looked up at the snow with a grin. "This is pretty with the fire." He ruffled my curls, no doubt making them messy. "I like it. It creates a nice ambience."

I pushed him off me and we tussled.

"I'm not a *snow* globe," I sniffed haughtily but laughed as he shook the melting snow off his hair and got me wet.

"Um." Malum cleared his throat awkwardly. "I think we should explain what happened in the forest."

I grimaced. "I don't think you should. I think it's perfectly clear that you are serial killers—stay away from me."

Orion's eyes widened.

Scorpius snarled, "That's not funny."

I made a face. "Neither is PTSD, which I now have."

"Are we already leaving them?" John stage-whispered. "Do we have somewhere to go? I kind of like it here."

Luka sat down behind me and pulled me back, so I was tucked against his chest. I relaxed into his embrace.

The fire burned warmer, and the snow stopped falling from the ceiling.

"The bond sickness showed us your memories," Malum

blurted out. "Each time you had a nightmare about your mother at the camp, we were also experiencing it."

I parted my lips and my pipe fell to the floor as I stared at the stone-faced kings.

I'd had a *lot* of nightmares.

"We created a list of the fae guards who helped hurt you." Malum's baritone voice shook with rage. "Every chance we had, we RJE'd to the fae realm and hunted them down. We would have done it even if we didn't see your memories, they just showed us who to—spend the longest time on."

Scorpius nodded and cracked his knuckles. "We gutted them all on pikes in the woods and made sure they bled out slowly and painfully."

Silver eyes burned like molten steel. "I made a promise to you at Elite Academy—do you remember what I said?"

My tongue was heavy in my mouth. I thought he'd just been saying things. Only a crazy person would *actually* mean what he'd promised me.

"No," I lied.

He looked smug. "Let me refresh your memory."

Malum recited, "*I don't care that your mother's dead. That is not enough. Whoever served her will burn by my hand. Whoever failed to help you will burn by my hand. Whoever was within a hundred-mile proximity to her when she did this will burn by my hand. I swear it on the honor of the House of Malum. You will be avenged.*"

He smirked viciously. "Now do you remember?"

"Maybe," I whispered.

Snow fell in larger flakes from the ceiling as I gaped at the predator I'd mated.

"Are you not avenged, Aran?" His voice was deadly, and the hairs on the back of my neck stood up.

Scorpius and Orion smirked.

I stared back at the kings in silence.

All the times they'd disappeared played in my mind like a movie. They always came back covered in blood and trembling with rage.

Each time I'd woken up from one of my nightmares, I'd found them missing.

Malum had said something in the enchanted truth journals about killing people for me. He'd been serious.

The hearth blazed, and my face was feverish.

I was uncomfortably hot.

"We hated leaving you," Orion whispered as he stared down at me with wide, pleading eyes. "But we didn't want to distract you with your past, during the war."

I grimaced.

Luka continued to play lazily with my hair, and John yawned as he rested his head on my shoulder.

Malum rubbed the back of his neck sheepishly. "We really thought you would be excited to see them dead. We just wanted to show you the project that we'd been working on for months."

"The project was—murdering people?" I asked, not believing what I was hearing.

Scorpius smirked. "No, the project was—murdering people *who hurt you.* There's an important distinction."

I grimaced. "Is there really?"

"Yes," Malum snapped. "Now obviously this is not the surprise you wanted." His expression fell. "We can figure out something else to show you—"

"I didn't say that," I interrupted him.

Hope flared across his face.

I chose my words carefully. "I don't want to see any more dead bodies for a long time. *However,* I also kept a mental list of their names and faces and planned on hunting them down eventually—so technically, you saved me a lot of time and effort."

Scorpius beamed and threw himself onto the leather couch behind me. "I told you both. I knew she'd love it." Malum and Orion sat down with more grace.

The kings looked relieved.

"Love is a strong word," I said dryly. "In the future, try clothes first. I also like expensive champagne. And diamonds."

"Anything you want," Malum said quickly.

It was hard to stay mad at him when he sounded so earnest and eager to please.

I yawned as I leaned back against Luka. "What was the other surprise you wanted to show me? If it's also going to be traumatizing, do it quickly. I want to take a nap."

The twins stiffened and sat up straight.

My stomach plummeted.

"Oh sun god, it's also traumatizing isn't it?" I whispered. The twins' silence answered the question.

I picked up my pipe and inhaled.

Longing for Horse pierced me sharply. One day, you were a child with hopes and dreams, and the next day, you were a woman who needed her emotional support bird.

Life comes at you fast.

"It's not bad," John said nervously as he and Luka stood up in front of me.

I was not convinced. "If it's not bad, then why are you so nervous?" I asked him suspiciously.

"It's good." John paused. "But it might be a little shocking, so just promise me you won't freak out."

I pointed my pipe at him. "Too late. I'm already freaking out."

"It is a great thing," Luka said stoically, a fierce expression on his face. Since he was the same man who usually ignored everyone, I wasn't sure I trusted his judgment.

"I just want to be clear," I said slowly, "if you're going to produce a carcass. Don't."

"It's not a dead body," John said with exasperation.

Scorpius muttered behind me on the couch, "It was a *forest* of dead bodies."

"Not helping," I said, and the room went silent.

"So—" John chewed on his lower lip "—you know how your back hurts every time you get turned on?"

"No," I said dryly. "I forgot."

John glared. "I've put a lot of time and effort into this presentation, and you're making it *very* difficult right now."

"Oh darn," I said sarcastically.

John swallowed audibly. "Like I was saying." He paused and squinted like he was trying to remember memorized lines.

My eyes grew heavy.

"Oh my sun god," Malum groaned. "Just spit it out."

"Right. Because *your* method really worked well?" John snapped back. "Let me do my thing. I have performance anxiety, and you're *not* helping."

"Why is this a performance?" I asked with confusion.

I felt delirious.

I'd started the day in a war camp. Now John was struggling to put on some type of theatrical performance.

I yawned sleepily.

"It wasn't my plan to show her immediately," Malum said to John. "I went to Sadie for advice, and she said to surprise Arabella with our project as soon as I could. *She said she'd like it*!"

I pursed my lips.

Moisture built behind my eyes as my throat closed, and I asked hoarsely, "Sadie really wanted to do that for me?"

"Are you serious right now?" Scorpius asked.

Malum made a choking noise. "Why is it sweet when she does it but traumatizing when we do it?"

I wiped a tear out of my eye. "Because you're *men*, and you'd just showed me your house for the first time. Do you know how creepy that is for a woman?"

"No one's paying attention," John complained. "I can't do this. Luka, you're going to have to go on without me." He went to sit back down, but Luka grabbed his arm and stopped him.

John grumbled but kept standing.

"Good work. I love your performance," I said, sleepiness was making me more sarcastic than usual.

John glared. "That is just hurtful."

Luka punched him in the shoulder and ordered, "Take off your shirt."

Scorpius made a harsh noise, and I nodded in agreement. "Now, *that* is what I'm talking about. That's a good present."

Both twins pulled their shirts off.

I sat up straight and mentally prepared myself for a lap dance. I just needed to find some coins to throw at them and I'd be ready.

They turned around.

The pipe fell from my lips.

That did not go in the direction I thought it would.

If I were a fainter, I would have passed out cold on the floor. Unfortunately, I stayed fully conscious.

I couldn't breathe.

Ice spread across my fingers and up my forearm.

"WHORE" was carved into their skin, exactly the same letters and font on my back.

I felt queasy.

Snow drifted around the room faster.

"This isn't funny," I whispered, squeezed my eyes shut, and prayed to the sun god that I was hallucinating.

"Put your shirts back on right now," Malum barked. "Why the fuck wouldn't you just explain to her what you did?"

The men argued.

It snowed harder.

I lay down on my back as I hyperventilated.

It was all too much.

"The knife that was used on your back was a blood enchantment," John said quickly as he knelt above me and cradled my face. "You can only reverse blood with blood—it's a tenet of the natural world. Enchantment removal is an ancient practice still used in the Olympus realm. You won't feel pain anymore—I took the cursed enchantment from you."

I opened my eyes.

Holy sun god.

When I kissed Malum earlier, I hadn't felt any pain.

"But will you feel it instead?" My stomach knotted with fear.

"No." John flashed his dimples. "It hurt like a *bitch* for days after getting it, but then it healed. My blood neutralized yours." He smiled like everything was fine in the world.

My head spun.

He fluttered his fingers. "Surprise." Dimples flashed.

I turned my head to where Luka hovered behind him.

"But then why is your back also—" I breathed quickly as I tried not to think about how they'd mutilated themselves.

Luka's expression was hard as he said, "Our aunt discovered that there was a second enchantment in the blade."

"What?" I asked numbly.

"The enchantment restricted your ability to fly." He shook his head and frowned. "Your mother was a heinous bitch. We didn't want to tell you until our wounds had healed because we wanted to make sure the process worked."

I asked cautiously, "Did it work?"

Luka nodded and said gravely, "It did"—everything tunneled out, and his lips moved in slow motion—"you should be able to fly now."

This time…

I passed out.

CHAPTER 63

CORVUS MALUM
HOARDING

PULCHRITUDINOUS (NOUN): physically beautiful.

I carried my sleeping Revered against my chest. Her curls were disheveled, pink lips pursed, and brow furrowed like she was thinking hard.

We shouldn't have brought her to the woods so soon after the war.

We should have given her more time to recover.

It had been stupid, but we'd been eager to show off. Even Sadie had thought it was a good idea. We'd been stupid.

Arabella was powerful, but not innately vicious.

I stroked my thumb gently over the purple bruises smudged beneath her eyes. She said she would have hunted the fae down herself, but I'd come to know her over the last few months.

She wouldn't have killed them.

That was why we'd done it—so she wouldn't have to. It was time for us to take care of her. *Really* pamper her.

I thought about the second promise I'd made to her back

at Elite Academy. I'd whispered to her, "*I'm the Ignis of the illustrious House of Malum. I'm the twenty-seventh immortal king to serve the sun god since the dawn of time. I don't deal in shades of gray. I hurt those who hurt what's mine.*"

I squeezed her tighter against my chest and bent my head toward her, inhaling her intoxicating scent—danger and frost.

It mimicked the duality of her personality.

The woman in my arms was both fierce and mellow.

She was a survivor.

In her sleep, she nuzzled her face against my chest, and I swallowed a groan at the feeling of her rubbing against me.

It was divine torture to hold her, the woman of my every fantasy.

She shifted again, and I frowned at how easy it was to readjust her in my arms. She'd lost weight and was too light.

The war had taken its toll.

I mentally made a note to feed her rich cheeses and fruits as much as possible.

My *mate* would never be malnourished another day in her life. I'd spend my immortal days making sure of it.

She shivered as I continued to climb the many stairs that led to the top of the house. Ice coated her hands like gloves, and flurries of snow drifted inside the warm house.

I hovered a scarlet ball of fire atop her chest, and she reached toward the warmth, even though she was unconscious.

That was another thing I'd make sure of.

My ice queen would never suffer from the cold again.

If I had to stalk her with scarlet balls of fire everywhere she went, then that was what I would do.

After I climbed the last set of winding stairs, I arrived at our A-frame loft bedroom.

Nowhere else was good enough for my Revered to sleep in.

It was the safest space, nestled underneath the *v* of the roof and farthest from the door in case intruders entered.

I laid her down gently on our custom bed that spanned the entire width of the room.

The feral part of my devil nature loathed putting her down, even for a few seconds. I wanted to hold her and growl at everyone who entered her vicinity, so they knew she belonged to *me*.

I stood over *my* Revered.

My soul.

Mine.

There was a reason the Ignises from the House of Malum were renowned for our possessiveness. It ran hot in our blood. We hoarded our mates like a dragon with a priceless treasure because that was *exactly* what they were to us.

One did not simply neglect one's soul.

You protected it.

With every fucking breath you took.

It was well known through our society that Ignises from our House would go to extreme measures—like locking their Revereds away and never letting other men so much as look at them. One of my ancestors had cut the tongue out of every person—man or woman—who'd dared to talk to his Revered.

Flames multiplied across my arms as I thought of all the ways I would hurt people who challenged her. No way would she be fighting anyone in the fae realm; I'd kill them all first. I'd tear them to pieces and—

Scorpius dug his nails into the back of my neck and yanked me back harshly. "Calm the fuck down," he snarled into my ear. "You will not ruin this for us with your posses-siveness."

He shook me back and forth.

Flames came out of my mouth as I breathed heavily.

"Calm. Down. Right. Now." His voice was sharp as glass, and his nails dug deep, drawing blood.

I concentrated on the pain, and it slowly brought me back to reality. The haze of anger lifted from my vision.

"Don't forget who she is," Scorpius warned, awe in his voice. "She's more powerful than all of us—don't be an idiot."

Orion patted my arm. "He's right," he whispered as he stood on the bed and opened the skylight windows.

A warm breeze filtered in.

Cricket chirps and frog noises filled the space.

Millions of stars glittered above.

"Breathe in," Scorpius ordered, and I obeyed. I exhaled my Ignis aggression.

I inhaled calm.

Strangers who didn't know me thought I was unfeeling. I had the opposite problem.

My feelings were *too* much.

They'd always plagued me.

Scorpius and Orion were the two people who'd always understood that about me. They related.

My world was shades of scarlet; I burned with obsession and rage. Scorpius's world was shades of black; he yearned for pain. Orion's world was shades of gold; people were shiny toys for him to play with.

For the longest time, it had only been the three of us.

Now Aran joined us.

In her memories, I'd felt what she felt. I'd seen through her eyes.

Aran's world was shades of gray; she was numb, unable to process the terrifying capacity for violence that lived within her.

She deserved so much more than gray.

I pulled away from Scorpius and walked over to the bed so I could play with my Revered's blue curls.

I'd channel my obsessive nature to not only protect her but to help her heal. To help all of us heal.

So help me sun god, her world would be shades of vibrant colors.

I refused to accept anything less for her.

As I twined the silky lock around my finger and made silent promises to my sleeping mate, Scorpius gathered our softest throw blankets and tucked them around her.

My ball of fire hovered toward the stone hearth in the room's corner, then it whooshed to life.

When I was fully satisfied that my Revered was comfortable and warm, I pulled off all my clothes.

John made a choking noise.

Turning, I realized Luka and John were standing awkwardly in the doorway.

I rubbed the back of my neck—I'd never expected them to be my mates. It was unheard of for a devil to have five mates.

But here we stood.

Warmth expanded in my chest as I looked down at Aran. *She* was the reason that all of us were connected. I'd gone from suffering because I was missing my mate to having more mates than I knew what to do with.

It was insane.

Life felt like a dream.

Pressure built behind my eyes, and I wiped it away

discreetly with the back of my hand as I gestured at the twins. "You can come in."

John glanced at Scorpius, then our Revered. "I don't want to intrude," he said slowly.

"Get in here. You're our mates," Scorpius snapped.

All of us were haggard.

Worn down from the war.

"Okay, then," John's eyes widened as he and Luka stepped inside the cozy space. They stared at the giant dragon that was carved across the walls.

"It symbolizes the power of the House of Malum," I explained. "All our power—*her* power."

"She's amazing," Scorpius grinned viciously. "She's terrifying." He gnashed his teeth. "She's perfect."

I rolled my eyes at my sadistic mate.

"Don't be shy, John," Scorpius sneered wickedly as he climbed into bed and patted the space beside him. "I won't bite—much."

Luka and Orion shared a glance as they shook their heads.

I ignored everyone and climbed in so I could hold my Revered in her sleep. No one complained, because they knew I was fire, and she was ice.

She needed me to warm her.

It was my life's purpose.

When all six of us were tucked under the covers, lying beside one another, we stared in silence at the glittering sky.

Our Revered was the only one who slept.

The rest of us were painfully awake, echoes of the war were tangible around us. Adrenaline still strummed among us.

I stared down at Aran's furrowed brow. My raspy voice was loud in the silence. "We need to let her heal."

There was a beat, then John responded, "Obviously. She's been through hell."

Scorpius frowned.

Orion sat up against the headboard and stared down at her, Luka scrubbed at his face, and I twisted more of her silky curls around my hand.

I already knew that letting her go in the morning was going to pose a problem.

"So what exactly does letting her heal mean?" Luka asked. "Just so we're all on the same page."

I was so startled that the quiet twin was conversing with us that it took me a moment to process what he was asking.

Scorpius answered for me, "It means we don't touch her. Not until she's 100 percent ready."

The five of us looked at one another with grave expressions.

"We have all of immortality," John agreed. "We need to make sure she's well. That's the priority."

I nodded as I tucked myself tighter around her protectively. *Mine. Mine. Mine. Mine. Mine.* A possessive voice repeated in my head.

My fire wanted her.

I wanted her.

"We all need to heal," Orion whispered, as he grabbed Luka's hand.

Scorpius sighed. "One day at a time, that's all we can do."

"For her," I whispered, and the men chorused back, "For her."

She was our soul.

Our hearts.

Our Revered.

Our treasure.

CHAPTER 64
ARAN
FLYING

ETHEREAL (ADJECTIVE): extremely delicate and light.

A warm breeze blew through my curls as I whooped aloud with joy.

Fresh grass and sweet florals filled my nose.

Crystalline wings flapped behind me as I spun higher into the air. The weight of my wings was a comforting presence that felt right, as opposed to crushing.

I was built to take to the sky.

It was my destiny.

The rising sun kissed my rosy cheeks, and morning fog gave everything a whimsical quality. Goats, sheep, and miniature ponies trotted about without a care in the world.

The sunshine was golden and hazy.

Life felt like a watercolor painting.

Bubbles of excitement jumped in my stomach as I twisted onto my back and spread my wings wide, then lazily spiraled toward the land.

Again and again, I flew toward the heavens, then turned, and drifted back down.

Flying was better than anything I could have ever imagined, and there were no words that could capture the feeling of pure euphoria.

It felt like freedom tasted.

For the first time in my life, I was completely, exquisitely, and wonderfully alive.

When my lungs strained and sweat dotted my brow, I landed gently in a soft patch of sun-warmed grass. Fog wrapped around my ankles in a caress as I walked across the rolling hills toward the stately tree I'd claimed yesterday as mine.

Its sweeping branches cast a welcoming shade.

Collapsing onto my pastel blanket, I lay on my back and marveled at the sensation of stillness after exertion. My flowy white silk pants and top were cool against my warm skin.

I closed my eyes and dug my toes into the grass.

Blood pounding through my veins, I spread my arms wide, wings fanned out beneath me as I embraced the stillness.

Tipping my head back, I swore I could feel the realm spinning.

I sighed with relief.

Ice spread across my fingertips.

Here—in a faraway countryside—I was nothing but a woman in a field with pastel ribbons in my blue curls.

A small pang of emptiness stabbed my heart.

I gasped.

Closed my eyes.

For a terrible second, I felt despair. A piece of my soul was permanently missing, and I was never going to get it back.

I struggled to inhale.

My throat seized.

I opened my eyes. Golden sunshine and the peaceful sounds of nature helped chase away the panic attack.

I pressed my hands over my heart.

Warmth strummed inside my chest as five mate bonds filled what once had been broken.

I didn't lose a piece of my soul, I gained five new ones.

I was going to be okay.

I exhaled shakily and soaked in the rich colors of the present.

Time passed at a lazy pace. All was exactly as it was supposed to be.

"Aran!" Malum yelled angrily as he walked toward me across the hills.

He cut a fine figure, his wide shoulders and impressive thighs on display in his loose button-down shirt, tan riding pants, and knee-high boots.

It was a good look for him.

The scarlet flames on his shoulders appeared significantly less fearsome with a miniature pony whinnying and neighing as it ran beside him. It cut him off as it sprinted toward some ducks.

I laughed as he stared at the small creature with exasperation.

As he got closer, I arched my brow expectantly.

He panted like he'd been sprinting and said, "I panicked when I woke up and all the men were there—but you weren't. I thought we went over this yesterday? It's not safe for you to fly yet. You're still missing a lot of feathers. We need to visit the angel realm and have you checked by a doctor."

Endorphins made my head light, so instead of arguing, I

smiled at him indulgently. "I'm fine. Also, if you recall, I fell asleep before I agreed to anything."

He glared at me.

Flames multiplied across his shoulders.

I shrugged my shoulders. "I can feel the missing feathers when I try to fly fast, but if I go slowly and use the air currents, I'm one hundred percent in control." I patted the space beside me on the blanket. "Have a seat and chill. The weather's divine."

I retracted my wings so he'd have space.

Malum stared at the pastel cloth with trepidation, then gingerly lowered himself beside me.

I yawned and draped my arm across my eyes.

I'd woken up with the overwhelming urge to fly.

"It is nice out," Malum said gruffly.

I moved my arm and squinted at his stiff figure. "Lie back and stay a while. Why are you so rigid?"

"What do you mean?" he asked with confusion.

I yawned again. "Have you never just lain down under a tree and enjoyed the stillness of this landscape? For sun god's sake, it's like living in a painting."

Malum's cheeks turned pink, and he shook his head like he was embarrassed by the thought of leisure.

"Lie down," I said, and satisfaction filled me as he sprawled out beside me.

He grimaced.

"Now just stare up at the leaves and flowers and enjoy how they flutter on the breeze."

I loved that I was giving out life advice like I'd mastered mental health.

It was called being delusional.

This morning, I'd had a panic attack in the bathroom

because I'd remembered the twins now had slurs on their backs. We were all mutilated.

Now, I stared up at nature like it could save me.

I focused on the good. The scenery was stunning, and I could fly with ease. Exercise endorphins coursed through me.

I ignored the bad.

Malum squinted at the tree like he had to concentrate on following my instructions, and I laughed at his ridiculous expression.

"What?" he asked defensively. "I'm watching the leaves like you said."

"It's not that serious." I watched a bird flit between flowers.

Time passed.

It was much slower than usual.

There was no warping, no twisting.

I felt a million miles away from my memories of the war. My time at Elite Academy felt like a bad dream. The ungodly didn't seem real.

"What are you thinking about?" Malum broke the peaceful silence, and instead of watching the leaves, he stared at me.

"How nice it is here," I whispered, "I feel like I'm dreaming."

He stared at my lips. "Me too," he whispered as he inched closer.

Whiskey and tobacco were softened by the sunny, floral scents of summer.

Our fingers touched, and there was a sizzling sound. Cobalt fire spread onto his fingers, and scarlet ice coated mine.

It didn't hurt.

The alchemy law of extremes: At its hottest temperature,

fire mimics the properties of ice. At its coldest temperature, ice mimics the properties of fire.

It struck me just how similar we were.

We were so perfectly in opposition that we were the same.

It didn't seem like an accident.

It felt like the universe itself had conspired to create us.

Apparently, my antithesis was a flaming homicidal man who breathed fire, had obsession issues, and owned ponies with bows.

It checked out.

"What do we do now?" Malum asked softly.

I stretched my hands above my head. "We lie here and do nothing all day. No war. No training. No stress."

We were all soldiers without a war.

We knew who we were in times of extreme duress, but we didn't know who we were in peace.

It was time to discover ourselves.

Silver eyes twinkled. Malum stared at my face like he was memorizing my features. "Can we talk, like we did before?" he asked self-consciously.

His cheeks blushed pink.

The warmth in my chest flared, and I smiled like a fool. "I'd like that," I whispered. "What do you want to know?"

His expression was serious. "Everything. What's your favorite hobby? What do you love to do most? I want to know every single thing about my Revered."

Crossing my arm beneath my curls, I stared up at the trees and told him about how I used to love fashion. I explained how different materials could make beautiful designs. Once again, I admitted things to him that I'd never told anyone.

I told him how I'd made Mother's gossamer silk dress.

How I'd sneak into the kitchen and help curate different enchanted wines.

Our conversation changed. I told him how the half warriors were my first friends. I told him how my mother made me hurt them. How they hated me for it. I told him about the role they played in mother carving my back.

I admitted that a small part of me thought I deserved the punishment because of how I'd treated them.

When I said that, Malum recoiled like he'd been hit. "No," he rasped harshly. "They were grown men, and you were a child. They knew about your mother's cruelty, and yet they blamed you."

I sighed. "It's not that simple. They thought I betrayed them."

He reached over and tangled our fingers together. "Listen to me, Aran." His expression was dire. "It's the most obvious thing in the entire world that you are softhearted and *nothing* like your mother."

I scoffed.

He shook my hand.

"I'm being dead serious," he said. "They blamed you because they wanted someone to hate. Someone they could bully. They couldn't do that with your mother."

I gnawed on my lower lip as I considered his words.

"Can we not talk about it anymore," I whispered.

"Of course," he said.

"Let's just enjoy the nature." I breathed deeply and reveled in the warm scents of summer.

He squeezed my hand three times.

An hour later, I shifted self-consciously because he was staring at me again.

"What?" I asked.

He propped his head on his hand. "Do you know how unique you are?" He wet his lower lip. "*Aran*."

I pursed my lips and tried to hide my smile at how liberally he was using my name.

"You're just realizing how special I am, *Corvus*?" His name felt weirdly intimate on my lips.

He leaned his head over and whispered against the sensitive shell of my ear, "Say it again."

"Mitch?" I played dumb.

He lunged and tickled my sides. I gasped and shrieked as I kicked against him with futility.

"Say it again," he demanded.

"No." Gasp. "You have to." Gasp. "Earn it."

He stuck out his bottom lip and pouted. "Come on, Aran." He stopped tickling me.

"I'm not falling for it." I flopped over and lay on my stomach, eyes closing with exhaustion.

He gave me a gentle kiss on my forehead.

When I leaned in for more, he pulled back with a playful smile. "With time, darling," he drawled.

I rolled my eyes.

This was the same man who'd pulled his pants down and fucked everyone he could at Elite Academy. The same man who wrapped his hand around my neck and pinned me to my bunk bed. For sun god's sake, he'd almost taken me in a *public* dressing room.

Apparently fighting in war had transformed him from a pervert to a prude. *Distressing*.

I wanted to demand that he ravage me. However, I didn't want to ruin the peaceful vibes that had settled around us.

A long moment passed, then a heavy weight settled across my back.

He'd repositioned himself to sleep and had tossed his

arm over me. "So we're really just going to lie here and sleep all day?" he asked skeptically. "Even after we just slept all night?"

"Yep," I smiled. "It's called relaxing."

He pressed his side against mine, body heat warming me through our clothes. "Sounds good, *Aran*."

Birds chirped above us, and the leaves rustled.

The air was pleasantly warm.

Everything was golden.

I smirked into the pastel blanket. "Keep it up and I just might forgive you in the next decade, *Corvus*."

He stopped breathing. Every muscle in his body tensed and he asked slowly, "Do you mean it?"

"Yeah," I said. "You just have to shower me with gifts and prove you're not an ass for the next decade."

"Done." He tickled my side.

"You're ridiculous," I squealed as I kicked at him.

He tipped his head back and laugh, "And you're mine, Aran."

The warm feeling inside my heart expanded, and it felt like I was flying.

"That means you're also mine, Corvus." I rolled his proper name on my tongue.

He buried his face in the blanket and groaned. "Fuck, you're driving me insane. I can't keep my hands off you."

He said it like it was a problem.

"Then, don't," I said. "Ravage me."

A soft snore echoed, and I flopped back with a sigh.

He was already asleep.

He hadn't heard me.

CHAPTER 65
ARAN
HORSES

Oscitancy (noun): drowsiness.

I woke up to find drool on my face and Corvus sprawled atop me like I was a bed. If I'd been a smaller woman, I would have been crushed by his excessive weight.

Good thing I was big-boned.

I tried to push him off, but he just grumbled in his sleep and reached for me. He didn't wake up. After ten minutes of kicking and pushing, he finally rolled off.

I sat up and studied him.

Sunlight filtered through the rich green leaves, and his skin shone like polished bronze.

He seemed younger.

Softer.

Gentler.

He didn't seem like the same man that had stalked down dark corridors, setting people alight as he expertly wielded enchanted swords.

His features abruptly scrunched up, and he whimpered.

He flinched and rolled on the blanket like he was under attack.

His arms flailed. He yelled out like he'd been stabbed.

I knelt on top of him.

Using all my strength, I grappled with his flailing limbs and crossed his arms over his chest. Then I pushed down.

"You're okay," I said as I exerted pressure. "The war is over."

He panted harshly, sleepily fighting against my hold.

Finally, he breathed out—a long shuddering sigh.

He fell still.

I traced my fingers over his brow and whispered soft words as he resumed snoring peacefully.

Feeling exhausted, I climbed off him.

I fingered the ribbons in my curls. I'd found them in a craft drawer last night.

This morning, as I'd hyperventilated in front of the mirror, I'd placed dozens of them in my hair. Just because I could.

A rebellion against myself.

I was no longer the girl who liked pretty things, but I'd find her.

With my toes in the warm grass, I tipped my face towards the sunshine and stretched.

In this foreign realm, I was just a woman who could fly.

In a field.

With no plans.

This lifestyle was new for all of us. It would take time, but we'd heal.

Together.

Pipe hanging lazily from my lips, I turned and sprinted toward the back of the estate. I ran just because I could. No other reason.

My joints were still stiff, and my muscles were achy.

I didn't care.

I ran to the stables and chose a pretty white horse. We trotted aimlessly around the estate.

A few minutes later, I crossed paths with the twins, who were also riding horses across the countryside. I blinked, unable to process the sight of them casually trotting like aristocrats.

We were living a dream within a dream.

Their heads were tilted together, and they were whispering to each other with forlorn expressions. Their features were harder, less boyish than they had been before the war.

We were all rougher.

When John looked up and saw me, his morose expression transformed into a playful grin. "Last one to the pond loses," he shouted as I rode up.

He broke out in a fast gallop, and Luka grumbled but gave chase.

I grinned and spurred my horse forward.

Faster and faster.

Green and yellow blurred.

The warm breeze kissed my face, and I laughed with abandon as my stomach whooped with adrenaline.

Suddenly my horse reared back as a duck flapped its wings with fright.

I was thrown from my saddle.

For a long second, I lay on the ground, watching the fluffy clouds drift past as I struggled to breathe. My horse sprinted back toward the stables.

The twins shouted with worry.

I spread my arms wide in the grass.

"What the sun god do you think you're doing?" Scorpius shouted from far away—he projected his voice like he did when he needed to be heard in the middle of battle. "Orion told me what just happened. What's wrong with you idiots. She's still healing!"

I looked up to find Orion and Scorpius stalking over the hill, still dressed in their silk pajamas.

The twins dismounted and ran to my side.

"Are you okay?" Luka asked as John checked me over like a mother hen. I slapped them away.

"I'm super fine," I said, "I barely felt it." My muscles screamed in protest as I tried to move.

Scorpius kept ranting as he approached. "What is wrong with you? Do you have any…" *Blah, blah, blah.* Orion looked at me with wide worried eyes.

The twins helped me to my feet.

I groaned as I flexed my aching joints, then I turned and screamed, "Run for it!" I ran across the hills clumsily, sore muscles protesting as I clutched my aching sides and laughed uncontrollably.

"What is wrong with you people?" Scorpius bellowed, and I looked back over my shoulder. Orion smiled beside him.

I laughed harder as I ran, the twins jogging up behind me. John was laughing with me. Luka shook his head like he was disappointed in us.

"It's just a *horse*," I yelled over my shoulder at Scorpius as I ran pathetically, unable to pick up much speed because I was laughing so hard. "I survived the ungodly. Of course—" I gasped "—I'm fine."

Fine was a relative term.

If my laughter had a manic quality to it, that was none of my business.

My mental health was not my problem. It was everybody else's.

"This is *not* funny," Scorpius snarled as he gained on us, easily tracking the sound of our unsteady footsteps.

I turned around and flipped him off with both hands. "I'm flipping you off, *Princess*."

Orion laughed at my nickname, and Scorpius scowled.

"He's gaining on us," Luka pointed out dryly as he jogged behind me.

John picked me up like I was a fair maiden. "I'll save you!" he yelled dramatically and sprinted back toward the estate.

I vibrated in his arms as he picked up some serious speed, both of us laughing the entire time.

Over his shoulder, I was just able to make out Luka, Scorpius, and Orion gaping after us like we were idiots.

John ran us all the way to the kitchen.

He was a good man.

We feasted on rich jam, crackers, exotic cheeses, and colorful fruits until our stomachs hurt.

Time continued to meander forward lazily.

After eating and talking by the hearth for a few hours, the rest of the men joined us and we found cards. We went back outside to play on the lawn.

The sun set over the hills in shades of pink and orange.

Scorpius brought out a bottle of enchanted wine that was three centuries old, and we passed it around and drank greedily. Fuzzy yellow insects with rows of wings buzzed around us, drawn to the sweet alcohol.

Corvus joined us, and we all made fun of him for being so sleepy.

I didn't mention his nightmare.

But when I leaned down to give him a hug, he trembled in my arms as he held me, like he was afraid the mirage would break and we'd be back in dimly lit corridors, chasing monsters.

Drunk on wine, one another, freedom, and the shock of surviving the war, we lay awake for hours and talked under the stars. Galaxies swirled across the sky in streaks of purple.

When there was a lull in conversation, Orion whispered cryptically, "I always suspected it."

Everyone turned to him with confusion.

He pointed up to the sky and said, "The Ara constellation. It sits closest to Scorpius and belongs to the family of stars that includes Corvus."

I inhaled sharply.

"Ara" was engraved in gold on the mittens he'd given me. Even in the middle of war, he'd been trying to tell me. My chest became toasty and warm.

The quiet king whispered reverently, "Ara sits so close to Scorpius that it, too, is directly opposite Orion."

The men all made different noises of surprise, but Corvus stared at Orion with betrayal on his face. "Why didn't you tell me?" he asked. "I thought the engraver had made a mistake."

All of us laughed at his incredulous expression.

Orion shook his head wistfully. "I didn't want her to feel pressured or think that we only wanted her because of fate."

Corvus made an annoyed noise but didn't argue.

"But we are fated," Orion whispered. "We're all destined for each other." He turned to the twins. "You two included."

John made a warm noise of contentment next to me.

My heartbeat faster.

Scorpius shifted so he sat closer to me, and he pushed John away so he could put his arm over my shoulder.

John scoffed, "Hey, what do you think you're—"

He stopped talking as Scorpius draped his other arm around him, and he pulled us both close against him.

"I always knew these two were mine," Scorpius said, and everyone snorted.

"Bullshit," Corvus laughed while John tried, but failed, to get away. It was wrong, but it made me feel better to see someone else struggle.

I laughed and settled into the crook of Scorpius's arm as we continued to stargaze.

Luka played with my hair, and Corvus readjusted so Orion was sprawled against his chest.

The night was quiet and full of new beginnings.

Hope was a fragile, delicate thing.

It unfurled around us.

CHAPTER 66

ARAN

GIFTS

Troth (noun): loyal or pledged faithfulness.

Weeks passed in a semidream state.

The six of us spent our days riding horses, talking, feasting on cheese boards, and pretending the rest of the world didn't exist.

The strange euphoria of surviving the war was broken up only by moments of panic.

Every night, at least one of us woke up screaming in bed. On one night, early on in our stay at the estate, all six of us woke up shouting and kicking at one another, like we were in the middle of battle.

Little things would also set people off.

A door would shut too loudly, and Scorpius would snatch a knife from his pants and prepare to throw it.

Corvus would randomly burst into flames.

I tripped over a flower one day, and Orion screamed out in fright as I fell to the ground. All the men had unknowingly frozen in place.

Some days John would tell a few too many jokes like he was overcompensating, and Luka would refuse to let us out of his sight.

I left trails of ice across the estate and balls of scarlet fire followed me around wherever I went.

I'd reassured Corvus a hundred times that I wasn't cold anymore, but he refused to put out his flames. One time, he'd just grunted and said, "It's my job as Ignis to keep my Revered warm. Let me do my job."

My jaw had dropped. "Am I just a job to you?"

Steel eyes smoldered with rage. "Don't you dare twist my words," he growled like a feral creature.

I threw my head back and laughed mockingly. "Excuse me for being a person with thoughts and feelings. I forgot you don't listen to me because unlike the rest of your mates, I'm a filthy *woman*."

He exploded in flames and threw me over his shoulder. I kicked and screamed and punched his back as he carried me to the bedroom.

He sat down on the bed and pulled down my pants.

A flaming hand slapped my ass. "Take it back," he snarled. "Take it back, Aran, or so help me sun god." His fingers splayed possessively across me.

He said darkly, "You're not filthy."

A rough sound rumbled in his chest.

"You're."

Slap.

"My."

Slap.

"Woman."

I squirmed, hyperaware of the hardness pressing against me.

"Um, what?" I panted intelligently.

He caressed my ass, flames sizzling deliciously as they touched my frost-covered skin.

I squirmed.

He let out a low moan and ground himself against me. *"You're mine,"* he repeated like a man possessed.

I rubbed against him and nodded, unsure how we'd gotten here.

Snowflakes fell around us.

The temperature of the room plummeted; scarlet flames burned brighter.

"Are we going to fuck?" I whispered.

Corvus pulled himself away from me like he'd been stung. "I'm sorry," he whispered brokenly. "I shouldn't have done that."

"What?" I asked with confusion, but he was backing away.

"I need to leave before I do something we both regret," he said harshly.

Before I could tell him that I would *not* regret anything, he left the room.

It was obvious what the problem was.

He was afraid of how turned on he got around me. I was *too* sexy.

A mature woman would have respected Corvus's boundaries and let him leave.

I wasn't that woman.

I chased after him, yelling sexual innuendos, as he ran down the stairs. He'd looked back over his shoulder, and I burst into laughter at the pure fear in the big guy's eyes.

Objectifying him was my new hobby.

Time meandered forward.

Life wasn't perfect.

We weren't perfect.

But gradually as the warm days passed, we panicked less and laughed more.

Against all odds, our lives became *more*.

Every day, I practiced flying while the men watched with proud expressions. We weren't training for war or trying to hone our skills; we were just marveling at what we could do.

Life was simple.

I also woke up each morning to a new gift from the kings.

One day, it was a room full of sweet-smelling flowers in vases that I eagerly placed around the estate. The next day, it was a pair of priceless diamond-encrusted heels.

The days continued in a pattern.

One day, the kings would give me sweet, thoughtful gifts —like handwritten notes from Corvus that said all the different ways he was grateful I was his Revered.

Then the next day, they'd give me a ridiculously extravagant gift, like an ancient mirror that showed the viewer cityscapes of faraway realms.

The most surprising gift genuinely left me speechless.

All of us decided to try our hand at drawing.

Most of us were stick-figure level, but Orion drew a masterful landscape with fancy markers that looked like paint. After I failed yet again to draw a duck, I doodled ice and fire symbols onto Corvus's arm with a marker while we lazed together under our favorite tree. I also wrote, "Aran is the best," in cursive script for fun.

It turned out Corvus and I were the laziest out of everyone. We preferred to spend long hours lying on the blanket and doing nothing. Either I was flying or I was lying still; there was no in-between.

The rest of the men tended to keep busy all day.

Corvus didn't.

He liked to lie beside me in silence after I'd flown, and we'd watch the pond. The best days were those when one of the miniature ponies or sheep would join us.

The leader of the kings was full of surprises.

Case in point: the day after our drawing activities, Corvus rode off on his horse and yelled something about getting dessert from the local village.

At dusk, he shook me awake.

Groggily, it took me a second to process that my doodles on his forearm were now *tattoos* in enchanted ink, which meant they would never disappear for all of immortality.

My jaw dropped as I stared at the new *permanent* design declaring that I was the best. He gave me a kiss on the cheek and put a cookie in my gaping mouth.

It was lemon flavored.

My favorite.

The next day, I drew an obscene picture on his other arm, but he was a coward and refused to get it tattooed.

The days continued to pass, and the gifts kept coming.

Every day, I had no idea what I was going to get, but somehow the kings made it special each time.

The twins apparently felt left out, because they also started giving me gifts. As a greedy woman, I loved this turn of events. Thanks to the twins, my jewelry box was now overflowing with rare family jewels from the Olympus realm.

My favorite was a diamond tiara.

I placed it each morning in my ribbon-covered curls and wiped sparkly pink gloss on my mouth. I pretended I was an ordinary woman from an ordinary family, playing queen. The lore was not complicated or deep; it was simple, and the aesthetic was coquette.

It healed something inside me and also proved I was clinically delusional.

Time continued its peaceful stroll.

I stayed up late stargazing with the men, then woke up at first light to watch the sunrise from the sky. It was clear why birds were always in the air—it was pure magic to fly.

When my shoulder muscles ached and lungs were raw from exertion, I'd collapse under my favorite tree and nap. Then I'd stumble sleepily into the kitchen and gorge myself on sweet fruits and cheeses.

Once the twins convinced me to do a workout with them, but I got PTSD three push-ups in (I was lazy) and never did that again.

Instead, I went over to my tree and napped beside Corvus, who was snoring lightly and sprawled half on the grass; he'd made sure I had enough space on the blanket.

Warmth filled my heart.

One thing everyone saw coming was Luka and Orion.

They went on long walks together. For hours, they'd say nothing; sometimes they'd gesture or whisper, but for the most part, they were silent as they traversed the countryside.

Orion had found someone to share the quiet with, and Luka had found someone besides me and John.

At night under the stars, Luka played with both my ribbon-filled hair and Orion's golden locks. Their new relationship was unexpected and heartwarming.

Other connections weren't as touching.

By far the most amusing development was Scorpius and John.

It was a classic enemies-to-lovers situation; however, John hadn't moved past the enemies stage, and Scorpius wanted to be lovers.

From dawn to dusk, the blind king taunted John and made him squirm with sexual innuendos.

John acted like he wasn't interested, but I'd caught him blushing and checking out Scorpius's ass a couple times.

While we were eating around a bonfire one night, Scorpius's hand "slipped," and he stabbed John's thigh with his fork suspiciously close to his crotch.

John hobbled away from the bonfire and a few minutes later he'd come back on crutches that he'd found in the estate.

We'd ribbed him for his dramatics, while he moaned that he needed to see a doctor.

"Poor guy, it was an accident," Scorpius said. "I'm truly sorry. Please forgive me."

It would have been believable if he wasn't lapping at his bloody fork with an erection straining his silk pants.

"Do you want me to lick him better, my Revered?" he whispered seductively into the warm night.

"Um," I said eloquently as I struggled to remember what my name was.

Where was I?

Who was I?

Scorpius leaned over John's lap. Ever so slowly, he stuck out his tongue and dragged it across the bloody stab wound. Then he bit down, and John screamed.

Scorpius wiped the back of his hand across his red stained lips and smirked in my direction.

Unsurprisingly, John did *not* forgive him.

What was surprising was none of the men initiated sex.

There were lots of little moments.

I'd nap on the blanket beside Corvus and wake up to hardness pressing against my ass.

Scorpius would whisper "good girl" when I ate sweet

fruit. Once, Orion whispered to him that the juice was dribbling down my chin, and he ordered me to, "Swallow it all for me sweetheart. Get every drop."

I obeyed and licked my lips.

All the men groaned like they were in pain, and Scorpius openly grabbed at his crotch, but nothing came of it.

As a woman with *needs*, it was torturous.

Another time was when I went horseback riding with Luka he sat behind me, my back pressed flush against his front, and his hand kept accidentally stroking across my chest.

Nipples hard as rocks, I moaned and leaned back against him.

He tugged my head back harshly and kissed me wantonly with his tongue. His other hand stroked my nipples as I white-knuckled the reins.

But then he stopped and abruptly dismounted the horse.

He said something about a cold shower and disappeared.

On and on it went.

But the little moments never turned into bigger moments. I would have started to worry about the men's interest in me, but Scorpius woke us all up each morning with a detailed explanation of all the depraved things he was going to do to our bodies.

It was definitely more of a timing thing.

So I waited.

And each day somehow got better than the last.

I called John out for checking out Scorpius's ass, and he threw me into the lake, which had the unintended effect of freezing it over.

Orion found ice skates, and all of us took turns skating.

My power kept the lake frozen even in the summer sun.

Then Scorpius brought out more enchanted wine, and

the skating *really* began. John challenged me to a trick competition, and he tried—and failed—to throw a flip.

Scorpius and I spent the afternoon dressing the bleeding cut on his head with white bandages. John looked ridiculous, and we were all drunk enough that we laughed about it for hours.

He was definitely concussed because he finally let me paint his fingernails the shade of Fae Bunny Pink I'd been trying to get him to wear unsuccessfully for the past week.

When he woke up the next day with a clear head and saw his nails, he bellowed as he chased me around the estate, demanding that I take it off.

I took pity on him and painted a sparkly coat over the top while he was asleep.

He grumbled and pouted, but I caught him admiring his glittering nails in the sunshine and showing them off to Luka. I even overheard him bragging to Malum that we had matching nail colors which meant I liked him the most.

The next time, Malum's nails were also pink and all the men made fun of him.

"Do you like them?" he asked me during our daily lie-under-the-tree-together. His cheeks flushed red, and he groaned as he stared at my face. "Or do I look ridiculous? Am I being stupid?"

I leaned over and gave him a soft kiss on the nose.

"I've never been more attracted to you than in this moment," I said honestly. "I like that you're rejecting toxic masculinity—you're cute."

He grinned proudly, then scowled. "I'm *not* cute, Aran. I'm a fearsome warrior who breathes fire."

I rolled my eyes and patted his shaved head. "Okay, big guy. Whatever you say."

He crossed his arms like he was pouting but the corner of his lips twitched like he was trying not to smile.

"Whatever you say," I repeated as I yawned and snuggled against his chest.

His fingers trailed through my curls as he massaged my scalp.

"I'll always protect you," he whispered when he thought I was asleep.

Warmth surged inside my chest and radiated through my limbs until I felt like I was burning alive in the best possible way.

Time moved forward at a lackadaisical pace.

Days felt like years, and I found myself forgetting about the war for greater stretches of time.

Other days, I'd panic and spiral as I remembered the screams.

When the memories became too much, I'd unfold my crystal wings and shoot into the sky.

I didn't fly far.

I didn't want to leave.

Instead, I'd float among the clouds, then pull my wings in and plummet. Adrenaline and pure bliss would fill me. Then I'd unfurl my wings and whoop with delight.

It was impossible to spiral while flying.

Sometimes, when I hovered in the still-freezing air above the clouds, I'd think about Mother.

How she'd never known such peace.

A part of me was afraid that if she'd been able to experience flying, then she'd have never gone mad.

Maybe the High Court had taken that from her? Maybe she'd taken it from herself?

When the thoughts became too much, I'd close my eyes, pull my wings in tight, and fall back toward my mates.

Life was a haze of sunshine drenched skies, enchanted wine, coy smiles, naps, trembling hugs, whimpers of pain in sleep, and laughter.

We created a fortress to heal within that was isolated from the outside world.

Then one night, everything changed.

CHAPTER 67

ARAN
SUPRISES

CONSANGUINEOUS (ADJECTIVE): of the same blood or origin.

There was a loud, ominous knock on the front door, and when I opened it, Lothaire stood framed in moonlight.

Long moments passed as we stared at each other.

"Congrats, daughter," he whispered, and a smile curled up his lips. "I told you that you were powerful." He winked. "You're my daughter, after all."

I rolled my eyes and gestured for him to come in.

When he passed my mates, who were crowding behind me protectively, he turned to the kings and said, "I trust you used the RJE device I gave you wisely?"

Scorpius smirked evilly and said, "Over three hundred fae guards have been—eliminated."

Lothaire nodded and flashed his canines. "Good."

Then all of us proceeded to walk toward the hearth. I closed the door behind me before the men could step inside, because I wanted alone time with Lothaire and they would hover.

Corvus said something rude on the other side, but since the house didn't burn down around us, he was just being his dramatic horse girl self.

"So." Lothaire sat down on the couch and patted the seat next to him. "Tell me all about the war and your ice powers."

Gingerly, I sat down next to him.

A few hours later, I sleepily rested my head on his shoulder and beamed with pride as I explained how I'd killed hundreds easily.

I told him how I'd thought of him when I was trapped in the room with the infected.

"That's my girl," he whispered.

When he stood up with a yawn and said it was time to go, he promised he'd be back to visit me.

"It's great talking to you—I'm so proud of you, daughter," he whispered as he enveloped me in a hug.

I patted his back and said, "Thanks, Father."

When he released me, there was a suspicious sheen of moisture on his cheek, and he wiped at his face.

"I'll be back," he repeated as he said his goodbyes to the men and RJE'd away.

I stared at the place he'd disappeared from and wondered when I'd become so softhearted. My chest hummed with warmth, and my determination to never forgive him seemed silly.

Our relationship wasn't perfect, and I had a strong feeling it never would be, but there was relief in not having conflict between us.

There was peace in not holding on to hate.

I felt lighter as I thought about how my father had beamed at me with pride.

Life was weird.

That night after he left, while the rest of the men climbed into the kings' extra-wide bed, Scorpius pulled me into the bathroom.

Fully clothed, we sat in the fancy marble tub with warm water pouring over us.

He didn't make any innuendos or try to seduce me while we sat under the warm spray. He just talked about the estate. About growing up blind in a world that everyone said was beautiful to look at.

He told me how scared he'd been when I was missing.

How proud he'd been when I mated with them and became one of them completely. He said it was the best day of his life, seeing me uncover my potential on the battlefield. The sheer power I'd wielded had been like nothing he'd ever experienced. It felt spiritual.

I told him about how I was doing better but sometimes I still spiraled.

I admitted that little things still set me off.

A bird would screech and it would sound like a chittering, and I'd freeze with fear. Sometimes I'd wake up sobbing in the middle of the night, feeling like I was choking to death with no memory of how I'd gotten that way.

I explained how other times, silence would get too quiet and fear would skitter up my spine.

Every now and again, I'd escape to the bathroom and lie against the cool tile, panting while I tried not to pass out.

Shamefully, I admitted that I didn't forgive my father completely.

A tiny part of me couldn't stop wondering why he hadn't checked up on me when he knew Mother had a reputation for being awful.

Scorpius held my hand while I spoke and didn't try to interrupt me.

When I was done, he admitted he had nightmares about losing all of us to ungodly. He'd run down corridor after corridor, screaming, but he couldn't hear a thing and he couldn't find any of us.

He told me I had no obligation to forgive Lothaire.

Then we talked about our favorite foods to lighten the mood. His was steak with risotto, and mine was mango chutney on warm bread. We both liked enchanted wine.

Scorpius couldn't comprehend colors, but his favorite sound was B natural; he said it sounded like lying beside all of us under the stars.

When morning's first light peeked through the gossamer curtains, I yawned and told him we should go to bed and get a little sleep before all the men woke.

He told me that if you stayed up through dawn and didn't sleep, you'd actually feel more restful. I was skeptical, but he was so earnest that I stayed in the tub talking to him.

Corvus found us a few hours later asleep under the spray, holding hands.

Scorpius had lied.

I didn't mind.

A week after Lothaire's visit, Corvus tied a blindfold around my eyes and told me to be a good girl as he led me down the hall.

I shivered at his deep baritone voice, stomach tightening with need.

We slept together and shared chaste kisses, but the men said they didn't want to pressure me into anything. They said we had all immortality to be intimate and that I needed to focus on recovering from the war.

Personally, I thought sexual relations would *accelerate* my healing process, but that was just me.

"Surprise," Corvus whispered gruffly as he pulled off my blind fold.

I burst into tears.

Sadie and Jinx stood at the doorway with wide, excited smiles—well, Sadie was smiling, and Jinx was scowling while Cobra stood behind them with a scowl.

I threw myself at Sadie and nearly brought us to the ground.

"I missed you so much!" she wailed, and I mumbled unintelligible things against the top of her head as I peppered her with kisses.

After a few minutes (a good hour) of tears, we pulled apart.

"You look amazing," Sadie said as she poked my face. "I didn't know you could tan? You no longer look ill. I like it."

I brushed her white hair over her shoulders, and it glittered. "Did you get gold put into your hair?" She nodded, and my jaw dropped. "I'm *obsessed*."

The conversation continued with compliments for another twenty minutes before Jinx made a rude comment.

For the first time, I took her in.

Jinx was tall, really tall. She was my height and had a surprisingly voluptuous, unathletic-looking figure. I silently felt bad for her because her string-bean arms were not going to be helpful in a fight.

I made a mental note to give her mace to carry around.

"You got a prosthetic!" I exclaimed as I realized what was different. "You can't even tell."

She glared back at me and drawled, "*Obviously*."

Her words felt more hurtful now that I knew she wasn't going through a teenage rebellion.

Ignoring her squeal of disgust, I pulled her into a bear hug. "Are you okay?" I whispered quietly into her ear so no one could hear. "Are they still hurting you? Do you need help?"

She went stiff in my arms.

"I'm okay," she whispered back, then relaxed in my embrace and returned the hug. "I promise. I have a plan."

I held her back at arm's length and pinned her with a serious gaze.

Lately, I'd had a lot of time to think about my future, and I'd realized what an asset Jinx could be.

"If I claim the fae throne," I said slowly, "I'm going to need a regent to rule in my absence."

"What absence?" Sadie asked.

Corvus asked, "What do you think you're doing?"

Jinx's lips pulled into an evil smile as she understood exactly what I was saying.

She nodded and said, "I'd be honored to whip that realm into shape."

Sadie hit both of us to get our attention. "What's going on?"

I explained, "I have to reclaim the fae throne, but I don't want to rule because I'll probably suffer from PTSD." I shrugged. "So I'll go claim it back, and then Jinx can rule for me—if she wants to. Otherwise, I'm sure we can find someone else."

"I want to," Jinx said eagerly.

My men tried to interrupt, but I cut them off as I gave the girls a tour of the estate.

We spent the night talking under the stars. Well, Sadie talked. Jinx spent most of it in silence, but she voluntarily sat next to us, which for her was a declaration of undying love.

We used Sadie's inter-realm enchanted phone—still had no idea how they'd acquired such a device, because they weren't supposed to exist—and called all the girls back in the manor.

Apparently Jax was sheltering the girls. He still hadn't let Jess get tested because he was afraid of the High Court's machinations and didn't want her registered in their database.

She was disgruntled but understood.

Meanwhile, Jala was a ball of energy and kept going on about how Warren had hot friends that they'd been introduced to.

The phone was ripped away by tattooed fingers.

Ascher launched into a disturbing but highly educational lecture about boys and sexual relations.

We lost connection while he ranted, which was a shame because I was learning a lot and he was just getting to the juicy part. Apparently men had needs that women didn't because they had a prostate.

The rest of the night, Sadie planned our joint wedding.

According to her the House of Malum estate was perfect. She'd already decided we were having it at the pond, and it would be a five-hundred-person wedding.

I nodded in agreement while I mentally planned how to sabotage her—*our*—big day. No way was I letting people stomp around the estate.

It was our quiet home.

Our sanctuary.

However, I did not break it to her that we were having a small wedding because she was already acting like a bridezilla.

I'd wait a little.

Other than that, the night was perfect.

Sadie cried when she saw a miniature pony, and the next

day, Cobra had to throw her over his shoulder to get her to leave.

She promised to return for dinner.

Three hours later she came back, and we ate a delicious cheese board underneath my favorite tree.

That night, after she'd left—again, by force, I blinked with surprise when I entered the bedroom.

A tiny baby bird with tufts of fluffy red-and-gold feathers was lying on my pillow. He was no longer just smoke.

"Horse," I whispered, afraid to move and ruin the illusion.

He cawed with delight and flapped his wings at his name as he hopped across the bed toward me.

I sobbed and held his fluffy feathered body against my cheeks.

He smelled like fire and ice.

Somehow, against the most unimaginable of odds, we'd both risen from the ashes. The phoenix and the woman who was emotionally dependent on him were reunited.

Together again.

The next morning, the sun rose a little brighter.

We both rose with it.

CHAPTER 68
ARAN
THE ART OF SEDUCTION

WILE (VERB): to lure or as if by a magic spell, entice.

Like most great things in the world, it started with enchanted wine and a simple game of truth or dare.

The night was warm and comforting.

It was the first day when none of us had any sort of panic attack. No one had woken up screaming in the middle of the night.

It felt like a milestone.

The babbling brook gurgled, and in the distance, an owl hooted.

A speaker vibrated and pulsed turquoise in the grass as it played enchanted low-fi music.

The darkness was dreamy.

All six of us sat in a circle under the night sky, holding our breath with anticipation as we spun one of our empty wine bottles on the blanket.

A single scarlet flame hovered in the air above our heads and cast us all in warm shadows.

The bottle landed on John.

Scorpius grinned wickedly. "Truth or dare?"

John narrowed his eyes, then he stuck his chin in the air and said, "Dare."

Scorpius's wicked expression became downright evil.

"I dare you"—he enunciated each word carefully—"to seduce Arabella, right now."

"You don't have to do that," Orion whispered, eyes wide with alarm as he stared at me.

Scorpius tipped one of the wine bottles to his lips, and red spilled down his tattooed throat. He licked his cherry-red lips slowly and said, "You don't have to." He smirked. "It was just a suggestion."

John looked at me, and I winked.

He flashed his dimples, eyes glossy with intoxication as he crawled across the blanket toward me.

The low-fi music flowed around us.

Warm air blew on a comforting breeze.

"Hey, beautiful," John whispered when he got close to me. He reached out and grabbed my head in both his callused hands, then he pulled our lips together.

He tasted like sandalwood and tenderness.

The man who'd held me up in a merciless ocean for hours kissed me like he was drowning and I was oxygen.

He groaned into my lips.

His kisses became fiercer, and he pushed me back so he was straddling me. Hardness rubbed against my aching core, and I lifted my hips to increase the friction.

"Who's your best friend now?" he whispered roughly into my ear as his callused thumb stroked the delicate pulse points of my neck.

"Still Sadie," I gasped out.

He reached under my flowy shirt and cupped my heavy

breasts. I flushed all over, and he moaned gutturally as he pinched my nipples and sucked the delicate skin on my neck. He whispered, "You're lying to yourself."

My hips arched.

The fire in my lower stomach was like nothing I'd ever experienced before; without any pain to dampen it, I was dripping and breathless with need.

It seemed surreal that something could feel so good.

My head spun.

Stars twinkled above.

A heady warmth strummed inside my heart as jewels vibrated on my wrist and neck. I wore little pink bows and a tiara as I sprawled wantonly beneath my mate.

The world was hazy in the best sort of way.

When callused fingers traced along the waistband of my gossamer pants, someone cleared their throat.

We both paused.

Reluctantly, John crawled off me and went back to his place in the circle. His cheeks were flushed with arousal, eyes hooded, as he adjusted his pants and stared at me hungrily.

I focused on regulating my breathing as I adjusted my shirt.

No one spoke.

Luka passed me a wine bottle, and I gulped it greedily.

My head floated.

My core still strummed with need.

As John spun the empty wine bottle, colors and warm lights were fuzzy. It was lovely.

Orion reached his hand out and stopped the bottle so it landed on me.

No one argued.

John's voice was rough with desire as he asked me, "Truth or dare?"

"Truth," I whispered huskily.

"I *dare* you to take off all your clothes," John ordered, ignoring my choice. The outline of a dark crown formed atop his head, and a glittering cape of darkness was draped across his shoulders.

Ever so slowly, I tugged off my shirt and pants.

The men held their breaths.

Low-fi music swirled.

Leaves rustled, and night creatures called to each other.

Naked, I tipped back the enchanted wine bottle and chugged. Sticky wine spilled down my neck and across my chest.

Unashamed of my muscles and scars, I sat up straight and spun the empty bottle again.

This time, no one stopped it.

It landed on Luka.

"Truth or dare?" I asked hoarsely.

Luka's dark eyes were hooded with desire as he said, "Dare."

I whispered, "I dare you to also get naked."

He stared at me intensely as he pulled off his clothes and revealed the fine-line tattoos that covered his lean, muscled chest. Silver metal glinted below his waist, and Orion looked at it appreciatively.

Luka spun the bottle.

It landed next to me on Corvus, and the flame above our heads flickered.

My stomach knotted as Luka's expression darkened and his voice filled with steel. "I dare you to lick the wine off Aran's body until she's clean."

He didn't give him a chance to choose.

Corvus didn't protest.

The king of fire turned to me and leaned forward. "May

I, Aran?" He tried to sound polite, but the deep, scratchy baritone of his voice made the words depraved.

I nodded, unable to remember how to speak.

Fingers buried in my curls and yanked my head back so the column of my neck was exposed. His tongue left a scorching trail across my skin as he lapped at every inch of my neck, then moved lower.

He took his time on my chest, licking and suckling on my nipples for what felt like hours.

I mewled with need and ground against him. Lifting my hips desperately.

He was relentless on my breasts and didn't touch me below the waist. "Be patient, darling," he said roughly.

Wetness dripped between my legs.

He kept tormenting me.

When my skin was clean and shiny, Corvus released my nipple with a loud pop. He looked down at my tender, reddened flesh with satisfaction, and his pupils were blown wide, lips glistening.

He settled back down in the circle like nothing had happened.

I crossed my legs and squirmed.

He spun the bottle, and it landed on Orion.

"Touch yourself, sweetheart." His quiet, lyrical voice mixed with the low-fi music and caressed my skin.

My face flushed, and I ducked my head in embarrassment.

"Look at me," Orion whispered, and I looked up.

His pretty brown eyes were intense, long lashes fluttering as he softly ordered, "Part your legs and show me your pretty pussy."

I obeyed.

He let out a low noise, and the men shifted to adjust themselves.

"Now touch yourself," he said loudly, and the men froze around us.

It was just the two of us.

I obeyed.

Pleasure coursed through me, and I panted as I climbed toward release.

"Stop," Orion said.

I stopped.

"Good girl," he praised, and my stomach clenched. Warmth unfurled inside me and spiked to a dangerous level.

He crawled forward, leaned his head between my thighs, and dragged his tongue across my sensitive flesh like I was a lollipop.

I moaned in ecstasy.

He backed away and returned to his spot in the circle.

The men re-animated, none the wiser.

Orion spun the bottle, and Scorpius reached out to stop it so it landed on him.

His grin was depraved. "Flip over and lie on your stomach."

Arousal made everything hazy, and I eagerly complied.

"Prepare her, Corvus," Scorpius ordered.

Strong fingers wrapped around my hips and hoisted my ass up into the air. A warm tongue licked from core to ass.

I spasmed and moaned.

He lapped at me mercilessly, then lifted me higher and feasted on my core.

Luka leaned over me, and his wet fingers slowly probed my other hole as Corvus tormented me with exquisite pressure that pushed me close to the edge, but he pulled back before I came.

It was horrible, it was earth-shattering, it was torture, it was divine.

After what felt like hours, but could have been years, Luka announced, "She's ready."

I was rolled onto my side.

Silver eyes stared into mine, scarlet flames dancing off his shoulders, as he pressed his thick cock into me with painstaking slowness. He was so wide that every inch forward sent fire blazing across my clit.

I cried out as I came.

Corvus swore under his breath and shoved his tongue deep into my throat while I convulsed around him. He kept entering me slowly, and my orgasm kept coming.

As I convulsed and whimpered against Corvus's mouth, John kissed the side of my neck and whispered, "Be a good girl and relax for me." Even slower than Corvus, he entered my ass from behind.

The fluttering trailed off into little zips of pleasure as I came back down to reality.

However, the double pressure had my need sparking hotter.

John finally entered me fully from behind and held himself still. Corvus didn't move, his wide cock splitting me open from the front.

Ice spread across my hands as I clutched flaming shoulders.

Scarlet danced off bronze fingers as Corvus plucked at my nipples torturously. He was merciless, calluses tormenting my raw flesh.

I spasmed on his dick, and he smirked down at me with male satisfaction. "Feeling good?" he asked smugly, his voice like broken glass and whiskey.

"I've had better," I taunted, the effect ruined by my breathless voice.

He grinned like he knew I was full of shit, then leaned forward and bit down on my collarbone.

I yelped.

"Don't be a brat," he ordered roughly, then said around a mouthful of nipple, "not while you're gushing on my dick."

I mewled at his words.

"Fuck, you both sound so pretty," Scorpius groaned. He, Orion, and Luka stood above us, watching, and all three of them were stroking themselves.

Corvus chuckled, vibrations traveling down his wide cock. "Did you just call me pretty?"

Scorpius smirked. "I wasn't talking about you."

John's cock pulsed inside my ass as he realized what Scorpius meant and jolted.

Scorpius leaned over and grabbed both John and me by the throats, his long dick jutting across his cut abs. He squeezed until my head spun with dizziness, then he let up.

John and I gasped for air, and Corvus laughed roughly. "Don't play with them too much."

The cock in my ass swelled, and I squirmed.

Just when I started breathing normally, Scorpius licked his lips and muttered, "Too late."

He choked us again.

As I asphyxiated, Luka and Orion stroked themselves faster as they stared at me.

Scorpius released us and fell to his knees behind a gasping John. He lay down behind him, and Orion similarly positioned himself behind Corvus.

Corvus grunted roughly as Orion entered him, and John moaned as Scorpius wrapped both his pale fingers around his thick throat and did the same.

Luka stroked himself faster and kept staring at me.

After what felt like an eternity of Corvus torturing my nipples while he and John held themselves still, they started to move.

The pleasure was unimaginable.

I cried out as Corvus's impossibly wide cock split me in two with each thrust, my clit pulsing in rhythm.

John's hips jerked roughly as Scorpius slammed himself against him.

We both yelled out.

I sobbed as fireworks exploded and my orgasm tore through me, my limbs tingling as every cell in my body danced.

The men held themselves still, bellowing as they joined me.

When we all came back down, everyone panted and lay still for a few minutes. Then the thrusting started again, and we reached new heights.

At some point, we all pulled away from one another with exhaustion.

As I gasped for air, Luka stepped over my naked body, then knelt above my chest. "Good girl," he whispered as he fed me his throbbing, pierced cock. He'd admitted a few days earlier that he had an oral fixation with my mouth.

He pulled out and came across my lips.

Orion licked his cum off.

Someone opened up the food basket and passed around chocolate.

We lay in a pile of sweaty limbs and watched the night sky. A shooting star streaked bright, and John yelled, "Make a wish."

Scorpius said his wish was for John and me to suck him

off at the same time, and John grumbled that if you said your wish aloud, it wouldn't come true.

Apparently that was false.

A few minutes later, we knelt in front of Scorpius and pleasured him as he pulled our hair roughly.

Then Orion pulled away and entered me in one swift thrust. He stood up and held me by my ass with impressive strength as I bounced on his dick.

Luka fell to his knees behind him and prepped him, then he stood up behind Orion and took him while the quiet king took me.

We lay down after and rested.

I woke up to Luka thrusting inside me while Corvus strained my lips and took my mouth. After that, more wine was passed around.

Everything was hazy.

The music made it feel like nothing was real.

I spasmed as John ate me out while the first light of dawn crested over the hills. My fingers tangled in his messy hair, and I admired how his ass was reddened from Scorpius's rough treatment.

He pulled away and grinned up at me, dimples flashing.

I stared back, and a pang of gratitude snowballed into something bigger inside me. *Thank the sun god he was my first.*

I wouldn't have wanted it any other way.

John stood up, my juices glistening on his face, as he turned and sprinted buck naked down the hillside. "Last one to the river loses," he shouted back at me.

He was ridiculous, but I wasn't a loser, so I stood up and sprinted after him.

Laughing, I shouted, "You're going to traumatize the ponies, cover yourself!"

"Fuck the ponies," John yelled dramatically, then jumped

off the rickety wooden dock and cannonballed into the lily-pad-covered lake.

I followed closely behind and threw a flip as I entered the refreshing water.

"Now you're just showing off," he said as he splashed me.

"No." I raised my eyebrows, and the lake froze around him. "*Now* I'm showing off."

"Luka, help!" He yelled dramatically, "Scorpius, save me!"

We both burst into laughter at the idea of the sadistic king saving him.

I unfroze the lake, and we spent the next hour pretending to drown to see if any of the men would save us.

Corvus stomped over eventually and dove in to save us, but at that point, we'd already pretended to die at least thirty times, so we weren't impressed. Overprotective mates my butt.

"They're useless," I said to John as we lounged naked, eating jam and crackers under my favorite tree.

He nodded in agreement and licked his fingers. "Completely useless."

I threw my arm over my eyes and lay back.

"Useless," I whispered with a smile on my lips as I fell asleep.

I napped all day, and my dreams were full of sunshine and wine, pleasure and baritone whispers, laughter and family.

Another piece of me healed.

CHAPTER 69
ARAN
THE WEDDING

ZEPHYR (NOUN): a gentle breeze.

"Stop it, you're not supposed to see me this morning," I hissed at Scorpius as he slipped inside the shower. Pale muscles rippling, with one fluid movement that revealed his training as an assassin, he pinned me against the wall.

"Good thing I'm blind."

He spun me around so my front was pressed against the marble shower wall. Soapy hands trailed across me with deceptive gentleness, then there was a loud crack as he slapped my ass.

I jolted at the blow and tried to stifle my moan.

"You're going to walk down the aisle," he whispered into my ear, "with red cheeks."

I squinted with confusion.

His hand cracked down harder, and I jolted. The sharp sting turned into a dull heat that melted away.

I blushed as I realized what cheeks he meant.

"Perfect," he whispered. "You deserve a prize for being

so sweet for me." Fingers explored my slickness as he merci-lessly made good on his promise with his other hand.

When I was a quivering mess, he pushed himself deep inside me.

I convulsed around him, and it sent him into a frenzy.

His pace was brutal ecstasy.

He didn't give me time to catch my breath.

Then suddenly he pulled out and barked, "Get on your knees."

Head floaty from multiple orgasms, I did what he said without question. Knees slammed against tile as I obeyed.

He rewarded me sweetly.

An hour later, we both stumbled out of the steamy bath-room into the bedroom. Well, I stumbled; Scorpius sauntered with male smugness.

"I can't wait to feast during the dinner reception," he whispered in my ear as he cupped me through my towel.

I choked.

Yet again his expression turned sinful, and he backed me toward the bed.

"Scorpius, you better not be fucking in there, you know the rules!" Corvus bellowed as he banged against the door.

"Come on, man!" John shouted from outside. "It's not fair, we all aren't allowed to see her."

Scorpius nodded and looked grave as he picked me up and took me on the bed.

"Be very quiet," he whispered in my ear. "You don't want to break the rules."

Then he put one hand over my mouth and another around my throat as he proceeded to set a brutal pace. Stars exploded in my vision as I convulsed underneath him, but he refused to relent.

"So fucking perfect," he whispered as I swallowed my

moans.

When Corvus threatened to burn down the door, Scorpius came inside me. When he was done shuddering with pleasure, he ordered me to lie still and grabbed the crystal initialed thong I had laid out for the wedding.

He pulled it up and over my legs, then patted where he was still spilling out of me. "I want you to feel me as you walk down the aisle," he said gravely. "I want you to remember who you belong to."

"Yes, sir!" I saluted him mockingly, and he groaned as he clutched himself.

"I need to go before I ruin you for our wedding," he said, then he stalked out of the room.

There were loud shouts and smacking as the rest of my mates attacked him.

I rolled my eyes at their antics.

A pang twisted my heart.

Last night was the first night in months that I hadn't slept beside all of them. The nightmares had been the worst sort—memories. I'd woken up heaving in the dark, patting at my arms.

I shivered as I remembered the feeling of being lit on fire for hours.

Eleven, twenty-two, thirty-three, forty-four, fifty-five. The repetition calmed me down.

I was secretly grateful Scorpius had broken the rules.

Already, the tense, achy feeling in my joints from a sleepless night was receding.

Meandering around the room, I picked up the thousand-year-old engraved, enchanted wood champagne bottle Corvus had gifted to me.

The wood reminded me of my pipe. I'd discarded it in a drawer forever ago.

There was a time where I smoked every minute of every day.

It had been my crutch for so many awful months.

When I thought about the pipe, I thought about the infected screaming in my face as I gutted them, chasing monsters down dark mazelike corridors, convinced I'd never find my way out.

Never again.

When I'd first put the pipe away, the compulsion to smoke had made my tongue itch for days. I'd suffered night sweats and choked at random times.

But I hadn't given in to the urges.

Now months had passed, and the cravings were gone.

Never again, I repeated. The lungs held memory, and if the pipe was between my lips, then I wasn't living in the present; I'd be trapped by my past, coping in desperate ways.

It had served its purpose, and I'd survived.

It was time to move forward.

I popped the top off the champagne, brought the bottle to my lips, and chugged the sweet, bubbly liquid.

I'd stick to imbibing heavily on special occasions.

Instantly, the world mellowed.

A whispering melody started to play. I stared down at the enchanted bottle in awe and chugged some more.

The music was rich and melodious.

I felt like I was flying.

All worry drifted away, and I fingered the outfit I'd had custom designed for today.

Everything's going to be all right.

Hours later, I walked down a makeshift flower aisle that led to the pond on the estate.

The sun was setting and cast the cloudless sky in streaks of gorgeous pink.

It was a deliciously warm day with a slight breeze, but snow flurried overhead and drifted around us magically. I tipped my head back and smiled as I unleashed my powers.

It coated the grass in sparkling white.

My blue curls supported a crystal tiara and hung loose around my face. A gossamer white silk dress was draped across my shoulders, and it floated around me in an iridescent sheath of fabric.

In the dress, I felt like I was a fluffy cloud on a summer day.

My makeup was subtle but pretty.

Pink gloss shone on my lips and matched the pink on my nails.

I'd covered up the scar on my cheek, and my skin glowed tan from the sun. Vanilla-scented oil covered every inch of my body, and I smelled delicious.

My favorite part—cobalt ice covered my hands and crawled up to my elbows, creating the illusion of elegant gloves. Ice also wrapped around my skull-tattooed throat like a choker.

The Necklace of Death pulsed warmly against my skin.

Majestic red and gold feathers tickled my back. Horse sat on my shoulder with his chest puffed out like he was proud. A sparkly gold bow was tied around his neck.

Snowflakes drifted across my neck and down onto my chest.

In tall diamond-encrusted heels, I was Lothaire's height. He held on to my right arm with tears in his eyes.

Enchanted wedding music flowed throughout the quiet hills, and birds chirped as they passed above. The melody was extra sweet because of the enchanted champagne I'd finished off before I'd walked down the aisle.

I smiled, and a serene feeling bubbled up my chest.

It was exquisite.

Swans turned in the lake to watch our meandering ascent down the flower-lined aisle.

A mini horse trotted in front of us, and we stopped to let it pass.

I laughed as Lothaire gaped at the pink bows that covered its mane. Unsurprisingly, Corvus had been the one who gave all the animals extra accessories for the wedding because he didn't want them to feel left out.

He came across as a harsh psycho, but inside he was a big flaming softy—and a complete psychopath.

It was amusing because you never knew what came out of his mouth; were we going to get into a screaming match and fight to the death, or was he going to blush and put a bow on a small animal? Horse girls were a special breed.

As we walked further down the aisle, I smiled at the small crowd.

There were a handful of guests sitting in white chairs: Vegar, Zenith, Lucinda, Jala, Jess, and Jinx. That was it.

No one else was present.

We hadn't had a therapy session after we won the war because the High Court canceled our mandatory sessions, but I'd still invited Dr. Palmer.

She'd sent back a letter saying she refused to attend because she believed we should all be incarcerated because we were "a threat to civilized society."

I'd written back reminding her that we'd *saved* all civilized society.

She hadn't replied, which was too bad because some sunshine really could have done her some good.

I stopped our progress down the aisle to shake some feeling back into my fingers because my left arm had gone numb thanks to my best friend.

Sadie walked beside me down the aisle.

She wore the same gown and shoes as me, but she was struggling to walk in the heels. I shook my head at her because I'd told her she could just go barefoot, but she'd refused. She said we had to match.

Her white hair had new red highlights and hung low down her back in a silky sheet. She'd visited the estate every day as of late, and her golden skin had taken on a darker bronze hue that was reminiscent of Corvus's.

She looked like a sculpture of a princess.

She was stunning.

If you'd told me a few months ago that all three of us would be walking down the aisle together—her, Lothaire, and I—I would have said you were nuts.

Now it made sense.

During the wedding planning, Sadie had gone from maid of honor wearing white and walking me down the aisle to a bride herself. Mostly because she'd wanted to stand beside me for the entire ceremony and plan everything, so it was easier to also just make her a bride.

She took her role as bridezilla *very* seriously.

In fact, she'd had three mental breakdowns just yesterday because the swans weren't cooperating and letting her walk them down the aisle on crystal leashes (truly shocking).

When she'd waded into the pond and tried to put the chain over their heads, she'd been shocked by how uncooperative the birds were.

After an hour of wrestling with the wildlife—and losing while everyone watched—she'd stomped out of the pond and called the swans "mean sluts who were going to die alone."

At that point, the swans had taken offense to the slander.

They'd removed themselves from the water and chased her across the field with flapping wings.

She'd cried because "the most special day of Aran's life is now ruined."

I'd patted her on the back and walked away because she was clearly projecting.

Now she, Jess, and Jala sobbed for different reasons.

Both of us were getting married—together.

It was just a formality, since both of us were already mated.

But it was fun to dress up.

It was fun to put on makeup and pretend that we were two country girls living a provincial non-violent life under the sun.

We were just two ordinary women committing to the loves of our lives. Nothing more, nothing less.

Jinx rolled her eyes as we walked past, and I blew her a kiss. Warren was draped over her shoulder as a ferret scarf, and I gave him the evil eye.

When we got to the end of the aisle, which was a towering ice sculpture covered in flowers that Sadie and I had handpicked, Lothaire took his seat and Sadie and I faced our men together. Four shifters stood in black tuxedos to the left, and my five mates stood to the right in dark-green tuxedos with gold accents (I had a fashion reputation to uphold).

Horse cawed as he took flight and spiraled above.

I laughed when I saw Luka and John wore skull earrings that matched the kings. John smirked and fingered the jewelry.

"Don't scrape it with your nails," Scorpius said as he wrapped a possessive hand around the back of John's neck. "It's a wedding gift, you're supposed to cherish it."

John smiled back at the blind king fondly.

My heart swelled.

I realized everyone was watching us expectantly, and I cleared my throat. "I promise to love you all forever," I said to the men because we'd all agreed to keep it simple.

They smiled back at me and said the same.

I turned to indicate to Sadie that it was her turn to say vows, but Corvus grabbed my hand and pulled me back to him.

He pulled out a piece of paper with shaking hands.

"Aran," he said, voice quivering as he began to read.

"*Every morning* I wake up and thank the sun god that I get to wake up next to you. *Every day* I watch you fly across the sky like a goddess, and I thank the sun god that I get to spend my days with such a divine creature—*every night* I hold you in my arms as we watch the stars, and I thank the sun god I get to spend my nights holding you." His voice broke. "I experienced what this life was like without you in it—and it nearly broke me. It was sheer torment."

Tears streamed down bronze cheeks.

"Life without you—was no life at all. So thank you for reminding me what it feels like to have a heart, a purpose, a *life*. You've given me everything. My mates. My home."

His deep voice dropped to a tortured whisper. "You once told me that you were the *dragon* of the House of Malum, and I want to tell you today that you're wrong."

Silver eyes gleamed like starlight.

He pinned me with his gaze.

"Aran, you're the *angel* of the House of Malum." His voice broke.

Scorpius stepped forward beside him, his sharp features complemented by his suit. He looked dashing and dangerous.

The eye tattooed on his neck stared at me as he said, "You're *our* angel."

Orion nodded next to him, his long blond hair plaited back and his golden skin shining in the sun. He was breathtakingly handsome.

"You're ours forever, sweetheart," he said at full volume, cherry blossoms blowing around us like in a moment from a fairy tale.

The rest of the wedding was frozen by his voice.

It was just the two of us.

"I love you," he said, brown eyes wide and full of unspoken emotions.

I smiled back, feeling shy all of a sudden. "I love you too."

He stepped forward and kissed me, fingers gripping my jaw tightly he devoured me with his mouth.

Corvus abruptly yanked him back and growled "*mine*" like a wild beast.

There he was.

I sighed, leaned toward my Ignis, and threw my arms around his wide shoulders to calm him. Our faces were close together because of my heels. He trembled in my arms, and my vision misted as he whispered "mine" repeatedly like it was a prayer.

When I went to pull away, he refused to release me.

I patted his back because we all knew when he got like this, all you could do was help him calm down. Eventually he'd come back to reality.

"Three of three," John whispered as he stared at me, then looked around at the other men.

"Eternally," Luka whispered.

Their words didn't make any sense, but their dark eyes shone with moisture like it meant something sacred to them.

Crowns of darkness glittered on their heads, and capes hung majestically off their shoulders.

They'd grown out their hair, and what had once been messy was now luscious curls that hung to their shoulders.

They were breathtakingly handsome.

I wasn't the only one of my mates who'd noticed. Scorpius kept resting his hand on John's ass and Orion kept sneaking looks at Luka.

Sadie said her vows, but I missed most of them because I was so focused on the warrior trembling in my arms and the men who stood around us.

It hadn't happened overnight, and at times, it seemed impossible, but somehow the twins, kings, and I had meshed into one unbreakable unit.

Somewhere in the far past, a little girl with blue curls, who'd only known torment from those who were supposed to be closest to her, sobbed with gratitude.

She had a family—a *real* family.

We both did.

And it was everything.

When Sadie and her mates finished speaking, Cobra's eyes had transformed, and snakes crawled across his skin and hers.

The sun set in shades of fuchsia and magenta as the ceremony ended.

With teary eyes, we meandered as a group over toward my favorite tree, which was covered in little twinkling fairy lights. Tables of food were spread out and overflowing.

There were chairs to sit in, but everyone chose to eat on the blankets spread out across the lawn.

When the stars twinkled brightly in the sky, the enchanted speaker switched from soft music to a pounding beat.

Vegar grinned as he passed around bottles of expensive demon brew.

A few minutes later, everyone at the party was heavily intoxicated. We sang under the stars and ate the moist lemon cake with our fingers.

At one point, Cobra and Scorpius got into a fight to see who could handle the most pain. An hour later, Cobra was in a chokehold with his eyes popping out of his sockets, and he refused to call it quits.

Jax had to pull them apart, and they were forbidden from talking to each other the rest of the night.

It didn't work.

Later that night, Cobra pulled Scorpius behind the tree and stabbed him in the thigh with a carving knife. They both smiled at each other and watched blood drip.

I rolled my eyes at their antics and turned back to the party.

I was too drunk to judge.

The best part of the night was when John tried to fight Sadie because she kept boxing him out on the dance floor. Luka stepped in before his twin could get his ass beat.

It was a messy, chaotic night.

It was perfect.

At one point, in the early hours of dawn, I sat tiredly at a table to catch my breath from the dancing and sipped water while I watched everyone else frolic.

A tongue licked up my leg slowly, and I jolted.

The lemon-meringue-patterned tablecloth hid him from view completely, and I tipped my head back and closed my eyes as Scorpius made good on his promise.

When the sun crested over the rolling hills, the men took my hand and RJE'd me to a surprise location. I was convinced they were taking me to a beach somewhere.

I was wrong.

It was even *better*.

We arrived at the fae palace, and I gasped in shock.

"Surprise." Corvus smirked.

The men explained how they'd put in an announcement the week prior that I'd be returning to face my challengers; as a result, the palace halls were filled with fae who wanted my throne.

Corvus's expression became serious. "I trust you will eviscerate the competition. It is—hard for me to put you in danger like this. But I know what you can do."

There had been a restlessness among all of us the past few weeks. A small itch that needed scratching.

I smirked up at him evilly and patted his arm. "Don't worry, sweet cheeks."

He looked worried.

But Orion opened his mouth before he could argue, and together we unleashed our powers.

A blizzard rolled in.

Fae charged forward but ice spread through the halls and froze them in their tracks. Their eyes widened with surprise then went blank as I tapped my staff and ice cut them to pieces.

Word spread and the fae stopped running toward me, but away from me when they saw me coming down the hall.

I chucked my head back and laughed.

The power intoxicating as I tapped my staff and eviscerated them.

Five men walked behind me with knives drawn avenging angels ready to protect their woman if I needed their help.

I didn't.

Forty minutes later, I walked through the ice-coated

atrium and collapsed onto the seat of death with a smirk.

I raised my staff and slotted it in the arm holder.

The skull on top matched the black skulls that covered the throne.

It was a perfect fit.

I exhaled as I took in the body parts of the slain challengers that covered the floor of the throne room.

I didn't feel bad for them.

Okay, I felt a *little* bad, but I was really not trying to think about it.

Instead, I focused on the high of victory.

My mates kicked the downed bodies with vicious satisfaction as they walked toward me with proud smirks on their faces.

Palace aides filtered back inside the castle, staring at me in awe as they took in the carnage. An enchanted broadcast stone floated overhead.

The fae realm got the first glimpse at their new leader.

Days later, I found out that the broadcast had record turnout, and afterward they'd held a realm-wide poll. My approval rating was above one hundred percent because some people had voted multiple times.

The realm was delighted to see their favorite fae princess as a powerful queen. The pundits were quick to claim that they'd been the first to recognize my strength as a child. They wrote that I was the strongest water fae the realm had ever known. They speculated my half-angel heritage made me invincible.

I let them have their delusion because I was a merciful ruler.

Mother had been wrong—I was stronger than she could have ever imagined. Stronger than she ever was.

Because the seat of death was mine, and I didn't want it.

CHAPTER 70

JINX

SECRETS

THEOMANIA (NOUN): religious madness in which the patient believes that he is the Deity.

I was woken up by an electric shock to find two figures looming in the darkness beside my four-poster bed. Turning as I convulsed, I shoved Warren's sleeping ferret form under the pillow.

The two leaders had arrived.

Dick stood beside the cloaked figure with vibrant blue eyes.

Sadie and Aran thought the cloak concealed a man because of the person's deep voice and commanding size. You should never make assumptions without all the facts.

The figure pulled down the head of their cloak and revealed a gorgeous woman's face. She pressed on her thin silver necklace and canceled the enchantment that concealed her voice.

"Hello Jinx," her tinkling feminine voice filled the quiet room. She was a master of secrecy. As far as I could tell, I was one of the few people who knew she was a woman, but I still didn't know her name.

My limbs stopped trembling as I panted, "I've been expecting you."

I sat up and grimaced as I realized my prosthetic was across the room, leaning against the chair behind them.

Their positioning was purposeful.

Cowards.

I glared at them, and Dick scoffed as he walked into the light.

"You will step down as Regent of the Fae Realm immediately. We did not *authorize* you to rule the realm," Dick spat. "Also, your other shackle will be reinstated because you've clearly demonstrated that you have no control over your violent urges."

It was my turn to scoff.

Every move I made was carefully calculated and planned out; it was how I'd always lived. If I weren't so regimented, I wouldn't have survived this long.

Dick held up the gold shackle, and I cradled my bare wrist against my chest protectively.

Then I pulled up the sleeve of my nightgown to reveal the small word carved into my flesh: "LIARS." You wouldn't notice it unless you knew to look for it.

"Take a step closer and you'll regret it," I warned.

Dick stopped moving.

"What is that?" the woman asked.

I smiled. "Insurance against you two."

"Explain," Dick spat, his disguised features turning red with agitation.

My tone was blasé as I said, "Aran's scar got me thinking about the many uses of blood enchantments. They are quite versatile."

Dick's scowl deepened, and I kept my face a blank mask while inside I was a mess of nerves.

I had one chance to get this right or my life was forfeit.

I continued, "This blood enchantment is tied to my life force and—through a tricky bit of science, made possible by the resources of the fae court—it is also tied to an algorithm. You both know how talented I am when it comes to equations."

Dick's eyes flashed, and his plain features distorted as his true face showed through.

Both Dick and the cloaked woman understood that I was a genius beyond the scale level used for these realms. They were the ones who'd tested me.

They were the masterminds.

The planners.

The leaders.

I hadn't even gotten to the best part and Dick was already losing control. This was good.

My plan was working.

Now I just had to do the hard part and execute it fully.

I swallowed around the lump in my throat and explained, "If I'm killed, the algorithm is preprogrammed to override every enchanted broadcasting system in the realms and play footage of you both admitting just *who* you are."

The cloaked woman recoiled.

Dick scoffed. "No such footage exists."

I raised my eyebrows. "Are you sure? The manor in the beast realm has enchanted cameras in the entryway to deter thieves."

Dick's eyes flashed with recognition as we both remembered the day he'd strangled me in the manor's entrance. We both remembered what he'd revealed when he thought he was going to kill me.

He only let me live with his secrets because he needed me and thought no one would ever believe me.

His eyes widened as he no doubt was scanning his memories and recalling the glowing recording crystals in the room's corner.

Dick swore violently and paced back and forth.

"Fine," he spat. "We won't kill you. It doesn't change the fact that you're putting this cuff on and leaving the fae realm."

This was the tricky part.

I pulled the wickedly sharp knife out from under my pillow and pressed it to my throat. "No," I said calmly. "I won't be doing any of that."

The cloaked woman snapped, "You wouldn't dare."

She was just as powerful as Dick, perhaps more so.

I pushed the knife against the thin skin on my neck and winced as it stung, warmth pouring down my chest.

My heart beat erratically, and I tried not to think about what I was doing.

I tried not to hyperventilate.

"Are you sure about that?" I asked, my voice high-pitched with the strain of holding back screams. "You've already taken my life from me. I have nothing left to live for."

"Do it, then, little girl," Dick spat vehemently as his average disguise disappeared and a handsome, cruel man stared down at me. "Do it," he taunted.

"Stop it." The cloaked woman grabbed his arm and pulled him away from the bed. "What is wrong with you? You know this can't get out. Everything we've worked so hard to build would be ruined. Our names would no longer be synonymous with greatness, and we'd be slandered. The realms would have nothing to believe in and the peace would fall apart."

Dick glared over her shoulder at me with pure disdain.

I pressed the knife deeper and nearly passed out as the pain became unimaginable. It took everything I had not to scream in agony.

"Fine!" Dick raged, and I nearly sobbed with relief. "You better keep yourself alive, and we *will* be sending a representative to assist you in ruling the fae realm."

He activated an RJE device.

The woman's otherworldly blue eyes glowed as she lifted her cloaked head and stared at me. "Careful with the games you play, Jinx of Lazarus. We are very upset with you, and everyone knows—you don't want to upset the gods."

The truth of what she and Dick were hung in the air between us.

Crack.

They disappeared.

I dropped the knife and screamed for help as I clutched at my bleeding neck. Warren climbed out from under my pillow, and he transformed. He knelt over me, swearing as he bunched up the sheets and pressed them to my neck.

Fae guards burst into the room and summoned a healer.

An hour later, after I'd promised a reluctant Warren that I'd explain everything in the morning, I lay on fresh sheets with bandages wrapped around my neck and a sleeping ferret lying on my head protectively.

My teeth chattered from the force of my tremors.

There was a recording from the beast realm, which I did have in my possession, but such an algorithm was beyond my current capabilities.

It would take years to figure it out.

I rolled out of bed, holding on to furniture and placing Warren on my pillow as I hopped awkwardly over to the gilded desk and collapsed into the chair. I pulled out a golden ink pen and began furiously continuing my equations.

If I was ever going to follow through on my threat, I needed to start working.

Now.

As I wrote numbers and letters through the night, I only paused once to marvel that I'd really done the impossible— I'd successfully blackmailed the sun god and moon goddess of the realms.

I didn't know if they were actually omnipotent figures ruling over the masses, or if they were frauds masquerading as something greater than themselves. At the end of the day, it didn't really matter.

I was no longer at their mercy.

My teeth chattered from excessive adrenaline.

I got back to work.

When the first morning rays shone through my window, I picked up my enchanted phone and called Jax.

"How's my genius sister doing?" he asked warmly, answering on the first ring.

Moisture built behind my eyes, and I whispered, "I love you so much."

He chuckled, and as we spent the morning talking, the scared little girl who'd cowered for so long before terrifying gods finally healed.

CHAPTER 71
JOURNAL PROMPT #3
TRUTH JOURNAL TO HELP FACILITATE
RELATIONS AMONG THE CRIMINALLY
INSANE

Do you feel like your sexual needs are being met in your relationship? Why or why not?

Aran Alis Egan Malum

I can't believe we open these up for fun and this is the prompt. Isn't this supposed to be about prisoners making friends?

Orion Malum

I love this question.

Yes, I especially enjoyed fucking Arabella in the lake yesterday while Corvus took me from behind.

Aran Alis Egan Malum

To answer, yes, I'm very sexually satisfied. However, I'm still worried we got diseases from the lake.

.   .   .

Corvus Malum

I told you, my Revered, light of my life and subject of my every thought, the lakes are fresh water that is clean enough to drink.

My sexual needs are extremely satisfied, especially since we've all started going topless during the days. I love licking Arabella's nipples each morning and making them rosy. It's my favorite part of my morning routine.

Scorpius Malum

Personally, my needs are not completely being met. I tried to use a knife on John yesterday while he was fucking Aran, and he screamed like a little girl and kneed me in the balls.

It hurt my feelings that he wouldn't let me stab him, just a couple of times.

John Son of Hades Malum

ERROR

An unauthorized writer is detected in Aran's journal.

This is an automated enchanted message warning you that your messages are being monitored by an administrator. Privacy is of the utmost importance to us. If you do not have permission to write in this journal, you will be placed in a maximum-security holding cell and denied food, water, and contact with other people for up to a month.

Please disregard this warning if you do have permission. Your mental state is of the utmost importance to us.

Scorpius, you literally stabbed me in my butt cheek unexpectedly while I was having sex? The unexpected part was the thing that upset me the most.

What I'm confused about is why you don't try to shank any of your FIVE other mates. It's just me who gets a knife in the ass when I'm trying to have a special moment with Aran.

To answer the question, I didn't know it was possible for someone to be as sexually satisfied as I am.

Side note, do you guys think someone is going to arrest me for writing in this? I'm nervous, I don't think I'd last in a holding cell.

Aran Alis Egan Malum

First, John, it was a major turnoff watching you sob and scream at the ducks to save you while you writhed on the grass with a knife in your ass. It was hard to watch.

Second, aren't these tied to the underworld prison, the one you literally run?

John Son of Hades Malum

Oh thank the sun god, that's such a relief.

Next time Scorpius stabs you during sex, I'm going to try to walk away, just like you did to me.

Scorpius Malum

What if I stab her with my cock, will you walk away

then? What if I stab my fingers into her pussy? What if I stab my tongue into her asshole? What if I stab gently? What if I stab in quick successive jabs? What if I lick the wound after? What if I bite it?

John, if I stab Aran, you won't be walking away because I'll want to stab you too.

Aran Alis Egan Malum

Wow. That is quite a list. Let's stick with the first option.

John, my feelings are a little hurt that you'd leave me with Scorpius. You know how he is.

Scorpius Malum

What do you mean? What am I???

John Son of Hades Malum

Aran, I said "try" to walk away because we both know that I'd never leave you alone with him unsupervised. Especially not with how violently he attacked me the other day. He's getting restless and I think we should get him professional help.

Aran Alis Egan Malum

Aw you're so sweet John. Also, I completely agree. Do you think we should call Dr. Palmer and try to get him an appointment? Last week I caught him threatening Darlene with a butcher knife!

. . .

John Son of Hades Malum

Darlene? The sweet old lady who stocks our pantry and brings us cookies each week from the local bakery??? No. He wouldn't do that.

Aran Alis Egan Malum

He had her pressed against the wall with a knife against her throat because she forgot to stock up on peanut butter cookies! Can you believe that? I gave her his diamond cuff-links as payment for her suffering.

Scorpius Malum

Aran, that better be a joke. Those were my favorite.

Darlene <u>knew</u> I wanted those cookies, and she purpose-fully didn't get them. I know she has a vendetta against me. I just need to find a way to prove it.

Also, if either of you say one more word about me, I'm going to paddle you for hours as you scream and beg for my cock.

John Son of Hades Malum

Call Dr. Palmer immediately. I fear for Darlene's safety.

Luka Son of Hades Malum

ERROR

An unauthorized writer is detected in Orion's journal. Please read the above warning and proceed with caution.

I think you both are being dramatic. Scorpius just has a lot of energy. I think we should visit the Fae realm and help Jinx. She mentioned at our weekly dinner with the shifter legion that she needed help hunting down criminals.

To answer the prompt, my sexual needs are extremely satisfied. Making love to Aran and Orion on horseback last week was amazing. I also loved waking up this morning to Orion sucking on my cock.

Being a part of this family has opened my eyes to so many things. I never imagined I could interact with so many people. It's better than anything I could have dreamed of.

Corvus Malum

Thank you, Luka for taking this seriously.

I also think we should make a visit to the fae realm, it would do us all good. Aran keeps making me go on thirty-mile morning runs with her and I'm too afraid to tell her that I don't want to go.

To answer the prompt, my sexual needs are so satisfied that I cried myself to sleep last night because I was so grateful that I get to be mated to all of you. I never could have imagined in my wildest dreams that this would be what my life is like. I thought I'd never find my Revered, and now I have five mates. ~~I'm crying right now thinking about how much I love all of you~~.

.   .   .

Aran Alis Egan Malum

YOU TOLD ME YOU LIKED THE MORNING RUNS?!! What the hell man???

Also, I forgot how funny Corvus was in these journals. You're the most interesting scary/soft man I've ever met in my life, and I love you so much. That being said, I can't stop laughing right now. Something about the way you cry is so funny to me. I'm sorry, I know it's rude, but I can't stop.

Scorpius Malum

Corvus are you actually crying? Is that why you said you had to go to the bathroom?

Orion Malum

For real, man??? You're such a cutie.

Luka Malum

I don't know what to say.

John Son of Hades Malum

At least I cried because I'd been <u>knifed</u> in the ass. That's just embarrassing. But also, I understand what you mean Corvus. Sometimes I also get overwhelmed by my love for you guys. I don't cry, but my chest feels warm and tingly.

Corvus Malum

I held a baby goat yesterday while I sobbed thinking about how much I love you all.

I will not cross this out because I am proud of who I am.

Aran Alis Egan Malum

Is the goat okay? You probably traumatized the poor thing. I mean this with all the love and respect in the world, that is such a Mitch thing to do.

Corvus Malum

Please do not start calling me that name again. It has taken me months to recover emotionally from that hurtful nickname. It makes me self-conscious.

Aran Alis Egan Malum

Mitch.

Scorpius Malum

Mitch.

Orion Malum

Mitch.

John Son of Hades Malum

Mitch.

Corvus Malum

Thank you, Luka, for not joining in on their childish gestures. It means a lot that I have at least one mate who will stand by me.

Luka Son of Hades Malum

ERROR

Please be advised that this message was delayed because of a processing error. For optimal results, do not share journals with others.

Mitch.

Corvus Malum:
My heart hurts.

Aran Alis Egan Malum
Stop hiding and come back outside Corvus we miss you!

Please, I'll give you kisses and massage your head. I know that's your favorite.

Corvus Malum
Fine, but I want kisses…everywhere.

Aran Alis Egan Malum
There he is.

Maybe, if you beg me.

.   .   .

Corvus Malum

We both know that I'm not the one who does the begging in this relationship.

Take your clothes off Aran. I want you naked and open when I come outside, Love of My Life.

Scorpius Malum

Corvus, she's not taking off her clothes. Do you want me to get her ready for you? I have my knife…

John Son of Hades Malum

Aran, I really think we should get Scorpius an appointment with Dr. Palmer soon.

Aran Alis Egan Malum

Agreed. I'll call her later. She hates us, so we'll probably have to blackmail her.

John Son of Hades Malum

Do whatever it takes.

Orion Malum

Corvus, I'll get her ready with my tongue for you. My favorite three course meal is Aran's pussy.

.   .   .

Aran Alis Egan Malum

Scorpius don't you dare come over here with that knife. Use it on John. Even though we have real concerns about your mental state lately, John did tell me secretly that he likes when you stab him.

Orion I just want to say you're amazing at giving head. Literally, mind-blowing.

John Son of Hades Malum

OH MY SUN GOD, Aran, I told you that in <u>confidence</u>! How could you? Is nothing sacred anymore??? We were just talking about how terrifying he is, and then you do that?

I will get you back for this.

Corvus Malum

I'm coming out soon. You better be ready for me Aran because I'm going to do depraved things to you. I'm going to make you come so many times that you forget your name.

It's taking longer than I expected because I'm trying to find a pink bow for Bessie. Her old one must have fallen off. Aran, do you know where we keep our ribbon?

Luka Son of Hades Malum

Who is Bessie?

Aran Alis Egan Malum

Corvus, top right bathroom drawer.

Bessie is the three-hundred-pound pig he rescued last week.

Also, she didn't lose her bow, she ripped it to shreds. I watched her do it.

Orion Malum

Are you guys talking about the BOAR with the foot long tusks that's been terrorizing the estate???

John Son of Hades Malum

That thing is terrifying. It makes me feel scared in my own home.

Scorpius Malum

I've been hunting that thing all week, but it keeps evading me. It has a wicked bite.

I recommend using a long-range weapon because stabbing it did *not* work.

Corvus Malum

SCORPIUS, DON'T YOU DARE TOUCH BESSIE!!!! She is a member of this family and a very sweet girl once you get to know her.

Luka Son of Hades Malum

Do female boars have tusks?

John Malum

I just want to bring up the fact that Bessie is a carnivore. I saw her eating a duck last week. Should we be concerned?

Corvus Malum

You probably saw a different pig, John. My Bessie would never do that.

Luka, she is obviously a woman.

Scorpius Malum

Can I hunt the wild boar? Or can I not? I'm confused.

All this talk of bloodshed is making me horny. John, get over here and suck me off.

Aran Alis Egan Malum:

Don't you dare hurt her Scorpius! I swear I won't talk to you for a month if you harm a single one of the poisonous spikes on her spine.

Corvus Malum

Found the bows. Do you think Bessie will like purple or pink?

I'm coming out now, Aran you better be naked and ready for me.

Luka Son of Hades Malum

Corvus, you should hurry up.

Aran and John are giggling and running across the hills.

They said they're going to go hide behind some trees? Do you want me to chase after them?

Never mind, Scorpius is sprinting after them.

Should we be concerned that he's pointing a knife at them like a spear as he runs?

Oof looks like he overtook John quickly, and tackled him to the grass.

Yep, he stabbed him.

Aran is still running.

Holy shit, Bessie is running beside her!!!!

Oh no, Aran is trying to pet her.

Bessie does *not* look like she wants to be touched. Corvus, are her spines projectiles?

Orion Malum

Corvus, get out here, Scorpius is attacking Bessie!!!!

I think your pig is having diarrhea. Corvus, what have you been feeding it???

Wait, now Aran is attacking Scorpius.

Bessie has turned on John.

I can confirm, the spines are projectiles.

Luka Son of Hades Malum

Update, John has been hit. Three spines to the ass.

Scorpius is now attacking Bessie with his bare hands.

Corvus Malum

TELL HIM NOT TO HURT BESSIE!!! I'm coming out now!!!!

.   .   .

Luka Son of Hades Malum

Too late.

Please leave a review of Psycho Gods on Amazon, it allows me to keep writing books. Also, read a bonus Journal Prompt at **blog.jasminemasbooks.com.**

I plan on releasing a new book series, **Blood of Hercules,** sometimes next year. It will be a funny fantasy romance story, similar to the cruelshifterverse.

Thanks for reading!

About the Author

Jasmine Mas loves writing about fantasy worlds filled with humor, sarcasm, realistic women, and psycho men (also realistic).

She attended Georgetown University for Undergraduate and received her JD at the University of Miami. She's a full time lawyer who loves reading Harry Potter fan fiction. She lives with her husband and cat named Boo Boo in Miami, FL and loves hanging out with her readers on social media.

Sign up for sneak peeks and bonus content on the Cruel Shifterverse straight to your inbox at

blog.jasminemasbooks.com

Follow her on Social Media for book hints
and Character Art

TikTok: @jasminemasbooks
Instagram: @jasminemasbooks

THANK YOU

Thank you for reading the 6th book in the Cruel
Shifterverse! You're my hero!

Also, special thank you to my mother who pulled four
consecutive all nighters with me (I wish I was joking) so we
could release this on time. I will forever cherish the memory
of both of us sobbing with laugher at 4am over Bessie.

Printed in Great Britain
by Amazon